What an extraordinary story of Esther! This tender and touching tale of what might have happened in Esther's later years is simply—well, delicious. A wonderful depiction of life in Persia and the Jews who continued to live in that ancient land. In Roxannah and Esther, Tessa Afshar has given us two wonderfully charming heroines.

Angela Hunt, *New York Times* bestselling
author of THE EMISSARIES series

I loved this book! Tessa's brilliance shines on these pages. In her signature way, Tessa tells stories, weaves biblical themes, and unearths traumas we can all relate to. *The Queen's Cook* reminds us that our pain and past will impact our present until we face them head-on. And that our identity is God-given and God-breathed, not attached to who we've been. This story made me cry, cheer, and pray that all who are hurting will be healed and established in God's best purpose for them. Enjoy this book. What a great read!

Susie Larson, talk radio host, national speaker,
and bestselling author

Afshar's writing shines in this brilliant perspective shift on Queen Esther's story. I loved all the detailed recipes (like only Tessa could do) and the weaving of characters' lives in a way that reflects the true complexity of our everyday existence. Searching biblical fiction relatable for today's reader.

Mesu Andrews, bestselling and Christy Award–winning author

--------- Past Praise for Tessa Afshar ---------

No one brings the Bible to life like Tessa Afshar.

Debbie Macomber, #1 *New York Times* bestselling author

Tessa Afshar combines adventure and romance in a fast-paced novel that kept me turning the pages. I loved the way she brought so many historical figures to life. I highly recommend *The Hidden Prince*!

Francine Rivers, internationally bestselling
author of *Redeeming Love*

T0313453

Talented author Tessa Afshar brings to vivid life the heartache, growing faith, and powerful love story of a truly fascinating character. A stirring treasure not to be missed!

Julie Klassen, bestselling author of the ON DEVONSHIRE SHORES series on *Pearl in the Sand*

Land of Silence is a biblical novel in a category all its own. Moving, believable . . . This inspiring, uplifting story encouraged me at a heart level. A wonderful story—not to be missed!

Jill Eileen Smith, bestselling author of *The Ark and the Dove*

Tessa Afshar's captivating and emotive story is about one first-century woman's pain and struggle. But the hope she describes is real and for you and me today.

Chris Fabry, bestselling author on *Land of Silence*

A moving portrait of faith and a spellbinding evocation of biblical life.

Library Journal, starred review of *Land of Silence*

Afshar again shows her amazing talent for packing action and intrigue into the biblical setting for modern readers.

Publishers Weekly, starred review of *Thief of Corinth*

Tessa Afshar once again brings the New Testament to life.

World Magazine on *Daughter of Rome*

[Afshar] makes early Christianity spark.

Foreword Reviews on *Daughter of Rome*

THE
QUEEN'S
COOK

QUEEN ESTHER'S COURT

THE
QUEEN'S
COOK

TESSA
AFSHAR

BETHANYHOUSE
a division of Baker Publishing Group
Minneapolis, Minnesota

Published by Bethany House Publishers
Minneapolis, Minnesota
BethanyHouse.com

Bethany House Publishers is a division of
Baker Publishing Group, Grand Rapids, Michigan

Printed in the United States of America

Library of Congress Cataloging-in-Publication Data
Names: Afshar, Tessa, author.
Title: The Queen's Cook / Tessa Afshar.
Description: Minneapolis, Minnesota : Bethany House Publishers, a division of
    Baker Publishing Group, 2024. | Series: Queen Esther's Court
Identifiers: LCCN 2024026437 | ISBN 9780764243691 (paper) | ISBN
    9780764243974 (cloth) | ISBN 9781493448074 (ebook)
Subjects: LCGFT: Christian fiction. | Novels.
Classification: LCC PS3601.F47 Q44 2024 | DDC 813.6—dc23/eng/20240617
LC record available at https://lccn.loc.gov/2024026437

Cover design by Jennifer Parker

Published in association with Books & Such Literary Management, BooksAndSuch
.com.

Baker Publishing Group publications use paper produced from sustainable forestry
practices and postconsumer waste whenever possible.

25 26 27 28 29 30   7 6 5 4 3 2

To my mother,
The most elegant, generous-hearted woman I know.
Thank you for always believing in me.

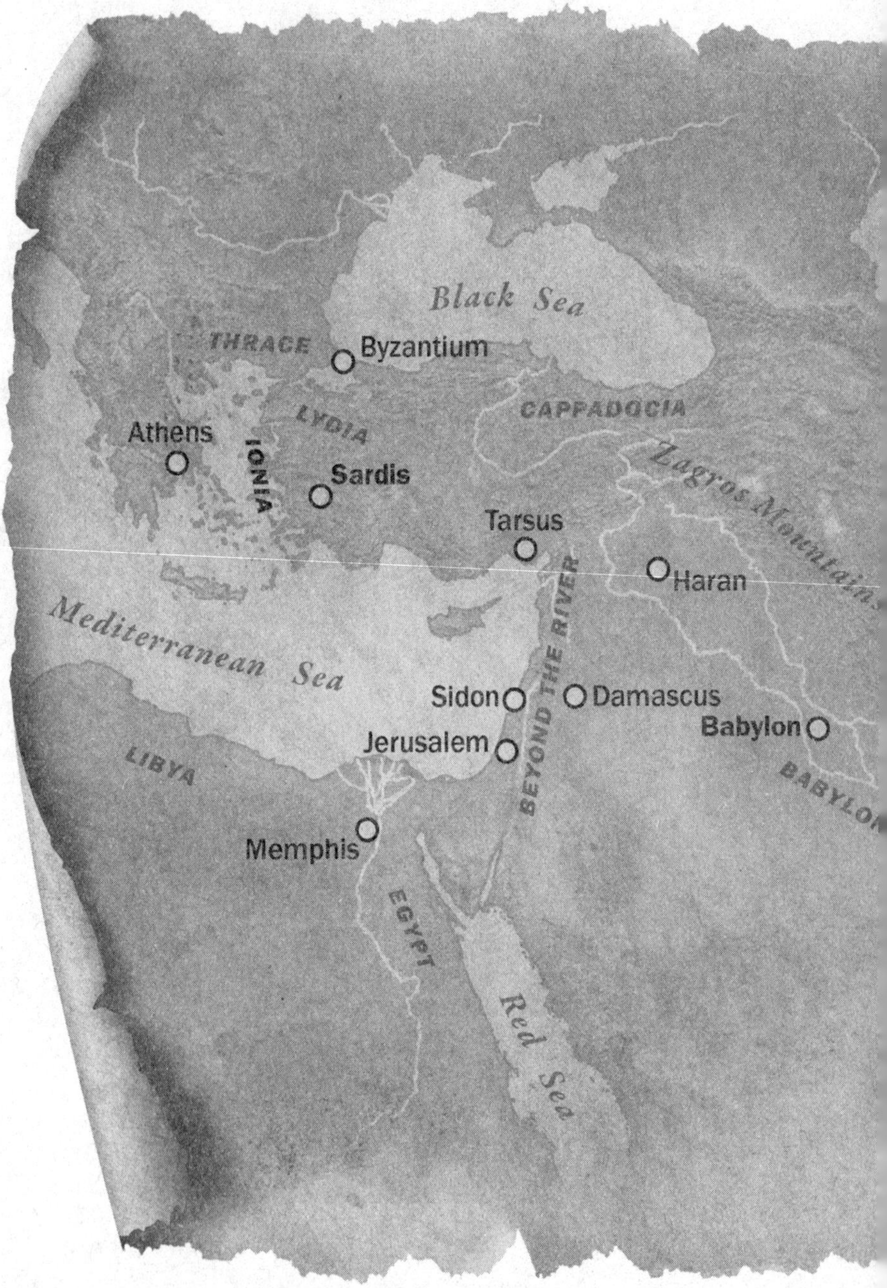

Black Sea
THRACE
Byzantium
CAPPADOCIA
LYDIA
Athens
IONIA
Sardis
Zagros Mountains
Tarsus
Haran
BEYOND THE RIVER
Mediterranean Sea
Sidon
Damascus
Babylon
Jerusalem
LIBYA
Memphis
EGYPT
Red Sea

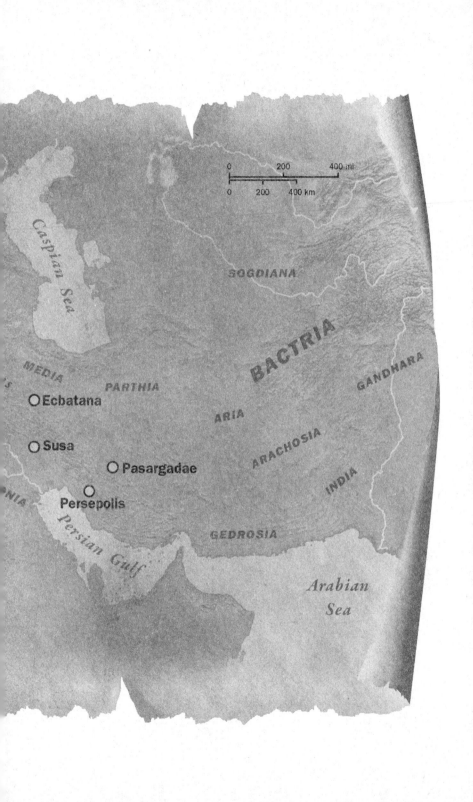

From the Secret Scrolls
of Esther

She who was once great among the nations
Now sits alone like a widow.
Once the queen of all the earth,
She is now a slave.

Lamentations 1:1 NLT

The Twenty-Fifth Year of King Artaxerxes's Rule

Let me tell you a secret: Being queen will break your heart.

Young women weave sweet fantasies of bejeweled crowns and magnificent honors when they dream of a title. How little they understand the weight of that crown or the cost of true honor.

They look upon me now and see an old woman whose ordinary life holds little to recommend it to the young. They have no notion that once I sat upon the throne they long for. The king's scepter lifted to welcome me, and a hundred backs bent low when I walked past.

They do not know who I am. And that is as I like it.

I have not survived this long without learning a trick or two.

The palace goes on as ever, its courtiers blustering, servants scurrying, scribes administering, wives and concubines scheming, armies marching. The empire grinds slowly forward as if the blood of the king I loved was never spilled by covetous hands. Kings are replaced as easily as dribbled ink, it seems.

His son sits on the throne now. *Her* son. She gave my king what I never could: a lineage to follow after him. She raised the boy well, I'll give her that. He has been a good monarch, with the steel-hard strength that won his forefathers an empire tempered with grace enough to make everyone love him.

I hope that makes her rest easy in her aristocratic grave.

She died clutching the crown she always longed for, while I sit in my simple house, my head bare save for a modest veil. Esther is gone. I am Hadassah again.

There is a peace that comes when you lose everything. Once, I wielded the power of an empire to save my people. That knowledge is my crown, the throne I sit upon when my losses haunt me.

I survived the sharp edge of palace intrigue long enough to complete the hard tasks that God laid before me. And somehow, on that arduous journey, I made a handful of true friends. You might even say I changed a few lives.

1

Roxannah

You are a hiding place for me;
you preserve me from trouble.

Psalm 32:7

THIRTY-THREE YEARS EARLIER
THE TWELFTH YEAR OF KING XERXES'S RULE
THE TENTH DAY OF SPRING

Sunsets had a lot in common with cats if you lived in Lord Fravartish's house; Roxannah never knew what they might drag in. This one had wrenched in the mangled corpse of her hopes for the evening.

She threw a hasty look at the door before scrambling inside the half-empty linen chest, her legs folding at an awkward angle in the cramped space. For once, her petite frame proved an advantage as she wedged her body inside the musty confines and pulled the lid closed over her head. At twenty-three, she had

13

long since passed the age of playing hide-and-seek. But finding a place of concealment tonight was no childish game.

The sound of heavy footsteps penetrated the smothering darkness of her hiding place. Her mouth turned dry as the steps reverberated inside the chamber, followed closely by softer footfalls.

A booted foot kicked the chest hard, jostling Roxannah. She pressed her face into the rough folds of a woolen blanket to muffle the sound of her gasp.

"Where is she?" The harsh timbre of her father's voice came slurred.

Wine was a thief.

It had carried off everything Roxannah cherished in her father and left behind a cruel husk. She had the bruises to prove it.

"Perhaps she is in the kitchen, cleaning up from your dinner." Her mother's voice trembled with strain.

Her father kicked the chest again. "Dinner, you call it? That bowl of peasant soup? I told her to cook me lamb."

He had. But lamb cost silver—silver that he had neglected to provide. The butcher refused to extend credit to their family anymore. Years ago, her father's noble name had meant something in Susa. But his unsteady temper and foolish spending had wiped most of that ancient honor from their neighbors' memories.

These days, they had no income other than the coin provided from a modest parcel of land her grandfather had long ago mortgaged to a farmer. It was the last of what remained of their family's once rich pasturelands and orchards. The paltry revenue stretched only far enough to fill her father's cup with cheap wine. He had long since sold off every other valuable inheritance he could. Her grandfather's precious herds had disappeared over the years, bartered off in exchange for her father's mounting debts.

Save for their house, with its leaking roof and creaky floors, a handful of dented furniture, and a few scrawny chickens, nothing remained of her parents' formerly ample heritage.

Hence, no lamb for supper.

The lid of the chest groaned alarmingly as someone leaned their weight against it. "Where has that useless girl gone? I have a thing or two I want—" The staccato sound of distant pounding brought her father's rant to an abrupt halt. Someone at the door seemed determined to gain entry.

"Who can that be at this hour? People have no manners." He belched loudly.

Speaking of manners . . . Roxannah's lips twitched with wry amusement. This was her best weapon against the despair that sometimes tried to wriggle inside. Laughter. She spent too much time hiding in chests, taking cover under stairs, finding shelter on the rooftop, trying to survive the wine-soaked hours. How else could she endure it if not for laughter?

The knock came again, loud and imposing.

"Where is that good-for-nothing boy? Why does he not answer?"

Her mother cleared her throat. "He ran away."

The last of their long-suffering servants, the boy had sneaked away during the night, tired of waiting for rations that came less frequently than his master's blows.

"That ingrate! After all I did for him."

He had, indeed, done a lot for the boy. He had taught him to run very very fast in the opposite direction.

Her mother coughed but held her tongue, as she always did. Her father cursed. "Must I always tend to everything myself?"

Roxannah listened to the sound of unsteady footsteps retreating from the chamber. When they disappeared in the direction of the courtyard, she lifted the lid a fraction.

"Mother?" she whispered.

The slim woman leaning against the wall straightened quickly, pasting a smile on her tired face. "I wondered if you might be hiding in that chest."

"I could tell it wasn't going to be a good night when he screamed at the wall for being in the wrong spot. His temper is sure to cool by morning. A few more hours out of his sight, and I might be safe."

Her mother shook her head. "Don't take his words to heart, daughter. That dinner was delectable. What you do with food is—"

The sound of shouting cut off her mother's words. Roxannah slid behind the half-closed door and watched the scene unfolding below. A hand lifted to her mouth. "Another bailiff."

It would be a while before her father returned, then. Roxannah crawled out of the chest and joined her mother. From where they stood, they had a clear view of the courtyard where her father stood screaming at a short, bald-headed man. The bailiff spoke in soft tones they could not make out.

Without warning, her father grabbed the wooden stool leaning against the corner of the gate, left there from the days when the family had enjoyed the services of a doorman. Before Roxannah could cry a warning, he swung the heavy stool sideways at the bailiff's head. The man had the nimble reactions of someone who found himself in the path of swinging furniture on a regular basis. The stool missed his head by a wide arc, but the momentum of her father's violent motion carried him forward, throwing off his already unsteady balance.

He swayed as he tried to regain his equilibrium and failed, crashing roughly into the stone wall. Even all the way inside the house they could hear the sickening crack as his head slammed into the masonry. Bouncing, he pitched backward, arms flailing as he fell and landed on the limestone path bordering the herb garden.

The bailiff took one look at the trail of scarlet that flowed from the still man's temple and beat a hasty retreat. Her mother screamed. Roxannah flew past her rigid form into the hallway and down the three uneven steps that led to the courtyard.

Her father stirred when she knelt by his side. With a moan, he opened bleary eyes. "My head!"

Roxannah swallowed as blood pooled on the worn stone. She laid a tentative hand on his shoulder. "You crashed into the wall. Can you sit up?"

He slapped her hand away. "You imbecile! Of course I can't sit up. Can't you see I am half dead?"

"Shall I fetch you a physician?"

Staring at the scarlet coating the fingers he had raised to his temple, he gasped. "Yes! Hurry!"

Roxannah sprang to her feet. By now, her mother had made her way to the courtyard and stood frozen, her face bone white. Roxannah gave her a quick embrace. "I am going for the physician. Perhaps you should cover him with a blanket? He is shivering."

She slapped her forehead. "Why did I not think of it? I don't know what I would do without you." She raced back inside the house.

Her father raised a hand as Roxannah turned to leave. "Girl! Not that idiot who tended me last time. He has the brains of a chicken."

"Who shall I fetch, Father?"

"That Jew from Elephantine."

Roxannah tried to remember who he meant. "The one who serves at the palace?"

He huffed an impatient breath. "His reputation is adequate."

Roxannah swallowed a groan. How were they to afford a court physician? They had barely managed to pay the fees of the neighborhood healer who had seen to her father's last illness.

She had no idea where this physician resided. Which way should she go? Their house was located in the old royal town, the

17

prosperous neighborhood that spread southeast of the palace. A half-hour's walk to the west lay a warren of five or six streets where many Jewish residents lived in proximity to one another. But another cluster of Jews had settled to the east, in the Artisans' Village, preferring to intermingle with the cosmopolitan people of Susa. Gathering her scarf more closely around her head, Roxannah ran west toward the Jewish quarter. Even if the physician did not live there, someone should be able to tell her where to find him.

By the time she arrived at her destination, she had a stitch in her side. A boy playing in the street pointed her to immaculate whitewashed walls encircling a sprawling property. Roxannah banged against the iron-studded cedar gate. She was about to bellow for the physician when a man of middle years opened the door softly. The pristine linen scarf wrapped about his head marked him a servant.

"My father . . . has been hurt!" She huffed the words in a winded gasp. "I need the physician."

Given her old, faded clothing, she half expected to be turned away at the door. But with a short bow, the servant invited her into a lush courtyard and indicated a stone bench. "Wait here, if you please. I will fetch my master." He spoke Persian in the cultured tones of an aristocrat, sounding like no ordinary servant she had ever met.

Roxannah pressed her palms together to keep them steady. "Hurry, please. My father hit his head and is bleeding badly."

The man nodded. "He will be with you in a moment." With a swish of his long tunic, he disappeared through the carved door leading into the house.

Roxannah knelt to rinse her hands in the clear waters of a shallow, rectangular pool. She grew aware of the perfume of hundreds of blooming roses and, turning, noticed for the first time the profusion of colors that surrounded her—soft pink, buttery yellow, rich cream, pearly white—dotting the roomy courtyard and climbing from a half dozen arbors. The physician had turned his home into a tiny paradise of calm and color. Sitting at the edge of the stone bench, she turned her back on the heavenly view and glued her eyes to the closed door instead.

It opened shortly to reveal a broad-shouldered man with raven-black hair and a neat beard. He looked more like a soldier than a scholar who had spent his years in the shade of libraries and schoolhouses.

Roxannah snapped to her feet. She expected him to demand payment before accompanying her, but he simply waved at her to join him. "Head injury, my man tells me. Is he conscious?"

She blinked, surprised at this no-nonsense greeting. "Yes."

"That's a good sign." He had a deep voice that seemed at once commanding and oddly soothing, edged by a slight accent that lent his speech an air of mystery.

Walking briskly, he led her to a plain gate at the opposite end of the courtyard, beyond which lay a wide lane. "It will be faster if we ride. My horse is in the stable around the corner. There is a donkey for you." He gave her a sidelong glance. "You needn't worry. It's a biddable creature."

"I can ride."

He walked ahead into a mudbrick stable, whitewashed to match the outside walls. His steps were long and loping, and she found herself half running to keep up. His servant had followed in their wake, his movements so quiet she startled when he appeared at her side to help her mount the donkey. The beast waited placidly as she settled on its broad back.

She caught the servant's eye and whispered, "What's his name?"

He shrugged. "We just call him Donkey."

"Not the beast. I meant the physician."

The servant's white teeth flashed against his salt-and-pepper beard. "Well, now. One might say that same name is not badly suited ..."

The physician held up a warning finger. "Don't finish that thought, no matter how great the temptation." Eyes the color of obsidian sparked with humor.

Roxannah looked from one grinning face to the other, marveling at the ease with which the master had allowed his servant's teasing insult to slide. In her father's house, any retainer with half the cheek would have been bleeding by now.

The physician merely smiled. "My name is Adin ben Zerah. And this impudent fellow is Darab."

"I am Roxannah, daughter of Lord Fravartish."

Adin inclined his head. "Let's tend to your father. Darab, my medicine chest, please."

While the servant secured a bulky wooden box to Roxannah's donkey, Adin led a black stallion out of a stall at the rear of the stable. Even the dire circumstances of her visit could not completely dampen her enthusiasm at the sight of the horse. "A Nisaean!"

Nisaeans were the most highly prized horses in the world, some costing more than what a man might earn in a lifetime. This one was a particularly fine specimen, his dark coat so glossy she could almost see her reflection in it. Long, powerful muscles flexed with each elegant stride.

Like most Persians, Roxannah had a deep affection for horses. "What a beauty!"

Adin cast her a short glance. "You know your horseflesh." Without waiting for Darab's help, he adjusted the straps on the stallion's felt saddlecloth and, holding lightly to the beast's withers, mounted with an agile leap.

Roxannah glimpsed a flash of tight trousers hugging muscular legs under his tunic. The practical garments of a military man rather than the finery of a palace healer.

He guided his mount toward the stable door. "Lead the way, Mistress Roxannah."

Feeling torn between the relief of having secured the services of a royal physician for her father and the anxiety of the hefty debt they were sure to owe, Roxannah steered her beast into the narrow lane and set it to a trot as soon as the street widened.

2

Adin

Be angry, and do not sin;
ponder in your own hearts on your beds,
and be silent.

Psalm 4:4

Adin followed the girl to what must have once been an elegant building but was now little more than a ruin, with crumbling walls and an old roof that surely leaked. In such a wealthy neighborhood, surrounded by lush villas of baked and glazed brick, the house's decrepit condition stood out all the more.

He secured his mount to the post by the door and turned to help the young woman from the donkey. Before he could reach for her, she dismounted with a sprightly hop and hastened to push the gnarled door open. Adin unstrapped his medicine chest and followed in her wake.

He saw his patient immediately, lying sprawled on the courtyard floor, tucked under the folds of a worn blanket. Adin's practiced eyes noted the blood spilled on the stone, the narrow wound at the hairline, and the pale, sweating skin. A woman sat by his side, her bearing still, her face white with exhaustion. Adin sensed a new tension coil through Roxannah as she approached her father. She perched next to the woman. "Father, Mother, this is Master Adin ben Zerah, Royal Physician." It was the mother's hand she sought, he noticed, not the injured man who lay covered by the blanket.

Adin gave a short bow of his head. "Lord. Lady."

Fravartish gave him a sour look. "Another useless physician, no doubt. I am likely to get better service from the butcher."

Adin bit down a smile as he knelt in the dirt. "I can fetch one for you, if you prefer?"

"Very amusing. Get on with it."

Adin ignored the man's cutting manner and bent to conduct a thorough examination. However rude his patient might be, Adin would do his best to help him. Carefully, he cleansed the wound before sitting back on his haunches.

"This gash requires stitches. I suggest I first help you to your bed, my lord. You will be more comfortable there."

Fravartish grimaced. "I knew you would torture me."

By the smell of him, his patient had imbibed enough wine to feel little pain. Bending, Adin slipped an arm behind Fravartish's broad back and gently pulled him into a sitting position. Roxannah sprang to his other side to lend a hand. He gave her an appreciative nod, and together, they drew the heavy man to his feet.

Roxannah's head only reached her father's shoulder, her delicate frame straining under his considerable weight. Adin hefted his patient closer against him, taking most of the burden. Fravartish's shifting body snagged the girl's tunic, drawing back the fabric of the sleeve and revealing a slender arm. What Adin saw sent an unexpected shaft of white-hot rage through him, making him want to drop the man back on the floor. Let him smash the other side of his head as well.

Black-and-blue marks littered the light skin of Roxannah's arm. Handprints left by some cruel beating. Noting his gaze, she flushed and pulled down her sleeve with a quick motion. As if *she* had anything to be ashamed of.

What kind of man would do that to so fragile a woman? His own daughter, no less. She appeared more than old enough to be married and mistress of her own home. Her dark blond hair, blue-grey eyes, and flawless skin surely drew many a suitor's eyes. He wondered what kept her bound to this dilapidated house and her cruel father.

It was no business of his.

Adin ground his teeth, tucking the man's arm more securely around his neck as he walked toward the house. He would do his best for his patient in spite of his rising dislike. It was all he could offer the young woman who had come to his door, eyes large with desperation.

He doubted he would ever see payment from Fravartish, who seemed more interested in the contents of his cup than in his responsibilities. But he had long since made a promise to himself and to God that he would not turn anyone away due to lack of funds.

Roxannah tripped under the weight of her father as they lowered him to his bed. Jostled, the man cursed. "Fool!" he hissed. "Can't ever do anything right, can you?"

Adin's jaw knotted. A surge of anger stopped him in his tracks. Instead of sewing up the man, he wanted to give him a bigger gash. He forced a few mouthfuls of air into his lungs until the fire of outrage calmed enough for him to keep a needle steady. At least the pain of its application would keep Fravartish's lips sealed, unable to serve anymore insults while the needle did its work.

Adin's practiced fingers made quick work of the stitches.

As he wiped his hands, he explained how the women should change the bandages and cleanse the wound to prevent suppuration. While the mother's lips trembled and she stepped away as if burned by his plain directions, the daughter stood her ground. Her irises had turned a dark grey, all the blue leached out of them. Clearly, she was no more comfortable with his medical direction than her mother. Still, she did not flinch. Not once.

Adin felt an unwanted flicker of warmth for her. An admiration he could not quite deny. He realized he was staring. Taking a hasty step back, he reached for his medicine chest. The daughter was turning out to be more dangerous than the father.

The sooner he left this house, the better.

3

Roxannah

See how my eyes have become bright because I
tasted a little of this honey.

1 Samuel 14:29

Roxannah pressed the poultice to her father's forehead.
"This will ease your pain and draw out the heat."

Her father grimaced. "It stinks."

"The physician left the herbs for me and told me how to
prepare them. They will protect you from fever."

"He thinks I'll get a fever? You better make sure he returns
to tend me himself. You can't get it right. My constitution is too
weak to live through a fever." He pointed an unsteady finger at
his empty cup. "Fill it."

"But he said—"

"Don't argue with me, girl! Get more wine."

Roxannah hesitated. His bottomless appetite for what
swirled in his cup was more likely to harm him than any fever

associated with his injury. Without comment, her mother rose from her seat at the foot of the bed and obeyed her husband. Roxannah fought a beat of exasperation. She knew that sometimes the only way to calm was by appeasing her father's demands and giving in to the monster that lived under his skin. But the need for compromise rankled even as it wore down her objections. The peace they purchased was hardly worthy of the name, a paltry reproduction that assuaged no one's pain.

He gulped down the blood-red liquid thirstily. "Don't forget to fetch the physician to me."

"Yes, Father." She did not bother to tell him that Adin would be at the palace now. Hopefully, he would fall asleep after finishing his wine and not awaken for hours.

Another visit from the royal physician would cost a fortune. Roxannah frowned. Adin had not demanded payment before leaving the previous evening. He had looked at her with his night-black eyes brimming with kindness, given his instructions, heaped upon her a generous hill of herbs, and left.

She had thought him a plain man until he had rested the intensity of his gaze on her. His face seemed transformed in that moment, coming alive with something she could not quite decipher, and for a moment, her breath had trapped in her chest, as if she had come across a dazzling sunrise after a week of grey skies.

With his dark hair and smooth skin, he seemed too young for the post he occupied at the court, a position that required the explicit trust of palace officials. She wondered how he had risen so high so quickly. He certainly knew how to be observant. Remembering his sharp scrutiny of the bruises on her arm, and the subsequent tightening of his jaw, she felt heat rise to her cheeks. Why did he have to witness the marks of her shame?

Leaving her sleepy father under her mother's watch, Roxannah sought solace in the kitchen, one of the few places she felt truly at home. Five years ago, when their cook had left to serve a wealthy household, she had taken charge of the family's meals. Thankfully the man, one of the few servants left from the days of her grandparents, had trained her before his eventual departure.

Roxannah had learned to be both cook and merchant, making an advantageous arrangement with a neighboring lord that kept her family from starving. The elderly Lord Zopyrus paid generously for Roxannah's dishes. His own cook was getting on in years and unable to keep up with the demands of the household. Zopyrus, who had an endearing attachment to his aging servants, refused to dismiss any of them. Instead, he had hired Roxannah to make additional food deliveries several times a week to his home.

This handy arrangement meant that Roxannah could keep her family from going hungry. Of course, she did not make enough to buy expensive ingredients like lamb whenever she pleased. Hence the need to hide in the chest.

She fetched a half-empty amphora of wheat from the storehouse, intending to take advantage of these quiet hours to make a cake. Lord Zopyrus said her pistachio cake tasted better than the pastries served at the palace.

She had learned the recipe from her grandmother who, in spite of being a highborn lady, had liked to dabble in the kitchen and learned a few tricks from the great cooks who served their family in those days. She had passed on her love of cooking to her only grandchild.

In the kitchen, Roxannah went through her familiar routine. Blocking the entrance with a large pot, she leaned a smaller one against it. These obstacles would slow her father if he decided to visit. Behind her, she ensured that the gap she had created as an escape route remained clear, in case she needed to make a run for it. Where would she hide today, should the need arise? Reason assured her that her father was too incapacitated to cause any harm, but old experience demanded safety. It insisted on the usual precautions. A taste of control in a chaotic world.

The storehouse. She could hide behind the empty oil amphorae today.

Satisfied, she turned her attention to her baking. Adding firewood to the hearth, she made a thick syrup by mixing rosewater and dark meadow-flower honey, a gift from Lord Zopyrus. Setting the pot aside to cool, she turned her attention to the cake's filling. From the storehouse, she fetched a sackcloth filled with pistachios that she had harvested herself the previous fall.

Pistachios always reminded Roxannah of her father. Not the man lying in his bed now, the one who had a barbed tongue and heavy hand.

No. Pistachios reminded Roxannah of the father she remembered from her girlhood. The quiet, amiable man who hadn't yet been ruined by the cruelty of war and too much wine. For a moment, her eyes welled.

When she had been little, her father had taken her on one of his rambles through their land. They had ended up in the pistachio grove. Plucking a young fruit from a fat cluster, he had peeled off the pink and green outer skin to show her the split seed inside.

"It takes a young tree seven years or more to produce its first harvest."

"Seven years? As old as me?"

He nodded. "Exactly that many years. You have to be patient with them." He gave Roxannah a handful of pistachios and taught her how to peel them. "But if you take care of them, they can be fruitful for a hundred years. Even a hundred and fifty."

Roxannah looked at the short, twisted tree with wonder. "That's even older than you."

The corners of her father's eyes crinkled as he smiled. "You are going to be a true mathematician, I see. You are correct. These trees are from the time of my grandfather. They will still be fruitful when you are grown up and have children of your own."

Roxannah's chest tightened as she remembered that smile. Its absence had been the first thing she noticed when he returned home after fighting for two years in King Darius's great army. He had started to drink to try and find it again. Instead, he had lost all the kindness and sympathy he once had. He had always been a reserved man. But wine had made him withdrawn. And then cruel.

She pushed the memory away as she shelled the small hill of pistachios. In the stone mortar and pestle, which had been in her family for two generations, she added the green and purplish kernels, along with a generous pinch of cardamom seeds, before pounding the mixture into a paste. Folding in a dollop of honey, she tasted the thick paste. The nutty flavor of the pistachios blended with the spiced perfume of cardamom and the sweetness of honey to create a mouthwatering blend that would serve as the perfect filling for the cake.

By now, her syrup had cooled enough to start the dough. In a large clay bowl, she mixed cow's milk with soft butter and the syrup, adding an egg and finally the wheat flour. It was only second-grade wheat, but it was good enough for a cake. She kneaded the dough just as her grandmother had taught her, until it no longer stuck to her fingers, and rolled it out into two thin rectangles. Laying one over a tray, she spread the pistachio filling on top, before stretching the second layer of dough on top, tucking the edges over the sides to seal the filling within.

The trick of baking tasty desserts was in getting the temperature right, an art in itself given their ancient clay oven. Roxannah had started the fire some time ago and, looking at the wood embers, judged them ready for a good bake. The delicate edges of batter would invariably char a little. These she would trim before cutting the cake into crisscross diagonal lines.

She had just removed the cake from the oven when a knock at the door made her almost drop the pan. Her shoulders drooped. What if another bailiff had come calling? The man would likely take the door off its hinges with his pounding if she did not attend him—or worse, he would awaken her father and put him in a dark humor.

A narrow crack between the wooden slats provided her with a handy peephole. Her stomach gave an odd lurch as she saw the man standing at their threshold.

Removing the bar, she swung the door open. "Master Adin!"

His expensive robe of midnight-blue linen, with its intricate silver embroidery and wide, pleated sleeves, lent him a formal air. It made him look lofty and unreachable. She found herself missing the haphazard clothing from the day before.

Adin smiled, and the air of formality cracked in half with that small gesture. "The palace grew quiet in the afternoon. I thought I might look in on your father."

"You are welcome. In fact, my father was impatient to see you. But he is sleeping."

"I will not disturb him, then. I suspect that might sour his mood." He did not add the words *even more*. But his expression made it clear he meant them, causing her to bite down a smile.

"Perhaps I could wait a while?" he said.

"That would be a kindness."

Roxannah led him to the covered porch that extended over their shallow pool. A common feature of the architecture in Susa, the water helped to keep the outdoor porches cool in the heat of summer.

Her grapevines climbed in woody tendrils around the four posts holding up the slatted roof. The vines had only awakened from their winter dormancy days ago, and the budbreak dotted the barren branches in tiny bursts of vivid green.

She pointed to the threadbare carpet and two rounded cushions that had lost much of their stuffing over the years. "It's not very comfortable, I am afraid. But it is clean."

He folded his legs into a graceful knot as he sat. "Very cozy."

"Would you like a piece of pistachio cake?"

His dark eyes brightened. "As it happens, I have a weakness for pistachio cake."

In the kitchen, Roxannah served two small pieces of the pastry on a glazed plate that had survived the years without a chip. She sprinkled a few dried, pink rosebud petals and slivers of pistachios on top of the golden cake and headed back to the porch.

She watched Adin take his first bite. His eyes drifted closed as he gave a low hum in his throat. "That is surely the best pistachio cake I have ever tasted." His lids opened. "You better not let anyone at court taste this, or they will pinch your baker from under your nose."

Roxannah relaxed against the post. "You can be assured I am in no danger of that. We have no baker."

He gave her a puzzled look. "But the pastry tastes like it is fresh from the oven."

She grinned. "Oh, it is. I baked it."

4

Adin

> She brings her food from afar.
> She rises while it is yet night
> and provides food for her household
>
> Proverbs 31:14–15

Was she fooling him? He remembered the scent of cardamom and rosewater clinging to her when she first opened the door. It had made him take a step closer before he realized what he was doing.

"You made this?" He could not hide the astonishment in his voice. That her family were impoverished she could not hide. But she was still a member of the Persian gentry, her father a lord with a long pedigree. Persian ladies did not slave in the kitchen.

The tiny dimple in the corner of her mouth peeped out at him as she suppressed another smile. "You picked a good time to come."

"You made this?" he could not help asking again. "All of it?"

She laughed aloud, a shy, restrained sound that somehow held a world of joy. He stared at her mouth, the single dimple in its corner, the merry blue-grey eyes unconquered by the man sleeping a few steps away, and something in his chest squeezed.

"Well, not the honey," she said. "We have the bees to thank for that."

Adin shoved a large piece of pistachio cake into his mouth lest he be tempted to make some flirtatious comment he would later regret. For a moment, he forgot about words as flavors exploded on his tongue.

"Good bees," he mumbled, and she laughed again. The cake disappeared in two more bites.

He gestured to the cushion across from him. "Please, join me," he said, and almost slapped a hand over his lips. What was he doing? Had he lost all sense? He should be erecting walls between them. Pushing her away with all the strength he could muster. Yet the mouthful of air that filled his lungs had the distinct taste of relief when she took up his invitation and settled down.

Everything about her was dainty. Her feet, her nose, her stature. Not her hair, perhaps. He wouldn't exactly call the fat braid that hung down her back, odd bits of curl sticking out with a mind of their own, dainty. He tried not to stare and failed.

"How did you learn to bake?"

"How did you become a royal physician?"

They spoke in unison, their words clashing and blending in an awkward rush. "You first," he said.

"My grandmother's influence. My father's mother taught me my first dishes when I was a young girl."

"I did not think Persian ladies soiled their fingers with kitchen work."

"My grandmother was a little ... unusual. She decided to learn to bake with the help of her illustrious cook."

"Your grandfather did not object?"

"He indulged her. Indeed, he took pride in eating her creations when she prepared something with her own hands. Of course, she did not have to contend with the drudgery of cooking. Someone else peeled and chopped and ground and plucked and cleaned and tended the fire. She merely mixed it all up and learned how to use the right herbs and spices."

Very different from her own experience, no doubt. He had yet to see a single servant in this household. Not only had she baked the cake, she had also served it. His voice softened. "Unlike your grandmother, you cannot avoid the drudgery."

She shrugged. "I do not mind it. I love to cook. Baking too. And the skill has proven useful. In fact, I can only dream . . ."

He leaned toward her. "What do you dream?"

She shook her head. "Nothing worth mentioning."

Adin ignored the surprising kick of disappointment he felt at her refusal to share her dream.

"Your turn. How did someone so young become a court physician?"

"Not so young. I am thirty-one." He meant to give her the short version of his life. The one he had smoothed and polished to share with company. But his words seemed to have a plan of their own. "My father wanted me to join the family business alongside my older brothers."

"What do they do?"

"For three generations, the men of my family have been soldiers in the Elephantine garrison on the banks of the river Nile." He shrugged. "My uncles, my cousins, my brothers, my father. We all worked together. I trained alongside them as a young man. The whole island serves as a defensive wall for the southern frontier of Egypt. Soldiering is a way of life. But when I turned eighteen, I decided that I wanted to become a physician."

He did not tell her what had precipitated that desire. The aching passion that fueled his work. Instead, he continued, "My father was horrified."

She gave him a questioning look. She had a way of eliciting information with little effort. A tilt of her head. A few simple words. Something about her seemed safe. Trustworthy. Comforting.

Without meaning to, he leaned toward her. "He might not have been quite so disgruntled if I had been willing to settle for a simple education, bound to the Isle of Elephantine. My father wanted me to keep on soldiering with my family and tend to my medicine on the side. Soldiers need a lot of sewing up." He gave a small smile. "Leaving Elephantine was never an option for my father. My family was like an unbroken wall before I left. Generations standing shoulder to shoulder, fighting together. No one dared come against us. They knew if they picked a fight with one of us, they picked a fight with all of us."

"But you chose to leave?"

"Staying became impractical. I was determined to learn as much as I could, and Elephantine did not offer the knowledge I sought."

"To become a physician, you had to become the chink in your family's wall. The broken place."

He gave her a surprised glance. "Yes. That's it, exactly."

"Where did you study?"

"In Egypt, at first. But the art of medicine has been on the wane there in recent years. The new center of study is Cnidus."

"That is in Ionia?"

"Very good. Their physicians are the world's leaders in medicine, teaching the way of observation and logic as a means of discovering the source of disease. An entirely new method of healing. Of course, the temples of Asclepieia still carry a lot of influence in the healing arts."

Her eyes grew warm with sympathy. "It must be hard to reconcile an Ionian god with your Jewish beliefs."

She had grasped his problem with astonishing clarity for a Gentile. He gave her a nod of approval. "Not so much hard as impossible. Which is why I have no interest in tampering with foreign gods and idols. Still, my whole family thinks I have lost my way."

He clenched his jaw before he could say more. Why had he blurted so much of his life to a practical stranger? He could not understand himself. With an abrupt move, he came to his feet. "I should see to your father."

"Of course." She stood as well and led him to Lord Fravartish's room. Just before they entered, she gave him a shy look. "For my part, I am grateful that you chose to be a physician. Many people in this world know how to wound and hurt. Few choose to bring healing."

She dropped her head and walked into the chamber before he could respond. He shoved his hands behind him, fisting them tight. He had an odd desire to reach for her. To draw her back to him. He quenched the thought, shocked at the intensity of the unexpected yearning.

What was it about this Persian girl who had the speech and manners of a lady, yet cooked and cleaned like a servant? A woman who bore the wounds of a cruel father? How had she managed to awaken these dormant longings in him?

He could not explain his attraction to her. He was a man who, by virtue of his profession, had seen and known more of women than most men would in a lifetime. A pretty face did not turn his head.

But something about her did.

He threw a look to the outside gate. For a moment, all he wanted was to scramble out of this house, get on his horse, and ride as fast and as far as the Nisaean could manage. Instead, he stepped over the threshold and followed her into the chamber.

5

Roxannah

For jealousy makes a man furious,
and he will not spare when he takes revenge.

Proverbs 6:34

What had possessed her to make such an intimate
observation about Adin's profession? At her words,
his eyes widened, and for a moment, he stared at
her like a cornered deer. Roxannah felt her face turn the color
of a fat beet. She led him into her father's chamber, and choking
out an excuse, escaped into the kitchen.

She berated herself for opening her mouth and a little too
much of her heart to a man she barely knew. She poured her
frustrations into the bread dough, kneading with too much
enthusiasm until her knuckles hurt.

"Mistress Roxannah?"

She gasped. How had he managed to weave through her obstacles without making a sound? She slapped a hand against her

chest in an unconscious effort to calm her palpitating heart, showering the front of her tunic with flour. "Master Adin!"

"Pardon my intrusion." He was all business now, the friendliness of earlier vanished behind a cool façade. "I only wished to tell you that your father is progressing well. No sign of fever or swelling. I am about to leave. I thought you might want to bar the door behind me."

"My thanks." She followed him into the courtyard.

At the gate, he turned to face her. "Lord Fravartish seems stable. I don't want you to worry. Yet his general condition is . . . more fragile than I would like. He will not listen to my advice."

Roxannah sighed. "Not if it concerns the contents of his cup."

He grimaced. "I'll return one last time tomorrow to ensure there is no relapse." He turned to reach for the door.

"Master Adin?"

He swiveled around so fast his pleated sleeves fluttered like wings before tangling against his side. "Yes?"

"Regarding my father's account—"

He waved a hand. "No need. No need at all. I hardly did anything. Glad to be of service to his lordship."

Before she could decide whether to argue or express gratitude, he had slipped through the door, his black Nisaean clopping down the lane with determined steps.

Roxannah returned to her father's chamber to find him sitting up, his brows drawn into a dark expression. She cleared her throat. "Master Adin is pleased with your progress, Father. He says there is no cause for worry."

Her father took a long gulp from his dented goblet. "Did you see what that healer was wearing? His tunic could pay for a month of my debts. Here I am, a Persian lord, my bloodlines pure all the way back to Mardian himself, and I have to put up with the indignity of wearing coarse wool. What does that nobody from Elephantine wear? Linen and silver embroidery! It's an insult, I tell you. An insult to my very blood."

Roxannah did not bother to remind him that the profligate life he led, riddled with poor decisions through the years, lay at the root of his increasing debts. "He refuses to charge you, you know."

"What do you mean?"

"He says he did so little that there is no sense in asking for payment."

Her father's eyes narrowed. "Does he dare offer me charity?"

"I think he was only being polite. He said he is glad to be of service to Lord Fravartish."

"Well. I doubt he treats anyone but a handful of servants at the palace. It's not as if he is the king's own physician. Must be a new experience for him, mixing with gentry."

Roxannah pressed a finger to her lips. "I am sure he is overwhelmed by the honor."

"Still, it doesn't excuse his rudeness. As if I need his handout!" He took a long swallow from his cup. "He can flash his embroidered tunic at the world all he wants. He's still a nobody."

He traced the neat bandage wrapped about his head. "At least he seems to know his trade." Roxannah inhaled sharply when her father tapped her cheek gently. "You did well to fetch him to me, child."

For a fleeting instant, the father of her childhood returned, a sweet gentleness sparking in his bloodshot eyes. Moments like this were rare. They made her ache with the impossible hope that one day he would abandon his obsession with wine and return to them whole.

She covered his hand with her own. He pulled back as if singed and, snapping his fingers, motioned for her to leave.

Roxannah could not sleep. For once, it was neither her father's temper nor the ever-present threat of financial catastrophe that kept her awake.

Instead, it was thoughts of Adin that had her sitting up in

bed, her arms wrapped tightly around her knees. His words replayed in her mind again and again, as if each one held some weighty revelation she could not bear to miss.

"What do you dream?" He had asked the question with a strange intensity, as though her answer mattered more than the exigencies of a casual conversation.

Lulled by his interest, she had almost blurted out the answer. He would have found it a challenge not to laugh in her face if she had revealed the silly dream of hosting the king and queen in her home for supper and cooking the whole meal herself. In her fantasy, every dish turned out perfectly, of course. And the king, impressed by her talent, presented her with a royal gift. Something she could hold up to her father to prove . . . to prove that she was not a disappointment, she supposed.

A childish fantasy she should have given up years ago. Adin would have been embarrassed to be on the receiving end of such silliness.

She flopped back on the mattress and pulled the sheet up to her chin. What was this ill-advised fascination she was forming for the physician? It was so unlike her, this odd longing for a man's regard. At twenty-three, she had long since outgrown that kind of desire. Roxannah couldn't live under Lord Fravartish's rule and keep dreaming those kinds of dreams.

Besides, why would such a man—wealthy and cultured—be interested in a woman with calloused hands, unkempt hair, and work-worn clothes? Worse still, why would a Jewish man devout enough to avoid Ionic temples of healing have any interest in a Persian woman?

Even simple friendship between them was an impossibility. They inhabited different worlds. She occupied the dominion of Lord Fravartish, a world that left little room for outsiders. The place of shadows and shame.

The crystalline currents of the river Karkheh flowed to the west of Susa, irrigating the thirsty city. It was said to have the purest water in the world. For that reason, no one was allowed to drink from its waters but the king.

Roxannah's favorite place was the river's fertile banks, which provided endless treasures for anyone patient enough to search for them. Here, she foraged for wild ingredients that had the advantage of being free as well as delicious resources for the new recipes she loved to create.

Walking by the river's banks at sunrise, Roxannah came across a cluster of wild, twisty fig trees. It was early for the first harvest. But a few handfuls of precocious fruit had ripened enough to be picked.

At home, she snipped the stems and washed the figs before letting them simmer with honey, adding a touch of her special blend of spices. They would taste delicious with the creamy yogurt she had made the day before.

Her mother navigated through her barricades with the ease of long familiarity. "What are you making?"

"Fig with honey." She spooned a bit of cooling jam over a small bowl of yogurt. "Taste."

"Oh my." Her mother made a swooning motion with her hand to her forehead. "You are a wonder, daughter."

Roxannah grinned. "I'll save you some."

"Taking the rest to Lord Zopyrus?"

"He loves anything with figs."

"He loves anything that you make because he is a man of good taste."

For every insult that Roxannah received from her father, it seemed that she received three praises from her mother. Her mother's warmth and bone-deep approval, along with the years of affection that her grandparents had poured into her before dying, now held her in one piece. Her father's darkness carried a lot of power. But not enough to vanquish the light of love.

Her mother tapped a gentle hand against her cheek. "You are the glue that keeps this family together. You do know that? You keep us from falling apart."

Moments like this were like eating a whole platter of honeyed butter pastries in one sitting, tasting the mouthwatering pleasure of every bite while feeling a little sick at the same time. Roxannah enjoyed the sweetness of her mother's appreciation. The delight of knowing herself useful to her family. But her mother's words also made her a little nauseous. She wished she did not have to carry the weight of their survival. The burden of it proved so heavy at times that it crushed even her ability to dream of better things, leaving behind merely the battle to endure.

The knock at the door interrupted her reverie. "That must be the physician. He said he would return today."

"He's a thoughtful man. I like him."

The problem was that Roxannah agreed a little too enthusiastically.

Adin lingered in the courtyard. "How is it that this house always smells a little of heaven, Mistress Roxannah?"

"That's how we pay our physicians, Master Adin."

"Sounds like a fair trade. What is it this time?"

"A bit of fig jam. And fresh yogurt. Come and have a bowl when you finish with Father."

He hesitated for a fraction of a moment. "How can I say no to such a generous fee?"

6

Adin

Guard your heart above all else,
for it determines the course of your life.

Proverbs 4:23 NLT

There were so many reasons to refuse Roxannah's invitation. He did not like figs. He was not partial to yogurt. He was a son of Abraham who should not encourage the companionship of a Gentile woman. He could picture his mother's horrified expression, his father's accusing glare. His own faith forbade any serious connection with a woman who did not love the Lord as he did.

Many of his people had loosened their ties to God's law in recent years. In Elephantine, where the Hebrew population had actually built a Jewish temple, a man could be seen worshipping the Lord there in the morning and paying a visit to an Egyptian temple in the afternoon. Even mixed marriages were not uncommon.

That life was not for Adin. He wanted, above all, to be a man after God's heart. In any case, none of these objections should even necessitate his consideration. *No* woman had a place in his life. Not anymore.

Still, here he sat on her rickety porch, new grape leaves sprouting on the arches over his head, a bowl of creamy white yogurt topped with fig jam in front of him. He tasted a cautious spoonful and frowned. It was like no yogurt or fig he had ever tasted. Sweet creamy flavors mixed with honey and a complex mix of spices that made him dip his spoon into the bowl again, this time with unfeigned enthusiasm.

"Mistress Roxannah, you should be famous."

Her mother climbed up the porch steps. "That's what I say." She placed a small ceramic bowl in front of him. She had covered the top with a bit of clean cloth. "For you to take home. Roxannah told me of your generosity. Yogurt and jam are hardly worthy of you. But your wife might appreciate it."

He blinked. She had maneuvered that with a deft touch. Many a mother had subjected him to more overt scrutiny. Roxannah had not missed the allusion either, if the tide of color flowing into her face was anything to go by.

"I have no wife, my lady. I am a widower."

"I am sorry to hear it."

"It happened a long time ago."

Roxannah's face softened. "When you were eighteen?"

"How did you . . . ?"

It knocked the breath out of him. How had she managed to cobble the story of his life together from the fragments he had given her?

"A guess, only."

"An accurate one."

Her mother rose. "I had better see to my husband. I only came to thank you for your excellent care."

He rose to give her a bow. She had handed him the perfect

opening to take his own leave. But he found himself sitting again on the flat cushion. He played with his wooden spoon. "What made you conclude my wife had died when I was eighteen?"

Roxannah clasped her hands together. "You told me you chose to become a physician then. Something made you change your whole way of life when you were eighteen. Something that gave you both the desire and the strength to leave everything you knew. To pursue a new vocation, in spite of your father's disappointment." She looked down. "I did not mean to offend you, Master Adin."

"You did not offend. I am intrigued. Not many would arrive at so accurate a conclusion from the little I revealed."

Her fingers twisted into a ligature. "Perhaps I know something about how hard it is to change your life."

"You have never married?" The question slipped out of him without his permission. Why did she do that to him? Why did she pull out what he meant to keep hidden?

"No." She drew her sleeve over her knuckles. "No dowry. No suitors."

"I find that hard to believe."

The little dimple peeped out at him. "Well, a few interested parties. But none who were acceptable to my father."

"I am so sorry."

"Not at all. It has always suited my own desires."

He turned his head toward the room where his patient lay half soaked in wine already. Remembering the bruises on her arm and the obstacle course that he had to navigate to the kitchen the day before, he grimaced. She had her own reasons to live a guarded life.

How strange that their opposite experiences had landed them in the same place. For him, it had been happiness that had encrusted his heart with ice because happiness had proven a betrayer. He had watched helplessly as illness engulfed Hulda's youthful body. As death's unbending hand claimed her. The pain of loss had brought him to the edge of sanity. To the precipice of despair. He never wanted to go through that again. Unlike him, Roxannah had learned to guard her heart because of unhappiness. Because her father had taught her that love could prove fickle and agonizing. The man was like an earthquake that struck when you least expected. An earthquake that leveled everything safe. She had been powerless to stop those tremors. So she had closed the gates of her heart, lest the quakes of pain dismantle the beams of her very being.

Their opposite experiences had taught them the same lessons. His chest tightened at the thought of the walls that surrounded her heart. It seemed like such a waste. What he could not feel for himself, he felt for her. She should know love. Know the joys of being held and cherished. Experience the contentment of being known—bone-deep known—and still wanted.

He could not give her any of that. His feet moved of their own accord, turning toward the gate as he rose to take his leave.

7

Roxannah

I will make a way in the wilderness
and rivers in the desert.

Isaiah 43:19

THE TWELFTH YEAR OF KING XERXES'S RULE
THE THIRTEENTH DAY OF SPRING

The following morning, before her parents had risen from bed, Roxannah left the house to purchase a shank of mutton with the silver Lord Zopyrus had paid her. The particular market she wanted to visit lay at the center of an oblong village east of Susa, occupied predominantly by tradesmen.

The city of Susa was too small to house all the artisans and servants necessary to support so great a citadel. Surrounding its ancient, walled boundaries, several villages had sprung up to sustain the homes and businesses of those who worked and served at the palace.

Roxannah preferred this market to the one located conveniently within Susa. For one, the prices were more reasonable. For another, her friend Tirzah worked at her family's stall, which meant Roxannah could enjoy a satisfying visit while tending her errands.

It was still dark by the time she arrived. The merchants, accustomed to keeping early hours, had lit the square with dozens of fat torches. Colorful stalls with leather rooftops were hung with patterned fabrics that served both as walls and decoration. Roxannah strolled by an endless array of merchandise: stacks of vivid textiles, exotic spices piled into aromatic hills, silver and copper platters, painted clay pottery, bright bird feathers, animal skins, and other curiosities from all over the empire.

The Artisans' Village imported the world's most beautiful objects while also providing the mundane necessities of life, offering something for everyone. Roxannah felt her heart lift as she walked through the vibrant stalls, the titillating scent of perfumes and oils mingling with that of fresh herbs and foreign spices.

As always, she purchased her meat from Tirzah's uncle, Avraham. He winked as he handed over the packaged mutton, charging her "the family rate" thanks to her friendship with Tirzah. But that wasn't the only reason she used him as a butcher. Whatever preparation was required by Jewish law rendered his meat and poultry the best in Susa.

On her way to Tirzah's stall, a bolt of mint-green fabric caught her attention. The merchant unrolled it so she could see it better.

"You will look like a flower in this." He kissed the tips of his fingers.

She shook her head. She would never be able to afford it. As she turned, a royal messenger clambered up the steps of a small dais and declared with a loud voice that he came bearing important news.

Like the other shoppers milling in the marketplace, she turned to listen. Royal proclamations were not rare. It could be a pronouncement about a new road the king had started to build or the celebration of another victory in some distant land. But this proclamation turned out to be nothing like she had ever heard.

"A letter to the 127 provinces of Persia," the messenger announced, "from Xerxes, king of kings, king on this earth far and wide, the son of Darius the king. I proclaim that on the thirteenth day of the twelfth month, which is the month of Adar, my people are to destroy, kill, and annihilate every single Jew, young and old, woman and child, in my entire kingdom and to plunder their riches."

Roxannah clapped a hand over her mouth to keep the sour bile from spilling on her shoes. Like everyone else in the square, she waited for an explanation. But none was forthcoming. In less than eleven months, before the arrival of the next Persian New Year, the teeming population of Persia were granted the right to kill and plunder an entire people.

The crowd sank into shocked silence for a moment before erupting. A confusion of sounds greeted the proclamation, which the messenger was once again repeating. A few people tore their tunics at the seam. Those must be the Jews, already grieving an incomprehensible edict.

Although the majority of those present looked dismayed, Roxannah also detected a few satisfied smiles on hard faces. For a moment, she was ashamed to be called a Persian.

Until now, Achaemenid kings had enjoyed a reputation for leniency in their conquests. They had become known for elevating foreigners to positions of power, according them honors when merited by hard work and talent. They certainly punished those who rebelled. No tame puppy had ever sat on the throne of the Persian Empire.

But never before had the royal line targeted a whole race

of people for annihilation. Never before had the royal house proclaimed the extermination of a whole people throughout the realm.

Roxannah stumbled through the crowd, hardly knowing where she went. Only two weeks into spring, the hot sun of Susa already beat down in waves of remorseless heat. Perspiration dampened her neck and back. Dizzy, she came to a stop at the side of the square and simply sank to the ground.

Good Light! The world had gone mad!

She dropped her head in her hands, thinking of Tirzah and her family. All—*all*—to be killed in a single day?

She must find her friend. By now the marketplace had turned into a roiling mass of people, running in confusion, shouting, searching for loved ones to share the news with. Roxannah rose and pushed her way through the crowd, arms and elbows finding frantic purchase as she made her way to Tirzah's stall. Spotting her friend, she waved.

Tirzah lifted tear-streaked eyes. "Did you hear? Did you hear that edict?"

Roxannah leaned against the table. Everything seemed so familiar. So ordinary. The colorful array of dried fruits, nuts, and seeds arranged tastefully on a clean tablecloth. She could almost make herself believe that the world had not tipped over on its head. "I am so sorry. There must be a mistake. It can't be true."

Tirzah's head gave a wild shake. "No mistake. My people! My poor people. I must tell my family. Will you give me a hand, Roxannah?"

Wordlessly, Roxannah helped her friend cover her wares and load them onto the cart waiting behind her. She watched as the weeping young woman slowly guided her donkey through the throng and onto the dirt road.

What could possess the king to write such a command into immutable law? There was no reversing this declaration. Like a stone carved, a king's law in Persia became a permanent thing. Even the king himself could not change it.

The Jews could not even take up arms to defend themselves. Only an army that served the king had the right to bear arms, to fight, to shed blood. If the Jewish population dared to protect itself from this attack, they would simply be arrested by the standing army and put to an even worse death. They had no choice but to give in to their fate or find a far corner of the world out of reach of the Persian Empire.

Not only Tirzah and Avraham and their whole kin, but the entire Jewish population of Persia would be annihilated.

Adin would be annihilated.

In eleven months, they would all die.

For a moment, Roxannah could not breathe.

She paced aimlessly through the now-subdued marketplace. Had the physician even heard the news? It was so early in the morning that she doubted he had left for the palace yet. He probably didn't know that his whole life had been upended in the span of a moment. Even once he arrived at the palace, he might not hear an accurate report. Her grandmother, who had been a common visitor to the palace in another age, had once told her that the place seethed with gossip, the truth often spiced with inaccurate tidbits of rumor. Unless he heard the edict read by an official messenger, Adin was bound to pick up a twisted version of events.

She could do Adin one service, at least. She could ensure that he received an accurate report. That way, he would not be caught off guard by some evil tongue-wagging, adding who knew what distortions to the already calamitous edict. Besides, the sooner he heard, the more time he would have to plan for his future survival. He certainly could not return home to the Isle of Elephantine. The Persians ruled over Egypt. The Jews living there were no safer than those living in Susa.

Roxannah headed west toward the Jewish quarter, racing through the streets of the Royal Village, ignoring dignified brick villas as she ran beneath the shade of leafy trees.

Darab opened the door to her frantic knocking. "Mistress! Did your father take a turn for worse?"

"He is well, Darab. But you must fetch your master. I come with dreadful news."

Before Darab could respond, the man himself emerged from the house, garbed in his formal attire, obviously bound for the palace. "Roxannah!" In his surprise, her forgot to call her *mistress*. "What has happened?"

Roxannah's throat turned dry. How was she to give such news? "I beg your pardon for coming to your house like this. It concerns a grave matter, or I would not have disturbed you."

He drew close. "Not your father?"

"No, no. He is well. I don't know how to tell you. . . . Adin, have you heard the royal proclamation this morning? Against the Jews?"

His brow furrowed. "What proclamation?"

"The king has issued an edict declaring that all the Jews in the empire are to be put to death in a single day, eleven months from now."

Adin's expression turned stony. "Where did you hear this poisonous rumor?

"It's no rumor, else I would not have come. I heard it from a royal messenger with my own ears while I shopped at the Artisans' Village not an hour ago."

"Tell me what you heard. As precisely as you recall."

"I will not soon forget the words of that terrible proclamation." Roxannah recounted the edict and described the crowd's stunned response.

Adin paled. A long look passed between him and Darab. The servant bowed. "I will find out what I can."

Outside, a woman's wail rent the air, followed by another cry, eerie and high-pitched.

Adin winced. "The news must be spreading."

Darab clasped his arm. "You had better go to the palace as usual. No need to draw attention to yourself."

Adin pulled a hand through his hair. His fingers were not quite steady. "Roxannah, I ask your pardon. I should not have doubted your word."

His simple apology had a strange effect on her. She felt as though a knot of hurt melted in some deep part of her. It had been long years since her father had asked her forgiveness. Adin's words, simple and sincere, felt like a soothing balm over not only his own cold words, but also upon that old ache. "I would not have believed it myself had I not heard it with my own ears," she said. "No need to apologize."

"I thank you for your grace. It was good of you to bring me the news."

"I am so sorry, Master Adin."

He bowed his head. For a moment, his face looked older than thirty-one years. "Who can understand what the Lord intends? Kings do not always have the last word, you know."

"Yes. Perhaps your God will intervene on your behalf."

The corners of his eyes crinkled. "He is not *my* God only. He rules over the whole earth. Even kings and queens are subject to him."

Roxannah smiled sadly. In her experience, it was human beings who ruled over gods. Their will seemed stronger. One had to spend just one night in her house to know that. Her father had once been a devout follower of Ahura Mazda, the Persian god of light. Of goodness. Yet his god seemed helpless to stop Lord Fravartish's destructive ways.

Adin released a long breath. "You must excuse me. I have to head to the palace."

"Of course. Perhaps you will be able to discover more there."

Darab swung the gate open for her. "Allow me to accompany you part of the way, mistress. I am headed in the same direction."

"Of course." They walked in silence for a few moments. Finally, she addressed the servant. "Darab, what will he do?"

The servant slowed his steps. "I am not certain. We will turn to God. He will guide us."

"*We?* You are Persian, I believe?" Everything from his speech to his name marked Darab as her own compatriot.

He bowed his head. "All the way to my roots, lady. From the Maraphi tribe."

Roxannah's brows rose. The Maraphi were an ancient tribal family, whose ties to Cyrus the Great had given them a permanent spot among the nobility. Darab's bloodlines were purer than her own. "Yet you worship the Jewish God?"

"I am devoted to the Lord. Yes."

"That is . . . unusual."

He inclined his turbaned head.

"Is it because of your God that you are a servant?"

"It is because of God that I am alive. I am a servant because my friend needs me." He flashed his white smile. "And besides, he pays generously."

Roxannah had seen enough of the relationship between the men to know that with or without pay, Darab would not leave Adin's side. Her mind burst with a thousand questions.

Before she could voice a single one, Darab offered her another of his regal bows. "I must part company with you here. My way takes me in the opposite direction from your home."

"Oh." Roxannah tried to hide her disappointment. "I hope you will find there is some mistake in the messenger's pronouncement."

"And even if not, the Lord shall make a way."

She watched Darab stride away, his steps swift. What a mystery the man seemed. A servant lord. At once higher than her father and yet more humbled. He must have lost everything to have been reduced to the position of a servant. And yet he seemed utterly content with his lot. He could not be more dignified if he wore a crown.

How did a man fall so low and yet live so high?

From the Secret Scrolls
of Esther

For the LORD of hosts has purposed,
and who will annul it?

Isaiah 14:27

Thirty-Three Years Later
The Twenty-Fifth Year of King Artaxerxes's Rule

You might say my menses shaped my destiny. The Lord designed my body with a strange timing. I was closer to seventeen than sixteen before I became a woman. My cousin Mordecai shrugged his shoulder when my friends were betrothed one after another while I sat at home, shamed by my backward body.

"The Lord has his plan, child. You can trust him."

Easy for him to say. He had never been late for anything.

When my menses finally arrived, I wept because I could finally be like everyone else. Women didn't throw pitiful looks in my direction. I was one of them. I was no longer different, and that was all I wanted.

God must have had a good laugh at that.

Mordecai lost no time in arranging a marriage for me. He had the kindness to ask for my approval first, allowing me all the freedom I needed to refuse if I wished. It was typical of him, this quiet thoughtfulness, and one of the reasons my parents had entrusted him with my care before dying of a fever within three days of each other. But that's a different heartache. We were speaking of my betrothal.

My cousin Mordecai, a low-level magistrate at the court, knew most of the Jews who worked at the palace. One of his friends, a man who supervised the king's poultry in Susa, had a son my age. I remember Gideoni's gap-toothed smile for its charm, and the way he startled at any loud noise, like one of the chickens he cared for.

He always seemed dazzled when he saw me, his very long lashes opening and closing rapidly like a woman's fan in the heat of high summer. Strange what the mind chooses to retain and what it discards. Though we were betrothed for almost six months, the years have since worn out the edges of my memories of him. I should perhaps have held him dearer in my heart. But I have lived a long life, and Gideoni did not.

Two months before we were to wed, he died. Another fever. Another heartache. Had he lived, I would have been a respectable married woman ensconced in my own home, helping my husband care for the king's poultry by the time the royal search began. I never would have been taken into the king's palace.

Never entered that ridiculous competition.

No one had heard of such a thing. A competition to find a queen! It was a preposterous notion for a dignified Persian king. Royal marriages were forged by bonds of power and wealth. By connections and conventions. Not this farcical search for beautiful virgins, as though the palace suffered a dearth of such.

Later, my husband confessed to me as we lay together in his golden bed, surrounded by silken pillows and silence, that the competition was a straw he had clutched at. Years earlier, he had chosen Vashti as his queen over Amestris. Amestris with her ambitions and her pride and her pure bloodlines. He had never liked the woman. Pushy and sly, she schemed too much for his comfort.

Once he dismissed Vashti, however, he had no real choice. The daughter of one of the most influential men in the kingdom, Amestris's lineage alone gave her the right to the crown, to mention nothing of the fact that she had given birth to the boy Xerxes recognized as his prince regent.

Yet he could not do it. He could not bear to have her as his queen. He had done more than his duty by her, siring four children upon her. But he needed an excuse to snub her a second time. To withhold the crown without causing a bitter political storm.

He had latched on to that absurd competition as the perfect excuse. It hadn't been his idea, after all. His courtiers had come up with the scheme. It suited them to prevent Amestris's father, Otanis, from rising too high above them by becoming the father of the queen as well as the grandfather of the crown prince. Xerxes could blame the whole affair on his officials if Amestris and Otanis objected. If they wanted to take offense, let them be offended at the whole court.

I was approaching the end of my mourning period for Gideoni when the king's agents brought me to the palace. To the Persians, being chosen as a candidate was a great honor. The riches of palace life, the privileges it brought to the family of any woman accepted, made belonging to the king, whether they were chosen as queen or not, the cherished dream of most girls.

I felt differently. Though aware of the honor bestowed upon me, I would, nonetheless, have preferred a quiet life away from palace walls. But sometimes the doors that open before us are not the ones we long for.

Thanks to my year of royal preparation and mind-numbing beauty treatments, I was twenty by the time Xerxes laid eyes on me. Practically ancient for a virgin. That might have been part of the attraction. I was not a giggling child. I had a woman's conversation and interests. Nor was I an ambitious princess, sharpening my avaricious talons on the sword of his power. He could see I did not care. The less I cared, the more beautiful he found me.

Men are strange creatures.

So you see, it was really my menses that landed me on the throne of Persia. Had I bled earlier, I would have been a married woman by the time the competition came about. Had I bled later, I would have been disqualified.

A woman's blood. An unclean thing. A reason for rejection and separation. That is what God used to save our nation from the plot of Haman.

Between you and me, God is even stranger than men.

Else, why would he entrust the fate of a generation of his people to a woman ruled by fear?

8

Roxannah

He is faithful in all my house. With him I speak mouth to mouth.

Numbers 12:7–8

Remembering his bitter resentment of Adin's success, Roxannah decided to keep the news of the king's edict a secret from her father. The temptation in that wicked proclamation would prove too much for a man already bent toward violence. She would have to devise excuses to keep him home for the next week. In a few days, the excitement surrounding the attack on the Jews would fade. The people of Susa would find something else to occupy their fancy. Hopefully, her father would never hear of that day of destruction.

She entered his chamber bearing a bowl of rich mutton soup and several squares of warm bread. "Your supper, Father."

61

He greeted her with a cheerful wave. "Smells good." Dipping his bread into the bowl she placed before him, he allowed it to soak. "Have you heard the news?"

Roxannah's heart lurched. "What news?"

"The wine merchant brought me the very best tidings." He slurped from his bowl. "Our troubles are at an end."

A shiver ran down her spine, as if her body already knew what her ears had yet to hear.

"I need not worry about the moneylenders for long. In eleven months, we shall have all the silver we need."

"Eleven months!" Her voice quavered. "You can't mean—"

"The king has handed me the perfect means to pay off my debts while enjoying a little justice."

"What manner of justice is this?"

"It is justice for a lord to take his rightful place and help others to theirs."

Making an excuse, Roxannah escaped her father's chamber and headed for the kitchen. She set up her pots against the door and, with half a mind, established an escape route in case of trouble. None of it made the world safe.

She stared at the pile of onions she had brought out of storage, and instead of chopping, sank down on the dented stool to stare into space. Images of what might happen in eleven months paraded before her eyes.

Her father, the veteran warrior of numerous battles, dressed in armor, sword strapped to his side. Her father attacking the Jews in the marketplace of the Artisans' Village. Her father shedding the blood of Tirzah and Avraham and their family to walk away with chests full of their hard-earned merchandise.

Her father attacking Adin.

Adin lying senseless on the ground. Her father riding away on Adin's black Nisaean, wearing his expensive silver-embroidered robe, its hemline scarlet with blood.

She pressed her fists into burning eyes, denying the tears

that longed to release. Grabbing her knife, she sharpened its edge against an old leather strop, her strokes haphazard and unfocused. As she chopped the first onion, its pungent smell did what her mind would not allow, and the tears flowed, salty and bitter.

Eleven months! A lifetime away. Anything could happen in that time. Rescue might come in ways she could not imagine. A thousand goblets of wine stood between now and that day. Likely her father would forget his deadly intentions. She pushed away the horrifying images.

Though they disappeared, the fear they had dragged into her heart lingered.

Her mother often told Roxannah that she kept the family from falling apart. In truth, she didn't know how they hadn't unraveled already, how they held together somehow, day after day. She thought of the way a dollop of yogurt in a tub of warm milk would thicken the liquid and transform the whole thing. Was she supposed to be that spoonful of starter yogurt? If so, she felt like there was a little less of her in every spoon. One of these days, they would look and all they would find was spilt milk disappearing into the ground, with nothing to give them the strength they needed to hold their lives together.

The last of the mutton simmered in water made fragrant with onions, garlic, and turmeric. Roxannah let the meat cook until tender enough to fall off the bone. It was the season for young almonds, and she had harvested a bowlful of the soft, green pods from the tree growing in the corner of the courtyard. She added the fuzzy pods to the stew and left them to boil until tender. They would give the meat a delicious tang. It was a recipe of her own making, one she had experimented with until satisfied with its consistency and flavor.

Cooking gave her what life often did not: the satisfaction of being in control. Even when a recipe went wrong, she had another chance—an opportunity to learn from her mistake and make an improvement in the next batch.

She set aside a portion of the stew for her family and poured the rest into a clay bowl with a lid. She needed to find out what Adin had discovered about the king's proclamation. Perhaps he would tell her that the decree was a misunderstanding. She clutched the only comfort she had to offer him—a bowl of mutton stew—and set off for the Jewish quarter.

A little girl was playing by the side of the wall with a dirty ball of twine. She clasped her twine to her chest and sidled close. "Are you here to visit Adin?"

"I am."

Her rosebud mouth rounded. "Why? Are you sick?"

"I hope not."

A grin revealed a gap where the two front teeth used to be. "He is nice."

Roxannah grinned back. "He is very nice."

"Did you bring him a gift?"

"A bowl of stew."

The girl nodded sagely. "Women are always cooking for him."

Roxannah coughed. "He receives a lot of dishes, does he?"

A little shoulder lifted in a shrug. "It's because he's always helping everybody. He helps me and my *ima*. I'm Leah. I'm seven."

"Goodness. You are very wise for your age."

"Everybody says that. How old are you?"

"Almost twenty-four."

Leah whistled. "Nice. You have pretty eyes."

"You have pretty everything."

Leah gave a regal nod of her head. "Everybody says that too. Here, I will knock for you since your hands are full."

Hearing about all the women bearing gifts to Adin had made Roxannah reconsider her visit as well as her offering. She suspected she had made a grave miscalculation. Adin had no need

64

of her comfort. Or friendship. But she needed to hear if he had any more information. The child banged on the door with single-minded determination, her tiny fist surprisingly loud.

"Oh dear," Roxannah said when Adin himself answered.

"Leah. And Roxannah! You know each other?"

"We do now." Roxannah held out her stew. "Another meal to add to your collection."

"My collection?" Adin took the bowl from her outstretched hand and sniffed at the steam rising from the bowl. "How thoughtful. Meat, is it?"

She noted his slight frown, though he was quick to smooth the lines of his face into a pleasant smile. "Purchased from Avraham the butcher in Artisans' Village," she said. "All his meats are prepared according to the laws of your people. He assured me this recipe would meet with the rabbi's approval."

His face relaxed. "If the aroma is any indication, Darab and I will be feasting tonight."

"I came to see if you had found out anything else about the king's edict."

He invited her into the courtyard, somehow managing to send Leah back to play in the quiet street. No words had to pass his lips for her to know his news. There had been no mistake. The edict was true.

"How can I help?" she offered hopelessly. She couldn't even help herself or her mother. One man kept her bound. How could she stand against a whole nation?

"It is enough that you want to." Looking into his kind eyes, she believed him.

He motioned for her to sit on the familiar stone bench across from his pool as he rinsed his hands in the water with slow, methodical movements. "This is one of those moments when God alone is the answer. Our friends can accompany us through the journey, and that too is a gift. But only God can open impossible doors like this."

His face looked tired and drawn. Just under the surface of that strain, she sensed a strange peace that held him the way a hand might cradle a fragile ceramic dish. For a moment, she envied his faith. "Must be a help to you, having been raised with such a strong belief in God."

The faraway look on his face sharpened and became focused. "I grew up with the outward trappings of my religion. Keeping certain rules, attending the Jewish temple in Elephantine, obeying the dietary laws. But my heart was ignorant of God. Rules make a poor bridge to his love. Then I met my Hulda."

My Hulda. His wife. Roxannah leaned forward, her whole body attuned to his every word. "She must have been very special."

His smile held a world of sorrow. "One of a kind. I think half the men of Elephantine were in love with her. But for some reason, she chose me. Her father was the newly appointed general of the Elephantine fortress. He had hopes of a better match for his only child. But in the end, his heart softened. Not long after my eighteenth birthday, we were married. Seven months later, she became sick."

"That's heartbreaking."

"I will not disagree."

She resisted the temptation to pelt him with questions. Curiosity was not a good companion for pain. She watched the emotions flit across his face like clouds in the wind.

After a stretch of silence, he settled himself next to her on the bench. To her relief, he took up the story again. "Hulda had a quiet faith that ran deep. She studied the Scriptures, not like a scribe for the knowledge, but with a sweet devotion that guided her life. In the throes of her illness, she turned to God in a way I could not understand. When I was railing and ranting, she was worshipping and praising.

"It finally dawned on me that she was beyond help. That our small island lacked the medical skill that could offer her hope of healing. I was about to lose her, and I could do nothing. My world shattered. The religious rules of my childhood did nothing to help me. God seemed more like an empty hoax than a source of our salvation."

She nodded in understanding. She had felt that same helpless shattering more than once. The same frustrated betrayal by a religion that did nothing to assuage her pain. The darkness that always seemed to overcome the light. "How is it that you changed your mind?" It was the place their paths diverged. He had returned to his God. She had left Ahura Mazda behind.

Adin bent to dip his hand in the water again and drew it down his face as if to wash away some putrid memory. "I had nowhere to turn. People tried to comfort me with platitudes, or worse. They tried to blame Hulda. They said she must have some hidden sin for God to strike her down in the prime of her youth. Poor dove. To the pain of her body, they added the embers of shame and guilt."

"I am surprised you have any faith left after that."

"I almost did not. People are not always good ambassadors for God. But Hulda held firm. To her last breath, she praised him. And I saw in her what I had never seen in empty religious observance. I saw the joy that comes from the presence of God."

Roxannah crossed her arms over her belly. "Even when she was dying?"

"Even as she lay dying. One night, toward the end, as I sat by her bed, weeping, she laid her hand on my head. 'Adin, you must be like Moses,' she said. I stopped my sniveling and stared at her in shock. She had not spoken for several days by then. 'Moses?' I stammered."

Roxannah gave him a puzzled look.

"He is our greatest prophet," Adin explained. "Hulda said, 'Remember how God spoke to Moses mouth to mouth? You must learn to speak to him like that.'"

"What does that mean?"

"In our language, speaking mouth to mouth is an expression of closeness. It means you are on intimate terms with someone. Friends who share their hearts openly. God spoke to Moses mouth to mouth. With the familiarity of a friend. Hulda wanted me to understand that true faith leads to that kind of friendship with God."

Roxannah went still. A strange longing opened its sleepy eyes and stretched like a puppy inside her. The longing for a God who would be a friend. A God so close that death itself could not devour his joy. "It does not sound like a simple lesson."

Adin chuckled softly. "It sounded impossible. At first, I placed all my focus on my medical learning, determined to pit myself against death and sickness. But the more I studied, the more I realized my limitations. I could not beat death.

"I had carried few things from home when I set off for Cnidus. Among them were the Scriptures Hulda clung to so faithfully. The scrolls were a sentimental reminder of her, worn thin from her touch. I hadn't meant to study them for myself. But as time passed and knowledge proved a poor companion, I began to turn to them.

"They brought their own questions. Yet they also opened the door to a quiet I had never known. That was the start of my faith. So you see, Mistress Roxannah, my youthful religion can do little to help now. Like Hulda, I am turning to God. And like Hulda, if this proclamation proves to be the death of my people, even here, I will praise him."

She sat in silence, digesting his words. Something about his faith struck her as beautiful. But also impossible.

Then she realized that he had addressed her as *Mistress Roxannah* again. After sharing his heartache, his suffering, after treating her like a trusted friend, he had remembered to push her away, holding her at arm's length once more.

In spite of his kindness, she sensed in him a reluctance, a distance, as though her presence brought him more discomfort than consolation. Roxannah rose to her feet. "I am honored you trusted me with your story, Master Adin. Call on my mother and me if we can ever be of help."

She said the words knowing he never would. As her steps carried her back home, she determined never to return, regardless of how much she wanted to.

Two weeks later, Roxannah stopped at the market to spend a little time with Tirzah. The pall of the king's edict had settled over her friend like a foaming wave on the deck of a small boat, and she staggered beneath the weight of it. Tirzah, usually chatty and full of news, seemed quiet and ill at ease, her eyes darting to and fro, her frame jumping at every loud noise.

"What will your family do?" Roxannah helped Tirzah clean up a puddle of something sticky that had spilled near her stall. "Will you leave Persia?"

"If we must. We hope for a miracle, of course. For now, we plan to remain in Susa. Our home is here. Our land and everything we own."

"Of course. You still have months before the edict takes effect. Who knows what will happen before then?" She wished she could offer her friend more than mere words. Offer her, if not shelter, then at least some manner of comfort by welcoming her into her home. But her father forbade visits from any of Roxannah's friends—not that she wanted to expose anyone to her father's mercurial temper. Still, this limitation was one of the reasons she enjoyed so few friendships. Even Tirzah's companionship had to remain limited to snatches of conversation in the marketplace.

Roxannah's gaze fell upon the next stall, and instantly she lost her train of thought at the sight of Adin examining a collection of silver amphorae.

"Master Adin!"

His eyes widened in surprise. For a tiny moment, she glimpsed a spark of pleasure in their inky depths. Then a curtain fell, and his voice, though perfectly pleasant, held a tinge of the old, familiar distance. "Mistress Roxannah."

For some reason she could not fathom, the formal address made her want to weep. The daughter of Lord Fravartish did not cry at every minor scrape. She must have lost her mind in the hot sun of Susa.

She pasted a cheerful smile on her face. "You should try Tirzah's dried fruit. No one has better in the market." Dried fruit? She hadn't lost her mind. She had turned into a fool. She sounded like a self-appointed peddler for the dried fruit merchants of Susa.

"I am well acquainted with Tirzah's delicious wares. Good day to you, Tirzah."

Tirzah blushed. "Good day, Master Adin." The girl had turned as dark a shade of red as Roxannah. Lovely. Now there were two fat beets staring back at him.

"I must return home."

"I must return to the palace."

They spoke in unison. They had a talent for that, it seemed. Roxannah gave an airy wave. "Give my regards to the king." She wanted to bite her tongue the moment the words left her mouth. Obviously, she had lost her mind *and* turned into a fool.

Adin laughed softly. "I wish I could. His Majesty is too preoccupied with running half the world to have time for a mere court physician." But the laughter washed away the brittle, detached air he had worn like a shield, and he seemed once again to become the friend who had whiled away an afternoon in her company.

It was a bittersweet moment, filled with a yearning for what could never be and the realization that, once again, she had to bid him good-bye.

From the Secret Scrolls of Esther

And who knows but that you have come to your
royal position for such a time as this?

Esther 4:14 NIV

Thirty-Three Years Later
The Twenty-Fifth Year of King Artaxerxes's Rule

How inaccurate is the measure of time. You may claim
that two days have exactly the same number of hours.
That one day in Susa equals one day in Bactria or Lydia.
But it is not so. That scale is an illusion.

One hour of conversing lightheartedly with your
friends does not last as long as an hour of toothache.
One evening with a broken bone drags much longer than
an evening devoid of pain.

By this measure, thirty days can last an age. You can
spin the stars out of their axis in thirty days. Make and
unmake worlds in thirty days.

You can crush a heart in thirty days.

A month of loneliness. Of uncertainty. Of rejection.

I do not call that thirty days. I call it a lifetime.

When destiny knocked upon my door in the form of Mordecai's message, it found me at my lowest. My husband, who had long since entrusted me with his heart and his secrets, had withheld himself from me for a long month with no explanation.

I wondered what had finally sundered him from me. Was it my barren womb? The son I had never borne him? Had he simply tired of my company? Had he found another beauty amongst his wives and concubines to replace me? Or had my rival Amestris, brimming with jealousy and contempt for me, finally managed to depose me by some clever scheme?

I did not know, and the not knowing cut me like the sharp edge of an unsheathed dagger.

I jumped at the sound of every messenger, fearing he carried a letter commanding me to vacate the queen's apartments so that I could make room for a more nubile woman. I wept when I could hear no messenger, fearing the king would never call for me again.

Into that vortex of confusion and pain, Mordecai's message came.

Save your people.

Whispered in the back corners of the synagogue in Ecbatana, over the years I have heard Mordecai's now-famous words to me: *"And who knows but that you have come to your royal position for such a time as this?"* They say the words lovingly, as if they were a sweet encouragement whispered in my ear. They hold on to those words because it reminds them that God's provision undergirds the times and places of our lives.

I have no quarrel with that. His provision has indeed proven trustworthy.

But the truth is that when Mordecai spoke those words to me, he meant them as a slap on the back of my hand. They were a poke into my wobbling spine to help me straighten. He meant them as more of a rebuke than an encouragement.

Here is the honest version of my story, without all the embellishments of years. When my cousin first told me about the plight of our people and asked me to intercede, I told him, *"I cannot."* Perhaps not those words, exactly. But I made him understand that any interference from me was impossible.

Go to the king? Intercede for our people? Mordecai did not understand.

My husband had not sent for me in a month. A century, you might call it, when you are a wife, unwanted. I saw my whole world through that lens. The lens of a woman rejected. It shaped my answer to Mordecai. To our people. To my God.

Thirty days earlier and I would not have hesitated. I had thought myself loved then. I had believed Xerxes would shield me from death, even if I came into his presence unbidden. Even if I broke the law.

Now, I knew I would die. Knew he would not choose to protect me from the death sentence that came with such a bold violation.

I was not like Amestris. My power did not lie in my bloodlines or my connections. It did not come from my children or my wealth. I had only ever had one power. Love. And now that it was gone, I had no influence with the king.

My people were condemned to death, and I could not help them.

That was my answer to Mordecai. My answer to God. *I cannot.*

So Mordecai rebuked me. He told me to take my eyes off my thirty days and put them on God's *such a time as this*. If God had brought me here to this position, if he had placed the crown on my head, then with or without a king's love, I would be able to save my people.

I could not refuse him. Not Mordecai who had been father and mother to me. I swallowed my *I cannot* and asked for the intercession of a three-day fast.

In truth, I had little hope. I thought in three days I would come before the king, my husband, and be condemned to death.

Mordecai might hold tight to God's *such a time as this*. But I still wallowed in my thirty days.

9

Adin

I am not able to carry all this people alone; the
burden is too heavy for me.

Numbers 11:14

THIRTY THREE YEARS EARLIER
THE TWELFTH YEAR OF KING XERXES'S RULE
THE LAST DAY OF SPRING

Adin arrived early at the synagogue and found it already
teeming with people. They spoke in excited whispers.
Mordecai ben Jair had asked the Jews of Susa to gather
together that day, for he had news of great import.

Adin had met Mordecai many times on his way into the
palace. The magistrate occupied a spot in the square across from
the Royal Gate, a favorite location for many minor officials
to conduct their business. Always ready with a smile and an
encouraging word, the magistrate seemed to Adin as solid and
stalwart as a plank of seasoned oak.

He liked Mordecai. More importantly, he trusted him. If the magistrate said he had important news, Adin wanted to hear whatever pronouncement he had.

The meeting hall in the synagogue was packed with hundreds of people, women crammed in their own quarter, which a fili-greed silver wall separated from the men's segment. Everyone quieted when Mordecai raised his hands.

"Brothers and sisters, you all know me. I am a widower with no children of my own, except that I raised the daughter of my uncle, one Hadassah whom you all remember as the sweetest flower of Israel. When she was eighteen, I told everyone I had sent Hadassah away, where she could have the company of other women, and the following year, I let it be known that she had married."

Adin frowned. This supposedly crucial proclamation had taken a strange turn. What import could Hadassah's marriage have to the Jewish community of Susa? He was not the only one to have that thought. A murmur arose in the synagogue, drowning Mordecai's voice.

Sheber ben Ziph, the ruler of the synagogue, snapped to his feet. "Please, friends! Be patient. Let our brother Mordecai finish."

Again, the congregation grew quiet so the magistrate could take up his tale. "I never lied to you. Hadassah did marry. What I did not tell you was that she married the Persian king, the same Xerxes who now rules over us. Indeed, Xerxes chose her for his queen."

A stunned silence met this pronouncement, followed by the sound of muted laughter.

Adin's brows rose. What madness was this? The queen of Persia was a woman named Esther, a beautiful creature he had glimpsed from afar. He had never met this Hadassah. But even he knew that the Persian queen could have nothing to do with a Jewish girl from an ordinary family, no matter how well-bred.

Once more, the ruler of the synagogue bade everyone to settle down. "You will never hear the full story if you do not quiet yourselves. And since I have been in Mordecai's confidence from the start, I will tell you that your very lives depend upon what he has to say."

Mordecai sent Sheber a grateful look. "You all remember five years ago when the king scoured the land for virgins, one of whom might be chosen as his next queen? Hadassah was among the women taken. From the start, I advised her not to reveal her Jewish heritage, worried for her safety in a Gentile palace fertile with perilous schemes." He paused. "That is when Hadassah disappeared and Esther was born."

Adin felt the breath knocked out of him. Could it be? Could Mordecai's claim have any merit? He did not appear to be suffering from delusions. In every sense, save for this outlandish story, he seemed to be in full possession of his mind.

The ruler of the synagogue stepped forward. "My friends, listen to me. Mordecai speaks the truth. I was there when Hadassah was taken in the street. It was I who brought the news to Mordecai."

"I have seen the queen from afar," a woman cried from behind the filigreed wall. "I work in the palace as a cleaner. Esther is a great lady. She looks nothing like your Hadassah."

"Does she not?" Mordecai turned to face the women's quarter. "Remember she received a full year of special treatments before she was chosen. It isn't merely that five years have passed since you last saw her. In those five years, she has learned to walk differently, to speak regally, to use cosmetics and clothing as a queen rather than an ordinary girl. Beneath five years of transformation, could you not see the resemblance to my dear Hadassah?"

A small gasp came from behind the filigreed wall. "Yes!" A moment of stunned silence passed. "God be praised!" the woman cried. "There is a Jewish woman on the throne of Persia!"

For a moment, nothing could be heard but a tremendous cheer.

"What now, Mordecai?" a man shouted from the front of the room. "If what you say is true, what can this mean for us?"

Mordecai raised a hand to hush the excited congregation. "This evil scheme to murder the Jews of Persia comes from the villainous plotting of one Haman the Agagite. Esther has agreed to intercede on our behalf with the king. She will seek an audience with him."

The applause that met this announcement shook the walls with its thunder.

Adin was starting to get a queasy feeling in the pit of his stomach. "Has Xerxes sent for her?" His cry rose above the din, silencing it.

Mordecai's expression became grave. "The king has not asked for Esther. Not for thirty days."

Adin's hand fisted. He had worked in the court long enough to know what that meant. The king of Persia was surrounded by a veil of mystery. Of majesty and awe. Even his friends did not dine at the same table with him. He was kept apart, held aloft like some divine being. No one tore through that curtain of separation to invade his presence as though he were some peddler in the Artisans' Village.

Adin inhaled sharply. "Anyone who dares to come into the presence of the king without being summoned is condemned to death under the law."

Mordecai's gaze fell. "There is an exception."

"A rare one." Adin shook his head. "Only if the king raises his scepter of authority over her. If he has not wanted her company for thirty days, then do you not think he is likely to be riled by her bold approach?"

Mordecai wiped a kerchief over his perspiring face. "For this reason, I have gathered you here today. Esther has asked us to fast for three days on her behalf. I beseech you to seek God.

Pray for an open door. A dark force has raised its hand against us. God alone can press it back. Fast and pray with me. On the third day, Esther shall approach Xerxes."

Grey clouds gathered over Susa for three days, but it never rained. Thirsting from his fast, Adin battled an anxiety as murky as the skies for this woman he had never met. Their lives depended on the outrageous plan that endangered not only her position, but her very life.

On the evening of the third day, an urgent knock made Adin scramble to his feet. Darab had already opened the gate by the time he made his way to the courtyard.

"Mordecai!"

The magistrate had lost weight in recent weeks, the loose folds of his tunic hanging on his bony frame. "We need your help. Esther has twisted her ankle. I fear it may be broken. The king and Haman are due at her apartments in a couple of hours. This is no ordinary meeting, as you can imagine. Can you tend to her?"

"I will head for the palace at once."

No words passed between him and Darab. Years of close friendship, of living and working together, had taught them what the other needed in moments of urgency. Adin was astride the Nisaean, his chest strapped behind him before Mordecai had a chance to mount his donkey.

Although Adin had never attended the king, he had been selected as physician for the courtiers who populated the palace and saw to the needs of several of the commanding Immortals, the specialized guard in charge of the king's security. After successfully treating a number of complicated cases, his reputation had grown. As a result, in recent months he had been invited to treat two of the king's concubines. But he had never met the queen.

At the Royal Gate, he found the queen's chief eunuch, Hathach, already waiting for him. Beardless and dark-skinned, the man carried himself with the smooth confidence of a giant, though he was short of stature. He treated Adin to an intense scrutiny. "You comprehend the import of the situation, Master Adin?"

"Yes, Lord Hathach."

"One can only hope so. Follow me." He conveyed Adin into the residential part of the palace, his short legs pumping surprisingly fast, so that Adin had to jog to keep up with him.

The guards on duty, recognizing them both, allowed them to pass without comment as they wended their way through several long hallways until they arrived at an intricately carved threshold. A pair of Immortals raised their spears in unison to bar their way. The distinctive golden apples that served as a counterbalance at the base of their weapons looked charmingly decorative. Adin knew too much about the elite force to be fooled. In the right hands, even the apples could prove as deadly as the spearhead. Hathach flashed the scroll bearing the queen's seal, and the Immortals gave them entry into the queen's apartment.

Adin followed Hathach to a hexagonal audience hall exquisitely tiled in shades of turquoise and teal blue. Numerous silver lampstands cast dancing shadows upon priceless carpets. A carved silver table at the center had been laid out for two, and another set apart for the king, who always ate alone. An arched silver framework surrounded the throne-like chair, enclosed within folds of purple and white silk curtains, a diaphanous fabric hanging in the front to give the king both privacy and free visibility into the room. Fresh lilies and roses had been draped over the arch, perfuming the air.

Hathach led Adin through a side door into a short hallway until they arrived at a smaller reception chamber on the left. Here, the queen sat on a plain leather chair, her elegant robes at odds with her unadorned surroundings.

Hathach bowed low. "The physician, Master Adin of Elephantine, my lady."

She lifted her head and smiled. For one moment, that face stopped Adin in his tracks. In her mid-twenties, she was tall and long-necked, her perfect posture making the most of a figure that could not be improved upon. But it was the sweetness of her expression that caught Adin off guard.

This was not a woman to put on airs. Her face, dewy soft and delightfully formed by the hand of the Almighty, held no self-importance, no testy awareness of her own dignity. Her smile held about it a tinge of sadness, as if she was about to bid farewell to something precious.

That very morning, she had braved death to come into the king's presence uninvited. God had heard the fervent prayers of his people, for the king had simply lifted his scepter to her and bid her to ask for anything she wished.

Esther had asked for nothing, save this banquet.

Adin would do everything in his power to fulfill that desire. He did not understand her strategy, the delay she had created by welcoming the king and her enemy together into her home. But he felt an odd conviction that he could leave the burden of his people in her young hands.

He knelt by her side. "I am at your service, my lady."

He offered no empty words to this woman who carried so mighty a weight. In that moment, with those few words, something shifted inside him. He became the queen's man for life. He might be hired by palace officials with long names and longer pedigrees. But something within him knew that he owed his duty to this woman. There was nothing amorous about this conviction. She did not engage his heart in that way. He only knew that God wanted his allegiance bound to the queen.

She stretched her foot toward him. "I was careless. I stumbled on the edge of a carpet in my haste. Is it broken?"

He examined the ankle carefully, the anatomical texts of his rigorous training in Cnidus as well as years of experience guiding his hands.

"You are a Jew, Hathach tells me." Her voice emerged softly. Almost girlish.

"I am, lady." He twisted her ankle this way and that, making her wince. "Pardon, my queen."

She waved a dismissive hand. "You must do what is necessary." She remained silent for a moment as he pressed against the bones through the swollen flesh. "You know who I am? Not in position, I mean. But by birth."

"Yes, lady. Every Jew in Susa knows by now."

She nodded as if satisfied.

He set her foot back on the floor and reached for his bag. "It is not broken."

"Well. That is good news. If I go to the gallows, I will go with my ankle intact."

He laughed in surprise. He had not expected the dark humor. "Shall I be able to stand on it tonight?"

"I will rub some ointment to diminish the pain and bind it carefully. Your long skirts will hide the bandages, and none shall be the wiser. It will help if you wear comfortable shoes."

"And tomorrow evening? If all goes well tonight, I plan to host another banquet. Will it bear my weight then?"

"It will bear *your* weight."

She chuckled. "But not the weight of our people, you mean?"

He threw a concerned glance in Hathach's direction. She waved her fingers like an open fan. "You need have no concerns there. Hathach is my faithful friend."

He bowed his head to the eunuch. "In answer to your question, lady, I fear no one can carry so great a responsibility. That weight is for God only."

Had he said those words aloud? He dropped his chin, feeling the heat as it crept up his neck. "I beg pardon, my queen. I am a fool to lecture you."

The sad smile returned. "I understand. You care for more than my ankle."

"Indeed." He put the leftover bandage neatly into a side pocket of the chest. "Rest your foot all day tomorrow. Keep it elevated on a cushion. I shall return to rebandage it for you. We will ensure that it holds you up through another banquet."

Early the following evening, just after the heat of the sun had dissipated, an inexplicable sight greeted the people of Susa. The Jewish magistrate, Mordecai ben Jair, dressed in gold-embroidered garments, rode slowly upon a festooned horse whose bridle bore the seal of Xerxes himself.

While seeing the king's own clothing upon Mordecai's back was strange enough, what truly made Adin stop in his tracks was the man who led the horse by its beribboned lead. Haman, the courtier known for his hatred of Jews, walked ahead of the horse, shouting, "This is what the king does for someone he wishes to honor!"

Adin shook his head as he rode on to the palace. In Esther's simple chamber, he found the queen once more seated upon her leather seat, pale but composed.

He knelt at her feet. The strict code of conduct in the palace forbade him from speaking unless first addressed by her. But Adin was beyond protocol. "My queen, you will perhaps be surprised to hear what I saw on my way here."

Hathach's frown was so fiery, Adin shifted, wondering if his fancy tunic might go up in flames under its heat. Esther merely waved a hand, signaling him to continue.

"I saw Haman the Agagite playing servant to Mordecai the Jew. You have heard of him, I think?"

She smiled at his discretion. "Indeed, I am familiar with the magistrate."

"Haman led Mordecai through the city square astride a magnificent horse." He unwound the old bandage as he spoke. "Was that your doing, lady?"

"Not mine. It seems God himself may have had a hand in

that particular event. The king could not sleep after my banquet last night. He ordered an attendant to read from the Royal Chronicles, and what passage should the scribe happen upon? None but the one describing how a certain Mordecai had saved the king's life from a deadly plot devised by guards of the threshold. The king asked his attendant how this Mordecai had been rewarded for his service. Discovering that nothing had been done for him, His Majesty decided to remedy that shortcoming immediately."

Adin forgot he was holding the royal ankle. "But how was it that Haman of all men received the task of honoring Mordecai?"

She laughed, and for a moment her face transformed into that of the carefree woman she might have been had she not worn a crown. "According to dear Hathach here, Haman himself suggested it. And I will tell you that Hathach is never wrong!" She pointed a rounded chin at the eunuch. "Tell the physician what you heard."

Hathach shrugged a shoulder. "Lord Haman happened to be in the outer court when the king discovered that Mordecai had never been rewarded. It was early morning by then, so he bid Lord Haman into his presence and asked what reward should be bestowed upon a man who truly pleases the king." He gestured at Adin's hand still holding onto the queen's ankle. "Either finish unwrapping that bandage or put Her Majesty's foot back on the cushion."

Adin flushed and proceeded to return his attention to his patient.

Esther giggled. "You mustn't be too severe on the physician, Hathach. Haman holds a particular interest for our healer. As a son of Abraham, he understands the damage the Agagite has caused his people." She returned her gaze to him. "We can only imagine why Haman suggested such an extraordinary reward. Likely, he must have thought the king meant to honor *him*! I spent a whole evening in Lord Haman's company, and I can assure you of one thing: he has a very high opinion of himself." She gave a peal of laughter. "Can you imagine his surprise when he discovered it was Mordecai the Jew who the king intended to reward all along?"

Adin chuckled. "He would have needed my services, I should imagine. For a very sour stomach."

Hathach's solemn face cracked into the barest suggestion of a smile.

"And tonight, lady?" Adin tested the ankle to ensure the binding did not sit too tight. "What do you plan for this banquet?"

"Tonight, I risk all." Her laughing eyes turned somber. "Tonight, I reveal all."

"Your kingdom in exchange for your people?"

The shadow of some terrible sorrow silenced him. "A kingdom? What is that to me? I risk my marriage for my people."

10

Roxannah

Good news refreshes the bones.

Proverbs 15:30

THE TWELFTH YEAR OF KING XERXES'S RULE
THE FOURTH DAY OF SUMMER

Roxannah fetched a bag of wheat from the storehouse. The bag was not heavy, but her hands wobbled, and she spilled the grain on the floor before she could empty the kernels into the mill. With an annoyed sigh, she fell to her knees to gather up the runaway wheat. The closer the dreadful day of the king's edict approached, the clumsier she seemed to grow.

Over two months of spills and stumbles. Two months of sleepless nights. Two months of waiting with no relief in sight.

In eight months, every Jew in Persia would be destroyed.

The nightmare had come to roost even closer to home. Her

father had not forgotten his plan to participate in the annihilation of the Jews. On the appointed day, he and the wine merchant planned to take up arms and march into the Jewish quarter. At least that meant he would not target Tirzah and her ilk who lived in the Artisans' Village.

But she knew Adin was in danger.

She could not understand Lord Fravartish. She could not grasp his reasoning. As if murdering a people simply because of their race could be the solution to anyone's problem. Such great evil could only beget worse evil. Hatred only birthed more hatred.

Roxannah made dough for bread and, covering it with a clean rag, placed the bowl on a shelf so it could rise. She fetched her old linen scarf and headed for the market to buy turnips for a mutton braise. Her own garden yielded many of the basic herbs and vegetables she needed for cooking, but for some reason, half her turnips had refused to bulb this year, and she was running short.

Tirzah was serving a customer, so Roxannah decided to stop at the root seller's stall first. Engrossed with sorting through white-and-pink roots, she missed seeing the royal messenger leap upon the dais in the center of the market. Royal messengers were trained for elocution and projection so that their voices could carry over large crowds.

They could also make an innocent woman jump out of her skin.

She dropped the turnip back on the pile and turned her gaze toward the messenger. Now what?

The man lifted a clay tablet out of a leather satchel and began to read. "To all the residents of the 127 provinces of Persia, and to the people of the great citadel of Susa: Hear this decree from your king, Xerxes, son of Darius, beloved of Ahura Mazda. Regarding the attack upon the Jews, which is to take place thirteen days before the start of spring, receive now this codicil."

Roxannah froze. There was a codicil? What else had the king added to that awful edict?

"I, King Xerxes, give the Jews in every city and province the authority to unite in order to defend their lives on that day. I put into law their right to kill and annihilate anyone who chooses to attack them and their families.

"As I gave permission to those who would attack the Jews in my kingdom to take their property, so I give the Jews that same right. If on that day they kill an enemy in self-defense, they may keep his property as their own."

The messenger turned the tablet toward the crowd. "This message has the seal of the king." A small blob of red wax sat unbroken at the bottom of the clay tablet. That seal turned the pronouncement from a declaration into permanent law.

The crowd expelled a collective breath.

The king could not abolish his earlier edict. For all his power, he could not overturn a law once it became established. But the new proclamation meant that anyone who planned to attack the Jews could now expect to face a powerful opponent rather than a helpless victim.

The Jews had been granted the right to fight for their lives. They had received permission to act like an independent military within the Persian kingdom, defending themselves by all possible means for a single day. To arm themselves. To gather their best fighters and protect fortune and family.

This was a unique privilege. The king did not normally allow the civilian population to behave like a small, independent army any time it suited them. That way lay mayhem and rebellion.

His unusual edict would force anyone who intended to attack a person of Jewish heritage to think twice about their plan. They weren't looking at an easy conquest anymore. The king's new command offered the best protection the Jewish population could have under the circumstances. Xerxes could not turn back the original edict he had issued. Instead, he had handed them a powerful defense. A chance at life.

It took a moment for the crowd to comprehend the full import of the messenger's words. A great shout of joy rent the air. Two men grabbed the messenger, who had finally finished his second reading, and placing him upon their shoulders, began to parade around the square to the cheer of the crowds. The market burst into an impromptu celebration. Many of the people of Susa had Jewish friends just as she did. They now celebrated their good fortune with typical Persian exuberance.

The root merchant dropped a large turnip into Roxannah's palms. "Enjoy! Enjoy! It's a happy day!"

Grinning, Roxannah thanked the man and, paying for two more turnips, shoved them all into her sack and turned to look for Tirzah. She found her friend, tears streaming down her laughing face, passing out dried apricots to anyone who walked by her colorful stall.

When she saw Roxannah, she jumped on the balls of her feet and clapped. "We are saved! Did you hear?"

Roxannah felt her heart lighten for the first time in weeks. "I heard, my friend. I am relieved and delighted."

Tirzah gave her a hearty embrace. "Not near so relieved as I, believe me."

"I wonder what caused Xerxes to change his mind?"

"It is the Lord's miracle!"

"This kind of reversal is certainly unusual. Kings rarely change their decisions for fear of looking weak. Do you think your God used one of Xerxes's officials to convince him to help your people?"

"Perhaps it was the queen," Tirzah said.

"The queen?"

Tirzah looked to the left and the right. She squeezed Roxannah's hand. "I know I can trust you." Dropping her voice, she said, "It will not remain secret for long, in any case."

Roxannah was intrigued by her friend's cryptic remarks. "What?"

"Queen Esther is Jewish. She feels deeply for the plight of our people."

Roxannah frowned. That sounded unlikely. The Achaemenid royal line had never chosen a foreign queen. They were famous for marrying blood relatives. Besides, a Jewish queen would neither gain the king great wealth nor political influence, the prerequisites upon which royal marriages were built.

Someone must have fed Tirzah false information. She supposed it was natural for her friend to believe such tall tales. They made her precarious world feel safer.

Tirzah reached for her hand. "I must run home to tell my family," she said. "They will be so relieved. Will you look after my stall for an hour?"

"Of course."

Tirzah shoved a few handfuls of nuts and raisins into Roxannah's sack. "With my thanks."

"You need not—"

"It's not payment. Consider it a celebration. The whole world will be feasting this day."

But Roxannah noticed not everyone seemed content with the king's latest declaration. Small bands of men and women gathered in the dark corners of the market, whispering, their faces hard and uncompromising.

It appeared Tirzah's God still had more work to do. Roxannah bit her lip and wondered if the king's new edict would prove enough to dissuade these people.

To dissuade her father.

11

My father seeks to kill you. Therefore be on your
guard in the morning.

1 Samuel 19:2

The Thirteenth Year of King Xerxes's Rule
The Sixty-Ninth Day of Winter

I am a seasoned warrior. I can handle a few inexperienced
men. You needn't worry about me." Roxannah's father
leaned against the thin cushion on the porch.

Months had passed since the king's new declaration. The
day of the edict was only a week away. Roxannah had done her
best to dissuade her father from his ugly intentions. Nothing
had worked. Even the possibility of danger to himself did not
seem to sway him.

He plucked a twig from the brittle grapevine and crushed
it between restless fingers. "We used to have a large vineyard.
Did you know that? We shall have another soon. And fields of
wheat. We shall replace the orchards I had to sell as well." He
pressed her hand. "You and your mother will not have to wear
these tattered tunics anymore."

The pleasure that came from this rare sign of his affection was swallowed by the horror of his intentions. "I don't mind the old tunics, Father. Can't you see how wrong this plan is? We can't restore our fortunes at the cost of someone else's life."

He withdrew his hand from hers as though burned. "You dare lecture me?"

He swung his cup at her head. Roxannah ducked to the left, barely avoiding the blow, else Adin would have to come and give *her* a few of his dainty stitches. She rushed to the kitchen and barricaded herself behind extra pots. In the back of her mind, she planned her route of escape, lest her father decided to pursue her.

Her mother found her instead. "What possessed you to argue with him, child? After all these years, you know that never ends well."

Roxannah crossed her arms. "It is wicked, what he intends."

"When did that ever stop him? Most of the time what he wants to do is wrong. How do you reckon this to be different from any other day?"

"He doesn't merely mean to hurt you and me. He intends to commit murder!"

Her mother leaned against the kitchen counter. "I am sorry, daughter. I am sorry you have to contend with the pain of our broken home."

Roxannah drew her mother's fragile form into her arms. "You've done all you can. It's not your fault."

"Nor is it yours." She caressed a loose curl away from Roxannah's face. "You don't have to try and make peace for everyone around you. It isn't your responsibility to keep the world safe."

Roxannah went still. Is that what she was trying to do? Protect everyone as she had tried to protect herself and her mother since girlhood?

If so, she had set herself a laughable task. She could not even keep herself safe.

Nights in Roxannah's home were like vegetables left too long in the storehouse: She never knew what she would get when she put her hand into the basket. A shriveled, mealy root that caused stomach pains, or the goodness of a healthy vegetable that had somehow weathered its overlong storage. Some nights arrived with the quiet of her father's sodden sleep, or a sad but calm wakefulness that caused him to withdraw from the world around him. Others dragged in his violence. Erratic as mercury, her father's moods remained predictable only in their unpredictability.

It had made a poor sleeper out of her, the not knowing. The bone-deep realization that bad things could happen with cruel regularity. She had learned to be vigilant. She had learned to take charge of her own safety. To take charge of her mother's security.

Except she knew that she was not qualified for the job. The more vigilant she became, the less safe she felt.

She pressed her face into the pillow. The sound of her father's voice mingled with the drunken murmurs of the wine merchant. Merry with hope and avarice, they were making all manner of plans. Roxannah turned on her side, shoving the pillow over her ear, trying to drown out the sound of their boisterous laughter.

For all its benefits, the new edict could not offer the assurance of a perfect outcome for the Jewish population. The worst could still befall her friends. They could still be victims of violence.

They could still be victims of her father.

She listened to the voices coming from her father's chamber and reached an uncomfortable conclusion.

She would have to go behind her father's back. She would have to betray the bonds of familial loyalty and forsake the fealty she owed her name and her blood.

She had promised herself never to seek him out again. If Adin wished to see her, he knew where to find her. But there was no help for it now. To caution him of the danger posed by her father, she had to go to him one more time. Just this final visit, she assured herself, and then no more.

A short distance from Adin's house, the clatter of horse hooves behind her forced Roxannah to the edge of the road. To her surprise, the horse came to a stop.

"Roxannah!"

She whipped around. "Master Adin." It had been months since she had seen him. Her breath hitched at the sight of the plain face that turned inexplicably appealing with a smile, the sudden flare in the dark irises as he greeted her.

He dismounted with an agile leap and took a few steps toward her, holding on to his horse's lead. "Is anything amiss?"

"No one is ill, if that is what you mean."

He gave her a curious look. "But you are on your way to my house?"

She gave a quick dip of her chin in assent. The stallion nudged him in the back and neighed. Roxannah patted the beast's velvety neck. "He seems keen for your attention."

"He is hungry." Adin looked toward the alley that intersected the road to their right. "Why don't you walk with me to the stable? We can speak while I feed this fellow."

Roxannah fell into step beside him as they made their way down the narrow passage, the stallion nudging Adin in the back every few steps to hurry him along. The third time Adin found himself shoved forward, his feet tripping, he cleared his throat. "Excuse my horse. He has no manners."

She caressed the stallion's withers and laughed.

"The problem is," Adin said, "he thinks he is royalty and has a right to be demanding."

"And you give in to him because you agree."

Adin grinned. "That is an accurate summation. I find his antics amusing."

In the stables, Adin took off the felted blanket from the back of the horse and hung it from a nail. "Won't you sit down?" He pointed to a plain stool next to the stall. "Tell me what brings you to my door. I will feed this beast as soon as I take off his lead and cool him a little."

"Why don't you tend him while I prepare his feed? That way, he won't have to wait long." Adin looked uncertain, so she added, "Don't worry. I won't give your stallion colic. I know how to feed a horse." She walked to the neat bale of hay she had spotted in the back of the stable but waited for him to give her a nod of approval before separating a flake of hay from the bale.

She inspected the bundle with care. "Alfalfa. He'll like that."

Adin raised a brow. "You do know your feed. I shouldn't be surprised. You are not an ordinary lady."

Except for her family lines, she could hardly be called a lady at all. Taking the flake of hay to a clean stall, she sniffed it for mold, and smelling nothing but the tangy scent of sundried grass, she shook the hay loose and spread it into a heap, making it easier for the stallion to consume. "My grandfather loved horses and insisted on looking after his own mount. He used to take me to visit his stables. Though it's been many years since I tended a horse, some things stay with you long after they are gone."

"Was that the same grandfather who encouraged your grandmother's cooking?"

"My father's father. Yes. He only had one son, in spite of having a wife and two concubines. And since my father only ever had me, I spent a lot of time with my grandparents." It had been her family's generational sorrow, their lack of children. Their lack of sons.

He looked up. "Some blessings can only be born out of disappointments."

"That, also, is an accurate summation."

She watched as Adin checked the stallion's hooves, looking for damage to the soles before running his hands down its powerful legs, feeling for heat or swelling. "Always the physician," she jested.

He grinned. "It's a hard habit to break." He drew fresh water from a bucket and brought it to the stallion, who drank greedily. "Whoa, boy. You don't need to drown yourself in it." He ruffled the horse's mane fondly. "Hot, are you?"

Pouring water over the horse's back, he let it wash away the dust of the road and the heat of the day. His hands, large and self-assured, held a mesmerizing gentleness about them. Finishing, he rinsed and dried his hands. "I think this prince is ready for his hay."

They watched in silence as the Nisaean chomped down lusty mouthfuls of his feed. Roxannah appreciated Adin's tactful silence as he waited for her to begin. She fumbled with the words she would have to speak. The betrayal of family loyalties that was inherent to her warning.

Everything in her culture, her upbringing, and the bonds of her heritage demanded obedience to her father. Demanded that she keep his plans secret from Adin.

The stretched silence did not seem to bother him. He leaned against a wooden wall, his shoulder tucked into a beam as if he could stand there all day if need be and wait until she felt ready.

She blinked back awkward tears. Wordlessly, he came to stand near her. A gentle finger traced the half-moon beneath her eye. "Not sleeping?"

"No."

"Tell me." He sounded so perfectly accepting, so utterly reassuring that the words stuck in her throat released.

"You're aware, of course, that the king's new edict gives the Jews of Persia the right to defend themselves from the coming attack next week. But I'm afraid that provision alone won't keep you safe. Not entirely. There are those still intent on attacking the Jewish people. For the sake of land and property, you understand? This edict presents a . . . a terrible temptation."

Slowly, he nodded. "Are we speaking of anyone in particular?"

She dropped her head, hiding behind a curtain of hair that had come loose from its braid, hoping he could not see the heat that spread over her cheeks. "The wine merchant from the Royal Village, for one. And . . . and my father. They are plotting together. I know of no particulars. My father has certainly not mentioned you by name as a target."

"But?"

"Months ago, after you tended him, he spoke of you with . . ." She looked away, at a loss. How was she to explain her father's behavior without making him sound monstrous?

She could either betray the man to whom she owed every allegiance, or she could protect Adin. She saw no way of doing both. And she had already made her decision by coming here.

"Yes?"

"I would take care if I were you, Adin. On the appointed day, be prepared for an attack. My father served in the military once. Fought in wars under the great King Darius. I imagine he still remembers that training. Don't be fooled by his wobbly exterior. He is a powerful man, strong enough to cause you great harm."

Adin took a half step until they stood toe to toe. He placed a finger under her chin, raising her face until she had to stare into his eyes. Had she once thought them ink black? She had been so wrong. They were as luminous as a star-filled night.

"You have my thanks for coming to warn me. Your courage does you credit." His thumb rested on her chin, warm and slightly calloused. "I can look after myself, you know."

Her skin tingled at his touch. "Don't underestimate him. Sometimes I think he is invincible." She frowned, unconsciously leaning into him. "He was not always a bad man. I still hope he will come back to us as he was. That he will be restored."

That confession caused her to remember what this moment had cost, and she took a step back. She had betrayed her father to protect the physician.

12

Adin

And do not be afraid of the people of the land,
because we will devour them. Their protection is
gone, but the LORD is with us.

Numbers 14:9 NIV

THE THIRTEENTH YEAR OF KING XERXES'S RULE
FOURTEEN DAYS BEFORE THE FIRST DAY OF SPRING

Adin whispered a distracted thanks when Darab placed
a plate of boiled chicken in front of him.

"Shall I bless the bread, or will you?" Darab asked.

"You go ahead."

Adin tried to attend the words of Darab's prayer but could
not wrangle his preoccupied mind into focus.

"Worried about what we have to contend with tomorrow?"
Darab asked. "The coming fight?"

"Actually, I was thinking of King David."

"Lofty. I was merely wondering if we have enough blankets

for everyone who plans to stay." He broke a piece of bread and dipped it into broth. "Were you remembering David's battle against Goliath?"

"I was thinking about what happened just before that fight. David had stopped to deliver food to his brothers. Remember that part of the story?"

Darab's brow knotted. "If I recall, his eldest brother rebuked him. What was his name?"

"Eliab." Adin tapped a restless finger on the table. "He accused David of being conceited and wicked of heart for presuming to reproach Goliath."

"And why are you thinking of that conversation? Are you feeling particularly conceited? If so, I can help." Darab waggled his eyebrows.

Adin's lips twitched. "Thank you for the offer. But you need not worry on that score. I was only wondering what it does to the heart to be thought of as worse than you are. How David coped with being falsely accused day after day."

"Why do you say *day after day*? What makes you think it was a common occurrence?"

"Because in answer to his brother, David said, 'What have I done now?' *Now*, meaning this was not the first time Eliab had chastised him unjustly. It was a habit with him."

Darab returned his bread to the plate without taking a bite. "Ah. You are thinking of Mistress Roxannah?"

Adin's smile held a wry edge. His friend always had a way of reading him like a scroll. "Can you imagine it, Darab? Growing up under constant criticism? Being told you are less than what you truly are? Feeling unsafe in your own home? It must leave a deep wound. The kind my craft cannot heal. An empty crater where there should have been love."

"Your medicinal arts may not be able to fill that crater. But God can. He did so for David."

Adin rubbed the back of his neck. "I cannot imagine what

it cost her to betray her father to me as she did. Darab, if Lord Fravartish does come tomorrow, we must shield him from harm.

It never even occurred to Roxannah that her father might be the one who is hurt in the melee. She has lived for so long under the shadow of his brute strength that she cannot see his vulnerability. She thinks him undefeatable. She only thought to protect *me*."

"I pray the man does not come at all."

"Yes. But if he does, we must send him home to her in one piece."

"Given the kind of father he is, it might be a mercy if he does get himself killed in this fight."

"I have committed myself to saving lives. I do not want to shed blood. Besides, Roxannah still hopes Fravartish will mend his ways. He is not much of a father. But he is the only one she has."

Darab wiped the breadcrumbs from his hand. "We can do our best to protect him. But the man has a will of his own."

Adin thought of the sacrifice Roxannah had made by coming to him. The courage it had required. Her sweetness, her unconscious protectiveness pulled on him like an irresistible force. The months of intentional separation had done nothing to lessen the attraction. Her stalwart desire to do right, the uncanny way she had of seeing through him and into him, and even her humor made her enthralling to him.

A dangerous temptation.

She was no Ruth. No outsider who entered the assembly of the Lord by proclaiming, *"Your God is my God, your people my people."*

Something in his soul stubbornly whispered, *not yet.*

Adin helped Darab hand out blankets and pillows to the women and children. There were more than a dozen of them who had taken up his invitation to find refuge in his house, with half as many men nervously waiting in the courtyard. With its high walls and iron-enforced door, his house provided a more secure gathering place than many of the other residences in the neighborhood, and five families had decided to find sanctuary within.

Tomorrow was the appointed time. The dreaded day of attack.

His guests had arrived at noon. They had decided to prepare for the worst by gathering early. No one knew when, or even if, their enemies might strike. Would they arrive in the dark of the night, with only moonlight to cover a stealthy offense, or make a bold advance in the daylight?

The men had arrived well-armed, though most were not fighters. Adin's upbringing had prepared him best for such a violent encounter. He had trained for combat from the age of seven, able to kill a man before he turned twelve.

He had used the past few months to refresh his training in preparation for this day. It had been fourteen years since he had picked up a sword. But as soon as he hefted one into his palm, he found that the old balance and rhythm returned to him with shocking ease. His body remembered the basic mechanics that had once been second nature—the correct posture, the placement of his feet, the right spot for his free hand. He still had the strong thighs of a swordsman, which would give him the dexterity he would need if it came to a fight.

The comfortable way his weapon sat in his hand left a bitter taste in his mouth. He had spent the last fourteen years saving life, not taking it. Would to God he wouldn't have to lift his sword for anything other than a gesture of threat that set their foes to flight.

As a soldier, he had learned early that one should never pick up arms unless he meant to use them. Unless he was committed to his course. Now, he felt a divide in his heart.

After sunset, he made his way to the courtyard, leaving Darab to look after the women and children. Something about Darab's quiet presence could reassure even the most anxious matron in a bout of panic.

The two mercenaries he had hired patrolled the back of the house, leaving the front to him and the neighborhood men. He trusted the mercenaries he had hired, Jewish soldiers from the garrison in Elephantine. Soldiers for hire were hard to come by just now, with all the Jews in the empire scrambling to employ them. Adin only managed to lay his hands on these two thanks to old connections and a generous stipend.

The hour was approaching midnight. But none of the men were sleeping. Adin was disappointed to find them huddled in a large group, watching the walls with tense attention. Their present formation would not be very useful if someone did try to climb in. By standing so close together, they had left several dark corners defenseless.

Over the past months, Adin had used his free time to train these men, to teach them the basics of fighting. Not that any of them had turned into real warriors. Between work and family responsibilities, none had had the time to develop any true skills. And he supposed the growing tension of the coming attack had wiped all the training they had received out of their heads.

He joined them on silent feet, making several of the men whip around and gasp at his greeting. He tried to inject calm into his voice. "Any sign of trouble?"

Avi the butcher adjusted his belt. "None so far, God be praised." He was the handiest with a sword, though he would probably do better if his victim were already lying prone on a stone slab.

"Let us remember our shifts and locations. Three hours per watch until morning. First watch, spread to your corners." He pointed out the strategic locations he had worked out with them in advance. "Keep your lamps burning. Make sure the torches don't die in the night. If you feel sleepy, awaken your relief early. Better for you to rest than leave a corner defenseless because you fall asleep. You can make up the time during the next watch. Remember, the Lord is with us; do not fear them."

When the men took their posts, Adin turned his attention to a smoking torch. From the corner of his eye, he saw a small shadow separate itself from the house. He whirled around. Before he could call a warning, a little form catapulted itself against his legs. Two arms wrapped about his waist with surprising strength while a warm face pressed into his belly.

Adin exhaled. With a shake of his head, he signaled the three alarmed guards to return to their posts.

"Little Leah!" He tried to make his voice stern, but mostly he sounded relieved. "You were told to remain inside with the other children, weren't you? Not to mention tucked in bed at this late hour."

The curly head bobbed up and down.

"And yet here you are. Do you see any other children here?"

The curly head burrowed deeper into him. "I can't see anything at all. It's very dark."

"That might be because you are trying to bury your head in my stomach." Exasperation mingled with a rush of tenderness as he pried the child loose from him and knelt before her. "You could have been hurt. Everyone is very jumpy tonight."

"Because of the bad men?"

"Yes."

"But you will stop them? You won't let them hurt us?"

"By the grace of God. Now, you must answer my question. Do you see any other children here?"

She jerked her head up, the Persian signal for no.

"Then why are you here, little mistress?"

"I wanted to be with you."

His heart squeezed. He pulled the child into his arms for a quick moment. "That's very commendable. You show good taste. However, your timing is bad. Tonight and tomorrow, you must remain within the house. Don't leave it for any reason. It is dangerous out here. You understand?"

She nodded.

Adin held out his hand for her to hold. Her small fingers seemed lost in his palm. "Let's go find your ima."

"Are you coming back to the courtyard?"

"I am."

"But what if the bad men hurt you? I don't want you to be deaded like my abba."

"I see." He came to a stop. In the light of the torch, he could see tears shimmering on her smooth cheeks. She wiped a hand under her nose, and Adin handed her a handkerchief. "You will be happy to know that I have no plans to be deaded by tomorrow."

She gave him a troubled look. "You promise?"

"I promise. Now, in you go. And I better not catch you out here again until you have permission to leave the house."

The child regarded him with grave eyes. Adin exhaled as he watched her return indoors. The men were so tense, they might have harmed her before realizing who she was. He walked the perimeter of the property. Earlier in the week, Darab had taken the Nisaean and the donkey to a friend's stables, a Persian merchant who, horrified by the edict against the Jews, had opened his home to help any in need.

The animals were safe. His house was well-protected. His hired mercenaries marched prominently around the perimeter of the house, one keeping a constant vigil over the back wall. Bows and quivers of arrows slung over their shoulders, swords glinting in the starlight, they presented a formidable picture. He hoped their mere presence would prove enough to discourage any would-be attackers. Why take the risk of coming against professional fighters?

Adin spoke encouragingly to the men on watch and slipped

indoors. He knew he should rest. But he could not slow the blood that thrummed in his chest. Patrolling his property, he listened for sounds of approach.

In the darkest hour just before sunrise, he found one of the men asleep in a corner wall. The man snapped to his feet when Adin shook him roughly, ashamed to be found sleeping on watch. Drowsy, he stumbled, his dagger clattering noisily to the ground. Adin bent to lend him a hand before sending him to the other side of the courtyard where Darab had set up several cots.

Drawing a tired hand down his cheek, Adin turned. An odd scratching sound made him look up. In the light of the torch, a head and shoulder appeared over the top of the courtyard wall, followed by another. Adin cried a warning. All around them, the wall seemed to swarm with men, a half dozen at least, climbing down with spears and swords in hand.

Drawn by the alarmed cries of their friends, the men resting on the cots ran into the front of the courtyard, sleep forgotten in an instant as they faced the hard visage of armed men intent on murder.

By now their attackers had lowered into the courtyard, their faces hidden by the shadows. One of the Elephantine soldiers slipped over the wall and stood behind them, holding still at Adin's signal. Good. That meant the second man had remained in the back of the house as instructed, guarding their flank, lest there was a second attack.

Adin took a step forward. "You see we are well-armed and prepared. Do not be foolish. You cannot win. Some of you will certainly die. Go home. Go to your wives and children. Leave this madness."

One man moved forward. In the light of the torch Adin recognized the dissipated features of Lord Fravartish. "Don't be ridiculous, physician. You think a bunch of weakling merchants can stand against us and win?"

His words emboldened the rest, who laughed nervously and stepped forward.

Adin ground his teeth until he felt his jaw crack. "I have mercenaries here."

Fravartish shrugged. "And I have beaten better men than they."

Adin took the measure of the bloodshot eyes and saw implacable determination. But the hand holding the sword was not quite steady. Either he had drunk too much, or he had tried to come stone-cold sober, a condition that would certainly be a shock to his body. Adin knew he could take the man without causing too much harm. A block with his sword, a fast twirl of the wrist, a hard jab, a left hook, and the man would be disarmed and on the floor. Unconscious and bruised, but well enough.

Fravartish took a lunging step forward. Adin unlocked his knees and raised his sword, at the ready.

A small shadow passed between them to the left of Adin. His breath stopped as an insistent form catapulted against him, head buried in his belly, right where Fravartish's sword was descending.

"Don't hurt him!" she cried.

The world slowed. Adin felt his vision tunnel, a rush of acute senses making his heart pound. He smelled the sour sweat of Fravartish's clothes mingled with the faint perfume of roses.

For a tiny moment, Adin hesitated. His initial plan for a downward swing on Fravartish's sword was now rendered useless by Leah's trembling form between them.

Fravartish, who had rushed in with a powerful lunge, could not check the momentum of his body. His sword drove in, headed straight for where Leah now stood, aimed at her little neck.

Fravartish's eyes widened. A stricken gasp escaped him. A younger man with better training and less wine in his veins might have managed to turn the point of his sword at the last moment. But Fravartish simply could not move that fast.

Adin twisted his body, his free arm wrapped around the girl's shoulder, knowing all the while that it would not be enough. There was no time to reposition her. No space for some clever countermove that would disarm Fravartish without hurting him.

He had one choice. Save Leah, or save Fravartish.

He felt an odd sense of calm descend as his sword arm rose a fraction, aimed, and thrust.

13

Roxannah

Reproaches have broken my heart.
Psalm 69:20

The sun had barely crested the sky when Roxannah gave up pacing her chamber and descended upon the dormant vegetable beds. Susa's hot climate meant that gardens could be planted before the end of winter.

For two hours she toiled, preparing the winter-tired soil for a new season of planting. But her mind was not on her work. Every few moments, her gaze drifted to the door, willing it to open. It refused to budge.

Sighing, she fetched the roots and seeds she had prepared the previous autumn and sorted through what had survived the winter. Still no sign of her father by the time the sun sat high to the east and she had finished planting three neat rows of carrot seeds.

In the dark before twilight the night before, she had tried to stop him when he had marched to the door, grabbing his old army sword.

"Father, please don't go!"

"Mind your own business, girl."

She had fallen on her knees before him. "Don't do this thing, I beg you."

"I do nothing wrong! My actions are within the law as the king himself has proclaimed."

"The law is not always just. Please, Father. Stay home. Don't become guilty of bloodshed."

He had kicked her then. Hard. She would have a boot-shaped bruise on her side. But she was too preoccupied to feel the pain.

Now, she gave up on the carrots and began to pace before the door. Where had he gone? Who had he attacked? Whose property had he seized?

Whose blood had he shed?

She dropped the small basket of seeds she had thoughtlessly clutched to her chest. She might burst like a gourd left too long in the field if he did not return soon. She unbarred the gate and stared into the street. It stood empty. Nothing stirred.

She straightened when she caught sight of a cart in the distance. Taking a few slow steps in its direction, she stopped. It did not belong to the wine merchant—its sole occupant, the driver, a stranger to her.

A trader delivering goods house to house, she thought. Shading her eyes from the sun, she slid her gaze past the driver and set it upon the patch of road that stretched behind the cart. No sign of her father.

Her attention was drawn back to the clattering cart. This close, she realized that the driver was no ordinary merchant. He had the air of a soldier about him, muscular arms pulling on the donkey's lead with ease. His long sideburns, tied in the back with a leather thong, proclaimed him a Hebrew. A mercenary? He brought his cart to a stop just outside her house. "Is this Lord Fravartish's house?"

She felt her breath catch. Noticing the way he waited for her answer, she jerked her chin down.

The man avoided her gaze. "I have a delivery to make."

"What delivery?" Her voice shook.

He did not answer. Silently, he walked around to the back of his cart and drew something toward him. From where she stood, Roxannah could see that it was a large bundle wrapped in blankets. Setting a wide wooden board against the edge of the cart, the driver pulled and tugged on the bundle. He was a tall man, thick with muscle. Still, he grunted with effort, face glistening with sweat before he succeeded in sliding the blanket-wrapped bundle onto the board.

The sun had turned too hot, or else she had forgotten how to breathe. Her head swam as she watched the man tie the bundle to the board.

"What do you have there?" Her lips formed the words, but they made no sound.

The man looked up. A trace of pity softened his stern lips. He lifted the end of the board and began dragging his burden toward their door.

Roxannah tried to swallow and failed. She followed him into the courtyard, wobbling with every step. "Is that . . . is that my father?"

The man grunted as his board jarred and bumped over the stones of the courtyard. "If your father be Lord Fravartish."

Roxannah's knees gave out, and she dropped on the upturned earth of an empty vegetable bed. The driver of the cart bent to untie the layers of rope from the blankets. She forced herself to her feet and stumbled toward the macabre package delivered to her door.

Perhaps there had been a mistake. Perhaps they had erroneously sent someone else's father to her door. Lord Fravartish could not be dead!

She had to know. With a trembling hand, she reached for the blankets and, layer by layer, spread them until a man's face was revealed.

Gasping, she lurched back.

Her father's expression seemed oddly peaceful, as though in death he had finally found what in life had eluded him. His eyes were closed, hair combed away from the high forehead, the usual knots untangled by some kind hand. No bruise marred his face, save for the bloat of too many years of wine.

Her gaze slid lower. A single bloodied gash, the breadth of four fingers, stained the old woolen tunic at the chest. The matching wound gaped upon his flesh, the edges clean, as if made by some sharp instrument. A sword, she assumed. It must have been blessedly quick.

The driver held out a hand, a leather purse dangling from his fingers.

"What is that?"

"For you. For his funeral."

Roxannah's eyes widened. She looked into the purse to find enough silver to cover a magnificent burial fit for a nobleman. Her father would have liked that.

She clutched the little bag to her chest, feeling sick. "Who sent this?"

"The physician. He tended the body and bade me to deliver him to you."

The combed hair, the clean face, the tidy state of the body. Adin had tended her father's corpse.

Adin had been there.

A chill traveled through her body, making her shiver violently. "How is Adin? Was he injured?"

"No. He is well."

"Did my father die in his house?"

The driver nodded. "The physician was sheltering several neighbors in his home. Some men attacked the house before dawn, your father among them."

Roxannah dropped the silver purse from nerveless fingers.

"He would have come himself. But the day has only begun, and they expect other attacks. He could ill afford to send me. But he did not want you and your mother to wait in ignorance."

Roxannah's mouth tasted bitter. She had warned Adin. And he had certainly taken her warning to heart. He had prepared well for her father's attack.

This was her doing. She might as well have plunged the sword into her father's heart with her own hands.

14

Adin

You have made your people see hard things.
Psalm 60:3

din sat on the roof's edge, feet dangling over the side,
the light of countless stars shining like shards of ice in
the obsidian sky. Again and again, he relived the gut-
wrenching moment his sword had pierced Fravartish's chest.

To save Leah, he reminded himself.

The reminder proved cold comfort. He had been determined
to shield the man from harm. For Roxannah's sake, if nothing
else. He had failed miserably.

If he had been just a little faster on his feet. If he had not
hesitated. If he had thought with greater agility. A thousand
ifs tormented him with the thought that he might have been
able to spare the man.

His only consolation, ironically, was Fravartish himself. The
look of horror on his face as the tip of his sword had found

Leah's fragile neck, the spray of first blood wetting his blade. He was no child killer, whatever he was. Lying in Adin's arms, gasping with his final breaths, he had asked, "Is she dead?"

"No. No." Adin had given him what assurance he could at this, the hour of his death. "She is safe. It is a superficial wound only and easy to remedy."

The dying man had exhaled. "I'm glad. I wouldn't want to die with that . . . not that too . . . on my conscience."

Too. So many words unsaid in that one huffed-out exclamation. Blood mingling with regret. Years wasted. Ruined. Years that he carried with him on his stained soul. But not Leah's life, at least. Fravartish had been glad to be free of that final sin.

A balm for Adin's squirming heart, those last words. A sort of confirmation for his decision to keep Leah safe. Fravartish did not want Leah dead any more than he did.

He sighed and rose to make his way down the wide stairs. The sun would rise soon. The attacks were at an end. He had heard from Darab, who had heard it from an official that they estimated five hundred men to have been killed in one night during the attacks that had spread throughout Susa.

And one of those deaths had been at his hands.

Later, he would go through the required cleansing ritual, for he had touched a corpse. He was unclean. But first, he needed to perform one more duty.

Roxannah stood before him, pale as bone. He wanted to pull her into his arms and offer what comfort he could. The irony did not escape him. The irony of a man whose hands were stained by the blood of her father wanting to offer solace for what he himself had caused.

If only he had found a way to save them both, the man and the child.

Roxannah stood before him, more dignified than a royal princess. Her wounded eyes, grey as a stormy sea, were almost his undoing. He expected a blistering accusation. He deserved it, God knew.

"Roxannah." He reached out a hand. She stepped away, as if stung. He dropped his arm to his side. "Let me explain what happened."

"No! I don't want to know. I don't want those thoughts in my head."

He exhaled. She deserved that small mercy. He would not add to her burden by trying to lessen his. Trying to justify his actions.

He inclined his head. "One day, you might want to know. For your own sake. When you are ready, ask me."

She said nothing, her expression flat. So unlike her. So unlike the spirited woman full of life and laughter he had come to know. This, too, was his doing.

He swallowed past the stone in his throat. Holding up another purse of silver, he offered it to her. "Allow me to help, then. It's the least I can do."

She slammed the door in his face.

15

Roxannah

A dream comes when there are many cares.
Ecclesiastes 5:3 NIV

Lord Fravartish's dignified funeral was a dry-eyed affair. Regret and guilt turned into a tight knot in Roxannah's belly. She was not hypocritical enough to pretend that what she felt most prominently was not relief. Like a big exhale, his very absence brought ease. The relief only added to the guilt.

Few friends attended the ceremony, though the function brought a half dozen creditors out of the woodwork. Appetites whetted by the luxurious ceremony, every man who had loaned Roxanna's father a few coins over the years lined up at the door, demanding immediate payment.

Roxannah wondered if she should have saved some of Adin's funeral money to stave off the creditors, or to at least allay some of their mounting daily expenses. But she could not bring herself to do it. That bag of silver felt too much like blood money.

"What are we to do?" Her mother lay curled on her mattress, hugging her pillow. "We have nothing to give these people as payment. Without your father to protect us, they will take our house. We will end up on the street. We'll become beggars."

Roxannah reached for her mother's hand. "We still have the annual payment from the mortgaged land. Without Father's expenses, that can go toward our debts."

"Another payment won't come due for four months. You think these jackals will wait that long? Or be satisfied with so small a pittance?"

Roxannah went to the window. The courtyard was beginning to show signs of new life. The cilantro and savory were peeking out of the dirt. Even the spinach had survived the mild winter temperatures. Her seedlings had unfurled their delicate green leaves, fragile shoots poking out of the compost with the promise of another harvest.

"I have an idea."

Her mother sat up. "What idea?"

Roxannah dropped her head. A version of this plan had already failed once, when she had offered herself as a full-time cook to Lord Zopyrus.

Their neighbor's mouth had opened and closed soundlessly, a fish flapping on desert sand. "My dear! What would my old cook say if the daughter of Lord Fravartish were to take over his kitchen? He is already ashamed that I buy your food to help him. But to bring you here?"

"I wouldn't take over his kitchen, my lord. He could be in charge of me, and I would obey whatever he said. He could teach me, and I would be his apprentice."

Lord Zopyrus shook his head sadly. "Impossible. You must see that. The moment you step foot in here, he will feel that I have brought you to replace him. There would be no peace in the kitchens." He pulled on his thin beard. "Truth be told, I cannot afford another servant. I have so many already, you see."

Roxannah knew it to be true. He had never let a single retainer go, not even the ones who were too old to work. He still fed them and housed them and looked after their needs.

The old lord cleared his throat. "I will continue to buy your dishes, you know. Do what I can to help you and your mother."

"What idea?" her mother repeated, pulling Roxannah out of her reverie.

Roxannah had spent hours thinking through her plan. It had come to her like the fading tail of a shooting star, dim and undefined. The last embers of a once-cherished dream—the dream to host the king and queen in her own home and to serve them the finest meal they had ever tasted. A meal she had cooked.

That had been the naïve dream of a child desperate for approval. Now, she had cobbled that dream into something hard and realistic. There would be no king or queen. No childish fantasy. Merely a practical means of saving her mother and herself from destitution.

"I will offer my services to one of our neighbors as a cook," she said. "You can ask if one of your old friends will hire me."

"Light preserve us! You must have lost your mind, daughter! Work in the kitchens?"

"I already work in the kitchens."

"Of our own home, not as a . . . a hired servant."

"What is the difference? My hands are rough now. They would be rough then. In any case, a true cook isn't really like other servants."

Head cooks in Persia enjoyed a higher standing than other servants. They were considered artists and artisans. On rare occasions, kings had even been known to present their cooks with priceless tokens of their esteem—not that Roxannah had such high aspirations. She was a mere woman with little experience. The best she could hope for was a small kitchen in a private home.

"At least I will have an income. Perhaps even make enough to save this house."

"I have only known of two women who served in the homes of the gentry in such a capacity. And both were daughters of famous bakers, born to their trade. No one has ever heard of a lady running a kitchen before."

Roxannah smirked. "Do you see a lady here?"

For a moment, her mother looked fierce. "Indeed, I do." She crossed her arms. "Roxannah, none of my friends and acquaintances will be willing to set aside their cooks to hire the daughter of a lord. They would expect their kitchens to turn into mayhem. Besides, it has been years since I have seen these people. Their invitations dried up a long time ago."

Roxannah sighed. For the same reasons that she could have no friends to their home, her mother had been deprived of companionship as well.

She took Roxannah's face in gentle hands. "For your sake, I will try, my dove. But don't expect much."

Over the next week, her mother did what she could. But as she had predicted, no one accepted such an extraordinary arrangement. Several offered a small gift of silver, which her mother refused with the same alacrity Roxannah had shown Adin. They might be destitute, but they still had their dignity to stand on. Poverty had not reduced them to surviving on the dregs of people's pity.

By midweek, Roxannah knew she had reached the end of her rope. It was time for extreme measures.

"I will offer my services as cook to the Jewish physician," she told her mother.

"Work for a single man with no wife? Your reputation would be in shreds!"

"You speak of reputation when I have lived most of my life as the daughter of a drunkard? I am not ashamed of honest work."

"You are going to ruin your life." Her mother's chin wobbled.

"I am going to save our home."

She didn't mind the hard work. The servitude. What made her cringe was the thought of Adin. Having to see him every day. The hourly reminder of her own betrayal. And his.

She had warned him so that he could shield himself from harm. She had never imagined that he would in turn cause harm to her father. Even if he personally had not raised his sword against him, Adin still carried some responsibility for allowing her father to be killed in his house. Couldn't he have protected Lord Fravartish? Knocked him senseless, bound him up? Anything but have a sword run through him?

Working in that house, she would be reminded daily of what they had done, each in their own way, guilty of blood on their hands.

So be it. She could think of no other home, no other master who would have her.

She had caused her father's death. She would make up for it by being the means of her mother's salvation.

This thought alone gave her the strength to put one foot before the other and trudge all the way to the Jewish quarter, back to the house where her father's blood had been shed.

16

Adin

When he opens doors, no one will be able to
   close them;
when he closes doors, no one will be able to
   open them.

Isaiah 22:22 NLT

The Thirteenth Year of King Xerxes's Rule
The Second Week of Spring

She was the last person he expected to find at his door.

Four weeks had passed since that dreadful day. Each crawling hour had been like a dagger's point at his neck, sharp and excruciating. He had started the journey to her house a dozen times and turned back before reaching her threshold. What would be the point? She had made it clear that she did not wish to see him.

Now here she sat on his stone bench in the courtyard, as unexpected as snowfall in a Susa summer. As if the mere shock

of her presence wasn't enough to knock him sideways, she then
made her request.

For a moment, he could not speak. "Work in my kitchen?"

"As a cook, yes. We have debts, you see." She turned the color
of pink rose petals, and the hue, at once lovely and painful,
twisted something inside him. "The creditors have grown impatient. I need to work. And I know how to cook."

"You cannot work in my house, Roxannah."

"I know you observe dietary laws. Tirzah will teach me all
I need to know."

"It isn't that. For your own sake, it's not possible. I have no
wife. No mother living under my roof. It would ruin you to be
in my house all day."

Her jaw squared. He saw what he had suspected all along.
Under the delicate features, she had iron in her bones. "I don't
care."

He almost smiled at the stubborn tilt of her chin. Worse, it
made him want to pull her into his arms and hold her. He raised
a placating hand. "Give me a week to find a better arrangement.
If I fail, then we will do as you wish."

"What kind of better arrangement?"

"I cannot say as yet. I will make some inquiries. Perhaps there
is a situation more suitable to your position."

"If not, you will hire me?"

He studied the patch of stone in the corner of the courtyard,
still stained the color of pale rust in spite of Darab's careful
scrubbing. "If not, you can have whatever you wish."

Hathach studied Adin's letter before him. "Merely because
you tended Her Majesty's ankle a few times does not give you
the right to ask for favors, physician."

Adin bowed his head. "It certainly does not."

"Yet here you are." Hathach waved the scroll in Adin's face.
"Asking."

"Favors, yes. But to whom?" Adin raised his hands in question. "Perchance it is the queen I favor by introducing her to the greatest talent of our time."

Hathach rolled his eyes. "Best you leave courtly talk to the courtiers and stick to your breaks and bruises."

Adin dropped his arms. "Will you deliver it to her or not?"

The eunuch's narrow chest lifted as he took an exasperated breath. "Hasn't she done enough for your people?"

"More than enough. But I am not asking for our people. I am asking for a Persian lady who has fallen on hard times."

Hathach tucked the message into his belt. "I suppose she will chide me if I keep it from her."

Adin exhaled as he bowed and took his leave. He prayed Esther would allow this unlikely door to open—prayed the queen would give Roxannah what he himself could not. A safe haven. An honorable income. And a means of providing for a family who had already suffered too much, thanks in no small part to Adin's own actions.

17

Roxannah

Establish the work of our hands upon us.
Psalm 90:17

THE THIRTEENTH YEAR OF KING XERXES'S RULE
THE THIRD WEEK OF SPRING

Though early in the season, the weeds were already trying to take over Roxannah's diminutive garden in the courtyard. The warm climate of Susa meant they sprung up robust from their dusty cradle. She never understood why they proved so much heartier and more prolific than the herbs and vegetables she painstakingly tended.

For a whole hour, she had been pulling one useless, covetous plant after another, piling them on the stone paving until her back ached. She grasped and tugged and pulled, and still they seemed to be winning. Or she was losing, depending on how you looked at it. Losing seemed more apt, given the general lay of her life.

By the time Adin arrived unexpectedly, Roxannah was covered in sweat and dirt. She had known he would come. Known, in spite of their short acquaintance, that he would prove a man of his word. And yet when he arrived, she found herself unprepared for the sight of him. The push and pull on her heart, at once hungry to see him and desperate to get away, made her dizzy. Too eager to hear his news, she did not budge, not even to excuse herself to wash her filthy hands.

The hem of his formal tunic swept through the pile of weeds as he approached, dirtying the embroidered hem. "I bring tidings."

He seemed to have drawn a veil over his features, making his expression inscrutable to her. "Good or ill?"

"Good." He rubbed his neck. "I think." He waited a beat, which felt like a month. "I could not find you a position as a cook."

Roxannah twisted her fingers into one another, making a great knot.

"Not at present. Not until you prove yourself. But you can have a job in the queen's kitchens if you wish."

A squeaking sound escaped Roxannah's throat. "The queen's kitchen?"

Adin held up a cautious hand. "It is only as an assistant's assistant. You will be starting almost at the bottom. But in time, if you show yourself capable, there may be a chance for you to climb a little higher. To the position of assistant cook, even. Working directly under the queen's own head cook."

"The queen's kitchen?" Those three words seemed the only thing she felt capable of saying. With sudden poignancy, she remembered her childhood dream to cook for the king and queen. Certainly, Adin's offer was not a dream come true. She would not cook in her own home. She would not even prepare the whole meal. But she would take part—a very small part—in preparing the queen's food.

For a moment, all the heartache and guilt and fear of the past few weeks faded. She clapped her hands. "When do I start?"

Adin's tense face softened. "You would have to live at the palace, Roxannah, as your hours will demand your constant presence. You can return here once a week to visit your mother. But you will have to leave your home."

She went still. Leave home? Leave her mother? Could she do that? Could she abandon everything she knew and live amongst strangers? Navigate the bustling, hustling life at the palace that would leave little time to herself? Could her mother manage without her, alone in this house?

"There's more."

"More?"

"There is an awkward situation I should mention."

"What situation?"

"I often use the queen's kitchens to prepare tinctures and ointments and the necessities of my practice. The king's kitchens are always crowded, leaving little room for my work. The queen has kindly granted me a corner in her scullery to make my preparations." He studied his shoes. "It means we will see each other often. It cannot be avoided."

Roxannah wanted to ask if it was for her sake or his own that he considered the situation awkward. Did he feel the need to keep an even greater distance between them than he had before her father's death?

For her part, she had made peace with that possibility when she had proposed to work in his house. Being around him regularly would be hard. But she could live with it. "Thank you for the warning. I can manage."

"I also have a condition."

She crossed her arms. "What condition?"

"You must allow me to handle your creditors, at least at the outset. They will not be satisfied with the wages the palace will provide you. You will have enough to look after yourself and your mother, but not such a surplus as to make a dent in your father's debts. Those men will press to take away your home. They will not care if they displace you or your mother. Like wolves lured by the smell of blood, they are drawn to the vulnerable financial situation in which you find yourself. They are clamoring to take advantage of it." His voice grew hard. "I will deal with them."

For the first time she sensed a steely implacability in Adin, as if they had arrived at a point where he would prove immovable. "What do you mean you will *handle* my creditors?"

"I mean I shall pay them."

She turned hot. "I think not."

His gaze bore into her with the precision of one of his surgical knives. "It's not a suggestion or a request. Take my offer, or find yourself another position."

"You mean to shame me!"

The determined set of his jaw gentled. "This is not your debt to pay, Roxannah. It is mine. I intend to look after your father's widow." He flushed. "It is *my* obligation. In any case, it is a responsibility that you are unable to shoulder at present."

She slumped, unable to refute his last point. She was in no position to repay their creditors. And yet, of all the people who lived under the blue dome of the sky, he was the last one to whom she wanted to be indebted.

She gave him a fierce look. "I cannot fight you." She could not understand her own adamant determination to resist being beholden to him. She only knew that she would fight tooth and nail to repay him. "I will settle this account, Adin. If it takes my whole life, I will pay you every gold *daric*."

Roxannah had never walked through the Royal Gate or seen the sprawling palace complex that sat hidden behind high walls. In the days when her family had been elevated enough to partake of an occasional royal meal, she had been too young to attend. By the time she had been of an age to be a guest, her father had long since lost the favor and position that would have earned him an invitation to royal functions.

In front of the Royal Gate, Susa's main square had been laid out in honey-colored limestone with avenues of trees shading its four sides. Here, the lesser magistrates conducted their business within view of the Gate without actually entering the palace grounds.

Roxannah lingered outside in the square as the first rays of daylight caught the many shades of turquoise glaze on the thousands of bricks that made up the palace wall, turning them into a vast, living waterfall. Lifelike reliefs of fierce lions prowled along the lower edge of the wall like roaring guardians.

She stepped inside the main arched entrance of the Gate and froze. Unlike other city gates, this was not a mere entry point. A square chamber with high ceilings held up by four elegant columns in the center welcomed the visitor. Gold, carnelian, ivory, and ebony embellishments transformed the space into a chamber fit for a king's throne room.

The chamber was flanked by two painted statues of Darius, the great monarch who a generation earlier had taken the old, tired city of Susa and transformed it into one of the most majestic royal citadels in the world. Distracted by the imposing figure of the old king, she missed the guard just inside the entrance arch until he pressed the cold shaft of his spear into her chest.

She gasped. "Pardon!"

"Name? Homeland? Profession? Reason for visit?"

"I am Roxannah, daughter of Lord Fravartish of Susa." She unfurled the letter from the queen's scribe and displayed the seal proudly. "I have come to work in the queen's kitchen."

"Good for you," the guard said in a bored voice after checking her letter with minute care. "That way." He pointed to the archway at the opposite end of the hall. "Turn left, follow the wall, and then turn right."

As she passed through the Gate, she had a quick impression of two side chambers with stone columns topped with massive cornices made of black onyx and gold. And this was merely the entrance! Its stupefying splendor was enough to make any visitor feel inconsequential.

Two more soldiers checked her credentials again before allowing her into the interior courtyard. The palace complex had been laid out like a small city, spread out upon acres of elevated, man-made terrace. Numerous buildings and courts intersected with carefully laid out gardens. The whole effect was one of grandeur rather than charm.

Twice, she lost her way, distracted by the sight of spectacular friezes upon brightly glazed bricks: winged sphinxes ornamented with gold, archers marching on the walls in profile, decorative rosettes and lotus flowers. Even the ground upon which she walked had been carpeted with priceless stones.

A passing guard directed her to the kitchens, a group of clay buildings that lined the south wall. She had a glimpse of the ovens and roasting pits, over a hundred of them stretching alongside the western wall as far as the eye could see, set well back from the buildings to reduce the risk of fires.

The queen's kitchen consisted of a two-room structure, interconnected by a wide opening in the middle. Though the sun had only just risen, more than a half dozen people were already busy chopping, whipping, cutting, and stirring. The stone and wooden counters where they worked were cluttered with baskets of eggs, cheese, butter, herbs, and flour.

The ordered mayhem of the kitchen set her heart to thrumming. Her fingers itched to get in there with them, to work in this harmonious frenzy that created some of the world's most sumptuous cuisine. It only took her a moment to identify the head cook. That he was in charge of this place, there could be no doubt. He shouted directions at the assistants while working on a lump of dough. His voice, his bearing, even the way he surveyed the small domain spoke of a quiet confidence.

Roxannah stood unobtrusively against the wall. It would be better to wait for a quieter moment to introduce herself.

When breakfast preparations came to a lull and the head cook grabbed a silver cup to sip from, Roxannah approached him.

"Master? I am Roxannah of Susa. I was told to report to you today."

18

God will help her when morning dawns.

Psalm 46:5

The cook, a tall, balding man who carried little flesh on his long bones, glanced at Roxannah's scroll before handing it back. "Hathach said you would be coming. You ever worked in a kitchen with a large staff before?"

"No, master."

"You'll learn." Turning, he addressed a young woman sweeping the floor. "Sisy, put that broom aside and show this one around."

The girl tucked her bristly broom into a corner and bounded over. "Right away, Cook."

"She'll be sharing your quarters. Take her there first, and ask the queen's handmaiden to supply bedding for her."

He pointed at the lumpy bundle Roxannah had carried from home, which contained most of her worldly goods. "You can stow that in your chamber before you trip over it."

Though he had delivered this last instruction in a brusque manner, the fact that he had taken note of her heavy burden at all revealed a thoughtful nature. At least, that was Roxannah's hope. She tried to swallow the buzz of anxiety that had accompanied her every step to the palace.

"Thank you, master."

The cook shook a bony finger at Sisy. "Mind you don't waste time flirting with the boys who handle the spits."

The girl giggled, flipping her long braid over one shoulder. "As if I ever would."

The cook rolled his eyes. "As if you ever wouldn't. Be back before lunch preparations start. I have too much to do to be left shorthanded."

Sisy gave Roxannah a shy smile, revealing a missing tooth near the front. "What's your name?"

"Roxannah."

"I am Sisygambis. But everyone calls me Sisy. Follow me, Roxannah. I'll give you the grand tour." Her musical accent placed her home in a village somewhere to the north in the vicinity of Ecbatana, Roxannah guessed.

She studied the younger woman curiously. She had a genial, open face that seemed pleased with the world and all that was in it. "You and I are to share a chamber, it seems."

"You and I and three other women."

"There will be *five* of us in one room? It must be a large dormitory."

The girl scrunched her nose. "Not very large. You'll have room for your bedroll. Don't you worry."

She led them through a narrow lane until they reached a plain courtyard surrounded by identical rectangular buildings. Sisy darted down a dark hallway past the first set of chambers. Just beyond them, she pushed aside a brown wool curtain. "Here we are."

Roxannah studied the windowless alcove with its painted green walls and stone floor. In a neat row, four bedrolls with folded sheets and blankets lay against the wall. "Five of us are to sleep here?" Accustomed to her large chamber at home, she could not imagine it. Though they had few luxuries, their home provided an abundance of space. How would so many women even fit in such a tiny alcove?

"It's very pleasant," Sisy said. "Warm in the winter. Dry in the rain. It does get hot in summertime. And Indu snores like a wounded bear. But other than that, you'll have a grand time." She pointed to the shortest wall in the room. "Why don't you put your bundle there, and I'll go look for the queen's hand-maiden." Sisy threw a furtive look into the hall. "She is only the lowest of the queen's women. But she scares the Light out of me."

Roxannah sank on the cool stone floor, glad for a moment of respite. She examined her surroundings curiously, finding them to be more a closet than a chamber. Still, to a village girl like Sisy, having stone floors and painted walls with clean sheets and blankets must seem a luxury.

She had spent most of her life under the cloud of her father's disappointments, always bringing to mind their lack rather than their blessings. She was now reminded how fortunate her family was in spite of the losses of recent years.

The sound of brisk footsteps brought Roxannah to her feet. In her midthirties with severe but handsome features, the hand-maiden had managed to comb and curl every unruly hair on her head into perfect submission. She gave the impression of a woman who would treat the people under her with the same iron rule as she did her coiffure.

"What is your name, girl?" The brisk way she spoke hinted at a determination not to waste a single moment.

"I am Roxannah, mistress." She bowed her head as she had been taught by her mother and grandmother, just low enough to demonstrate respect without seeming like a flatterer, making sure her fingers did not fidget as she did so.

"Well, you have some manners at least. And you don't smell offensive."

Roxannah kept a straight face. As compliments went, this

one was anemic. Then again, having lived with her father, she had heard worse. "My thanks, lady."

The handmaiden gave her an assessing look and nodded, seeming to arrive at a conclusion. "You'll do. I'll have one of the servants deliver your bedding before nightfall. Sisygambis will tell you the rules."

"What are the rules?" Roxannah whispered to Sisy as they wound their way back down the dark hallway.

Sisy held up a finger. "You make your bed every morning before you leave." Another finger rose in the air. "You deliver your sheets to the laundry once a month." Another finger. "No visitors, no food, no noise, no lice." She shrugged. "I don't have enough fingers. But the most important rule is: Don't get caught when you break the rules."

Roxannah grinned. She was starting to enjoy this irrepressible girl. After a few convoluted turns, they emerged at the western wall. Sisy honed in on the roasting spits. "This is where the most handsome boys work."

"I see." Little wonder the cook had cautioned the girl about flirting. "Why are there so many spits?"

"They slaughter a thousand animals a day to feed this place. Oxen, deer, waterfowl, ostrich, and beasts I never saw before I came here. Even a few older horses and camels are brought to be roasted, though they feed those to the soldiers. The fine folk eat the more tender meats."

"A thousand?" In spite of her grandmother's stories of the feasts at the royal palace, she was astounded by the sheer quantity of game. "Do they slaughter them here?"

"Never. The slaughterhouses are beyond the palace walls. They stink too bad to be anywhere close to the royal residences. Cartloads full of prepared animals are delivered to the spits from the slaughterhouse every day. The best cuts are brought to the kitchens to be prepared by the cooks. The rest of the meat is handed directly to the spit masters."

Roxannah pointed at dozens of domed clay structures that looked like fat artichokes. "And the ovens?"

"All the kitchens have small fireplaces for simple frying and boiling and such. But the ovens for baking breads and cakes are out here. Most of these are assigned to the king's kitchens."

"So many?"

Sisy gave Roxannah a don't-you-know-anything glance. "The king's kitchens don't just cook for the king and the high-and-mighty guests who visit him every day. They bake for the king's guard as well. Soldiers eat a lot. In fact, there's many hungry bellies here about."

"I am beginning to appreciate that."

The girl flashed her wide smile. "You sure talk funny."

Roxannah flushed. "Beg your pardon?"

"There you go again. Begging and pardoning and all them funny words."

Roxannah's accent, which had been drilled into her after a lifetime of gentrified speech, was not something she could conceal any more than Sisy could hide her village pronunciation. She would have to grow accustomed to comments like this.

She swallowed a sigh. "And where are the queen's roasting spits and ovens?"

"Only the oven at the end of this row belongs to the queen's kitchen, and over there, on that far corner, those two spits are for the use of the queen's staff."

Roxannah took care to memorize the locations.

Sisy tightened the thong at the end of her braid. "The queen's kitchens are small, really. One dairy assistant who doubles as a beverage maker; one bread baker who works half days; one dessert assistant; one who specializes in meats and braises; and another in vegetables. I help with the cleanup, mostly. The assistants are supposed to pick up after themselves. But they leave a lot of the work to me. Cook oversees us all and makes the most important dishes."

Roxannah could appreciate why the girl called the queen's kitchen small. Her grandmother had once told her that 290 cooks, most of whom worked as assistants, served in Persepolis, the relatively new Persian capital built by Darius and expanded into something from a dream by Xerxes. A staff of seven was diminutive in comparison. Well, a staff of eight, now that she had joined them. She felt a small thrill at the thought.

A position in the queen's kitchen seemed like a perfect fit for her. She would have been utterly lost in the king's vast and boisterous culinary domain.

Although Roxannah had more questions than answers, Sisy brought their tour to an abrupt end, declaring they needed to help with lunch preparations. No sooner had they stepped into the kitchen than the head cook rounded on Roxannah.

"Time for your test."

"There's a test?" Even to her own ears she sounded like a mouse.

The head cook handed her a tiny papyrus scroll. "Fetch me all the items on this list. They are here in the kitchen. You pick the best. Go."

Roxannah read the list, aware of seven pairs of eyes converging on her. She studied her surroundings for a moment before setting off. Asparagus, first. She had seen a basket of them when she first arrived. She looked for firm stalks and compact tips, rich in color. Next, she collected eggs, looking for a dozen eggs of the same size. She sniffed each to ensure their freshness.

The head cook had asked for two kinds of flour—one of the finest grade, another a degree coarser, but not inferior, obviously testing her ability to tell the subtle difference. Bit by bit, she collected every item on the list and delivered them to the cook.

After making a quick examination of the items she had fetched, he gave an approving nod. "You can read. That's a good start. And you haven't missed any items. If you are to work in my kitchen, I need to know that I can rely on you. When I tell you to do something, you will do it and do it well."

"I will try, master."

"You can call me Cook. Now fetch these." He handed her a second list.

The assistants chortled as if she was about to encounter an unpleasant surprise. Nervously, she unfurled the piece of papyrus.

19

Jealousy is fierce as the grave.

Song of Solomon 8:6

Another list. Only, this one was in Persian. The first list had been written in Aramaic, a much simpler language to read and write due to its compact alphabet. The common people of Persia who could read often used Aramaic. Written Persian—like Elamite and Akkadian, all complex languages that required intense study   was the domain of scribes and the aristocracy. Roxannah understood why the assistants had snickered at this second part of the test. They did not expect her to be able to decipher Cook's list.

She wouldn't have, except that as her father's only child, her grandfather had chosen to have her tutored in Persian. The tuition had only lasted four years, and Roxannah was certainly no scholar. But she could work out the items on Cook's list: a pinch of saffron, salt, four onions, twelve cloves of garlic, a mortar and pestle.

The kitchen grew quiet. The assistants gave up all pretense of work and stared at her as she fetched her items.

Cook gave a short nod. "Let me see you dice the onions. I want them real fine."

Roxannah chose a knife that was slender enough to fit in her palm. She peeled the onions, leaving the root head intact, which would help keep her eyes from tearing up. Tucking three fingers in the front of the bulb, she used her knuckles to protect her fingers as she made several quick long cuts along the flesh and added a couple of transverse cuts before chopping. Lastly, she cut the root and discarded it. In a few moments, she had a hill of finely chopped onions.

"Nice and even," Cook said, examining her work. "Good technique. You didn't teach yourself that."

"I learned from my grandmother's cook."

He tapped the table as if in thought. "Now go to the queen's roasting spit and ask the boy there what meats were delivered today."

Good thing she had paid attention when Sisy had given her tour. At the spit, she found a young man with huge arms cleaning up ashes.

"Pardon. Might you be able to tell me what meats were delivered for the queen's kitchen today?"

The young man straightened slowly. "And who wants to know?"

"The queen's cook."

"The queen's cook," he mimicked. "Is that who you be? I thought it was that skinny fellow."

"Oh, no. Certainly not. I mean, I am not the cook. I am Roxannah."

"If you take that long answering a question, I'll be an old man by the time you hold my hand."

Roxannah's mouth fell open. He certainly moved fast.

He wiped his hands against his none-too-clean tunic. "When are you free to step out with me? Bet I can teach you a thing or two."

This was beyond fast. It was disrespectful. "Teach me?" He took a long step toward her. "What are you, simple? Isn't that what I said?"

Blood thrummed in her chest. She took a furtive glance to the left and right, searching for an escape. "Beg your pardon. I am not able to step out with you."

His eyes narrowed. "Think you're too good for me?" There was just a hint of menace running under the words. Something hard and threatening.

Lord Fravartish's daughter froze. Best not to rile him. Her fingers twisted, hidden by the fabric of her loose tunic. She had to find a way to appease him. "Not at all. If you please—"

He took another step toward her, forcing her back against the wall. "I don't please. Now, what's it to be?"

"Cook needs that list," she said, her voice trembling with desperation. She felt the familiar shivery feeling she used to get when her father was in a nasty mood.

A giant hand shot out to grab her around the wrist, leaving ash marks on her skin.

Across from the spit, a white-haired man emerged from a shed and approached them. "What's going on here?"

"Nothing," the young man said quickly, loosening his hold. Roxannah gave the man a pleading look. "The queen's cook wishes to know what meats were delivered today, if you please."

"Is that all?" He gave the young man a small shove. "Be off with you. Go fetch the meat." Turning his attention back to Roxannah, he rattled off his list fast as the Immortals shot their practice arrows. "One lamb, three goslings, five pigeons, and a leg of gazelle. And tell him I am short on firewood and kindling."

Roxannah doubled back, not wanting to be around when the young man returned. She tried to calm her racing heart as she headed back to the kitchen, hoping she could remember the meat list through the jumble of her thoughts.

Once again, she found herself the center of attention as seven pairs of eyes trained upon her when she entered the kitchen.

The dairy assistant grinned. "I reckon you met Miletus, if your face is anything to go by."

A couple of the men tittered. The head cook shook his giant spoon at them. "Settle down." He turned his attention to her. "Well?"

Roxannah repeated the list she had rehearsed all the way back from the spits. "And they are short on firewood and kindling," she remembered to add.

Cook gave her a level look. "Miletus did not give you that."

The titters turned into guffaws. "Bet he gave you something better," the dairy assistant said.

"If by Miletus you are referring to the nasty boy with too much muscle on his forearms and nothing at all between his ears, then no. He did not give me the list. A man with white hair obliged me."

Cook's lip tipped up. "You'll do. Let's put you to work."

She was assigned a corner and given the thankless task of chopping another mountain of onions. Her spot was next to the vegetable assistant, who was cleaning asparagus spears. "Aren't you all high and mighty," he hissed under his breath. "Don't think you'll get treated special just because you talk fancy."

Roxannah dashed at a stinging eye with the back of her hand. *You've already treated me special. Especially bad.* "Is this enough onion?" she asked instead.

By the time she was finished with her tasks for the day, Roxannah felt like an old pair of shoes that had lost their soles. As they plodded to their chamber, she listened to Sissy's chirpy babble. She was grateful that her new companion never seemed short of words. For her part, Roxannah could not manage a single sentence with or without a fancy accent.

In their cubicle, Sisy introduced her to the other residents of the alcove: an older servant and her daughter, both of whom served in the laundry, and another girl about Sisy's age, a helper to the queen's senior handmaiden.

Roxannah made up her bedroll, choosing a spot pressed into the wall as far from her companions as she could manage but with easy access to the door, lest some unforeseen threat should present itself in the night. She placed her small bundle near the foot of her bed and an ewer of water near her head, where anyone intending to reach for her in the darkness would stumble and make enough noise to warn her of their presence.

Some habits were hard to break.

Bone-weary though she was from the exertions of the day and the sheer newness of everything, she still could not sleep. Small unknown sounds made her jump. Quiet footsteps passing in the hallway made her hold her breath. She longed for her mother and missed home with an intensity that caught her by surprise.

Slumber finally came just before sunrise. No sooner had she finally closed her eyes than she had to open them again, fold up her sheets, and head back to the kitchen.

The second day, she was assigned to help the dairy assistant. She could tell the man did not want her there. He snarled every order and kept her rushing around doing work better suited for Sisy. She was fetching a large amphora of milk when she noticed Adin walk in. He spoke softly to Cook before settling in a corner by himself.

She felt an odd kick of joy at the sight of him. Clearly, she was so desperate to see a familiar face that their painful history managed to get lost beneath the relief of his presence. He inclined his head to her but did not single her out for a greeting, which she appreciated. The men would probably tease her mercilessly if she received any particular attention from the physician.

Before lunch preparations got underway, Cook approached her. "What have you done today?"

He snorted when she listed her activities. "If I wanted another fetch-and-carry servant, I would have hired one. I brought you here to assist my assistants. Now let's see what you can do. Do you know how to make a *kuku*?"

Kuku, a fluffy egg dish with herbs, had numerous varieties. "What kind?"

His mouth tipped up in the corner. "You choose."

Roxannah had learned her first kuku from her grandparents' head cook, a man who hailed from a populous village near the Caspian Sea. He had taught her this recipe, a specialty of his region. Quietly, she collected the ingredients she needed: dill, cilantro, parsley, a bit of fenugreek, barberries, onions, garlic, and chives. Sisy showed her where to find the spices. When Roxannah reached for the eggs, the dairy assistant threw her a filthy look. But he could do nothing to stop her since she was obeying Cook's orders.

The trick to making a good kuku lay in achieving the right balance of herbs and eggs. Sautéing the onions and garlic until golden, she set them aside. In the same pan, she added a touch more butter and fried a large handful of barberries, sweetened with a spoon of honey. Their tangy flavor and ruby-red color would create the perfect topping for the dish.

When she turned to fetch the mountain of herbs she had washed earlier and set aside to dry, she noticed Adin watching her. Her cheeks heated. But oddly, his gaze felt like a warm hand on her back, cheering her on.

Roxannah returned her attention to the herbs, chopping them very fine, using her knuckles to protect her fingers from the sharp knife. The eggs came next. They had to be properly whipped or the kuku would turn out too flat. To the eggs, she added the fried onions, garlic, and chopped herbs. She needed one more ingredient to give the egg dish an extra dimension. Crushed walnuts. These gave the kuku a subtle crunch in every bite. A final dash of spices elevated the flavors of the simple dish to something elegant. At least, that was her hope.

Now came the hard part. She couldn't see the bottom of the kuku. She had to be able to tell from the jiggly feel on top when it was cooked enough to turn over. Get the timing wrong and she would end with an ugly mess that fell apart, or worse, with a burnt bottom.

Roxannah stood over the pan and stared at the lid. What if she ruined her first dish? The assistants would snigger for a whole week. Worse, Cook would never give her another chance.

She sneaked a peek under the cover and judged the egg dish ready. Covering the pan with a flat sheet used for making bread, she flipped the kuku onto the sheet with a deft movement. Adding another dollop of butter and sesame oil to the bottom of the pan, she slid the kuku back inside.

When ready, she served the vibrant green kuku onto a glazed platter, decorated it with the fried scarlet barberries and a few dill flowers before bringing the dish to Cook. Perspiration dampened her brow as he studied her presentation before cutting a piece and placing it in his mouth. He closed his eyes for a moment as though focusing every sense on what sat on his tongue as he chewed.

"Good," he said in his usual no-nonsense tone. "Make another one. We'll serve it with the queen's luncheon."

Roxannah sank on a stool. "The *queen*?"

The bowl of cheese the dairy assistant had picked up clattered back on the counter. "The *queen*?"

Roxannah tucked her fingers under her arms.

"That's what I said."

The dairy assistant turned the color of a plump grape. "But she only just arrived!"

"Perhaps." Cook shrugged. "But that kuku tastes better than anything you ever managed to make."

The meat assistant poked a finger into the kuku. "Don't get too excited, girl. It will be one of a dozen dishes."

The dairy assistant wrinkled his nose. "True. Likely the queen won't even taste it."

Sisy took a whiff of the aroma rising out of the fluffy egg dish. "Well, *I* want to taste it. I'm starving, Cook. Can I have a piece?"

"Go on, then."

Cutting a wedge, she plopped it into her mouth. "Good Light! Can I eat another piece?"

"Wait until everyone has had a chance to try it." He turned to Adin. "Hungry, Physician?"

"I thought you'd never ask." Adin left his corner and picked up a large wedge of kuku to take back to his own spot. With his first bite, his eyes drifted closed. "God be praised for giving us something so delicious in this fallen world." He turned to Roxannah. "You are, indeed, talented."

She tried to quell the smile that was rising somewhere deep inside. Her lips insisted on having their own way, spreading as wide as a cart door, refusing to shut.

Cook snapped his fingers. "Well? Why are you lounging on that stool, grinning like a hyena? The queen's kuku won't make itself. Hop to it."

20

You place your hand of blessing on my head.

Psalm 139:5 NLT

R oxannah felt as if she had sipped a few too many gulps
of wine. *The queen! The queen! The queen!* She could
not stop saying the words in her head.

The queen of Persia was about to taste her cooking. Her old
childhood dream, the one she had thought a silly fantasy, did
not seem so silly now.

But what if this time the kuku tasted terrible? She couldn't
cut a piece to test it beforehand. It had to be served whole.
What if she made a mistake? What if Queen Esther hated it?
Everything that could go wrong paraded in her mind like well-
trained soldiers in Xerxes's army.

She ignored the slight pounding that had started behind
one eye and fetched the eggs, stacking them in a clay bowl.
She was on her way to her counter when something tripped
her feet. The bowl soared into the air. Roxannah went sailing,
landing spread-eagle on the ground. She watched the eggs flying in six different directions, somersaulting elegantly on their

way down. Five eggs smashed against the stone tiles. The sixth cracked against Roxannah's head.

The assistant cooks were howling with laughter. Sisy stood frozen in a corner, two hands pressed over her mouth. Cook had left the kitchen to supervise the bread baking in the ovens, thank the Light. At least he had not seen her humiliation.

Roxannah closed her eyes and exhaled. Someone had tripped her on purpose.

Adin crouched on one knee next to her. "Can you sit up?" he asked gently.

She nodded.

"Let's make sure you're in one piece."

"The only things broken are the eggs." She scrambled to her feet and stared in dismay at the mess on the floor. A finger to her head came away wet with runny yolk.

Adin pressed a hand to her back. "Sit and catch your breath." He guided her to the stool she had occupied earlier. "Pardon me for a moment."

He whirled around and marched to where the dairy assistant stood, finger pointing in Roxannah's direction, laughing himself hoarse.

"You tripped her. I saw you."

"Don't know what you mean."

Adin took another half step forward. His bearing shifted, feet slightly apart, arms loose by his side as though getting ready to lunge. He pressed the tip of his finger into the dairy assistant's fat chest. "Touch her one more time," he said slowly, his voice soft, "and that will be the last day you work here. It will give me great pleasure to ensure that you leave bouncing on your broad backside. Understand?"

The dairy assistant gasped as Adin took another threatening step toward him. Mutely, he bobbed his head, the fat under his chin jiggling for emphasis.

Adin lowered his pointed finger and readjusted the man's

tunic. "Glad we agree. I hope we never have occasion to discuss the matter again. Now, do you want to clean up the mess you made? Sisy has better things to do than to pick up after your pranks."

Roxannah's eyes widened. No one had ever stood up for her. No one had ever fought for her. Some sweet emotion rose up and reached out to Adin with longing arms.

Shocked, she realized that the fascination she had held for him from almost the first day of his acquaintance had not been vanquished by her father's death. If anything, it had deepened, growing under the ground of her heart like a root, hidden from her own eyes. It made her feel like a nation in civil war, half of her battling the other half. Longing and resentment crashed against each other, leaving her a little nauseous.

Sighing, she shoved away both the bitter and the sweet. She had work to do. She came to her feet, still shivery with reaction. "My thanks," she whispered to Adin, and before he could reply, she knelt next to the dairy assistant to help clean up broken eggshells.

"It will go faster if we do it together," she said.

He ignored her. She shrugged and smiled when Sisy came to help too. Those few moments on her knees made her resolve harden. She was not going to allow any man to steal her chance of cooking for the queen.

She wiped the egg yolk from her hair as best she could and determined to make another kuku even better than the first.

Once again, the kuku flipped out of its pan with ease, looking golden in the center and around the edges. Cook took over its decoration, and Roxannah watched in fascination as he used the fried barberries in an intricate design rather than a fat heap as she had done. By the time he finished, her humble egg dish looked worthy of a royal table.

Servers in white tunics arrived to carry the queen's luncheon on gold and silver trays. Esther was entertaining a handful of guests that day, though the meal was a simple affair by palace standards. Cook disappeared behind a drawn curtain and emerged a few moments later wearing a clean tunic, looking fresh and smelling of agarwood trees, his sparse hair combed neatly.

Sisy wriggled her eyebrows in his direction. "Dresses like that whenever he thinks there might be a chance the queen will summon him to praise the food," she said to Roxannah.

It wasn't until they had finished cleaning up from luncheon that Queen Esther sent for Cook. Their own meals would be taken from the leftovers of the queen's table, a common practice that ensured not only honored guests but also all the royal retinue received a share in the king's table. That was part of the reason jobs at the palace could prove hard to come by. If one liked to eat a square meal, no employment could beat palace jobs.

Roxannah sat on her stool, her knee jerking up and down with a mind of its own. Too many years of strict training had made chewing her nail unthinkable, a circumstance she regretted at the moment.

She jumped to her feet when Cook came in, whistling. "Well done, everyone. The queen sends her compliments. She especially enjoyed the stuffed gosling." Roxannah's shoulders drooped.

Cook grabbed a date from a dish and popped it into his mouth before sinking on a stool with a sigh. "Leftovers are being sent to the kitchen as we speak. We can eat soon."

He spat the date pit into a rag. "Too bad there is no kuku left." He directed his glance at Roxannah. "Not one bite. The queen and her guests finished it off. She said it was the best kuku she's had in years."

Roxannah would have fallen and smacked her shins on the stone floor for the second time that day if she hadn't been leaning against the wall. The queen hadn't despised her kuku! She hadn't sent it back untouched. She had actually—dare she believe it?—liked her cooking! Somehow, with egg yolk on her head, and scraped hands and shins, she had managed to survive the first hurdle. She had pleased Cook. She had even pleased the queen!

It was not exactly a royal gift. But the queen's compliment came so close to the substance of her dreams that Roxannah went to bed feeling like she might be floating on a bed of fluffy clouds.

The next morning, Cook assigned her to Halpa the baker, a quiet man with prematurely white hair who kept to himself most of the time. Unlike the other assistants, he showed no interest in baiting her. Instead, he took the time to teach her a new recipe. When she made a mistake, he corrected her without making her feel a fool.

He only worked half a day, arriving before everyone else and finishing by the time lunch was served. Roxannah learned more from her few hours with Halpa than she had from all the other assistants put together.

Still, her time with the others was not wasted. Though they kept her busy with menial tasks, she found herself introduced to lush spices, exotic vegetables, and meats with which she was unfamiliar. Every peeled, diced, crushed, and pounded ingredient taught her something new. A fresh flavor. A distinctive aroma that made her imagine new recipes.

Each day, she gained skill in using the alien implements of the queen's kitchen: round-bottomed pots, ceramic pans, bronze kettles, shallow trays, and deep cauldrons. There was no end to the tools with which she could work. Even the fire became her friend as she learned just how much kindling and wood to feed each oven in order to arrive at the desired temperatures. She felt as if she was doing the work she had been born to do.

By the time Roxannah went home at the end of the week, her joints hurt like an old woman's, but her feet felt as if they walked on air. She could not wait to see her mother. To recount for her the adventures that had kept her occupied in the queen's kitchen.

Roxannah's greatest worry when she had left home had not been adjusting to a new environment, performing her job well, or even being accepted by her coworkers, although she had struggled with all those concerns. Rather, it was the thought of leaving her mother alone that had pursued her with the persistence of a toothsome panther.

For the first time in her life, her mother had to contend for herself. To live in that sprawling house alone, no daughter to keep her company, no servant to help, no companion to assuage her solitary hours with conversation.

Her mother had assured Roxannah that she would have no trouble coping with her absence. That she would enjoy the peace of living in a quiet house. Though neither had said it, both knew she meant the peace that came as a result of her widowhood.

Her mother had practically pushed Roxannah out of the door. "Go. Go live your life," she had said. Her insistence had been the only reason Roxannah had felt free to accept the job in Queen Esther's kitchens. But it had not relieved her of worry.

She had earned an early leave from Cook by working late in the kitchen a few nights in a row. By showing up three hours earlier than expected, she hoped to put a smile on her mother's face.

But it was not her mother who opened the door when she arrived home.

"Darab?"

Her mother appeared behind the servant and, with a joyful cry, pulled Roxannah into her arms. "You are early!"

"Cook gave me special permission."

"Perfect." Her mother clapped. "Wait until you see the house.

Master Darab and Miriam and even little Leah have been helping me prepare all the rooms for your arrival." Her eyes held a sparkle that had been missing for too many years.

"Miriam and Leah?"

Two dark heads appeared in the courtyard. She recognized the little girl at once, though there seemed to be a shadow in her downcast eyes. "Ah, that Leah! Of course. And you must be Leah's mother?" she asked the woman with the round face and shy eyes, whose rag showed signs of good use.

She dipped her head.

"Thank you for helping us." Roxannah had a good idea who was behind this added service that couldn't have come free. She would be in debt to the man for the rest of her life.

Darab bowed. "Not at all, mistress. We were pleased to do it. Now, we shall take our leave. No doubt after a week of absence, you have much to say to your mother."

Her mother reached a hand that did not quite touch Darab's arm. "Thank you for all your help, my friend."

Roxannah's brows rose. *Friend*, was it?

He bowed again, this time deeper. "It is my honor, mistress."

Roxannah knelt to give Leah a good-bye cuddle, surprised when the child hid behind Miriam's flowing skirts.

"Forgive my girl." Miriam placed a comforting hand on the child's curly head. "She is a little shy these days."

"But we're old friends, aren't we, Leah? Remember me? We met at the physician's house."

The girl retreated farther behind Miriam's legs. Roxannah frowned. This was something weightier than mere shyness. Leah pulled on her mother's skirt and whispered something. Miriam straightened. "We have to go."

"Of course. And thank you for your help."

After their visitors had departed, Roxannah wrapped her arm around her mother's waist. "So. Darab?"

Her mother grinned. "He showed up a few hours after you

left for the palace last week, bearing a bowl of hot stew and warm bread. His cooking does not compare to yours, of course. Then again, it is much better than anything I could prepare."

"How kind of him."

"He's been here four times. Twice with Miriam and Leah, and twice alone, though on those occasions he would not come inside, lest there be any shadow of impropriety. He is the soul of discretion." She sank onto the well-dusted cushions of their living room. "I do believe he is a Persian lord in spite of his station. Do you know, I never had to cook once since you left? And this house is cleaner and more ordered than it has been in years."

Roxannah realized that the visits from Darab and Miriam had provided more than practical help. They had given her mother the gift of companionship. "I see I worried for you needlessly."

"Indeed. I have been well cared for. What of you? I am impatient to hear of your adventures."

Roxannah regaled her mother with a long account of the past week. When she told her about her kuku and the queen's compliment, her mother pressed her hands to her chest. "Darab prayed for you, you know? Every time he came. He prayed for your protection and blessing. For favor to cover you as a shield. And it seems his prayers have been answered." Her mother grinned. "There's such peace when that man prays, Roxannah. I've never felt anything like it. Even when the little girl, Leah, prays, it's as if the heavens listen." She played with a tassel on the corner of her cushion. "Darab says he and Adin pray for us at home. They pray for you every day."

Roxannah's mouth slackened. "For me?"

"Every day, my girl."

It had been many years since Roxannah had felt the desire to turn her mind to the spiritual realm. As far as she was concerned, the gods who occupied heaven and earth were impotent. They could not interfere in the affairs of humanity. And yet knowing that Adin and Darab prayed for her daily melted the hard crust around her heart a little. She wasn't sure if it was the thought that they cared enough to spend their time on her or the idea that some divine force might actually listen to their intercessions. She only knew that she felt warm and oddly safe at the thought of their prayers.

The following week, the queen announced that she would entertain the king's sister and several other ladies for dinner. The kitchen turned into a hive of activity.

Roxannah had been assigned to the meat assistant, who was preparing a lamb braise for the evening. She watched the pot worriedly as it simmered. The meat had reached that point in tenderness where it could fall apart with a gentle touch. Boil it any longer and all flavor would leach into the broth, making the meat soft but bland. Besides, the white beans and chives she had added would soon disappear into the sauce if overcooked.

But her supervisor had glanced at the braise only moments ago. Replacing the lid, he had walked away, allowing the lamb to continue simmering. Roxannah bit her lip as she considered her options. Coming to a decision, she removed the pot from the fire and set it aside before returning her attention to the hen she had been given to stuff. She would return the pot to heat ten minutes before dinner was served. That would give her enough time to warm it.

But before she had a chance to follow through on her plan, an outraged cry rent the air. "What have you done, you imbecile? You have ruined my braise!" The meat assistant rushed at Roxannah, brandishing an open hand, as though ready to strike.

Roxannah stood paralyzed, her mouth open in dismay.

"What ails you?" Cook said, his voice sharp. "And put that hand away. If any beatings are to be meted out around here, it will be my hand that delivers them."

"This . . . this upstart woman has ruined my braise." The words spewed with venom. "She needs to be thrown out."

"Throwing out is also my job. Now calm yourself and tell me what she has done."

"She took the lamb off the heat before it was ready! It has just been sitting there like a lump. It won't be tender enough. She did it on purpose to make me look bad."

Cook gave Roxannah a considering look. "Did you do that?"

Roxannah jerked her chin down once. "I took the braise off the heat because it was ready, Cook."

"Let's try it." He cut a piece of meat using the edge of his wooden spoon, poked at it with his bony finger, and put it in his mouth. "Well. There is at least one imbecile in this kitchen." He looked at the meat assistant. "And it isn't her. This is the first time your braise isn't overcooked. If you had kept your mouth shut, you would have earned my praise. As it is, she gets all the credit."

"But it's cold," the man cried. "You can't serve that to the queen."

"It will take a moment to heat it, just long enough for me to add the spices without them losing their flavor. Now move aside and let me do my job." He crooked a finger at Roxannah. "You, girl. Next time you want to do something, speak up. Come and stand next to me so you can watch me add the spice."

Roxannah's legs couldn't move fast enough. Cook's invitation may have sounded casual. But being trained by a head cook was the highest honor any assistant, not to mention underassistant, could receive. Established cooks often kept their secrets to themselves. They only chose to train those they considered the very best.

21

Adin

As soon as I pray, you answer me;
you encourage me by giving me strength.

Psalm 138:3 NLT

THE THIRTEENTH YEAR OF KING XERXES'S RULE
THE FOURTH WEEK OF SUMMER

Adin set up his chest in the usual corner of the kitchen. His gaze sought Roxannah, unable to resist a glance. He had not spoken to her since the day the dairy assistant had tripped her. For her sake, and for his own, it seemed best to create an invisible wall between them. But he could not avoid her today. He needed her help.

She seemed to possess an exhaustive knowledge of the herbs and trees that grew wild in Susa's fields and riverbanks. He had seen her collect them for some of her dishes. If anyone could guide him, it would be her.

She was busy chopping a mound of red meat into tiny pieces

and then chopping them into smaller pieces still. Her brows rose when she found him standing at her elbow. "Master Adin?"

"I need your assistance, Mistress Roxannah."

She hesitated for a small moment. "Of course."

"I am running out of marsh mallow root. The palace gardens don't have them. Do you know of any that grows wild?"

She thought for a moment. "I saw a patch by the river not long ago."

"Can you tell me where?"

"The location is hard to find. If you can wait for me to finish the meat, I will show you."

"I am loath to interrupt your work."

"As long as it does not interfere with meal preparations, Cook encourages us to search for fresh ingredients. I can spare the time."

"That would be a kindness." As he waited for her, he took inventory of the contents of his medical chest. The court might soon be on its way to Ecbatana, and he needed to prepare for that long journey.

The Persian king and his entourage were not sedentary, a reality that Adin found at once exhilarating and inconvenient. The court divided its time between five different citadels over the course of the year: Susa; Ecbatana; Persepolis; Pasargadae; and for shorter periods, Babylon.

Some of the royal servants and retainers were chosen to go on these seasonal migrations, while the rest remained to look after the local palace. It was a mark of distinction to be among those selected to accompany the royal house, an honor Adin had never missed since he began working at the palace.

Although the court should have traveled to Ecbatana by now, a flood had damaged the royal apartments in the ancient palace, delaying departure. Hence, they all remained captive to the steamy heat of a Susa summer, awaiting news from the builders in Ecbatana. If the gossip was to be believed, the repairs to the palace were nearing completion, which meant they could be on the road within weeks.

Though he longed for the comfort of his home while he traveled, Adin had to admit that being away from Susa during the sweltering summer months would be a relief. Ecbatana sat in the cool foothills of Mount Alvand. Green and well-watered, the refreshing climate of the seven-walled city made a welcome change to the endless sweat of Susa.

He examined the clumps of *mastiha* resin that he kept in a folded piece of papyrus, satisfied he still had a good amount left. Noticing Roxannah looking his way, he tipped the package toward her. "Resin from mastic trees that grow on the island of Chios. It's very effective in the treatment of wounds and even snake bites."

To his surprise, she drew close to poke a finger at the resin. "That's all very nice. But the real question is, does it taste good?"

He laughed. "Can't say I've ever tried it. And I'm not keen to start either." He folded the papyrus and set it aside.

"I have finished the meat. If we leave now, we'll still have plenty of sunlight left when we arrive."

"Lead on." He tried to shorten his stride to match hers so that she wouldn't have to run every few steps in order to catch up with him. "How are you enjoying your work in the queen's kitchen?"

She had a pretty blush that seemed to bloom at odd times when he expected easy answers. "I am happy there. If only—"

"If only?"

"Well, the queen has not mentioned my dishes. Not since she tasted the kuku, and that was over a month ago."

"She loves them, you can be certain of that. I know because I have eaten your cooking."

The single dimple peeped out at him, making him long to reach for it. Did it feel as tantalizing as it looked? He wrapped his fingers around his wrist behind his back, like a man arresting himself with manacles. The pull of her company was bad enough. But this added physical attraction had become a distraction he could do without.

The dimple disappeared like the moon behind a cloud, and her head drooped. "I fear I may be losing my touch in the kitchen."

"That's an empty fear, I assure you. I speak as an expert. I may know nothing about cooking. But I am an authority on eating. Take that chickpea cutlet you made yesterday. I took some home, and it left Darab speechless. You should appreciate that as a momentous occasion since it's a rarity. He says he might have to give up cooking entirely."

"But why?"

"Because if what you do is cooking, then he has been doing something else all these years."

He was rewarded with a tiny smile.

He grew serious. "Mistress Roxannah, you cannot measure your success by how often you are praised."

She gave him a quick glance. "I think I was hoping for assurance rather than praise." She was quiet for a moment. "Growing up, my mother often bolstered me with encouragement. To make up for my father's sharp tongue, I think. I suppose I have grown accustomed to receiving that constant affirmation. It feels like something is wrong when it's not there."

Adin digested her words, savoring this rare moment of openness between them. "Perhaps you have outgrown that season of your life," he said. "Perhaps God wants you to find a new source of assurance. One that doesn't depend upon others."

"I do not have your faith, Master Adin."

She had said nothing he did not already know. And yet the depth of his disappointment shocked him.

This ridiculous yearning was an impossibility. It had been impossible before Fravartish had climbed over the wall of his house. He had had no room for her even then. Now, it was like a star wishing to take residence in the sea. Other than a pale reflection, it could have no part of those deep waters. She belonged to a different world.

But Ruth had once been an outsider too, his heart murmured.

22

Roxannah

The wicked draw the sword and bend their
bows.

Psalm 37:14

Some of the mallow plants were as tall as Adin, though they only bore a few lateral branches. By the time they were close enough to examine the bushes, they were ankle-deep in warm, muddy water. They waved away the mosquitoes and kept a sharp eye for snakes.

Roxannah plucked an early-blooming flower, white with the faintest tinge of pink and a red pillar at the center, though most of the buds would not open for another month. "What do you think?"

Adin, who had been examining a thick stalk and some of the broad leaves for damage, held up his trowel. "Perfect. I don't know how you even found these plants all the way out here." He knelt and started to dig. "When we were children in Elephantine, my mother used to make sweets with the sap of the marsh mallow. It's an Egyptian delicacy. In ancient times, it was reserved for the pharaohs. Thankfully, these days the rest of us can enjoy it too."

Intrigued, Roxannah dropped down next to him. "Cook is always telling us to discover new recipes. How did your mother make it?"

He looked up from his digging. "As I mentioned earlier, my expertise lies more in the area of consumption than production."

"A talent every good cook appreciates."

He shifted his trowel to get around a stubborn root. "I do remember the ingredients since I helped to gather them. Honey, nuts, and mallow sap. Simple, eh?"

"I can experiment with that." She broke off a narrow stalk and gingerly put a dollop of the sap on her tongue. "Very sticky."

"I think that's the secret. The sap pulls everything together into a chewy treat." He wriggled the plant at its base to test how securely anchored it was to the ground. "Sit back, if you please. I am about to pull this one out. I don't want to elbow you in the nose."

The root emerged from its marshy bed with surprising ease. Roxannah leaned closer to study its cluster of long tendrils. They seemed quite ordinary. "What are they used for?"

"Fermented with grape must, the root heals wounds and abscesses. In a decoction, it will rid you of kidney stones." He shifted, turning in her direction to hold the root for her inspection.

For a moment, their faces grew level, so close she could feel his breath on her lips. Her chest felt like dough, rising and rising, as if she had forgotten how to exhale.

She had only come because he needed her help—or so she had told herself. She owed him that small courtesy after all he had done for her and her mother. But sitting this close to him, that firm conviction flew straight out of her head. In this deserted spot, there was no Jew and Gentile. No dead father, no painful disappointment, no impossible lines that could not be crossed. There was only a man and a woman.

Adin sprang away, but not before he could hide the dull color that rose up his cheeks. He cleared his throat. "You can cut the stalk from this one if you want to experiment with the sap."

They maintained a careful distance from each other after that. Adin dug up roots in silence as she gathered a bundle of stalks.

Why did this man draw her? The one person she needed to avoid. The one man in the world who could hurt her without even trying because his mere presence felt like an indictment. A reminder of her own betrayal, not to mention his.

And yet she seemed unable to resist the pull of him, like a bumblebee heading straight for the sweet nectar in a spring bloom.

Not far from them, Roxannah could hear the splash of feet. She looked up but could see no one from her vantage point this low to the ground.

"You will have to kill her soon," a man hissed, sounding agitated.

"Her household is guarded tighter than a maiden's virtue." The voice, low and cold, sounded oddly dispassionate. "I haven't been able to get close enough. Even poison needs some access."

Roxannah's eyes widened. Adin raised a finger to his lip, motioning silence.

"Then use something else."

"You forget. It's not enough to kill her. He has ordered that I get the book as well. We can't let that fall into the wrong hands."

A frustrated cry. "Where is she keeping the wretched thing?"

"I am working on that. There will be more opportunity to access her and the book when the court moves to Ecbatana. They are bound to let their guard down in the chaos of packing."

"You will never find any chaos under her rule. Not even during packing. She runs her household like a military outpost."

"During the long travel to Ecbatana, then. No one can maintain perfect guard in the mayhem caused by all those carts and animals on the move."

"She's not just anyone. Do not underestimate her. How do you think she has risen so high?"

A dry laugh. "The name of her father hasn't hurt."

"That is not the only reason. She makes a dangerous enemy. Only last month, the body of a man who had cheated her was found rotting in a field. Did you not hear of it? She is not a woman who is afraid of getting her hands a little bloody."

Roxannah covered her gasp with a hand. They were speaking of Amestris, the mother of the crown prince! The would-be assassins were too careful to name her outright. But she had recognized the story of the dead man. The rumor that Amestris was behind the murder had taken the palace by storm so that even she had heard of it.

All the allusions to her power, her guarded household, her father's rank fell into place. These men wanted to kill *that* Amestris. She gave Adin a wild look. He gave her a slow nod, as though he had recognized the same facts.

The faint rustle of someone pacing. "What if she leaves the book behind in Susa?" asked the more cautious man.

"She is not likely to do that, not when she went to so much trouble to lay her hands on it. As soon as I discover its whereabouts, I will make my move."

Adin motioned for Roxannah to remain where she was. Creeping silently, he slid amongst the bushes. Roxannah wanted to grab the hem of his fine palace robe and keep him from going another step.

What was the man doing? Didn't he realize they were in danger? They had overheard a plot to murder the most powerful woman in the court! Those men were not merely going to smile and wave hello if they spotted unintentional eavesdroppers. Should they catch Adin, they would kill him.

Roxannah would have followed in his footsteps to offer what assistance she could in case of trouble, but she feared she would prove more nuisance than help. Frustrated, she squeezed her eyes shut. For a physician trained to live a sedate life, that man managed to get himself into deadly situations with appalling regularity.

She shoved the end of a mallow stem into her mouth to keep herself occupied with something other than the desire to scream. Raw sap, sticky and slightly sweet, made her her lips purse.

Without warning, Adin reappeared by her side. Startled, Roxannah landed flat on her backside. "What are you doing?" she hissed. "Are you trying to get yourself killed?"

He wrapped a gentle hand around her wrist and pulled her back to her knees. "Pardon. Didn't mean to scare you. It's all right. They are gone."

She peeked around the clump of bushes. "Are you certain?"

He stood, stretching his back. "Watched them leave myself."

Cautiously, she rose to her feet. Curiosity won over ire. "You saw who they were? Did you recognize them?"

"I only saw one of them, and that in profile. He was a stranger to me." Rapidly, he collected his roots in the bag he had brought for the purpose, stowed his trowel, and bundled the stalks Roxannah had prepared. "We must return to the palace and speak to Queen Esther."

She froze. "Whatever for?"

He gave her an are-you-daft look. "To tell her of the plot against Amestris."

Roxannah shook her head. He could be so naïve for such a brilliant man. "For all we know, Queen Esther is behind this conspiracy. Everyone in court knows they hate each other. What do you think she'll do to us if she discovers we know about her plot?"

He choked. "Esther would never do such an underhanded thing, I assure you."

"Fine. Let us assume you are right. The queen is not behind this conspiracy. But why would she even care? What business is it of hers if her enemy has an enemy?"

"Be that as it may." He narrowed his eyes. "You are the queen's retainer. And I, for all that I am a palace physician, also owe her my allegiance. It is our duty to report to her."

Roxannah had spent a lifetime keeping her head down and minding her own affairs. She had survived by guarding her tongue. The only time she had decided to interfere, she had caused her father's death.

Having grown up with stories from grandparents who had lived through many a royal intrigue, she had developed a bone-deep wariness of anyone who interfered with palace business. "You don't stick your nose into plots and intrigue without getting burned in this place."

Adin's expression softened. "I know. I know what I am asking may be precarious. You don't have to come if you don't wish. For my part, I have no choice. This is the right thing to do, and I must do it."

Roxannah's mind stopped whirling, arrested by his speech. All the years she had lived under her father's rule, she had longed for someone to speak those very words. For her. For her mother. Someone willing to stand up to her father on their behalf. Someone willing to do the right thing, no matter how hard.

For the first time since she had been a little girl, she looked up to a man and felt the nascent power of respect. For the first time in years, her heart overflowed with the threadbare beginnings of trust.

"Hathach, we must see the queen most urgently." Adin had somehow managed to run the eunuch to ground in the royal stables.

Hathach crossed his arms over a narrow, though impeccably garbed chest. "The queen is otherwise engaged. And you stink of the swamp, Physician." His nose crinkled at Roxannah. "You reek even worse." Retrieving a delicate kerchief from some hidden pocket, he waved it in front of his face, releasing a burst of perfume into the air. "How did so much putrid muck smear upon your person?"

Adin flapped his hand in Hathach's face to draw his attention away from Roxannah's deplorable state. "Hathach, I regret the condition of our attire as well as the inconvenience to the queen's schedule. Believe me, I would not disturb you if it were not important."

"What is this about?"

Adin surveyed the heavy traffic of the stables. "It is a private matter."

"Of course it is." Large brown eyes looked to the skies as if seeking patience from some supernatural source. "Very well. Follow me."

Hathach led them to a deserted courtyard. In a few words, Adin and Roxannah described the plot they had overheard. Hathach frowned. "Amestris? What has that to do with my lady?"

"That's for her to decide, surely." Adin stared hard at the eunuch.

Hathach shifted his weight from one foot to the other. "Trouble. That's all this is."

"A truer word no one ever spoke," Roxannah mumbled under her breath.

Hathach blew out his cheeks. "Fine. Remain here. I will return to fetch you."

Roxannah leaned against a lion-topped column, her shoulders drooping. They were in for it now. Embroiled good and proper into the affairs of royalty where no prudent nose had any business sticking itself.

But what else could she do? As hard as she would like to avoid the coming interview, Adin had a point. This was the right thing.

From the Secret Scrolls
of Esther

Though I walk in the midst of trouble,
you preserve my life;
you stretch out your hand against the wrath
   of my enemies,
and your right hand delivers me.

Psalm 138:7

Thirty-Two Years Later
The Twenty-Fifth Year of King Artaxerxes's Rule

The day you occupy the throne is the day you will make
enemies.

I had no notion, when Xerxes selected me as his
queen, that the very crown on my head was an offense to
Amestris.

She saw me as an upstart. A nobody being given the
title that rightfully belonged to her. From the moment
Xerxes chose me, she despised me with a malignant hatred that could have no rest until she disposed of me.

It wasn't as if I stole her power. As the mother of
the king's eldest son, her apartments were larger, her

169

servants more numerous, her properties vaster, and her tongue more influential than mine. Her blood was royal. Through her mother, she was a first cousin to Xerxes. Her power spread in both directions—through her parents and through her son.

That was the woman who turned the blade of her enmity on me. No pup, she. Amestris knew how to knock down, how to demean, how to destroy.

The most famous story about her has been twisted in the mists of time, save for one detail. She did, in truth, kill her sister-in-law, the wife of Xerxes's brother, Masistes. I have heard people accuse her of jealousy as the motivation behind this violent murder. As if Amestris cared whose sheets Xerxes climbed under!

That was my burden. She was far too pragmatic for such things.

If you had any familiarity with the laws of the Persians, then you would know that the particular way Amestris mutilated and killed her sister-in-law followed the punishment reserved for those who betray the crown. Those who rise up in rebellion.

She had caught scent of her sister-in-law's embroilment in a plan to overthrow Xerxes. Instead of waiting for proof and diplomacy, she wheedled a sly permission out of Xerxes to take the woman in hand. I doubt the king expected Amestris to go so far. Swift and shockingly brutal, she did her own dirty work. If it was meant as a warning to the woman's husband, Masistes—a man so high as to be even beyond *her* reach—it failed.

Not long after, Masistes and his sons rose up in revolt. A savage battle ensued, leading to their deaths and the end of their rebellion. He had been one of Xerxes's favorite brothers. One of the few men he felt he could trust. Coming so close on the heels of the king's defeat in Greece, his brother's treachery almost broke Xerxes.

A mere handful of months after so personal a betrayal, the king set into motion the wheels of that silly competition that brought me to him. What else was he to do? Deny Amestris yet again? She had proven loyal when his own brother had not. In her own way, she had done Xerxes a service, though not in a manner he would have wished. She had little grasp either of discretion or finesse, that woman. Well. She had her own array of talents.

Still, in spite of the gift of her fierce loyalty, Xerxes could not bear her company. She was hard and unsentimental, the precise arrangement of mind and temperament to put Xerxes off. He respected her, I think. He might even have been a little in awe of her. But he could not love her.

I told the king once that as brutal as the loss of Masistes had been, God had used it for good, for in the end it had brought us together. I doubt the king would ever have given the idea of that competition any credence if he had not sunk so low.

He had lived his whole life in a deep well of loneliness. Having been born the son of a great king and the grandson of another, he never knew who his true friends were. Everyone wanted something from him.

By the time I met him, disappointment and the ever-present razor edge of rebellion had driven him to find solace at the bottom of his cup. The sting of his defeat at the hand of the Greeks in Thermopylae and Salamis had ground him down more than he ever admitted. After all, the Persians returned home with the loot of Athens piled into their carts. The military commanders hailed the war a triumph. But Xerxes knew better.

That failure tormented him. Foe and friend had gouged him out.

I remember at one of his lavish birthday feasts when the whole family had gathered, dozens of in-laws and blood kin filling the audience hall, he pointed to his half brother Arsames, and Amestris's brother, Hyperanthes. Whispering so that only I could hear, he said, "Here are the only men I can trust. The rest all want something from me."

He looked so devastatingly alone in that crowded room, I almost wept.

In that sea of grasping ambition, he held on to me with an endearing desperation, knowing I wanted only him. That, I think, made Amestris hate me even more than the crown upon my head. I had made her lose face in a palace that sneered behind her back when it called her mother of the crown prince, but never queen.

23

Roxannah

If your enemy is hungry, give him bread to eat,
and if he is thirsty, give him water to drink.

Proverbs 25:21

Xerxes had chosen the way of kings by marrying three women and filling his house with concubines. But according to Persian tradition, his choice of queen was uncommon, to say the least. Instead of giving the crown to Amestris, the mother of Xerxes's eldest son, he had chosen an unknown woman who had come to the palace by means of an unusual competition. This was the woman who now held Roxannah's future in the palm of her hands.

Before being presented to the queen, Roxannah and Adin took turns washing hastily behind a curtained alcove in the servants'

173

quarter. Hathach had declared they were not fit to appear before Esther in their mud-soaked tunics and had given them the loan of a couple of white robes used by the royal waitstaff.

Wordlessly, the eunuch conducted them to the women's building, a long rectangular structure with a shorter square edifice tucked at the end. Its walls had a row of decorative crenellations, with two stairways that connected directly to the main palace where Xerxes had his quarters.

The queen's apartments occupied the discreet square building nestled privately at the end of the main property. Hathach led them past two Immortals and into a hexagonal room tiled with glazed bricks in a thousand shades of blue and turquoise.

Roxannah felt as if she was standing inside a peacock tail.

In contrast to the richly ornamented chamber, the queen sat simply robed in a long-sleeved lavender tunic, hair unbound as her handmaiden worked aromatic oils into the long tresses. Unadorned as she was, stripped of cosmetics and jewelry, she seemed the most beautiful creature Roxannah had ever laid eyes on.

Tall and willowy, she turned with swanlike grace to watch them bow. "Physician. This is a surprise. And you have brought a friend?"

"My queen, this is Roxannah, daughter of Lord Fravartish of Susa."

The perfect brows puckered. "Ah. The little cook who has been making all those delectable dishes."

Roxannah almost fell on her head. She did not know which shocked her more—that the queen knew of her, or that she had been enjoying her dishes.

At her slack-jawed expression, the queen's laughter tinkled, girlish and teasing. "Did you think I had not noticed because I did not send my compliments?" She leaned forward in her chair so that her handmaiden had to let go of her hair or risk pulling the royal scalp. The queen shook a finger at Roxannah. "Let me tell you a secret: It's not good for your health to be the center of too much attention when you work in the palace. At least not until you make a few powerful friends. Sometimes, the best gift you can receive from a royal hand is a bit of anonymity."

Roxannah considered the mean treatment of the assistants over the past few weeks. How much worse it would have been if the queen had made a pet of her. She bowed her head. "Thank you for your gift, Your Majesty."

The queen waved a gold and ivory fan. "What brings you to my door, Physician? As you see, your visit is not entirely convenient."

Adin bowed again. "I would not have dreamed of this rude intrusion had it not seemed urgent. It concerns the Lady Amestris."

"Oh." The queen closed her fan with a snap. "That woman! What is she up to now?"

"It isn't so much what she is up *to* as what she is up *against*." Adin described what they had heard on the banks of the Karkheh River.

Esther grew quiet as she considered his words. "And you do not know the identity of these men?

"No, Your Majesty."

She came to her feet, gauzy lavender fabric swaying as she paced from one end of the chamber to another. "Well," she said under her breath, "this is unexpected." She whirled on the eunuch. "What think you, Hathach?"

The eunuch cleared his throat. "It seems to me that particular lady is capable of fighting her own battles."

Esther's lips twitched. "You always have a way with understatement." Sighing, she returned to her seat. "And yet we have knowledge that might save her life."

"Had she such, she would certainly not bother to share it with you."

"No. She would clap with glee and celebrate her good fortune."

The queen's hands wrapped around the handles of her chair, knuckles turning white. "Quite a temptation, this."

The lovely face had grown pale. She sat unmoving for long moments. To Roxannah, the very silence became mesmerizing, for she suspected that just beneath that fragile exterior, the queen waged a battle. Walk away and leave her enemy to deal with her own problems, or dip in her oar and try to save a woman who had, according to gossip, made it her mission to take away Esther's crown.

As Hathach had pointed out, this was a simple matter. Few royals, bred to defend their position and territory, would have experienced such inner turmoil over it.

Roxannah found herself drawn to this woman who had withheld her praise on purpose to protect a minor retainer and who turned white at the thought of refusing help to her enemy.

Here was a monarch worth serving.

Esther leaned back. "Once, not so long ago, I was afraid to help those who stood in grave danger."

She caressed the bejeweled curves of her golden fan where it lay in her lap. "I was told, then, that I may have been brought to my royal position for such a time as this. A slap on the back of my hand, that reminder. It is not a lesson I would easily forget. That time, in spite of the risk, I used my influence to save those I love.

"Now, I must use it to save someone I . . . do not love." She directed her attention to Adin and Roxannah. "So, my physician and little cook. It seems you have also been brought to your own positions for such a time as this. Off you go, then. You had better tell Amestris what you overheard."

Roxannah forgot the warm feelings of a moment ago. This was worse than she had feared! Go to Amestris, the most feared woman in the court?

The queen smiled. "What is it, little cook? You look like you have swallowed a mouthful of sour milk. Speak freely."

Roxannah decided that facing Esther was far less dangerous than facing Amestris. "Lady, surely such a revelation would be better coming from you?"

Esther pointed the bejeweled fan at her. "You think so, do you? Amestris would deny me an audience for the sheer joy of turning me away. No, you will have a better chance of making her see reason.

"Go through her household eunuch and petition the proper requests. Do not tell him or anyone else what you have overheard. We do not know who is involved in this plot. Best you keep what you heard to yourself. You must share it with the lady and no other unless she trusts them without reservation."

She sighed and sat back. "She will not want to see you, that is true. But she will also be too curious to send you away. You work for me, and that will pique her interest. She will want to know if perchance you are selling some damaging information about her rival."

The appropriate response at this point would be to thank Her Majesty with humility and take oneself off with utmost alacrity. But Roxannah felt incapable of an appropriate rejoinder just then.

"Your Majesty, I am not even an assistant cook." Hathach glared at her for breaking protocol. Roxannah swallowed past the knot in her throat. Even Hathach could not be as scary as Amestris. "It seems to me that the Lady Amestris would as soon dangle me by my hamstrings for having the effrontery to approach someone so far above my station than to grant me an audience."

Roxannah did not dare add that Adin's Jewish heritage tied him too closely to Queen Esther, who had shocked the whole court by announcing her own Jewish roots. Amestris would instantly dismiss him as biased. Or worse, her spy.

Esther laughed, seemingly amused by Roxannah's plain speaking. "You may serve in my kitchens, but you are such a well-spoken kitchen helper that one might even say you have the manners of a lady. I am sure you won't be picking your nose in the presence of the princess.

"As to the physician," she said, as if she had read Roxannah's mind, "he is one of my people. That cannot be helped. But he does have a reputation in the palace for integrity. Who knows. Perhaps between the two of you, you might make one halfway credible witness. It's the best we have to offer her, in any case."

In one final ditch effort to turn her world the right way around, Roxannah addressed the eunuch. "Begging your pardon, Master Hathach. Perhaps you might consider going in our stead?"

Hathach looked like he might have a fit from suffering so many breaches of his precious protocol. Roxannah could not blame him. She could not understand what had gotten into her. Her mouth, well trained after years of her father's unpredictable ups and downs, had inexplicably chosen this inconvenient moment to run loose.

The queen exhaled. "Calm yourself, dear Hathach." She came to her feet, back ramrod straight. "My Hathach is as unwanted as I. Everyone knows he is my man through and through." The sweet face turned hard. For all that she had once been a commoner, she knew how to play the royal. "The sooner you leave, the better your chance of warning her in time."

What could she do? Roxannah bowed and, walking backward, followed Adin out of the peacock chamber.

"You are very quiet," Adin said as they walked down the length of a fragrant garden.

She came to a stop. "*I* am quiet? Why did you not say anything, Adin?" In all the tumult of the past hour, she forgot to observe the formalities they had maintained so carefully between them in recent weeks. "Why didn't you try to sway her from this ridiculous course?"

He crossed his arms. "It seems to me you said enough for both of us."

Roxannah paled. She *had* spoken too much. What had possessed her? Was it because the queen seemed safe, somehow? But that was ridiculous. She did not even know the woman. She groaned. "I did say too much."

Adin's expression softened. "Peace, Roxannah. She was not offended. No damage done."

"What did I accomplish except to rile Hathach?"

"He'll get over it." Adin exhaled a long breath. "You ask why I did not speak. Because there was nothing to say. Esther had the right of it. We may not be the best people to approach Amestris. But we are the only ones she has."

"She will still hold it against us."

He huffed a humorless laugh. "You may be right." He removed his plain round hat and dragged his fingers through his hair. "Do you remember how the queen told us that she had been brought to her royal position for such a time as this? That was because she had to intercede on behalf of the Jewish people with the king."

Roxannah's eyes rounded. So Tirzah had been right after all. "Esther was the one who gained royal permission for your people to defend themselves?"

"Yes." His face became grave. They both knew that the new edict had purchased Adin his life. But it had also cost her father his.

This was dangerous territory between them. Roxannah pressed a hand against her chest, feeling torn once more by the civil war of her feelings for Adin. Now Esther and Amestris had unwittingly entered the mix, muddying the waters between them even more.

He dropped his head. "Receiving that permission was not a simple matter. Esther came before the king without being sent for. You know what that means. You know the risk she took. I tell you this because you need to understand that she does not send us where she herself has not gone before. You and I don't

179

face so great a danger as Esther did. There is no law that says we must be put to death if we come before Amestris without being summoned. We merely risk her ire."

Roxannah sank on the marble edge of the shallow pool that occupied the center of the garden. "I may not lose my head. But I face something worse."

"What could be worse?"

"I could lose my position, Adin. Amestris has that kind of power. Her influence would even reach into the queen's own kitchens. If she complains loudly enough to the king, he will move on her behalf. It is how monarchs keep peace. They sacrifice the little people." She dipped her hand into the pool and found the water too warm to be refreshing. "I don't want to lose my post." Her voice sounded small in her own ears.

Adin crouched before her. His fingers found her cheek as he tilted her chin. A jolt went through Roxannah at the touch. Their eyes caught and held. For a moment, they were frozen, his hand on her chin, gazes tangled.

Roxannah forgot about her job. Forgot about Esther and Amestris and murder plots and the whole benighted court.

24

Adin

Cast your burden on the LORD,
and he will sustain you.

Psalm 55:22

A strange lethargy spread through him, slowing time, making Adin feel like a man drugged with the juice of the poppy. For a moment he stayed frozen, one knee to the ground, everything in him locked on her. He felt tethered to her the way a man is tethered to the very ground he stands on.

It took all his will to rise and take a step away.

He had intended to comfort her. To remind her that no job was as important as she thought. He wanted her to know that her life did not hang in the balance of some abyss, to be snatched and tossed at the whim of monarchs. He had intended to tell her about the God who had stayed the hand of death over Esther. The God who could certainly shield Roxannah from the temperamental venom of a royal princess.

Instead, he had fallen into some bottomless well, betrayed by an emotional longing that had taken his breath away. In a blinding flash the longing had turned into desire, like a punch to his chest, knocking him sideways. He was long past the age when the sight of a lovely woman scrambled his brains. What was happening to him?

He grabbed the yearning that still burned too hot and, taking it by the throat, throttled it back into submission. Just under the surface of the sudden and unexpected physical desire, he felt the other need. The one that had brought him to his knees before her in the first place.

The need to reassure and protect this woman.

Before he could think of a way to do that, she stomped upon his thoughts with yet another unexpected twist. "My mother says you pray for me."

For a moment, words were lost to him. "I do," he admitted.

"Why?"

He crouched before her again, this time maintaining a safe distance between them. *Because I can't seem to stop thinking about you.* Or perhaps because of a memory, etched in blood and regret, which he could never untangle from her.

"Because I know of no place safer than in the arms of God." That bit of truth would have to satisfy them both for now.

Her irises had turned a river-blue, turbulent and questing. He could see a hundred questions forming in their depths. "But I am not one of his people."

"Israel's twelve tribes are populated by many outsiders. You can choose to belong to him if you wish, Roxannah."

"Like Darab, you mean? He worships your God."

"With all his heart. It does not matter that his blood is Persian and mine flows from Abraham. God binds us to himself, and through him, to each other. He and I are closer than if we had been born from the same womb."

She twined her hands in her lap. "It's been long years since I have put my trust in any god." The dimple peeped at the corner of her mouth. "And I am not about to begin merely because of your splendid recommendation. But I want to tell you that I . . . I value your prayers."

"Then I won't stop. In fact, do you want to pray now? Before we seek out the Lady Amestris?"

She gave a cautious nod.

He came to his feet and collected his thoughts. *Help me find the words. The ones that will touch her.*

"O Lord God of heaven, open a way for us. Defend us as we seek to do the right thing. Find a way for us to help Amestris. Give Roxannah the perfect peace of your presence. You are faithful, O God, and worthy of trust. Blessed be your name in all that we undertake." He stopped, not wanting to rattle on and on, lest he bore her.

Roxannah gave him a curious look. "That was not so bad."

He grinned. "I see I have to ply myself harder if I am to impress you."

She smiled back. "Pardon. I meant that I enjoyed it, and I had not expected to." She threw an anxious glance over her shoulder. "I need to tell Cook that I will not be able to help with dinner. I was supposed to prepare the braise for the queen tonight." She looked crestfallen.

"I am certain Hathach has already sent him a message. And you are doing something more important for Esther than preparing her supper."

They returned to the courtyard outside the women's quarters. When they asked for Onophas, the eunuch in charge of Amestris's household, they were shown to a tiny alcove, smaller than one of the storerooms in Adin's house. He was surprised that such a high official would be assigned so modest a study. But it was only Onophas's assistant undersecretary who met them.

"Purpose for visit?" he asked in a nasally voice.

Adin sighed. "Private."

"I need to record a purpose."

Adin's stomach grumbled. The dinner hour was fast approaching. He was hungry, thirsty, tired. He longed to go home and sit in the quiet of his chamber and think. He shoved his nose into the assistant undersecretary's face. "Record this: Private."

The assistant undersecretary sniffed. "Return in an hour."

"My thanks." His stomach grumbled again.

Roxannah threw him an amused glance. "Let's wait in the queen's kitchen. I can give Cook a hand while you find something to eat."

"That is a worthy suggestion."

"I speak stomach-growl fluently."

He laughed. The tight muscles of his neck started to loosen. She seemed to have that effect on him.

They found the kitchen already winding down from the dinner hour's activities. At the sight of them, Cook filled two bowls with roast fowl, slapped a piece of warm bread on top, and told them to start eating. Adin did not have to be told twice.

For some months, Adin had been treating the queen's head cook for a heart malady and, having come to know him more as friend than acquaintance, held him in high regard.

Cook jerked his head to the door, motioning for Adin and Roxannah to join him. Adin cradled his bowl to his chest as he followed down the narrow lane, his curiosity piqued.

They stopped when they arrived at a deserted corner near the perimeter wall. Cook mopped his brow with a clean rag. "Is it true what I hear? You're going to meet with Amestris?"

Adin wiped the surprise from his face. "And where did you hear this?"

He snapped his rag at a fly that had dared come too close. "You were heard making an appointment in her assistant undersecretary's chamber."

Adin set his bowl on the ground, his appetite ruined. "Why does the king waste his silver on spies when the servants do a perfectly credible job? What else do you know?"

"Nothing. Only that you and my new helper wish to meet with Amestris. No one knows the reason. Seeing as you came out of the queen's apartments before you headed there, I assume this is not some villainous plot against my lady."

"Your trust warms my heart." Adin crossed his arms, not bothering to hide his annoyance. "Is there some purpose to this conversation?"

Cook raised a mollifying hand. "Peace, Physician. I only want to warn you and the little one here. Amestris is no kitten. She will bite your hand off if you don't have a care. Which is why I am going to do my best to prepare you for whatever is bringing you to that woman's door."

Adin's racing pulse slowed. "I thank you for your kindness, Cook. We would welcome any guidance from you."

He nodded. "For a start, few know this, so keep your mouth shut about it. Amestris's head cook is my cousin and boyhood companion. Which means I know a few things about her preferences."

Roxannah drooped against the wall. "It won't matter if we know her favorite foods."

"Who said anything about food? When you come into her presence, you have to greet her, don't you? What will you call her?"

She frowned. "The right term would be *princess*, I believe."

"Well, don't use the right term. She will take offense."

Adin whistled. "Of course! When I say *princess*, she will only hear *not-queen*."

"Right."

"What, then? Should I address her as Your Majesty?"

"She would be even more mortified at that title, knowing it is not rightfully hers. She prefers the Elamite title *duksis*. It may mean princess, but it is ancient and more venerable because of it. Few in the court merit it. But her bloodlines go back far enough to give her a better right to it."

"You have done us a real service," Adin said. "That scrap of information will save us from stumbling before we even begin. Anything else?"

"Her court is much more formal than Esther's. Be sure to observe every protocol. And whatever you do, keep your mouth closed until she gives you leave to speak."

25

Roxannah

If they had listened to the warning, they could
have saved their lives.

Ezekiel 33:5 NLT

Roxannah cast a longing glance in the direction of the
kitchens, where she wished she could hide. "I'm sorry
I failed to prepare the braise tonight, Cook."

"Hathach sent a message saying you might not return in time."
He shrugged a bony shoulder. "There will be other braises. You
must go where duty takes you." He lowered his voice. "I will
let you in on a secret. The queen herself does not eat meat or
poultry. She only partakes of vegetables, legumes, and dairy.
The meats are served to her household and guests. That's why
she enjoyed your kuku so much. So you need not worry about
that braise. She wouldn't have tasted it in any case. Besides, I
assume your matter is important to the queen, else she would
not have involved you."

Roxannah exhaled with relief. She had worried that Cook might be annoyed about her absence.

Adin picked up his bowl. "We best keep our appointment with Amestris's eunuch or we shall make no headway."

Cook took the dish from him. "And how often will you be taking my new helper off with you on these palace adventures?"

Adin made a face. "As often as it takes, I fear."

"I am not reassured."

"Neither am I, my friend."

Roxannah's head swiveled from one man to the other. "Well, think how I feel!"

Once they arrived at the assistant undersecretary's office, instead of being led to Onophas's chambers as they had hoped, they were directed to another nook, only marginally larger. This one was occupied by the undersecretary.

"At least we are rising in the world," Adin said.

The undersecretary cradled a stylus in his stout fingers. "Name? Homeland? Profession? Reason for visit?"

Amestris's household had obviously laid out its visitation protocols on the strict guidelines of the Royal Gate. The undersecretary stifled a yawn as Adin explained that they needed to meet with Onophas. "Much too late, now. Return tomorrow."

"What time?"

"After breakfast."

"And we shall meet with Master Onophas then?"

"You shall meet with me. I will give you an appointment with Onophas then—if you explain yourself properly."

At this rate, they would never access the man in charge of Amestris's household, let alone Amestris herself.

———

Roxannah rose early the next morning and visited the servants' bathhouse to strip the last vestiges of the swamp from her skin. She asked Sisy to comb her damp hair into a more formal style than its usual braid, arranging it in a neat circle at the base of her neck. Donning her best tunic, she hoped she would manage to keep it clean as she worked through the morning shift.

When breakfast preparations were finished, she cleared her counter from the detritus of the mad morning rush. Unsure when she might return to the kitchen, she wanted to leave everything tidy for the lunch shift before leaving on her unwelcome errand.

"And where were you last night?" The dairy assistant's voice was sour with resentment.

"Mind your own frying pan," Cook told him. "She had my leave." At the door, he slipped a small package into her hand. "The undersecretary has a sweet tooth. He will appreciate this little gift. It may even dispose him to be kind to you." He tilted his head. "See? Knowing people's favorite foods does make a difference."

She grinned with appreciation. "You are craftier than the king's advisors."

He rolled his eyes. "Possibly. However, in this case, I am only doing what Hathach told me."

Once she'd met Adin outside the kitchens, Roxannah waved the package under his nose. "For the undersecretary."

"Bribe, is it? Heaven help me. I have begun the slippery slope to corruption."

"Not a bribe, exactly. Merely a sweet from Cook to mellow the man's disposition."

"That's a relief. I am feeling marginally less corrupted."

The undersecretary opened the package at once, revealing sweet plum rolls made from slow-cooked fruit that had been spread thin to dry under the sun like sheets of papyrus. Deftly, he retied the package and set it aside.

"Master Onophas will see you today. Wait in the courtyard and I will send him to you when he is free."

Adin winked at her when they made it into the deserted

courtyard. "Well, that went better than expected. Perhaps we can see the duksis today after all."

"It's a sad day when getting to see Amestris is cause for celebration."

Adin grinned. His expression, a warm mix of compassion and humor, tugged at her like a fishing lure in a trout's mouth. She looked away. The whole business of this plot had thrown them together in intimate companionship, whitewashing over the trouble between them. She could not help wondering when their past would seep through like mold, ruining everything between them.

She snapped out of her reflections when he nudged her. A stately figure approached them.

"No wonder Cook didn't send *him* any fruit rolls. Looks like he prefers sour to sweet," Adin said under his breath.

Roxannah felt the air whoosh out of her lungs. His expression could not have been stonier if Onophas had been a marble statue. He looked as if his lips had never smiled—and might crack if they tried. His silken robes billowed behind him like the sails of a warship.

"What's this about?" he snapped.

Adin bowed. "Master Onophas, I am—"

"I know who you are, Physician. I know also the woman you attend." He turned his inscrutable gaze upon Roxannah. "As for you, kitchen maid, I can't believe you even have the temerity to ask for an audience with my lady."

Roxannah found herself shrinking under that haughty examination.

Adin laid a reassuring hand on her arm. "Then you know that we do not approach you lightly. We come bearing delicate information for the Lady Amestris."

"What information?"

"As I said, delicate. Not the kind to be bandied about in common courtyards."

Onophas glowered. "You expect me to welcome you to my lady's inner court based on that pathetic excuse? You must be mad. That manner of reasoning might work for your mistress. Here we do things properly."

"Then we must take our leave of you. We only came because we wished to do the lady a good turn." To Roxannah's shock, Adin bowed. "The Light be with you, Master Onophas." He grasped her wrist. She barely had time to bow to the eunuch before she found herself pulled in the opposite direction.

That had not gone the way she expected. She could actually go back to the kitchen and start working on a new recipe. Her steps grew lighter. She was just considering the merits of using barberries in a sauce when the eunuch barked, "Stop."

They turned to face him.

"I did not dismiss you."

"Begging your pardon, Master Onophas. But that was exactly what you did."

Roxannah studied Adin with admiration. The eunuch's glower seemed to have no effect on him. Calmly, he returned stare for stare.

Onophas tapped an impatient toe. "I warn you, put one foot wrong and you will both regret it."

Roxannah wanted to tell him that she already regretted it. Her stomach had turned into a roiling pot again. It almost boiled over when at the threshold, Onophas whirled on her. "You are clean enough, I suppose. Have you any idea how to behave in the presence of royalty?"

She gave him her best bow. "Yes, Master Onophas. I am the granddaughter of the Lady Phaedymia of Susa. My grandmother used to attend the feasts held in this very premises when the great Atossa reigned as King Darius's queen."

"Phaedymia's granddaughter?" The eunuch narrowed his eyes in thought. "That makes you Fravartish's daughter." His lip curled in disdain. "He had quite a reputation, your father,

I believe, for the quantity of wine he could consume in the course of one day."

Roxannah turned pale. Shame, sour as acid, stole her speech.

Adin's face tightened. "Mistress Roxannah, as you presume, *is* the daughter of Lord Fravartish. The same Lord Fravartish who fought bravely in King Darius's mighty army. The same Lord Fravartish who fulfilled his duty to his nation, to his king, and to his noble name. The same Lord Fravartish who paid a dear price for that loyalty. He may not have been a perfect man, Master Onophas, but it behooves us to remember his service. Mistress Roxannah deserves the honor of an old and worthy name. Even if she does help in the queen's kitchen."

Roxannah threw Adin an astonished look. He had already protected her once. But this time, he also spoke up on behalf of her father. The same man who had tried to kill him and take away his possessions. The scales of her divided heart tipped seriously in Adin's direction.

Some unseen scale must have tipped in Onophas's heart as well, for the man flushed. "This way" was all he said.

He left them in the dark, narrow antechamber of Amestris's reception hall. "Don't move until I come to fetch you. Light help you if I find you snooping. Understand?"

Roxannah leaned over to Adin as Onophas retreated. "After Onophas, perhaps the Lady Amestris will seem quite"—she raised her brows—"maternal?"

He stretched his foot and tried to find a comfortable spot on the hard stool. "Downright affectionate."

"Why, we'll probably end up eating honey cakes and swapping amusing stories by the end of our visit."

"She is sure to invite us to her next private banquet. I hope you have something suitable to wear."

"I am thinking she will probably entreat us to work for her. That will prove awkward. How shall we refuse her without giving offense?"

Adin shrugged. "She is too understanding and affable to be offended by anything we say. By then, she will be thinking of us as family."

Roxannah laughed aloud. She sounded only a little hysterical. "I think it's more likely that after meeting with the Lady Amestris, Onophas will seem like a friendly kitten."

"You have the right of it, I am sorry to say."

In the windowless antechamber, they had no idea how much time had elapsed. Was it noon already, or did the strain of waiting only make it appear so late?

Finally, Onophas returned. "My lady has agreed to hear you." He pointed a threatening finger. "Briefly."

Amestris's audience hall was much grander than Esther's, both in proportion and decoration. Instead of blues and greens, she displayed a surfeit of gold, punctuated with generous embellishments made of semi-precious stones. At least a dozen people occupied the chamber already, most of them women, alongside a handful of eunuchs.

In spite of its grandeur, the chamber smelled musty, as though months had passed since anyone had aired the place. In the center of the room, a woman sat on a gold chair, her back straight as an Immortal's spear. Roxannah walked the length of the room without stumbling, despite the way her knees were knocking together. She and Adin bowed deeply a good distance from their hostess. They maintained that posture for an uncomfortably long time before the lady's handmaiden gave them the signal to rise.

Roxannah knew better than to gaze directly at the object of their visit and kept her head lowered as she straightened out of her obeisance. But her lashes lifted of their own accord, and she found herself secretly studying the infamous mother of the crown prince.

A handsome woman with strong bones, well-defined brows, and a square jaw, she had eyes cold enough to freeze water.

Under their wintry scrutiny, Roxannah feared her teeth might start chattering.

Amestris adjusted the sheer veil that flowed from her narrow crown, pushing its wide border of bejeweled ribbon out of the way before signaling her senior handmaiden with a wave.

"State your case." The woman had a deep rumbling voice that made her sound like a court gong.

Adin made a show of surveying the room full of visitors and cleared his throat. "Forgive us, Duksis, for this intrusion. We bring no presents worthy of your high office, no gifts to show our regard for you. Our only offering is information, which we hope you will find useful."

The handmaiden looked at Amestris, and at her nod, returned her attention to Adin. "Speak."

Roxannah cringed. They could not reveal what they knew before all these people. Esther had made that clear. They had to convince Amestris to empty the room of all, save her most trusted servants, and even that would be a risk.

Adin seemed unfazed by the lady's icy demeanor. "Duksis, we bring you a matter of utmost delicacy. It would be unwise to speak before so many witnesses. I ask your forbearance for a little longer. Would you honor us with a private audience?"

A whispered consultation before the handmaiden snapped, "Speak or leave."

Adin bowed his head. "It concerns your safety, Duksis. I can say no more in this company."

Amestris was apparently done with speaking through her handmaiden. She came to her feet in a whisper of silk and linen. Her ruched skirts swayed about her feet like a silent bell. "You think I don't know who sent you? You think I am unaware that you are here to make trouble? You must be soft in the head if you believe I will fall for your warnings and ominous hints.

"Go tell your servant girl I was weaving intrigue before she had learned to read and write. If she thinks I will fall for her schoolgirl machinations, she is a greater fool than I took her for. Now get out."

Roxannah winced. That could have gone better. There was no arguing with the lady. She had dismissed them most emphatically before they could even mention the book.

Bowing, they walked backward. The large double doors of Amestris's chamber yawned open behind them. As they stepped into the hall, Roxannah halted. She had only a moment to consider the insanity of the idea that had popped into her head.

Before she lost the courage, and more importantly, before the double doors closed behind them, she turned to Adin and in her loudest voice said, "Master Adin, isn't it a pity we did not have an opportunity to tell the duksis about the book?"

Through the slowly swinging double doors, her voice was loud enough to carry into Amestris's audience chamber. Roxannah had broken no rules. She had not spoken in the presence of the lady. They were already outside her private chamber, and she had merely addressed Adin.

Adin's brows rose. He turned to guide them toward the exit. No one stopped them. They continued to stroll until they passed through the outer door and into the courtyard. Still, no one followed.

Her gambit had failed.

26

For you shall not go out in haste,
and you shall not go in flight,
for the LORD will go before you,
and the God of Israel will be your rear guard.

Isaiah 52:12

They were almost all the way to the kitchens when behind them, footsteps clattered on the stone floor. "You there. Wait!" Amestris's senior handmaiden huffed to a stop.

Roxannah's heart slammed against her chest. They turned to face her. "Yes?"

"The duksis requests your return."

"With pleasure," Adin said.

This time, the audience hall was empty, save for the senior handmaiden. Even Onophas was glaringly absent.

Amestris was pacing before her golden chair. "You better not be playing me for a fool." She pointed her chin at Roxannah. "I gather you are something more than a kitchen maid. You obviously have brains enough to think on your feet. You talk this time. To what book were you referring?"

"The one they intend to steal from you, Duksis. After they kill you."

Amestris sank back into the golden chair. "Who are *they*?"

"We do not know, Duksis. Master Adin and I were gathering plants at the river's edge when we overheard their conversation. There were two men. But we did not recognize them."

"Tell me exactly what you heard. Leave nothing out."

Roxannah obeyed. "Master Adin saw one of them in profile," she added as she finished her tale.

Amestris leaned forward. "Will you be able to recognize him if you see him again, Physician?"

"I believe so, my lady."

"And your mistress? Does she know?"

"She knows what we know, Duksis," he said. "We went to her first."

Amestris sneered. "At least you appear to be honest." Folding her hands, she bowed over them in thought. "She sent you here, did she?"

"Yes, lady."

Her smile held a bitter edge. "Probably a clever ploy to gain my trust."

Roxannah wanted to defend Esther's motives. To disabuse this woman of her unfounded suspicions against her queen. It dawned on her that in the course of her short acquaintance with Esther, she had come to believe in her, heart and soul. Believe in her worthiness. It was an offense to hear her name besmirched. But speaking up would break protocol, which would only make Amestris angrier. She bit her lips to keep them sealed.

The princess turned to address Roxannah again. "This book. Does your mistress know what it contains?"

"The man never elaborated on its contents, Duksis. He only referred to it as *the book*. Neither we, nor the queen, know more than that." Amestris had carefully avoided calling Esther by her rightful title. At least this one service Roxannah could do for her. She addressed Esther as she deserved.

Amestris sat back as though slapped. "She may be queen now, girl. But that will not last. Not with her empty womb. Her days on her little throne are numbered, I assure you." She waved an irritated hand to dismiss them.

Roxannah and Adin began the familiar route to the exit.

"Wait!" Amestris slapped a hand against the chair's handle. "You may run into him again. You say he was dressed as befit a courtier. If so, he is slithering about the place somewhere. Bring word to me immediately, Physician, if you see him. Understand?"

Adin bowed his head. "You can count on it, my lady."

And that was the conclusion of the harrowing audience with the mother of the crown prince. She never thanked them. Never acknowledged their service. She had doubted the sincerity of their motives and, worse still, doubted the sincerity of the queen's motives.

But Roxannah felt certain that Amestris had taken their warning to heart. At least now she was sure to take extra precautions with her safety, not to mention that of her mysterious book.

Halfway down the formal garden, Roxannah was finally able to exhale a sigh of relief. "It's over, Adin. We did as the queen bid us. We managed to warn Amestris. And by some miracle, she did not even threaten to ruin us."

Adin looked at his shoes. "That was a clever ploy, the way you managed to snag her attention."

She grinned. "Do you think so? I thought it hadn't worked when she let us walk right out without calling us back."

"Oh, it worked. Only . . ."

Something about Adin's tone made the hair on the back of her neck rise. The way he hemmed and hawed, that knotted frown and half-finished sentence. Something was definitely off-kilter. "Only what?"

"Well, if there was a spy in that room, someone who reports to one of the men at the river, she, or he, would certainly have been interested in the fact that you mentioned a book. Their curiosity would have been even more aroused when Amestris dismissed everyone and recalled us into her chamber."

Roxannah went cold. "I had not thought of that."

"It may be nothing. You spoke in very general terms."

His words failed to reassure her. She doubted they even reassured him. "What do you think will happen?" She pushed her shoulders back. "Speak straight with me."

"Most likely, nothing. But there is a chance, a very small chance..."

Roxannah stamped her foot. "Will you spit it out? You are making my head ache." In the back of her mind, she felt a small thrill of shock at her own boldness. She would have wondered more at the unusual trail of brash words she had left behind her in recent days if Adin's warning had not occupied her attention.

Adin gave her a rueful nod. "Plainly, then. Whoever is behind this plot will now be interested in what we know. Are we in possession of information about the same book that they are interested in? If so, do we know its location? Since I mentioned a concern for the lady's safety, does that mean we know about their assassination plans? Do we realize the book is connected to those plans? They will want to discover what it is exactly that we know."

Roxannah started to feel like she was clinging to a thin, waterlogged plank in the midst of swelling waves. "What will they do?"

"They may simply have us followed. They may pay someone to spy on us in an attempt to discover what we know. Or they may decide to interrogate us."

Roxannah's eyes rounded. "Interrogate us how?"

A wide shoulder lifted casually. "In the usual ways, I imagine."

"Illuminate me."

He looked away. "Questions accompanied by a few bruises. Perhaps a broken bone or two."

"Torture?" She groaned. "I knew we should never have become involved."

"Roxannah, what if we did not happen upon that riverbank at that particular moment by accident? What if God wanted us to overhear that conversation? What if there is an intention behind the situation in which we find ourselves?"

"What do you mean?"

"I mean that there is purpose behind this danger. It isn't empty happenstance. I do not claim to understand God's plans. But I know the One who set our feet upon this path will be with us as we complete our part. He will go before us and make a way."

Adin said the words with such firm conviction that for a moment Roxannah believed him. She realized that he had not once seemed overwhelmed by their difficult circumstances. The ground beneath him never seemed to shake. She wondered what it must be like to walk about with that much security beneath your feet.

He gave her one of his intense looks, the ones that seemed to burrow inside her heart. Her belly went tight and soft at the same time.

"I will do what I can to keep you safe. We will come out of this, Roxannah."

Wrapped in the warmth of his reassuring words, Roxannah decided that Adin was like a late-season apple. Thick-skinned on the outside, so that little seemed to overwhelm him, and sweet to the core on the inside.

"Will you do that prayer thing again?"

———

That evening, when Roxannah and Sisy finished their chores, they found Adin waiting for them outside the kitchen. "May I accompany you ladies to your door?" he asked.

Roxannah was not deceived by his offhand manner. There was nothing casual about this offer. He wanted to ensure nobody clouted her on the head and dragged her off in the dark for an "interrogation."

Sisy might giggle and bat her thin eyelashes all she liked. Roxannah knew better.

"I think the physician is sweet on you, Roxannah," Sisy said later as she unrolled her mattress and made her bed.

"Ha!"

"He is, I tell you. A man doesn't go out of his way to walk a girl home for nothing."

Roxannah rolled her eyes. She added a couple of extra obstacles to the perimeter of her bed and studied the hallways to establish an escape route in case of trouble. Somewhere in the back of her mind, she knew all her preparations would probably prove useless in a windowless room with only one exit. Still, she clung to old habits that gave her a tiny thread of control, and hence, an illusion of safety.

Long before sunrise, something clattered with a loud noise at the foot of her mattress. Roxannah gasped and sat up.

The queen's handmaiden crouched next to her, her neat tunic damp at the edges where she had knocked down an ewer of water.

"What's going on?" Sisy mumbled.

"Nothing that concerns you," the handmaiden snapped. "Get back to sleep. It's still early."

Sisy, recognizing the voice, did not make another peep and, closing her eyes, obediently lay as still as a terrified doe.

The handmaiden did not make the same offer to Roxannah. She wrung the corner of her tunic and watched water drip from her fingers onto the floor. She gave Roxannah an incensed look. Motioning with an imperious hand, she gestured for her to rise and dress quickly. Roxannah, still half asleep, pulled on a clean tunic over her linen undergarments and stepped outside the alcove.

The handmaiden was trying to straighten the wrinkles from

her wrung-out skirts. "Why do you keep a large ewer of water next to your bed where an innocent person can spill it?"

"Pardon, mistress."

"I didn't ask for an apology. I demanded an explanation. Why can't you just keep a beaker of water like normal people if you thirst in the night?"

"Because unexpected visitors don't stumble over small cups of water, mistress. A large ewer serves as an effective warning as well as a barrier."

"Do you have many unexpected visitors in the dead of night?"

"Not so far. But I find it's better to always be prepared."

The handmaiden blinked. She could not have been more than a decade older than Roxannah. But in moments like this, she made Roxannah feel like a child. "You are a curious creature. Well, what are you waiting for? Move."

"Where are we going?"

"To the queen's apartments, of course. Where did you think I would take you? For a chariot ride in the hill country?"

"The queen?" In truth, a chariot ride in the hill country would be less strange than an audience with the queen long before sunrise. Roxannah swung her sleep-mussed braid over her shoulder. "But I am not presentable."

"I will tend to you before you go in."

When they arrived in the queen's modest antechamber, the handmaiden fetched a box brimming with sundry items. From its depths, she chose an ivory comb and began to ply it with more energy than care to Roxannah's curls. Roxannah winced. She hoped the woman was gentler when using her craft on the queen.

Rubbing a bit of rose oil between her hands, the handmaiden anointed Roxannah's tresses before binding her hair into a tidy braid that she pinned in a half-moon at the base of her head. "You have acceptable hair. You should take better care of it. Most of the time it resembles sheep's wool."

Roxannah could not suppress a snort. Somewhere under that insult she detected the merest hint of a compliment.

"The condition of your hair is no laughing matter, young woman." From her box, the handmaiden extracted a couple of pale chewing sticks, soft yellowish twigs from the Persian miswak tree popular for brushing teeth. "Use this while I fetch you a washing rag." Roxannah obeyed with relief, flattening the end of the pale stick with her teeth. The refreshing taste of cress burst in her mouth.

She washed thoroughly using the wet rag the handmaiden had fetched. It smelled faintly of rose and jasmine.

"That will have to do." The handmaiden made a face as Roxannah put her tunic back on. "You will need a new tunic if you are going to make a habit of visiting the queen."

Roxannah threw the woman an alarmed look. "Make a habit? You needn't worry on that score, mistress. We can call this an exception and leave new tunics out of it."

"We shall see. Now stop talking and start marching."

To Roxannah's surprise, it was the queen's bedchamber to which the handmaiden directed her. Esther's hair lay around her shoulders in a tousled dark cloud as she sat in bed, her back resting against a stack of silk pillows. She was issuing the day's orders to her senior handmaiden in a leisurely tone. Lifting a richly embroidered cloak from the floor next to the bed, she buried her face into its folds.

"My lord forgot his cloak," she said with a smile as she handed it over to the handmaiden. "Best launder it before returning it to his chamberlain."

Roxannah noticed the smudged eyes and bruised lips. It dawned on her that the queen had not spent the night alone. For a moment, she did not know where to rest her gaze.

Like every Persian citizen in Susa, she had had glimpses of the king from afar when he rode off to some distant land, attending to the needs of his empire in war and peace. He had never seemed fully human, somehow. She had thought of him more as a symbol, imbued with the power to rule vast lands. Not a man of flesh and blood who would hold this beautiful woman through the night, leaving behind the mark of his passionate kisses.

Roxannah frowned. Ever since hearing the edict that proclaimed the annihilation of every Jew in Persia, she had lost her trust in the king. His actions had left a bad taste in her mouth. The thought of him in Esther's bed made her slightly sick. She would have imagined that Esther felt the same, especially given her Jewish heritage.

Yet the queen smiled when she mentioned her husband, and caressed his robe as though it were a precious garment. If she was miserable in her marriage, she certainly knew how to hide it.

From the Secret Scrolls
of Esther

Love prospers when a fault is forgiven.

Proverbs 17:9 NLT

Thirty-Two Years Later
The Twenty-Fifth Year of King Artaxerxes's Rule

I will tell you a secret: A queen must know how to forgive.

If you cradle every disappointment to your chest and never let go, you will not know happiness. Your retainers will betray you; your friends will disillusion you; even those closest to you may one day break your heart.

I learned that the day I walked into the presence of the king without his invitation. My mind was in a welter. I feared for my people. I feared I would fail them. I feared for my own life. I feared I would not manage to stay one step ahead of that toad Haman.

But underneath all that turmoil, my heart clung to other, more painful questions: *Why did you ignore me for*

205

a whole month? Why did you abandon me? Why did you let me down?

They were not questions I could ask.

I stood there with a hundred eyes upon me, wondering how the king would respond to my audacity. I barely saw them. All I knew was him, sitting on his throne, his face a stony mask. He had carved that exact expression in his youth; it came to him with practiced ease now. He betrayed no emotion at the sight of me as I stood shivering, hanging in the balance of his mercy.

Would he save me?

Then I saw it. For the merest instant, I saw his eyes widening, brightening. He stretched a foot toward me, as if part of him wished to stand and march over to my side.

The well-worn stony expression returned so quickly, I wondered if I had imagined the change. Then he raised the royal scepter, and the court knew that I would live.

You could hear the crowd exhale—in relief or disappointment, I could not tell. But the king made sure they knew where he stood. He promised to give me whatever I wanted, even to the half of his kingdom before I had a chance to speak.

He came to my apartments that night alongside Haman. I could tell curiosity had a hold of him. But he did not remain, not past dinner. He came as a guest and left the same way, as though he had not whispered a thousand endearments in my ears over the past five years.

He came again the second night. I was sorry for his sake to reveal Haman's perfidy to him. The Lord knew my husband had already borne the brunt of too many betrayals. Now he had to contend with another false friend. Another treachery that left him feeling foolish and used.

He hated me a little, then. I had always made him feel strong. I had made him feel enough. But that night, it was my finger of accusation that made him see his weakness. He had been beguiled into writing a terrible law at the hands of a man who had pretended to be his true friend.

He gave Mordecai and me the help we needed to shield our people. But he walked out of my apartments with his stony-faced mask firmly in place again. A king leaving the presence of a petitioner, not a husband leaving behind his beloved wife.

I saved my people, and it left me with a cracked heart.

I still could not fathom why he had rejected me for thirty days. Why the month of utter silence? Now, he would never return. Not after I had made him feel so small by revealing how Haman had exploited him.

He kept his distance from me as I knew he would.

Then, one night, without explanation, without the usual royal flourish, he came into my chamber and slipped into my bed. The proper protocol would have been to send for me, or on rare occasions, to send word well ahead of his arrival. Instead, he sought me out like an ordinary husband.

For a long time, he held me without a word. He cradled me to him as if I were the anchor to his storm-tossed ship.

In the morning, the questions spilled out. His touch had dragged them out of me. "Why? Why did you leave me? Why did you stop sending word?"

For a moment, he gave no answer. I thought he would refuse. He sat up, turning his back to me as though he could not bear for me to see his face as he explained.

"Otanes came to see me."

Otanes. One of the wealthiest members of the Persian

aristocracy, and a man who had been a mighty general during the reign of my husband's father, the great Darius. He might be too old to lead an army, now. But he was still a man to be reckoned with. The kind of courtier who could foment uprisings. Who could seize thrones. Who could snatch crowns.

And he was Amestris's father.

"He said I had made a mockery of his name by putting you on the throne, by favoring you over his daughter. He said everyone at court whispered that I came to you often while I neglected Amestris."

"Ah." It had been the father and not the daughter at the root of this separation. Amestris would have been too proud to spill those words of complaint. I liked her for that.

My husband's broad shoulders, muscled from years on horseback and wielding swords, bowed as though under an immense weight. "It was the best I could give you, Esther. A separation with enough sting to satisfy Otanes's pride. A public rejection. Everyone knew that I stopped coming to see you. Everyone saw me enter Amestris's apartments instead."

He shrugged. "It was the only way I could think of keeping you without turning Otanes entirely against me. To have you and reject you with the same breath. I could not send you word of my intention. He would have heard of it. He has as many spies as I." His voice turned bitter. "Some, better trained."

Finally, I understood. He hadn't rejected me. He had done what he could to hold on to me. And the day I had approached him with my request, he had protected me publicly, though no doubt it had cost him something with Otanes.

I put a gentle hand on his shoulder. "That was a clever

ploy, my lord. Far cleverer than anything I could have thought of."

He whirled around so quickly the bed dipped, and I tumbled against him. He grabbed me and held on tight, his fingers not quite steady.

He had expected me to criticize him. To point out the shortcoming of his plan. To complain of his insufficient power.

Instead, I gave him what he needed most. I made him feel safe in his own skin, because I always saw the best in him. I understood that the forces against him wielded too much weight and power, and I saw the strength it required for him to survive them.

Everyone called his father *Great*. He had always known he could never be a match to Darius. But what few had eyes to see was the strength it took for him to place one foot before the other and simply endure.

I saw.

He knew I looked up to him. Not as a king, but as a man. And that day, he learned that I knew how to forgive him also. I suppose that was why he loved me.

27

Roxannah

For I, the LORD your God,
hold your right hand;
it is I who say to you, "Fear not,
I am the one who helps you."

Isaiah 41:13

THIRTY-TWO YEARS EARLIER
THE THIRTEENTH YEAR OF KING XERXES'S RULE
THE FOURTH WEEK OF SUMMER

Well?" Esther leaned forward. "I hear you made it into Amestris's exalted presence. Twice. Tell me what happened, little cook."

Roxannah began with a general report, shorn of the unpleasant particulars. The queen waved her words away like they were a bad odor. Instead, she questioned every minute detail, forcing Roxannah to leave nothing out, not even Amestris's insults.

When she heard the lady had called her a servant girl, Esther laughed. "Close enough."

But when Roxannah told her that Amestris suspected their warning to be a clever ploy on Esther's behalf to gain her trust, the queen's lips tightened. "How like her to see something underhanded even in my efforts to save her hide. There is no pleasing that woman." She threw aside the pillow she had hugged to her chest. "But wait. You did not tell me why she called you back after she dismissed you."

Roxannah pleated her skirts between nervous fingers, a breach of court etiquette. Fortunately, no one had their eyes on her hands. Unfortunately, everyone was staring at her face with intense interest. "I fear I slipped, somewhat, Your Majesty."

"Slipped on what?"

"On my own tongue."

The queen raised a perfectly plucked brow. "I find that hard to believe."

Roxannah, well versed with the art of sarcasm, picked it up in the queen's tone without difficulty.

"Well? Continue. What is the nature of this slippage?"

She cleared her throat and rushed on. Perhaps if she said it quickly enough, the queen would miss the possible consequences of her words.

The senior handmaiden gasped as soon as Roxannah finished explaining her strategy. Esther paled. Apparently, no one had any problem understanding the ramifications of Roxannah's impulsive declaration. She had been the only one bright enough to miss it.

Esther sighed and in a graceful motion rose out of bed, limbs flashing long and smooth beneath the soft silk of her tunic. "This places you at some risk, little cook. For now, go nowhere alone. You understand?"

"That's what Adin said."

"Adin, is it? Well, *Adin* has the right of it. In fact, remain in his company as much as you can. He grew up in a soldiering family, as I understand. I can trust him to keep you both safe." She pulled on a purple bed robe before her maidservant had a chance to help. "The court will be leaving Susa once the apartments are ready in Ecbatana's palace."

"Will that be soon, Your Majesty?"

"I do not know when it will be. But I want you to come with us. Hathach will inform Cook."

Roxannah squealed in a most uncourtly manner. She had assumed that since she was the newest member of the kitchen staff, she would be one of the ones left behind in Susa.

"That is generous of you, my queen!" She bowed and bowed again. "I will do my best not to disappoint you. Or Cook."

Esther waved, reminding Roxannah to stop blathering.

It felt like a whole day had passed since the junior handmaiden had come to fetch her, but it must have been no more than an hour. Roxannah's roommates were just starting to rise when she returned to their chamber.

"Did I dream it," Sisy said, her mouth opening in a huge yawn that showed off a pink uvula, "or did the queen's handmaiden come to fetch you in the middle of the night?"

Roxannah folded her blanket. "She came."

"Are you in trouble?"

"Depends what you mean by trouble. But the queen is not displeased, if that's what you are asking."

"What a relief." Sisy rolled up her mattress. "Working in the kitchen has been a lot more fun since you came. Those good-for-nothing assistants boss me around. But you are kind. You never palm off your work on me."

The assistants did take advantage of Sisy. They were supposed to clean up after themselves. But as soon as Cook's back was turned, they dumped their dirty dishes and messy counters on the poor girl and left her to manage the chaos they had created.

Roxannah felt oddly touched by Sisy's praise. She wrapped an arm around her shoulders. "We women must stick together."

Sisy grinned. "You smell nice. All rosy and things. And your hair looks very grand. Did the queen's handmaiden do it up for you?"

"That she did. And I will tell you, Sisy, I would rather have you comb my hair than that lady any day. She pulled my scalp until my eyes smarted."

"Maybe. But it looks a lot prettier than when I do it."

Roxannah was due to work only a half day. After lunch, she packed up her portion of leftovers so she could share them with her mother. Cook had been particularly generous, as was his habit when a member of his staff went home for the day, knowing everyone who worked for him had other mouths to feed.

Outside, she came to an abrupt halt at the sight of Adin leaning casually against the wall.

"I thought you might want some company on your way to your mother's." He looked like she felt. Tired from too many hours spent tossing and turning.

"Your own personal bodyguard." Sisy, who had followed her out, gave her a meaningful glance. "You'll be spoilt with all these attentions." She sauntered off, not waiting for an answer, whistling off-key. Subtlety was a stranger to that girl.

"I hate to trouble you," Roxannah said to Adin.

"It would trouble me more if you were traipsing on the road by yourself."

"You sound like the queen."

"Esther sent for you?"

Roxannah nodded. She described her interview as they walked to her house.

"She knows I grew up in a soldiering family, does she?" Adin crooked a brow. "I shouldn't be surprised, I suppose. They would never have hired me as a palace physician without first scrutinizing my background. No doubt she asked for my full dossier before allowing me into her presence."

They strolled on in companionable silence. For the first time since her audience with Esther, Roxannah had an opportunity to truly absorb the queen's unexpected news. *I'm going to Ecbatana!* For an instant she had the urge to break out into a jaunty dance step, shaking her hips as her grandmother had taught her.

Then it dawned on her. Esther had likely wanted her along merely to ensure her safety. Cook would not be pleased to have her forced upon him all summer. At the thought, she felt like she had swallowed a big, glazed brick.

Adin stopped. "What's wrong? You look like a cloudy day."

She should not be surprised that he had noticed her change of mood. The way he could read her still caught her off guard. "The queen wants me to come to Ecbatana."

"That's wonderful news." For a fraction of a moment, she could have sworn that he wanted to break out into his own dance. Her chest tightened at the look on his face. Like he felt truly happy to have her close to him for months.

She cleared her throat. "I thought so too, at first. Then I realized she only wants me on account of the situation with Amestris. I wished she had asked me because of my cooking."

"You have the wrong of it, there. She is killing two birds with one stone. She gets to enjoy your excellent creations while also keeping you safe. I couldn't agree with her more. I can protect you better if you are near."

She must have imagined Adin's happiness at her news. That was the real reason he wanted her in Ecbatana. She swallowed the sour taste of disappointment.

He began to walk again. "And your mother?"

Roxannah frowned. Some servants brought close family members with them when they traveled with the court, though many could not afford the added expense. Roxannah had no intention of leaving her mother alone for long months. At the same time, she had no idea how to accomplish this feat. Where would her mother stay? How would they pay for her lodging? Who would look after their home in Susa? A film of perspiration broke out on the back of her neck.

"I will have to find a way to bring her along."

She was no longer surprised when Darab opened the door. He had been such a regular visitor that he was starting to feel like a part of the family. "Mistress Roxannah. Welcome home."

"Darab and I will not linger," Adin said. "We know your time with your mother is precious."

"Nonsense." Her mother beckoned them inside the house. "We would like you both to join us for lunch. We have plenty."

Roxannah gave Adin an apologetic glance. "Jewish law forbids them from eating with us, Mother."

Her mother grinned. "I have a solution. We have set up a separate table for them. We will sit close enough to speak to one another, but far enough to satisfy the law. Dear Miriam has already prepared a Jewish feast."

Leah's mother, the widowed Miriam, had also become a regular fixture in their home, giving her mother a hand with housekeeping in exchange for food.

"Will that suit, Master Adin?" her mother asked.

"You are most gracious, my lady. We would be honored to be your guests."

Her mother led them to the long living room, where two tables had been set up with platters of warm bread, mashed chickpeas, and lamb meatballs already waiting.

Adin sat where Darab indicated. "We are going to have a feast, I see."

Roxannah was about to begin serving when her mother said, "Master Adin, would you like to pray for us?"

"Indeed." Taking the bread in his hands, he said, "Blessed are you, O Lord, King of Eternity, who brings forth bread from the earth." Breaking off a small piece, he dipped it into salt and ate immediately.

Her mother seemed so at home with this ritual that Roxannah realized she must have already experienced it with Darab and Miriam. Soon the conversation flowed, and her mother described in glowing terms some of the long-needed repairs Darab had managed to complete in their home.

Darab held up a modest hand. "I enjoy it. I am a much better carpenter than I am a cook."

"I can attest to that," Adin said with a grin. "Though when I first met him, Darab had no idea which end of a hammer to hold, let alone how to use it. He has learned a great deal over the years. Which is why I still hold out hope for his cooking."

"A vain hope," Darab said, making them laugh.

"How did you meet each other?" It was a question Roxannah had always wanted to ask.

Adin smiled. "That is Darab's tale to tell."

All eyes turned to the man who wore dignity like an invisible mantle. "The circumstances of our meeting were sad ones, I fear," Darab said. "It is quite a long chronicle."

"I like long chronicles," Roxannah said immediately.

He dipped his head with that special grace that was so much a part of him. "Then you shall have it, Mistress Roxannah." Darab pushed away his plate. "I suppose I will have to start with the war. Like many men of my generation, I served in Darius's army. My company was among those who boarded the ships headed for Marathon, intending to teach the Athenians a lesson for breaking their oath."

Roxannah winced. Eighteen years ago, many Persians had lost their lives in a battle that had unexpectedly turned into a bloodbath, the first of their painful losses in Greece.

"We arrived confident of our coming conquest. After all, we had already vanquished half the world. The Athenians hardly seemed a threat. Hauling our ships onto the sand of the long promontory at Marathon, we watched with pride as our vessels extended along the curve of the beach as far as the eye could see. Our men swarmed over the plain, trampling the hard-won crops that had sprung from the broken backs of Athenian farmers."

Roxannah found herself spellbound by Darab's tale. He was a consummate storyteller, his narrative at once self-deprecating and vivid.

"I was a member of the cavalry. My company galloped up to the enemy lines, which somehow had managed to block both the roads to Athens. We wheeled and turned our mounts, mocking our adversaries who lacked our swift archers. They could only watch us helplessly from behind their shields.

"We mocked them, but we dared not break their lines. They had the advantage of higher ground. After a week, we received information that the army of Sparta would arrive to lend their numbers and brute force to aid their Athenian allies."

Of all the city states on mainland Greece, Sparta had the reputation for being the fiercest warriors. Roxannah forgot the lamb congealing on her plate as she listened raptly to Darab.

"In the cover of night, our general ordered the cavalry to embark the ships and sail behind enemy lines to Athens, thinking to conquer the city before the Spartans arrived. Only a skeleton crew of riders remained to guard the infantry. I was among them.

"It would have been a good plan had we not been betrayed. The Athenians discovered that our cavalry was away. At dawn, the Greek hoplites marched into the plain, sheathed head to toe in bronze. The sun rose upon shield and helmet, greaves and breastplate, turning them into a fearsome line of shimmering metal." Darab grew silent. When he took up his tale again, his voice had grown so quiet, they had to strain to hear him.

"We had the advantage of speed and mobility. But they were covered by an armor so hard, it resembled a city gate. At first, the dust of ten thousand feet obscured them from our view. Then we saw them come."

Like every Persian, Roxannah knew the ending to this story. Still, Darab held her rapt as he described the events of those four gruesome hours.

"Our men loosed a storm of arrows and slingshot. To our shock, they bounced off the bronze armor. The hoplites reached our line barely suffering injury and slammed into our men. The few of us cavalry who had remained could do little to aid them. I saved a life here and there only to watch it taken by the next Athenian in that unbroken line of metal." Darab's face had taken on a greyish cast as he relived those terrible memories.

"Our wooden shields smashed under the force of their bronze. We had chosen agility over protection, covered with little more than quilted wool and leather. Speed was no use to us now. The hoplites crushed us, their every stroke finding flesh, whereas our bows and arrows proved useless.

"Our lines broke. Those the hoplites did not kill drowned in the general stampede to our ships. I had made it safely to a vessel when I noticed an Athenian aiming for one of our boys. I saw his face so clearly as he scampered into the water. He couldn't have been older than sixteen. I could not bear it. Not one more life lost. One more boy slain. I wheeled my horse and managed to strike down the Athenian. The boy made it to the ship. I did not.

"The brother of the man I had killed captured me with the aid of several of his friends. I became his slave that day."

Roxannah and her mother gasped. The shockingly wretched treatment of Persian captives at the hands of the Greeks had become legendary. But having killed the man's brother, Darab would have become a special object of his master's loathing. He must have suffered unimaginable torments.

"I am surprised you survived," Roxannah said.

"They saw to it that I would. For six years." He said no more. He did not have to. She pushed away her bowl, pity choking her. "By then, my body was failing. My master had taken me to Cnidus when he traveled there. One morning, I collapsed, and no amount of beating could revive me. The physicians at Cnidus told him there was no hope. After treating me to one final kick, he abandoned me where I had fallen, so certain of my impending death that he did not bother to soil his dagger with my blood."

Her mother reached out a hand into the space that separated their tables. "Darab, I am so sorry."

His gentle smile swept away the gathering clouds on his visage. "It was the best day of my life. The day Adin found me." His smile widened and grew mischievous. "I became his pincushion. The drain down which he flushed his medicines. He sewed up every gash and poured his concoctions down my throat. He treated me like I was a treasure he had found on the side of the road."

"As a young physician, I had difficulty finding people I could freely practice upon," Adin jested.

Darab shrugged. "His prayers buzzed in my ears day and night. By now, I despised myself as much as my Athenian master had. What I had suffered in those six years had turned me into an object of scorn in my own mind. Adin taught me my worth in God. A worth that no indignity or violence could destroy."

28

From your presence let my vindication come!

Psalm 17:2

Adin took a sip from his cup. "It was a miracle he survived. I did not have the skill to save him. But God did."

Roxannah sat in stunned silence. Her father had never been enslaved, though he must have suffered his own monstrous hours of gore and defeat. He had returned home a changed man. But Darab had returned home a better man. He had come home with peace. There wasn't a shred of the slave in him. Not to anger or hatred or self-contempt.

Darab was free.

And the only explanation she could find for that freedom was the one he gave himself: his God.

"How is it that you never returned to your home and family?" her mother asked.

"Six years is a long time. My family had thought me dead. Before passing, my father left all his property to my brother." He shrugged. "It is hard for a man to give up the possession he has grown accustomed to owning, especially if the law is on his side. What wealth I had owned personally had been lost." He ran a hand down his beard. "After what I lived through, being poor is hardly a tragedy."

His easy smile underscored those final words. In it, Roxannah saw more contentment than she had observed in her father all the years of her life.

After the meal finished, Roxannah excused herself to greet little Leah. To her surprise, the child still hid from her, looking almost fearful. It was like seeing a different girl from the one who had, all those months ago, chatted confidently and complimented Roxannah's eyes.

"Leah, don't you remember me? We met at Master Adin's door."

Leah burst into tears. Roxannah stepped away hastily. "I beg your pardon, Miriam. I did not mean to upset the child."

Miriam pressed the girl's head into her middle. "It's not you, mistress. It's because of what happened the day of the attack. She feels guilty about your abba."

"My abba? You mean my father? . . . I don't understand. What has Leah to do with that day?"

Miriam paled. "My mistake. I thought you knew. Excuse me. Master Darab will be wanting me." She pulled Leah away and escaped into the courtyard.

Roxannah felt hot and cold, feverish and shivering all at once. What had her father done to Leah? Had her father harmed the child in some way?

For months, she had tried to escape the events of that foul day by burying them in the ground of her mind. She had refused to discuss whatever had taken place with Adin and Darab, and even asked her mother never to speak of it. Now, Miriam's remark about Leah's mysterious involvement had dug up the matter like a stinking carcass dragged out of the earth by a snuffling fox. And she found she could not push it away from her mind again. She had to know the truth.

Adin had once told her to find him when she was ready to know how her father had died. He had been wiser than she, recognizing her eventual need to discover the details of that day.

She found him standing rigidly next to Miriam, lock-jawed and ashen, like a man who was about to face his doom.

"Tell me," she rasped. "Tell me what happened to my father. Did he hurt Leah?"

He dropped his head. "Let us go to a private spot." Wordlessly, they walked to the opposite corner of the courtyard. Roxannah's heart was trying to crawl out of her throat.

Adin swallowed convulsively. "It was me. Your father died by my hand. My sword killed him."

Roxannah sank to the ground. In the back of her mind, she had always known. Of course she had. The funeral money, the prepared body of her father, the way Adin's eyes slid away from hers sometimes. But to hear him say the words left no room for pretense anymore. No fantasy that one of his neighbors had been responsible, leaving Adin only with a small failure. Something she could accept in time.

She realized this was the very reason she had never wanted to know the truth. Now she could never undo the knowledge that he was her father's murderer. It was a chasm too large to cross. Even the tiny, unrealistic hope that someday there might be something between them went up in smoke with those words.

Haltingly, he began to tell her the story as it had unfolded. "I am sorry, Roxannah. I had every intention of shielding your father. I knew exactly how to disarm him when he lunged at me with murder in his eyes. Then Leah threw herself at me."

"Leah?" she breathed.

"They were staying at our house with a dozen other women and children. Leah was convinced I would die, in spite of my reassurances. Somehow, she managed to escape from the house, and in the darkness and confusion of battle, no one saw her until it was too late. She thought to shield me from your father. Instead, she almost got herself killed.

"I would have spared Lord Fravartish if I could have, Roxannah. But I could only save one of them: Leah or your father. I am so sorry. I would undo it if I could."

"Was Leah hurt?"

"Only a scratch. Your father tried to turn his sword when he saw her, and I managed to twist her away a little." He looked at his shoes, his face flushed. "Lord Fravartish was distraught when he thought the child was dead. I will never forget his last words. He said, 'I wouldn't want to die with that . . . not that too . . . on my conscience.'"

A tiny weight lifted from Roxannah's shoulders. At the end, her father had cared, had reckoned with his uneasy conscience. Had sounded like the man she had once known. For the first time since his death, she felt a wave of true mourning, unsullied by the guilty relief of being rid of him. Good, clean grief for the loss of the father who had once loved her.

Tears washed her eyes. "How is it that Leah knows it was my father you killed that day?"

"She overheard the men speak his name. When she came to your house with her mother, she heard the name and made the connection."

"Is she angry with me because I am his daughter? Is that why she won't speak to me?"

Adin's brows rose in surprise. "Not at all. That night, she heard a couple of the men whisper that if she had obeyed her mother and remained indoors, Lord Fravartish wouldn't be dead. She knows you are his daughter. She is wretched with remorse for having caused your father's death."

"But she is not at fault."

"We have all told her so. Even your mother. But she cannot let it go." He turned his head away. "Guilt can be very sticky."

As she knew only too well. "I thank you for telling me everything."

"Roxannah." Adin gulped a mouthful of air. She caught the sheen of tears in his eyes. "Forgive me if you can."

She wanted to. She could even see why he had done it. But when all the explanations fell away, she still did not know how to let go of the principal fact. He had killed her father. "I will try, Adin."

"You knew?" she asked her mother after the others had left. "You knew what happened that day?"

Her mother nodded. "I asked Darab to tell me weeks ago."

From old habit, Roxannah reached to pull her braid over her shoulder like a drowning man searching for rope. But the queen's handmaiden had pinned it up too neatly. "It was my fault. I went to warn Adin."

"Don't be foolish, child. Adin would have been ready without your warning. He is a soldier trained, and a man intent on protecting his neighbors. He knew someone would come for them, no matter who it might be. Your warning merely made him determined to shield your father from harm." She shrugged. "No one could have foreseen Leah running into the melee. Might as well blame that child as yourself."

"Poor Leah. She is an innocent in all this."

"You all are." Her mother reached for Roxannah's hand. "The burden of that night's events belongs to your father. It was his decision to go. Adin, Leah, and you all have been wounded by his actions. It is time this wound stopped bleeding. It is time you let Fravartish rest in peace.

"Remember he did not want the child harmed by his hand. To my mind, what he said at the end means that he was willing for that exchange—his life for Leah's. The three of you need to accept that. Let Fravartish have that final reward. Let his death carry with it this one grace."

"I . . . I don't know how to do that."

"Find a way. This is not for your own heart only. Adin and Leah need your forgiveness, Roxannah. They cannot move on until you are able to give them that gift."

For a moment, she resented one more responsibility left to her by her father's actions. He had been the one to cause the harm. But the work of forgiveness rested on her.

Forgiving Leah required little. She did not hold the child responsible. But forgiving herself and Adin? That might prove harder.

In spite of these new burdens, she fell asleep as soon as she lay down and did not stir until the next morning. It was as though her soul had needed to know the details of her father's death before it could rest.

After an early breakfast, Roxannah finally had the opportunity to inform her mother of the queen's command. "I have big news. Brace yourself. The queen wants me to accompany the court to Ecbatana."

This announcement was likely to throw her mother into a proper panic. If she remained in Susa, then she would not see Roxannah for several months. If they found a way to settle her in Ecbatana, then she would feel overwhelmed by the prospect of living among strangers, not to mention the rigors of travel. She would fret about the expense and wonder how they could manage it all.

Her mother grew pale at the blunt announcement. But her response took Roxannah by surprise. "Of course you have been chosen, my love. I doubt there is anyone more gifted than you in that kitchen. They would be fools not to take you." She smoothed the skirts of her tunic.

"I want you to come with me."

"Then I shall come. It has been too many years since I have visited the seven-walled city. It will be good to escape Susa's scorching heat."

A new peace undergirded her mother's words. In spite of the ashen face, she seemed grounded, somehow. Roxannah wondered if this new calm had been born from her father's absence. But it had a deeper quality she could not finger.

"How soon will you be leaving?" her mother asked.

"I cannot say. Soon, I believe. Rumor has it that the repairs to the Ecbatana palace are close to completion. The servants' quarters have turned into a madhouse of activity. You'd think the hallway outside our little chamber is the royal highway, feet running every which way at all hours of day and night. I never realized the chaos that ensues when the court is about to move. And now we have to move with it." She studied her hands. "We still need to find a place where you can stay in Ecbatana," she cautioned, broaching the cold, practical reality of their situation.

"We will manage, daughter."

Roxannah faltered. When did they reverse roles? Usually it was her job to comfort her mother. Perhaps she had failed to understand? "Mother, I don't know where you will live."

"We will sort that out."

Roxannah stared, unable to hide her astonishment. "You are different."

"I am?"

"Not so long ago, the idea of having to travel to Ecbatana would have paralyzed you with terror. You would have turned white and started shivering."

"I do feel a little shaken."

"But not in the way you used to. Where did this new peace come from? Is it because Father is gone?"

"I will not lie. His absence helps." She sighed. "Do I sound hard-hearted? Forgive me. I have mourned him, of course." She paused before continuing. "The truth is, I did most of my mourning before his death. Bit by bit, as the man I knew and loved vanished. His body remained. But I lost my husband a long time ago."

She laid a hand on Roxannah's cheek. "The peace you sense in me is from God. I find strength in the Lord, my girl. He settles my heart in a way I cannot explain."

Roxannah shook her head. "But you're not even Jewish!"

"He does not care what blood flows in my veins. He cares only that I am his."

29

You shall treat the stranger who sojourns with
you as the native among you, and you shall
love him as yourself, for you were strangers
in the land of Egypt.

Leviticus 19:34

When it was time to leave for the palace, Roxannah found Darab waiting for her at the door. "Adin thought you might not wish to see him today. But he did not want you to travel by yourself."

"I see. Thank you, Darab."

"*Do* you want to avoid him?"

"I am not certain. Perhaps a little."

Darab grimaced. "Time does not heal all wounds. But it does help with some."

"Darab, do you mind if we go to the Artisans' Village first? I want to buy some meat from Avraham."

"Is the palace meat not to your liking?"

"It isn't that. Cook told me the queen does not eat meat. It occurs to me that her diet may be limited because of her Jewish faith. She does not wish to break God's law. I thought if I purchased the meat from Avraham and prepared it according to Jewish dietary rules, she might be able to enjoy it. If I am wrong, others will be happy enough to eat it."

"A good plan, mistress."

"You do not need to call me *mistress*. My name is Roxannah."

He bowed his head. "Thank you, Mistress Roxannah."

She rolled her eyes. "My mother seems to be following in your footsteps."

"How is that?"

"She is pursuing the Jewish God. But I fear she will be disappointed."

"Because?"

"For one thing, she is convinced that being an outsider will not prove detrimental. Yet from everything I have observed, Gentiles are considered lower somehow in the Jewish community. My dear friend, Tirzah, has never invited me to her home. In spite of our friendship, her parents would be horrified if I showed up for supper one day."

Darab hummed thoughtfully. "In their zeal to keep the law, some members of the Jewish community do hold Gentiles at arm's length. Not all are the same. God himself has a more expansive heart. Even in the early days of Jewish history when the Hebrews wandered the wilderness for forty years, they had foreigners with them. Those Gentiles were subject to the same rules and protections as any Hebrew. Why, their greatest king, David, was the great-grandson of a Moabite woman named Ruth."

Roxannah's steps faltered. "Truly? But how is that possible?"

"I think it is because of Ruth's heart. She told her Hebrew mother-in-law, Naomi, 'Your God is my God.' That is to say, she exchanged the gods of her people for the Lord. She also pledged that Naomi's people would be *her* people. In other words, she belonged to God and his people. Your mother is no less than Ruth."

Roxannah forced herself to move. Could such a thing be possible? Could the Jewish God be as open to outsiders as Darab made out?

Cook was the sole occupant in the otherwise empty kitchen, sitting in his usual corner, head bent over his list as he planned for the day. Roxannah collected onions and salt. "Lovely day out there."

"Hmm."

She wiped down the counter and began her braise. "Cook?"

"Hmm?"

"The queen wants me to come to Ecbatana with you."

He gave her a quick glance before returning his attention to his list. "The queen, is it?"

She cleared her throat. "I am sorry if my coming inconveniences you. I suppose you didn't want me along, with me being so new and all. I just wanted to say that I didn't put her up to it."

Cook set down his list. "Idiot girl. The queen wants you along, does she? Who do you think put the idea in her head in the first place?"

Roxannah's fingers went still. "You wanted me to come?"

"Good Light. Are you always this chatty in the mornings? It's getting so I can't hear my own thoughts."

Roxannah grinned. "No, Cook. I'm not chatty in the mornings. But, Cook? I want you to know I will work hard so that you won't regret my being there."

He growled. "If that's your not chatty, I am regretting it already. Now, take yourself off to the queen's spits and get me the list of the day's meats."

Roxannah grimaced at the thought of her least favorite chore. She dreaded coming face to face with Miletus. He harried her worse with every visit. Sometimes he would try to grab her, his actions full of a threat that chilled her blood. Sometimes he merely hassled her with words, browbeating her as he shook his giant ash-stained hands in her face, like a weapon he wanted to unleash.

Cook noticed her expression. "You've got to learn to stand up to him, girl. You can't climb up in this place if you show yourself scared of a rat like Miletus."

Roxannah's chest deflated. She might as well stand up to one of the mythical giant bulls of Susa.

When she asked if Sisy could accompany her, Cook did not even bat a lash. Hathach must have requested that Roxannah go nowhere unaccompanied. Sisy chattered excitedly, looking forward to her visit to the spits. She knew how to avoid Miletus, cutting a wide berth around him and finding the nicer boys who worked the king's spits. Roxannah did not have that luxury.

She stood a good distance from the big-muscled boy, but she could still see the tiny burns on his face from the flying embers in the spit. It must be unbearably hot here this time of year.

She inhaled, trying to prepare for the coming assault. "Miletus, Cook wants to know what meats are being delivered today, please."

Miletus looked up. "It's the snooty girl."

"Beg your pardon. I didn't mean to rile you."

He rolled his eyes and mimicked her. "'Didn't mean to rile you.' Well, you did. Your very existence riles me."

"All I need is the list of the meats."

"Come and take them from me." He opened his arms wide like he was ready to give her an embrace.

Roxannah waited a beat. "You don't know what's on the list?"

He threw a stick on the fire. "I know everything."

Roxannah turned, studying the escape route she had worked out. She took another deep breath and turned around. "You would have told me if you did. I'll tell Cook you don't know," she said over her shoulder.

He lunged. She was ready for him. Her legs sprang into action, carrying her out of his reach.

"Come back here, you wet piece of dung," he snarled.

He was fast. But she was scared. Terror had more power than rage. She stayed ahead of him. "The meat," she gasped as she ran. "Tell me, or I will send Cook."

He slowed to a stop. "You little snot. You aren't worth the trouble. I'll get you next time."

Roxannah skidded, hands on her thighs, breathing heavily. "May I please have the list, Miletus?"

"Ox, partridge, some kind of fish, and a peacock. Don't come back if you don't want to get your face smashed in."

Roxannah found Sisy flirting happily with a smiling spit boy. She took a long look at Roxannah's heaving frame. "Was Miletus awful today?"

She tried to swallow the bile rising in her throat, to calm the nausea that always plagued her when she spoke to Miletus. "He is awful every day."

"He isn't bad with the men when it's their turn to go. In fact, he is a great favorite with them. They always come back laughing at his latest antics. That's why he isn't dismissed. It's just us girls he hassles." She shrugged. "No one cares about that."

Roxannah frowned. She couldn't imagine either Adin or Darab not caring. "Some men care, Sisy. Good men care."

But it wasn't the men allowing Miletus's behavior to go unchecked that frustrated her. It was her own response to the muscle-bound young man. She had learned too well from her father. When someone threatened her, she made herself small and inconsequential. She either appeased them or, failing that, she ran.

There must be a better way. She just didn't know it. And even if she did, she wouldn't have the strength for it.

———

The braise, made from Avraham's lamb shanks, spinach, fried onions and garlic, grape molasses, and sour plums, was thick and aromatic. She showed it to Cook.

He tasted it and nodded. "Not bad. But I don't recall lamb on the meat list."

"Wasn't there. I bought it from Avraham, the Hebrew butcher in the Artisans' Village."

He stared at her blankly. "If you wanted lamb, why didn't you just ask for it?"

"Well, it's the way the Jewish butchers prepare it. They have strict rules, you see."

Cook raised a brow. "Thinking of the queen, are you?"

"Might be worth a try."

He considered the braise for a moment. "I'll serve it in a separate bowl. What should I tell Her Majesty? That the meat is from Avraham the butcher?"

"Also that it was prepared according to Hebrew dietary laws. Avraham gave me careful instructions."

"I'll serve it myself and make sure she knows." He gave her a considering look. "That was good thinking, girl."

When the dish returned half empty, Roxannah felt like she had sprouted two wings and could take flight into the blue zenith of the sky.

"Stay late today," Cook told her in his usual offhand manner. "I'm going to teach you how to take inventory and place orders for the kitchen."

Her mother's mouth tipped up in one corner. "Today, it's your turn to brace yourself. Darab knows of a respectable household in Ecbatana where I may rent a couple of rooms. The lodging he has in mind will include food and laundry, so you need not worry about me while you are working."

Roxannah stretched. It had been a long few days at work, with Cook keeping her late every night to teach her the administrative side of running a large kitchen. "Did he by any chance also reveal how we would pay for these rooms?"

Her mother gave a cheeky grin. The sight of it warmed

Roxannah to her toes. She hadn't seen that grin for years. It was as though her mother was blossoming before her eyes, turning into a new woman. "The rent on your grandfather's land came due this month. The farmer brought it to me directly."

"Every bit of that silver has already been promised to the creditors."

Her mother leaned over. "Yes. Except that he added three gold darics to his payment. We can give our debtors the usual amount and still have enough to rent rooms in Ecbatana."

"Why would he pay extra?"

"Because Darab, Miriam, and I have been praying for God's provision. Even little Leah joins in."

Roxannah fidgeted with her cushion. "That sounds very godly and sublime, and I am certain it availed much. But for someone earthbound like me, can you clarify how the farmer explained the added payment?"

"He said he owed it to your grandfather. Years ago, when his fields had suffered through a long famine and his pockets had grown empty, your grandfather loaned him the money. You know how generous he could be. He had told no one about it. Drawn no documents. Your father had no knowledge of it. It took some time for the farmer to make enough to return the payment. But by then, your grandfather was long gone."

"Why did he not repay Father instead?"

"I asked. He turned red and begged my pardon. Stammered and choked until finally he admitted that he had decided to save the money for you and me, knowing we would one day need it. He said he suspected that your father would simply waste it."

"He *was* very talented in that way," Roxannah admitted. She leaned forward. "You mean we really have the money?"

"We really do."

Roxannah shook her head, feeling a little dizzy. "What about the house? If we leave it empty for months, it will become a beacon for thieves."

"If you are willing, I want to invite Miriam and Leah to move into the servants' quarter. It will be a help to her, not having to pay rent. Being a widow is not easy. I should know. She already gives me a hand in exchange for food. You send so much from the palace that I always have enough to share with her and Leah. When we travel to Ecbatana, she can look after the house for us and take in a few odd jobs to make ends meet."

"You trust her?"

"Completely. Darab and Adin have known her for years and vouch for her."

Roxannah leaned back against her cushion. There might be more to this prayer thing than she suspected. She had experienced a weepy kind of hope when Adin had prayed for her. Now, she found a hint of the power that might be found when the followers of the Jewish God prayed. Three gold darics had fallen into their laps at just the right time, followed by the perfect solution to their empty house. She studied her mother's joyful face, the change in her so palpable that Roxannah sometimes felt like she had blinked and the world had tilted and become new somehow.

Her mother leaned over to tug a curl that had escaped Roxannah's braid. "Now explain why the queen wants you to remain in the company of the physician. It seems an odd kind of request for a queen to make of her kitchen staff."

Roxannah winced. "I did not have a chance to tell you last week."

"I know. Your mind was occupied with many things."

"I am afraid my explanation requires more bracing on your part."

"I am well-braced these days, child. Go on."

Roxannah recounted the story of the book, her audience with Esther, followed by her meeting with Amestris. When she finished explaining, her mother grew thoughtful.

"I can see you need more prayers, my girl."

30

Blessed is the one whose transgression is
 forgiven,
whose sin is covered.

Psalm 32:1

That evening, Cook announced that, along with Roxannah, he had chosen the dairy, vegetable, and dessert
assistants to go to Ecbatana. Halpa the baker, being
part-time, would stay behind, as would the meat assistant.

The meat assistant gawped. "You're going without me? Are
you mad? Who will take care of the braises and the stews?"

Cook wrote something on his ever-present scrap of papyrus.
"We'll manage."

The meat assistant glared at Roxannah. No doubt he blamed
her. She dropped her head. She had never meant to displace
anyone.

To her surprise, Cook also chose Sisy. "It will take almost six
weeks to meander our way to Ecbatana, and we are expected
to keep the same high standard while we travel as we do in the
palace. Sisy can help fetch and carry as usual." He studied his
notes. "Roxannah."

"Yes, Cook?"

"I am going to make a new recipe. Come and watch."

He had been teaching her more and more of late, a marked sign of his favor, which did not sit well with the others since they rarely received special instruction. After learning the new recipe, a variation of grilled meat that Cook served over warm bread, Roxannah had a free hour.

That morning, she had soaked almonds in water. Now their skins came loose with a touch, revealing the white flesh beneath. Using a sharp knife, she cut each kernel into delicate slivers, which she arranged in small clumps over a shallow bronze cooking tray.

She fetched the marsh mallow sap that she had already extracted from the stalks she and Adin had harvested by the river. She had tried to make the syrup twice before, both times yielding nothing but a pot full of disaster and a lot of scrubbing. A certain amount of failure was to be expected, given that she had never cooked marsh mallow before. But both times, she had been alone in the kitchen. Now she had an audience.

She kept a vigilant eye on the clear liquid as it simmered. Experience had taught her to keep the heat low. Gradually, the sap turned golden in color. This time, as the sticky syrup thickened, she added honey one spoonful at a time. She had to guess at both the right consistency and sweetness. But at least the syrup did not turn into a burnt mess.

Just before removing it from the fire, she added ground cardamom and cinnamon. When the mixture cooled a little, she spooned it over the clumps of slivered almonds that she had prepared earlier. She only hoped the syrup would solidify as it cooled. This could turn out to be an inedible, sticky disaster. Or it might yield a pleasant treat.

The best royal cooks were expected to seek out unusual ingredients and create new recipes. While this inventiveness provided the royal table with delightful culinary experiences, it also served a practical purpose. A great empire always needed more food. In years when one crop failed, they needed to know that another might take its place. Royal cooks helped the empire discover new ingredients that might feed the hungry populace during feast or famine seasons. They were part artisans, part researchers, and part students.

A good cook never stopped learning.

This was why Cook allowed them time to look for new ingredients. He always encouraged those who worked for him to try creative recipes, though Roxannah had noticed that his assistants showed little interest in this activity. They found the necessary experimentation too exhausting, given that their days often felt too long already. But Roxannah loved coming up with fresh ideas.

An hour later, the syrup on the almonds had solidified, creating golden clumps that looked like amber. Cook came to stand at Roxannah's elbow. "Looks good."

Roxannah twisted her dishrag nervously. "Want to taste one?"

"Hold a moment." Cook picked up a large knife and scraped at the bottom of the sticky candies. They popped off the sheet one at a time. He plopped one into his mouth. Every eye in the kitchen fixed on him.

Sisy set her bucket aside. "What's the verdict, Cook?"

He tapped a finger against his mouth. "There is a problem with this."

Roxannah sank slowly on the stool, her shoulders rounding with disappointment.

Cook pointed at the tray. "I really should set this whole tray aside for the queen. But I want to eat at least five more."

Roxannah's eyes widened. "You like it?"

"Try one." He pushed the mounds of sweet marsh mallow toward her.

She let the candy sit on her tongue for a moment. The taste of honey mingled with the perfume of cardamom and cinnamon, along with a hint of something buttery. She bit into the sweet, finding it chewy and soft after the first crunch. The combination of flavor and texture proved irresistible. She hadn't finished the one in her mouth before her mind began to demand a second. "Oh my."

"See what I mean?" Cook handed Roxannah a scrap of papyrus. "Write down what you did so you will not forget."

She noticed Adin, who had quietly returned to the kitchen sometime in the afternoon, eyeing the candy longingly. He had kept away from the place for several days. Out of deference for her feelings, no doubt.

She had appreciated the gesture. After his revelation, time had been something she needed. Then it had become an annoyance. She realized with him gone that her days felt dull and flat. Her mother's counsel had started to haunt her. She needed to forgive this man. To remove the lingering dregs of blame and disappointment from her heart.

What had he done but choose to save the life of a little girl? She would have made the same choice, had she found herself in his shoes.

She held up the tray of treats. "Would you like one, Master Adin?"

"More than anything." A look of understanding passed between them. At once, Roxannah felt something inside settle.

Adin bowed his head as he chewed, then swallowed. "I don't believe I have ever tasted anything so good."

Cook broke the quiet spell that seemed to be weaving them together when he stepped between them. "Don't grow too attached, Physician. I have plans for that candy." He fetched a silver platter from the special chest where he kept a few of the queen's expensive serving dishes. He had a genius for decorating food, using it as if it were an artist's mural. He arranged the clumps of sweet marsh mallow in the form of a little hill and sprinkled the tops with rosebuds.

"These will go out to the queen after dinner."

"Aw. Can't I try one, Cook?" Sisy put her chin in her hands as she stared at the decorated platter.

"Tonight, if the queen sends back leftovers to the kitchen. But don't hold your breath."

For a moment, Roxannah felt as though she would never fail at anything.

Roxannah sniffed the large bunch of mint leaves the gardeners had delivered to the kitchen. They lacked the delicacy of the variety she grew at home. Their sharp, pungent flavor would work well in some recipes. But she wanted to make an herb braise that required a more subtle flavoring.

It was possible that they had the particular mint she was looking for in the palace herb garden. If she hurried, she could get there and back before the dinner rush started.

Adin joined her at the door. "Are we going for a stroll?"

"We are going in search of mint."

"Ah. The royal gardens. Excellent. I meant to go there myself today." His face grew serious as they strolled. "I will tell you something. But you must never tell my mother."

She pretended to think. "I can't make any promises."

"Then I will take my chances. Because, you see, your marsh mallow candy tasted better than anything she ever made. And it will break her heart to find out. She prides herself on it. The candy of pharaohs, she calls it."

Roxannah grinned. "She'll never hear it from me. Is she—?" Roxannah's went silent at the tense expression on Adin's face. "What is it?"

"It's the man from the river. There!" He pointed to a walkway. "We have to follow him. Stay close." He took off toward a pathway leading east of the palace compound, his gait slow enough for Roxannah to keep up.

She spied the man ahead of them in the distance, at times visible, then hidden behind a wall or terrace. The light fabric of his long yellow tunic whipped about his feet, bright blue rosettes edging his hemline. For a breathless moment, they lost track of him as he turned a corner. Then he appeared again on a different path heading north.

Adin glanced her way, ensuring she could keep pace. She nodded and signaled for him to continue. Though they maintained a safe distance, something about their presence must have alerted their quarry. Abruptly, he turned around and looked behind him.

Lightning fast, Adin pulled Roxannah behind the shelter of tall oleander shrubs before the man spotted them. Roxannah sneaked a peek just in time to catch a glimpse of his profile. He had a strong nose, sharp and straight, and bushy eyebrows that poked out in multiple directions.

He resumed his walk, his steps growing rapid. Adin motioned for them to follow, keeping well back, choosing stealth over speed.

The man took a turn down a familiar alley. On either side, the stone-paved lane was guarded by a row of perfectly pruned cypress trees that had been planted with the mathematical precision of soldiers in rank. This was one of the most well-known sights in the palace.

It led to only one place. The Apadana.

Roxannah's feet stopped moving. There was no going beyond this point. She and Adin would not be allowed behind those walls.

The Apadana, the largest structure occupying most of the north terrace of the royal complex, had been designed to impress. The stunning colonnaded building erected by Darius two decades earlier and completed by his son Xerxes served as the main audience hall of the palace. Every important assembly, every significant function, every formal tribute ceremony was held in the Apadana. This gave the building an almost mystical importance, particularly since it was the only place most courtiers ever had a chance of catching a glimpse of the ruler of the Persian Empire.

This made the Apadana the kind of place one could not casually stroll into. Immortals guarded every nook. In her months at the palace, Roxannah had not even had a proper glimpse of the audience hall, except from a distance.

What kind of man could approach the Apadana with such confidence?

Adin clasped her hand and pulled her forward. Two magnificent gardens edged the Apadana's porticoes on opposite sides, one to the east and another to the west, connected to each other via a wide flowering border that ran across the main front entrance. A bronze gate guarded the border and gardens to each portico.

In order to go beyond this point, they needed letters bearing royal seals and official permissions. A couple of steel-eyed Immortals blocked their path, forcing them to turn around.

Roxannah bit her lip as she stretched her neck to try and see over the heads of the tall guards. "Are you sure it was him?"

"Sure enough."

"Did he walk straight into the Apadana?"

"Barely slowed down. I suppose we should have expected it. Anyone bold enough to want Amestris killed must hold a high rank."

"What do we do now?"

"We pay the princess a visit."

Roxannah groaned. "I don't want to miss another dinner preparation."

"I doubt she will keep us waiting."

She did not.

This time, they were met with a completely different reception at Amestris's apartments. Within moments of approaching the assistant undersecretary, they were ushered into a private audience with the mother of the crown prince.

"Well," she barked, "spit it out. What have you found?"

Adin bowed. "Not very much, I fear. Only that the man I saw has easy access to the Apadana."

She hissed in frustration. "His name?"

"We were not allowed past the gardens. I never heard him say it."

"Which door?"

Adin told her.

Amestris addressed her senior handmaiden. "Find out the names of the Immortals who were on duty this afternoon." She extracted a cinched linen bag from the depths of the cushion where she sat. Something jingled within as she handed it to her woman. "Get the names of all the visitors who passed through that door in the past two hours."

Amestris gave Adin a beady stare. "You are still here, I see."

"Yes, Duksis."

"And why?"

He tipped his head toward Roxannah. "Their spies would have heard what Roxannah said when we were here last. About the book."

"Yes, yes. What of it?"

"I am concerned for her safety, Duksis. If they are bold enough to set their sights on you, they will not hesitate to harm her."

"Or you, I suppose?"

He shrugged. "I can look after myself."

"Three generations of soldiers in your family. I suppose you can."

Adin smiled. "My lady is well-informed."

"As if you didn't know." She drummed her fingers on the handles of her golden chair. "What do you wish from me?"

"We will tell you everything we discover. Will you return the favor?"

Amestris glared. "Impudent pup."

Adin bowed. "Thank you, Duksis."

Amestris laughed, a full-throated sound that held the surprising ring of genuine enjoyment. *Why, she can be downright charming*, Roxannah thought with wonder.

"The more we know, the better we will be able to protect Roxannah," Adin said. "And serve you, my lady."

Amestris leaned back into her silk cushions. "The woman has good taste in servants, I'll give her that. I suppose it comes from having been one herself."

Roxannah opened her mouth to defend Esther. Adin stepped on her toe hard enough to make her puff out a gasp of air.

Amestris came to her feet. The soft blue fabric of her full skirts had been tucked and gathered to create a horizontal scalloping effect in the front. She looked like a sea wave. "I shall inform you of anything that might be useful to your situation. No more than that. Now take your leave before I lose my patience."

How can you lose what you so obviously lack? Roxannah wanted to ask. Fortunately, she kept her tongue inside her head where it belonged.

She had never been so relieved to be back in the queen's kitchen. As she plucked a brace of quail, she realized that in all the excitement she had forgotten to tell Adin she had had a glimpse of their nemesis. In profile, only. But she thought she would recognize that nose and those eyebrows anywhere.

She shoved aside thoughts of the man and all the unpleasantness relating to Amestris and her book and instead daydreamed of her upcoming trip to Ecbatana. By then, all this would be behind them.

31

Adin

> On that night the king could not sleep. And he gave orders to bring the book of memorable deeds, the chronicles, and they were read before the king.
>
> Esther 6:1

Adin stretched. It had taken two hours to stitch the long gash on the Immortal's leg, bandage his bruised rib, and put a splint on his finger. Even a friendly practice bout could turn ugly if a soldier's attention strayed at the wrong moment.

He tested the tension on the man's bindings. "That should do it. I will return to look at that wound tomorrow."

The soldier mumbled his thanks. Adin's tincture had him halfway to sleep already.

"Nice work, as always." The commander in charge of the battalion watched as Adin packed away his herbs. He straightened from his casual pose by the wall and extended a sealed scroll to him. "Message for you."

Adin examined the seal. Amestris. "My thanks."

"You keep exalted company these days, Physician."

He was not the first to notice. "I keep pesky company, Commander."

The commander grinned. "That's the truth."

Adin broke the seal and perused the brief message. *Western Gate garden. Come at once.* Not one for long-winded communications or pleasantries, Amestris.

Adin sighed. He would have appreciated a few minutes to himself. He combed his fingers through his hair, adjusted his belt, and made sure no blood splatters had stained his undertunic. He had removed his formal outer robe before treating the cut on his leaky patient, but blood had a nasty way of splashing. He did not suppose Amestris would appreciate the sight.

The Western Gate sat on the opposite side of the palace from the military court where he had spent the morning and thus required a long, brisk walk. Adin left his bulky chest in care of the commander and set off. He had to admit that Amestris's summons had aroused his curiosity.

The garden seemed empty. Adin wondered how long he would have to wait before Amestris deigned to send for him. To his surprise, her senior handmaiden emerged from behind the cover of a Persian silk tree, a few pink petals caught in the folds of her otherwise pristine garments. She motioned for him, and without a word, set out on a circuitous route that avoided the most crowded sections of the palace.

Clearly, she did not wish to be seen with him. So Amestris wanted to keep this meeting secret. He found himself following the handmaiden into a back entrance that led directly into Amestris's apartments. A hidden door! Adin wondered how many furtive meetings had been conducted by way of this well-concealed portal.

Amestris stood by a window, studying a small scroll of papyrus. Adin performed the usual courtly honors and awaited the lady's pleasure.

She turned to face him. "This is a task only you can perform."

"I am here to serve, Duksis."

She held out the piece of papyrus. Adin had spent enough time at the court to know not to reach for it. His commoner's hands were not allowed to soil her noble skin. Her handmaiden saw to the transfer.

Upon the scroll, he found four names written in a neat row. "The names of the men who walked through the Apadana Gate in the right timeframe yesterday?" he guessed.

"You're sharp. That's handy."

"I am also the only one who can recognize him."

"That's even handier."

Adin took a deep breath, trying to determine how to play the next few moments. Should he push for her help again or hold until he had some useful results that he could use as a bargaining tool? He prayed quickly for direction. For an open door. For anything that would help him keep Roxannah safe.

Amestris tapped her foot impatiently. "You're thinking too hard. It's giving me a headache. You may speak freely."

Adin exhaled in relief. "Do you want me to seek these men in any particular order, Duksis?"

"The top one is the most unlikely. You can leave him to the end. And, Physician? Don't let them see you."

"I shall try to remain invisible."

She looked at him with disconcerting frankness. "That will be difficult. You may not be the most handsome of men. But you have a presence about you that makes you hard to miss."

"My thanks. I think."

She smirked. "You won't get better than that from me."

"I am relieved. Duksis?"

She spun away from the window and headed for her golden

chair. "Oh, very well," she said as she settled down. "I will tell you what I know."

Adin huffed with relief.

She tapped an impatient rhythm on the handle of her chair. "About a year ago, the king spent the evening feasting with your skinny mistress and that fool Haman who got himself hanged from his own gallows." She adjusted her veil.

Adin was aware of the exact date to which Amestris referred. She was speaking of the first night Esther had entertained the king and Haman in her apartments, for on the second, Haman had been arrested.

"When Xerxes returned to his chambers," Amestris continued, "he could not sleep. The silly woman had probably fed him something too greasy and indigestible. Tired of tossing and turning, Xerxes requested the Book of Memorable Deeds to be read to him. Do you know what that is, Physician?"

Adin knew. "The book that chronicles the events of the royal house. It records all the important affairs of the court."

"As you say. We have a century's worth of these chronicles. Mostly they contain information boring enough to put a lawyer to sleep. Which I suppose was the point. Xerxes sent for one, hoping it would cure his insomnia.

"But as he listened, he made an interesting discovery. A certain man had done him an important service. He had revealed a murderous plot and thereby saved the king's life. That man was one of your people, I believe."

"His name is Mordecai. I know him."

"I thought you might."

Adin frowned. What did Mordecai have to do with the plot to kill Amestris?

"After that incident, Xerxes became convinced that he could unearth important information from these chronicles. He decided to have them read to him every night. Read in the order in which they were written, starting with the latest. That has become his practice for the past year. Then two weeks ago, someone broke into the hall of records."

"They tried to steal one of the Books of Memorable Deeds?"

"Ah. You see where this is headed. Yes. They tried to take the tablets from seven years ago. But they were not successful. A dutiful scribe, zealous for his records, got into a tug-of-war with the thief and managed to hold on to the chronicle. He received a deep gash in his shoulder for his pains and would have been killed but for the intervention of a palace guard."

Adin leaned forward. "Do we have the thief?"

"If only. The palace guards are not so well trained as the Immortals. The slippery maggot got away."

"So there is something in that particular book that someone does not wish revealed."

"That is my conclusion also."

"But if the book contains a record of public events, what could they possibly reveal that is worth killing for? Isn't it already a matter of common knowledge?"

"That is a good question."

"May I ask another?"

"You mean may you pose a more impertinent question than the ones you have already asked?"

Adin could not hide his smile. "That would be an accurate summation."

"Well?"

"Did you take the book?"

"I did. It's safe in my possession."

Adin didn't even want to know how she had managed that feat. Whom had she bribed, threatened, or charmed to get hold of a state document? "Why did you think this event merited your intervention? I imagine most of the court assumed the whole affair to be nothing more than an inconsequential theft gone wrong. Why arrange to bring the book into your keeping?"

"Because I am not most of the court."

"Only a fool would fail to notice that, Duksis."

"Meaning you are not a fool, I suppose? That remains to be seen. Having sharp wits does not exempt you from foolishness."

"I have often thought the same."

She huffed a laugh. "I arranged to take possession of the document because the day before the theft, the king had an accident. He fell from his horse. Xerxes has not been unseated from his stallion since he was two. So even though nothing about the accident pointed to foul play, it raised my suspicions. It was a nasty fall and could have proven fatal. By some good fortune, the king managed to twist his body at the last moment and merely suffered from superficial bruises instead of a broken neck.

"When the attempted robbery took place immediately afterward, I wondered if they might be connected. At that point, even I did not take myself too seriously."

"But if I may point out," Adin ventured, "it has been a year since the king started the practice of reading the Memorable Deeds. Why wait for so long? Why would they act now?"

"Probably because they assumed Xerxes would grow bored and stop. They hoped he would give up reading long before he reached this particular volume. Now, he has grown too close for their comfort. He is only a few tablets from reaching it."

Adin studied her angular face. "By taking the book, you are keeping the king safe from another attack. But you are also setting yourself up as a target."

Her finger rose in warning. "Don't paint me with your heroic colors, boy. I took the book because I was curious. I had no idea some boneheaded idiot would try to murder me for it."

"What is in those chronicles, Duksis? I assume you have read them. What do they contain that would provoke a man to murder?"

She frowned. "That is what irritates me. I have read that volume from top to bottom multiple times, and I see nothing that incriminates anyone. Whoever it is, they have tentacles in the court. The two men you overheard at the river. Those were his underlings."

"And yet one of them can come and go into the Apadana without a problem. If an underling of his is so high up, what does it say about the one behind this plot?"

"Hmm."

"Seven years, you say. That would be soon after the Persian campaign against Athens."

"Also the start of the revolt in Babylon, followed by another uprising in the coast of Ionia." Amestris made a face. "Every front seemed to have mutinied against Persia at the same time. Xerxes had a job of it stopping a half dozen bleeding wounds."

"Wasn't that also close to the time the king's own brother, Masistes, rose up against him?"

"Yes." Amestris's jaw tightened. "Masistes and his sons. He might have succeeded, too, had he made it to Bactria where he was *satrap*. His people loved him enough to follow him into a full-scale war against Xerxes. But the king heard about the insurrection in time, and his forces managed to cut Masistes off before they reached Bactrian territory." She shrugged. "None of these events are even mentioned in the book. It records nothing but tedious details pertaining to the running of the court."

She signaled her senior handmaiden, who had stood silently by her mistress throughout this conversation. The woman handed Adin an open scroll. At the bottom, it bore the seal of Otanes himself. Above, in neat writing, Adin ben Zerah received permission to enter the Apadana at will.

"Report to me as soon as you find his name. But do nothing. It's the head we must catch. The tentacles are of little use."

"May I ask one more—?"

"No, you may not. I have given you what you need to bring me the man's name. Now be off with you."

Adin barely had time to bow before the handmaiden bustled

him out of the chamber through the secret passage. He decided to head straight for the Apadana. The sooner he began his search, the sooner he would get his hands on their prey. And, with the help of God, cut off this plot at the knees once and for all.

A clutch of formally attired Immortals guarded the entrance to the audience hall. Their ornamental robes and pomaded hair did not fool Adin. There was nothing decorative about these men. They were the best trained soldiers the world had to offer. Most of them had seen war. Had faced death. Had killed without hesitation.

Under a veneer of politeness, they had an intransigent quality that seemed harder even than their rippling muscles. One examined his documents with minute attention while the other questioned him carefully before they waved him through.

Against the northern wall, the throne stood empty, as it often did when no special event was in progress. The king's person was accessible to a select number of courtiers, giving those chosen few great prestige and influence in the court. Without the tight ceremonial structures that surrounded the king's presence, Adin could walk with freedom through the magnificent building. Thirty-six columns topped by enormous double-sided bulls held up the intricately carved roof. Though the stone bulls were crouching, they would have dwarfed him had he been able to stand next to one—an impossibility in itself, given the sheer height of the fluted columns.

Adin stepped deeper into the hall. A perfect square, the Apadana was flanked by two rectangular porticos to the east and the west. He retired to the eastern portico and, leaning casually against a column, looked around him, seeking a familiar face. When he did not find the man he sought, he cast his mind back to Amestris's abrupt termination of their meeting. She must have known the nature of his final question and chosen to block it.

If the would-be murderer was so certain the king could spot his secret, why not simply hand the book over to the king with a warning? Surely he could decipher the whole mystery when he read this particular volume of the Book of Memorable Deeds for himself?

32

Roxannah

Commit everything you do to the LORD.
Trust him, and he will help you.

Psalm 37:5 NLT

ook dropped an empty silver platter in front of Roxannah. "You know what this is?"

Roxannah ran her finger through the crumbs. "A dish in need of washing?"

"If you are Sisy, maybe. But to you, this is a satisfied queen."

"The marsh mallow almonds? She liked them?"

"She ate one. Then three more. Then she had her handmaiden box the rest up and sent them off to the king with her compliments."

"She ate four in a row? That's a good sign. Wait. Did you say the *king*?"

Cook rolled his eyes. "You seem a bit slow today. You better pull yourself together, girl. She wants to see you. Sisy will walk you over."

"The *queen*?"

"Am I speaking Akkadian? Yes, the queen. The queen. Move."

Roxannah dropped the amphora of pomegranate paste on the counter and ran for the door, Sisy on her heels.

"You're going to see the queen again?" Sisy asked in an awed whisper.

"She sent for me."

"And I thought the junior handmaiden was bad."

"Cook says my lady enjoyed the marsh mallow candy. I am astounded. Being favored with an audience is a monumental honor."

Sisy whistled. "Not to mention a really big one."

"Oh no." Roxannah stopped abruptly.

"What is it?"

"I have a nasty grease spot in the middle of my bodice and my only other good tunic is in the laundry. I'll have to change into my old tunic. It may be frayed, but at least it's clean."

The junior handmaiden was already waiting for them in their alcove. "Where have you been? I have loitered here forever. Come. We must get you ready."

"Beg your pardon, mistress. I will just fetch a clean tunic and—"

"No need. Come, I say."

"But—"

"Don't waste any more of my time, girl. We must hurry."

Roxannah threw Sisy an anguished glance. Sisy grimaced and threw up her hands.

Roxannah traipsed behind the ramrod-straight figure of the handmaiden, dreading the reprimand she was certain to receive when she showed up in dirty attire. Once again, in the now-familiar antechamber, the handmaiden applied rose oil to Roxannah's hair and with an all-too-familiar rough hand, combed and pinned it in a half-moon braid. She handed her another perfumed wet rag to wash with before leaving the room. Roxannah stripped to her linens and scrubbed her skin, sparing a woebegone look for the stained robe that she would have to put on again.

But when she returned, the handmaiden grabbed the offensive robe with the tips of her fingers and, holding it at arm's length, threw it into a corner. Carefully unfolding a length of fabric, she extended it to Roxannah. "Put this on."

Roxannah's eyes widened. A cream undertunic peeked under a shorter sky-blue overtunic. She caressed the soft linen. "This is new!"

"Of course. A gift from the queen. I told you. If you are going to make a habit of coming before her, you'll need better clothing. She keeps a chest of garments for such occasions."

Devoid of the rich embellishments typical of a true royal gift, Esther's offering still implied special favor. And it was the first brand-new tunic Roxannah had owned in a decade. "It's beautiful," she breathed.

The handmaiden snorted. "It's plain. Put it on. The queen awaits."

The linen flowed in gentle swirls to the floor, hugging her body in loose curves. Unlike the robes favored among the wealthy gentry, the sleeves were tight, and the skirt narrow to save on fabric. Still, Roxannah found it more elegant than any garment she could dream of owning. She would have twirled if not for the handmaiden's scowl.

The handmaiden announced her before they entered the hexagonal chamber. Esther lifted her head from the clay tablet she had been studying in the light of her window. The smile that had captivated a monarch softened her lips. "You should wear blue more often, Roxannah. You look very pretty in that tunic."

"My queen, I cannot express my gratitude. I hardly know how to—"

, "Yes, yes." Esther waved her words away. She held out her hand to the scribe who stood at her elbow, and he exchanged her clay tablet for a papyrus scroll. From her vantage, Roxannah could see the unmistakable red seal, now broken, on the edge of the letter.

"Did Cook tell you that I sent a box of your sweet almonds to the king?"

"Yes, lady."

"I remembered he had once mentioned eating something similar in Egypt. He was quite fond of them."

Oh no! Roxannah groaned inwardly. He knew the taste of the original recipe. Had he found her version too great a departure? Her short nails dug into her palms.

Esther unfurled the papyrus. "I will read you what he said. The king writes . . ." Esther perused her letter to find the section she wanted. "'I thank you for the thoughtful gift. The candy from your kitchens was even better than the one I remember from Egypt. The spices gave it a distinctly Persian flavoring, which I enjoyed. Be sure and serve it to me the next time I visit.'" Esther closed her letter. "What do you think of that, little cook?"

Roxannah opened her mouth, but no sound escaped.

"You make a convincing trout impression. I will tell you what *I* think. You shall prepare more of your marsh mallow almonds when Xerxes comes for dinner in three days. And some of that herb kuku you made for me weeks ago. He would enjoy that, I think."

"You mean for the *king*?"

"Well, I don't mean for the bricklayer, dear. Do you think you can manage it?"

"I will do my very best, lady."

Esther settled herself on a comfortable couch and indicated a stool next to it. "Come and sit by me. I have something to discuss with you."

Roxannah sank on the edge of the stool, her back straight as a wooden pillar. She tried to corral her eyebrows back down from the middle of her brow, but they seemed stuck there permanently. What could the queen have to discuss with *her*?

Esther took a sip from a jeweled cup. "Cook wants to promote you to the position of assistant."

A small gasp escaped Roxannah. She had never heard of such a fast promotion. It took at least a year in the kitchens before someone was even considered for advancement. Trust built slowly in the palace.

Esther turned sideways so she could look Roxannah in the eyes. "Allow me to speak to you as a friend rather than as your queen. Cook honors you with this unusual favor. But there is also a disadvantage to his regard, a challenge for which I must prepare you. I want you to understand that such a fast rise will cause the other assistants to resent you. You will have to bear the weight of their displeasure. Their constant harassment. Their jibes and complaints."

Esther's smile looked like a crescent moon—bright and narrow. "I know something about the nature of a meteoric rise, and let me tell you, it is not painless." She placed her cup on the table. "You have to contend with one more challenge. You are a woman wearing what is usually a man's shoes. For this alone, your colleagues will begrudge you. Cook cares little for such things. He only sees in you someone who appreciates the culinary arts as he does. But the other assistants will hate having a woman as their equal. They will make their displeasure known at every turn. They will accuse you of being my spy. Of being Cook's paramour. And worse." She leaned forward. "Cook tells me you are the most talented assistant he has ever had."

"He said that?"

"He did. I am no expert, but I have tasted that talent for myself. You have earned this position, Roxannah. But you must prepare for the price you will pay for it. An open door does not always lead to an easy path."

Roxannah took a moment to absorb the queen's words. She could hardly recognize her own life. The woman who used to hide trembling under stairs and inside chests was about to cook for the queen and king of Persia. Her old impossible dream actually coming to life!

Adin would say that this fast rise was the hand of God at work. An answer to his daily prayers. He would say that her whole life was not a result of chaos and cruelty but the outworking of a carefully laid plan.

Was God real and good as Adin seemed to think? Had every hurt and danger brought her to where she was meant to be all along—in the royal kitchens of a queen who spoke to her as a friend?

Esther leaned close. "I will tell you a secret. If God has opened this door, he will help you with every hard step ahead."

"Do you believe it, my queen? That he is behind this open door?"

"I do not doubt it. The question is, do *you* believe it?"

Roxannah laughed. She could not help it. She was sitting next to the queen as if they were old chums, planning the royal dinner she had always dreamed of, speaking of a promotion she had no right to earn for at least a year. How could she deny that a hand greater than hers had come to her aid? She nodded carefully.

"Then you can place your trust entirely in his hands."

Cook gave Roxannah an assessing look when she walked in. "Well?"

She grinned. "You want me to be your assistant?"

The corner of his mouth tipped up. "Look around. I am not exactly spoilt for choice. You'll have to do. I will notify the scribe to raise your rations accordingly."

He clapped his hands until he had everyone's attention. "The king is coming to dinner in three nights." Everyone gasped. The king usually ate in his own private chambers and rarely partook of a meal in the queen's apartments. Cook's raised hand quieted the dithering agitation.

"I've been working on the menu, and it's a beauty," he said. "We're going to show the king's senior cook what a true royal meal is. So don't expect to get much sleep between now and then."

He waved his wooden spoon in the air. "One more thing. Roxannah has been promoted to full assistant." A shocked silence met this new announcement, followed by a volley of loud objections that overrode the excitement of the king's rare visit.

Cook narrowed his eyes. Years of ruling over his small domain had armed his gaze with an unspoken intimidation that cut through the protests like a knife through egg custard. "What are you, Athenians? You think this is a democracy? You think anyone is interested in your opinions? No. We live in a civilized nation, thank the Light. Which means what I say goes. Anyone have a problem so far?"

The kitchen fell silent.

"Didn't think so. Now, come receive your assignments."

Roxannah had no desire to hang around and listen to what her colleagues thought of her promotion. She needed to visit the shores of the Karkheh River to harvest more marsh mallow for the king's candy. She searched for Adin but found no sign of him. He had been missing all day. He must be occupied with a patient.

She suppressed a sharp stab of disappointment. When had he become the first person she wanted to run to with news?

She shook the thought and grabbed Sisy's hand. "We have work to do."

Sisy dug in her heels. "Is that a new tunic?"

Roxannah ran a hand down the front of her blue linen robe. She had forgotten she was still wearing her finery. "Yes."

"Good Light! It's beautiful. Did the queen give it to you?"

"The junior handmaiden gave it to me from the queen's chest. I suspect she was ashamed to be seen with me in my stained clothing. Now, you heard Cook. We have to hurry."

"You must have dropped your head in the queen's audience hall. We aren't going anywhere until you change. You can't work in that. You'll ruin it. Think what the handmaiden will do to you."

Roxannah groaned. "You're right. We'll stop at our chamber first."

Sisy poked her side with a bony elbow. "Assistant, eh?"

Roxannah could not hide her grin. "What do you think?"

"I am so happy I might burst. Those assistants have run me ragged since the day I arrived. You know when was the first time someone thanked me in that kitchen? The day you came. I loved watching their hairy jaws drop with dismay when Cook made his announcement."

From the Secret Scrolls of Esther

So the people went away to eat and drink at a festive meal, to share gifts of food, and to celebrate with great joy.

Nehemiah 8:12 NLT

Thirty-Two Years Later
The Twenty-Fifth Year of King Artaxerxes's Rule

The court may thrive on intrigue, but you must know it is also a place of unending delights. The nobility wallow in their pleasures with the enthusiasm of a pig in mud. They revel in their hunts and their music and their dancing. And they love nothing so well as a good banquet.

Whether a magnificent celebration that goes on for days and displays an extravagance that will be spoken of for generations or a more private affair, feasting is the heartbeat of the Persian court. Careers are made in the course of a drinking bout. Alliances are forged when delicate nibbles are served. Marriages decided upon as the flutes play.

I once saw Xerxes do the war dance of clashing shields, crouching down on one knee and springing up again to the measured beat of drums. It was a breathtaking sight that left the whole audience stunned, more so because he was rarely seen on display. The court could speak of nothing else for months, honored because they had seen what few ever would.

That was part of the king's power, this ability to share his presence with only a chosen few. Those he allowed into his rarefied world on a regular basis were destined to become the most powerful voices in the court.

It was no small thing for Xerxes to eat in my apartments. It showed a distinct favor rarely bestowed.

I remember on the occasion of one of his splendid birthday celebrations, when I was still fresh to court and everything a new discovery, I watched with amazement as he ate apart from his guests. I had not known that Persian protocol and fear of poison demanded the partition. He sat at his table, separated from the rest of us by a sheer curtain. Through some clever arrangement of lighting, none of us could see him, though he told me later that he could observe us with perfect clarity. After dinner finished, he invited several men to join him for wine. I had a glimpse inside his chamber when the curtain swished open for a server to bring in a large ewer.

Aside from his cupbearer, only four men attended him: Hyperanthes, Amestris's brother who was of an age with the king; Otanes, Amestris's influential father; and Arsames, the king's own half brother; and Haman.

Once, that circle had held other men. His disloyal brother Masistes, who had been killed during his ill-fated uprising only a few months earlier. Xerxes's beloved brother-in-law, Mardonius, who had been killed in Greece, his body still not recovered a year later.

Every time Xerxes lost someone to treachery or war, his circle shrank, and he seemed loathed to expand it again. I suppose he did not wish to deal with another Masistes. He preferred loneliness to the hurt of betrayal.

Which is why I wanted to make our little feast special for him. He rarely had the gratification of a night devoid of policy and maneuvering. A night of simple pleasures rather than the lavish affairs of the court. By coming to me, he had honored me. I intended to repay that favor.

33

Roxannah

There is surely a future hope for you,
Proverbs 23:18 NIV

THIRTY-TWO YEARS EARLIER
THE THIRTEENTH YEAR OF KING XERXES'S RULE
THE FOURTH WEEK OF SUMMER

The dessert assistant sidled over to where Roxannah was extracting sap from the mallow stalks. "You may rise now because you are the queen's pet. But it won't last. She won't remain on that throne much longer. Don't you know that?"

Roxannah ignored him, hoping he would grow bored and leave. He did not.

"What earns a woman a crown, do you think? A pretty face? A pleasing figure? No. The crown comes from the very thing she hasn't been able to produce. Six years she's been queen, and her belly stays as flat as Cook's thin morning bread."

Roxannah slammed her knife on the stone counter. Esther had treated her as a friend and a protector rather than as a haughty queen. Roxannah would not allow anyone to put her down within her hearing. "She is queen because the king wants her to be."

"You're a fool if you think that's enough. No king can afford to keep a childless queen on the throne. Looks bad, don't it? She's going to come crashing down. And she'll take you with her. So don't put on airs for us, girl. Any day now, you are going to topple right down with her." The assistant walked away, a satisfied smirk on his lips.

Roxannah smashed a stalk using the flat of her knife, pressing with unnecessary force until sap gushed over her fingers. Could it be true? Could Esther's position be that vulnerable? She remembered the queen's tender expression every time she spoke of the king. What would it do to her if he replaced her? A former queen had no place in a palace. Would he banish her? Or worse— Would she be at the mercy of her enemies? Of Amestris?

Without the king's protection, Esther would be crushed. Roxannah could not bear the thought. She had come to love Esther, the fragile queen who held her world together with nothing but threads of love and grace.

She could not protect Esther or provide an answer for the heartache that hung over her like the shadow of a teetering rock. But she could win for her a tiny sliver of the king's approval by making the best mallow candy this side of Egypt.

She had just finished extracting the sap from the stalks when Adin walked in. She set her pot aside. "I was starting to worry someone had kidnapped you."

He stretched. "I went off on a wild-goose chase for our new friend."

"She sent for you again? What did she want this time?"

"She had a list of possible names for me to hunt down. I found two. But they weren't the man we are seeking. I will look for the others tomorrow. I can walk you home now if you are ready. I am surprised you're still here."

"I doubt any of us is going to bed before midnight. The king is coming to dinner in three days, and we have a lot to prepare."

"The king, is it? No wonder everyone looks so serious."

Roxannah wove her fingers together. "I have some other news."

Adin waited. She tipped her head toward the others. Picking up on her reluctance to speak in the present company, Adin grunted. "Don't you need some vegetables or something? We can go to the gardens to collect them. They are deserted this time of evening."

"I need a large bundle of fresh herbs, as a matter of fact. I have to make another kuku."

"Kuku? That's urgent business."

"Calm your stomach. It's for the king's dinner."

"Amongst our proverbs, we have one that says, 'There is surely a future hope for you.'" Adin rubbed his hands together. "I refuse to believe my hope is cut off, king or no king."

In the herb garden they found a dew-soaked stone bench. Susa's bright stars shone like a sea of light above them. Roxannah exhaled. "Cook has made me a full assistant."

Adin jumped up. "Already? But that is extraordinary. Look at how far you have risen in three months."

"I'm not sure how I will manage. The other assistants resent me already."

Adin returned to his seat. He gave her one of his midnight-dark, melting looks that made her wish the handsbreadth that separated them would vanish. "You will win them over one day at a time. Now tell me about it, and leave nothing out."

She laughed, warmed by his interest. The shadow that had stood between them—the specter of her father's death and the part she had believed each of them had played in it—was diminishing with every passing hour.

She described her visit to Esther and how the queen had spoken to her as a friend. "She understood how the news would hit the others. Part of me was ready for their hostile remarks because she took the time to prepare me."

"I am relieved to know she has taken an interest in you. You can't find a better guide in the palace. She is wise beyond her years."

She told Adin what the dessert assistant had said about Esther. "Do you think he is right? Do you think she will lose her crown?"

His lips tightened. "That rumor has been flying for over a year, and she still occupies her throne. But, yes. She stands in considerable danger. It's a miracle she has not lost her position already."

"She loves him, you know."

"The king?"

Roxannah nodded. "It will break her heart if he banishes her."

"It might break his own. But those who rule nations owe their allegiance to something greater than their own hearts. Esther and Xerxes will pay the price required of their position."

"Will she be in danger once he removes his protection from her?"

"Yes."

Roxannah grew quiet. Everything about this vast palace with its astounding buildings, magnificent friezes, and lofty columns seemed to promise permanence. Pledge a solidity that could never be shaken. The casual observer would never know, walking down these massive stone-paved avenues, that all these buildings and monuments and the power they represented hung by a fragile thread. Lives could be changed—could be stolen—with the turn of a phrase. With a womb that refused to burgeon.

Roxannah had always felt that way about her own life. The uncertainty of it. The sheer vulnerability of opening her eyes to another day. It surprised her to realize that life at the palace was no different.

Then it occurred to her that Adin didn't live that way. Nor did Esther. They anchored their souls to something bigger than their circumstances. Bigger than their talents, their efforts, their clever devices. Bigger than their enemies, their insecurities, their lacks.

They anchored their souls to their God.

And in some incomprehensible way, he seemed to guide and guard them. To give them peace in the valleys of life. To impart strength for the hard choices.

As she sat facing the starlit gardens, enveloped in the scent of jasmine and tarragon, something in her reached toward this Being the way waves tumble for the shore. With the whole-hearted abandon of something she was born to do but forgot about the moment she took her first breath, her soul turned in the direction of God and sought him as an anchor. The God who had given her mother peace and Darab dignity and Esther courage and Adin healing. The God whose power opened impossible doors. She reached for him with all her strength.

Then, the storm came.

Even before they reached the kitchen, they could hear the shouts. Adin began to run, Roxannah a few steps behind. Sisy dashed out of the main door just as they approached it. "Physician! Come, quick. It's Cook."

Adin did not waste time asking questions. He leapt into the kitchen and within moments had shooed the small knot of men who had gathered around Cook's prone figure.

"He just collapsed," one of the assistants said. "Grabbed his chest and went down."

Adin told everyone to hush and laid his ear against Cook's chest. "He's alive. Barely. Sisy, fetch my chest. You." He pointed at the vegetable assistant. "Run and tell Hathach what has happened." He turned to Roxannah. "A pot of boiling water."

Roxannah raced to obey. Her fingers shook as she took the pot off the fire and brought it to Adin. Ignoring the sudden wave of nausea that clawed up her throat, she watched Adin mix his herbs into the steaming water.

Cook's eyes fluttered open. "What . . . ?"

"You've had a turn," Adin said, his voice calm. "Try to drink this." He spooned a bit of his tincture into Cook's mouth. Even his cough sounded weak.

"Too much fuss." He tried to sit up.

Adin pressed him back with a hand to his shoulder. "If you want to live, you will do as I say. Lie still and drink as much of this as you can."

"The king . . ."

"Is no longer your concern. Right now, all that matters is that you survive. Understand?"

Hathach appeared at the door, his forehead covered in a sheen of sweat. "How is he?"

"Still alive, by some miracle," Adin said.

Cook stirred on the ground. "I can hear you, you know."

Hathach bent over him. "Excellent. I will be sure to make my insults especially colorful."

With a sigh, Cook closed his eyes.

Adin laid his ear against his chest again. "Seems a bit stronger. We should be able to move him soon."

Hathach straightened. "I'll arrange it. He has a nook to himself in the worker's building. It's not far from here."

"I will accompany him. Sisy, can you carry my chest, please?"

Roxannah watched as Adin took charge. Being thrown in the midst of a crisis seemed to have made him calmer. More controlled. He had told her that in times like this, he turned to God. He sought his counsel and strength. It seemed to spill over, somehow, into the very atmosphere of the room. God's supernatural calm flowed through Adin and into the rest of them, washing away the panic that had choked the air.

Three burly servants arrived to carry Cook to his chamber. They rigged together a makeshift litter from a blanket and lifted Cook onto it. Adin barked a warning when one of the servants grew too rough. He and Hathach kept pace with Cook's slow-moving processional, Sisy bringing up the rear, hugging Adin's bulky chest to her breast.

Roxannah watched them disappear around a bend before quietly returning to her corner of the kitchen. She wiped her mouth with the back of her hand, trying to still the shivery feeling inside.

With a determined breath, she fetched a bowl of soaking almonds. Until they were told otherwise, she intended to follow Cook's plans for the king's dinner. It was the only way she could think of helping him. She started to skin the almonds. Exhausted as she was, the rhythm of the work steadied her. Her nauseous belly settled, and her hands stopped shaking as a hill of blanched almonds piled up in front of her.

The restless wave of her soul tumbled toward that unknown shore again. For the first time, she did not think of him as Adin's God or Esther's God. She saw him for himself. For her.

God, please help Cook. Please show Adin what to do. Her first prayer, alone and unaided. It felt right. It felt like she had come out from a far country and stepped into home. *Thank you for hearing me.*

"What are you doing, idiot girl?" The dairy assistant came to stand over her.

Roxannah jumped. Had he noticed her praying? She had not said the words aloud, had she?

He pointed at the counter. "There isn't going to be a dinner now."

"Oh, you mean the almonds? Well, even if there isn't a dinner, someone will enjoy them. Maybe it's you."

"I'd rather swallow elephant dung."

Don't know of any elephants, or I would oblige. Silently, she sliced through the softened almonds, creating a mound of slivers.

"Come," the dairy assistant said to his colleagues, "let's go to our beds and leave this one to tire herself out."

The other assistants followed him to the door. They came to a sudden stop when they ran into Hathach. For a small man, he certainly knew how to block a doorway. "Where are you going?"

The dairy assistant scratched his head. "To bed, Master Hathach. There's nothing to be done with Cook sick."

"Really? He told me he had already given you assignments. Why aren't you working on them"?

"What's the point? Without Cook, surely the king's eunuch will send one of His Majesty's own men to take over. They will change the menu. All our work will go to waste. We might as well rest while we wait for our new orders."

"What a fantasy you occupy. Who said anything about another cook?"

"Well, I assumed . . ." His words ran aground under the strain of Hathach's stare.

"You assumed?"

"I mean, with Cook away, who will be in charge? He has never even allowed one of us to take over a meal for the queen. He's sure not going to hand over the management of his kitchen with the king visiting."

Hathach straightened the man's tunic where it had grown twisted at the neck. "Never mind all that. You finish the work assigned to you." He waved his fingers like a broom at the assistant cooks. "Everyone to your counter. I will return in a couple of hours to check on your progress. Roxannah?"

Roxannah blinked. "Yes, Master Hathach?"

"Cook is asking for you. I will accompany you there."

Cook's face had turned the color of boiled parsnip, pasty white and glistening with sweat. He held out a small scroll to her. "Produce list. For the king's visit."

She took it. "Yes, Cook."

"You still have to manage the regular breakfasts, lunches, and dinners for the queen until then."

Roxannah settled down on the floor next to Cook's bed. "We'll be all right, Cook. You just focus on getting better."

He ignored her and signaled Adin. "The scroll I told you about."

From a modest wooden chest, Adin extracted a fat roll of stained papyrus. Cook shook his head when Adin tried to hand it to him. "Her."

Adin passed the scroll to Roxannah. She glanced through the papyrus quickly. Recipes. Years' worth of Cook's recipes, all written in neat Persian syllables. A good trick to keep other cooks from snooping. She gave him a confused look. "What shall I do with these?"

"Can you read 'em?"

"Yes, Cook."

"They don't have amounts. You'll have to figure that out."

"What do you mean I have to figure it out?" She felt like she had just stepped on a slippery rock. Like her body was about to go whirling into the air before landing with a painful thump. "Why are you giving me your recipes, Cook?"

"King's dinner. You'll find the dishes I selected in there. I want you to take charge."

Roxannah snapped to her feet. "You what?"

"You can do it."

She shook her head wildly. "No, Cook. I can't."

"You can, I tell you. Come to me when you have questions."

"I have a question right now. Have you lost your mind?" Beads of sweat broke out on her forehead. "It will be a disaster! Those assistants aren't going to work under the authority of a woman. They aren't going to listen to a word I say. Besides, do you realize I've never even made some of these recipes? And I've certainly not made so many dishes for one event without your oversight."

34

My flesh and my heart may fail,
but God is the strength of my heart and my
portion forever.

Psalm 73:26

Cook motioned for her to sit next to him again. She forced herself to obey, though what she really wanted was to run out of his small chamber and out of the palace compound and out of Susa if it meant finding a safe place.

Reaching for her hand, he gave it a weak squeeze. "I'll be here for you, girl. You've learned a lot in the past three months. All you have to do is what you've always done. Follow this." He tapped his chest. "You have a natural sense for cooking."

"I don't know what I'm doing half the time."

He smiled. "But you do it better than all the others put together. Hathach asked the queen before he came to fetch you, and she agrees. She wants you to take charge of the dinner."

Roxannah dropped her head in her hands. "The others will never follow my directions."

"Hathach will help with that."

"Couldn't we just ask a cook from the king's own kitchens to step in?"

"We could. But then the queen would look like she can't run her own household. Like she needs the king's help to serve him a simple meal. We don't want that, do we?"

"No. But we don't want her to look like a fool either, which is what's going to happen if I have charge of this dinner."

"It's only a small meal for two people. Forget that one of the guests is the king. Just prepare the food like it's for ordinary folk." He gave Adin a look. "Like it's for him. You'd do just fine cooking for him, wouldn't you?"

"He wouldn't dismiss me if I undercook his meat."

He growled. "I'll dismiss you myself if you keep talking. Get back to work. I want to sleep."

Adin walked Roxannah to the door. "You look as pale as Cook."

"What am I to do?" Her voice had the wobble of the tears she refused to shed. "I can't manage this, Adin."

"Cook believes you can. The queen believes you can. I believe you can."

"Well, you are all foolish and misguided, begging your pardon."

He couldn't quite suppress his blooming grin. "What did Esther tell us? That, like her, we also have been brought to our own positions for such a time as this."

She sniffed. "Adin, I prayed. To God."

His face took on the aspect of a polished apple, all aglow and inviting. "What did you pray for?"

"For Cook. That he would be healed."

"Your first prayer, and it was for someone else," he said, his voice soft with approval.

"Will he survive this, Adin?"

"I don't know." He reached for her hand. "Remember, you are not alone just because Cook is not there to show you the way. God will help you. When you feel weak, when you need wisdom, turn to him. He is faithful."

They were only words. And yet, they were more. They felt true. It was as though Adin gave her a staff to lean on for the climb up a steep and treacherous hill.

Outside, Roxannah almost plowed into Sisy, who yawned as she fell into step beside her. "Master Hathach said I was to wait for you. How's Cook?"

"Well enough to snap at me."

"What did you do wrong?"

"I told him I couldn't be in charge of the king's dinner."

"Good Light!" Sisy ground to a halt. "He wants you to cook for the king?"

Roxannah tugged at the neck of her tunic, which seemed to have grown a few sizes too tight. Her head whirled. How could something she had cherished as a dream hurt as much as a nightmare?

She knew the answer to that question—because even dreams came with the threat of loss. This open door could lead to an ending instead of a start. It could mean her dismissal.

Without her work, she could not support her mother. They would not be able to keep their home. Without her work, they would be destitute. So much hung in the balance of one dinner. It was easy for Cook to tell her to take charge of the meal. But he could not comprehend how one event could mean the end of the fragile security she had managed to forge for herself and her mother.

She thought of God, who had allowed Darab to be a slave for six agonizing years. Who had not helped Adin's precious Hulda when she grew sick after just seven months of marriage. Clearly, he was not a God who offered certainties.

Yet somehow, they clung to him. Even Esther, who had known she might die when she approached the king without an invitation, had chosen to obey him rather than pursue her own safety.

Roxannah exhaled. That seemed her own path now. Obedience, even though it meant walking under the ominous shadow of disaster. Adin said God would help her, and she believed him. Whatever the outcome.

Hathach was waiting for her in the kitchen. "Cook spoke to you?"

"Yes, Master Hathach."

"I expect an exceptional dinner from you."

"Oh, it will be exceptional. The king will never have tasted anything like it."

If he noticed the thick layer of sarcasm that ran through her words, he gave no sign of it. Turning to face the others, he snapped his fingers. "I have an announcement." The assistants left their stations to gather around the eunuch.

"Cook has put Mistress Roxannah in charge of the king's dinner."

Ice-cold disbelief met Hathach's pronouncement. The four assistants turned to glare at her. As if on cue, the hush in the room broke into a torrent of angry objections.

Hathach raised a hand, and the noise died down. "I didn't ask for your opinions. Did I? Not at all. I told you what was going to happen."

"But Master Hathach . . ." The vegetable assistant's words died at the look the eunuch gave him.

Hathach held up one finger. "The king is coming to dinner. You will serve him the best meal you have ever made in your sorry lives. If one part of that dinner is disappointing, I will personally hold the assistant in charge responsible. Whatever trouble you are thinking of making for Mistress Roxannah shall be visited upon your own heads. If you do not comply with her orders, if you are lazy, if you arrange for little accidents—in short, if you ruin this meal in any way—I will personally report you to the king's guard as an agitator and consider it a pleasure. Have I spoken clearly enough for your thick skulls to grasp?"

The assistants jerked their heads down.

"Excellent. Mistress Roxannah." He waved his hand at her, motioning for her to speak. Motioning for her to take charge.

Roxannah fought a wave of dizziness. She faced the hostile gazes of her colleagues like a condemned man staring at the gallows. "Between now and the king's dinner, we also have five regular meals to prepare." She swallowed, trying to still the quaver in her voice. "We'll divide into two teams before each meal. One prepares the regular food, the other works on the king's dinner.

"Tomorrow, you prepare the queen's breakfast." She pointed to the dairy assistant. "Halpa will help you. The rest of us will work on the first braise for the king's dinner. We'll keep lunch simple. A cream of barley soup, chickpea-flour meatballs, followed by saffron pudding. Sisy, you clean up after lunch while the rest of us work on the base for the second braise and the roasts.

"Hopefully, Halpa can remain with us all day tomorrow and the day after to prepare the breads, make the noodles for the herb soup, and give us an extra hand for whatever else we may need. Any questions?"

No one said a word. Not a single objection. With Hathach here to glower at them, their tongues remained still. But he wouldn't be here every hour of the day. He had his own duties to attend to. Hopefully, his threats would prove sufficient to keep the assistants in line. She cleared her throat. "You can go to bed for a few hours tonight. But be here before sunrise."

Roxannah rose out of bed three hours after collapsing into it. Outside her chamber, she plowed into the stone-hard chest of an Immortal who stepped in front of her.

"Pardon!" she gasped.

"Mistress Roxannah?"

"Yes?"

"I've been assigned to protect you."

Her jaw loosened. It was definitely too early in the day to cope with mysteries. "Assigned by whom?"

"The queen sent me."

"I see." How odd of Esther to have one of the king's guards planted outside her room overnight. What was she expecting? A midnight ambush? "Well, I thank you."

Outdoors, the world still lay asleep in the pitch-dark of a moonless night. To her shock, the Immortal followed her as she headed for the kitchen. "I'm going to work now," she explained slowly, as if speaking to a child.

He had a jaw that reminded her of an iron box—square and unmoving. "I am following."

If a palace column had knocked her on the head, Roxannah would not have felt more off-balance. She supposed with Adin watching over Cook, Esther had decided she lacked proper protection. But the queen had failed to take an important detail into consideration. How was Roxannah going to explain the presence of an Immortal to the other assistant cooks?

She had a ridiculous image of him standing at military attention, his spear perfectly straight as the kitchen staff tried to weave around him. How could she explain that? *He won't be underfoot at all. He can actually prove very useful. Try hanging your ladle from his sword belt.*

She exhaled. Just then, Sisy emerged, a huge yawn splitting her face. She came to a sudden stop in front of Roxannah. Her head swiveled between her and the guard. "And Cook calls *me* a flirt. First the physician, and now this one. They just line up, don't they?"

"It's not what you think."

"Whatever you say."

"We can all agree on that."

"I am only pointing out what's obvious. You seem to collect them. Must be the fancy speech. Maybe you can teach me some."

Roxannah sighed. "I'll leave you behind if you keep up this nonsense."

Sisy tucked her hand in the crook of her arm. "No, you won't. You need me too much."

"Light help me, I do."

Sisy grinned. They started down the path again, the Immortal making a good imitation of a shadow, silent and bigger than life. Sisy looked over her shoulder. "Coming, is he?"

"It's the food. He can't resist it."

The Immortal threw her a dirty look. She gave him a sweet smile and tried to ignore his hulking frame marching one step behind her. He should have made her feel safe. Instead, he seemed like one more reason for the assistants to resent her.

The sight of Halpa already at work in the kitchen cheered her. "You heard about Cook?"

He nodded. "Hathach sent a servant to explain." He raised a brow at the Immortal. "We must be shorthanded if you're recruiting the king's guard."

"It would take longer than the *Epic of Gilgamesh* to explain this one."

The hint of a smile softened Halpa's lips. "Things are getting more entertaining around here."

"I am so glad you're amused. Since you are in such a good temper, can you make me some noodles for the herb soup?"

"Only the best for you, mistress."

Roxannah washed and soaked chickpeas. She was rinsing the lentils when the dairy assistant walked in. He froze in the middle of the room and pointed at the Immortal in horror. "What's he doing here?"

"Him?" Roxannah did her best to look innocent. "The queen sent him."

"Why would the queen send the king's guard into the kitchen?"

"Why do you think?"

He sank on a stool. "Hathach has set his spy on us."

Roxannah raised a brow. Maybe that muscle-bound nuisance and his fat spear could prove useful after all. "You think so?"

In answer, the dairy assistant snapped up and busied himself at his station. She had never seen him work with such dedication. Roxannah fetched a bowl of clotted cream, a jar of honey, and a piece of warm bread and put them before the Immortal. He deserved a kingly breakfast.

35

And his name shall be called
Wonderful Counselor, Mighty God,
Everlasting Father, Prince of Peace.

Isaiah 9:6

The onions were singed.

The vegetable assistant glared at Roxannah as if she were to blame. "You told me to fry them longer."

Without a word, she began chopping another onion. Halpa joined her at the counter and matched his knife strokes to hers. Before long, they had an even-sized pile of onion slivers between them.

"I'll prepare the garlic," Halpa said. "Go."

Roxannah gave him an appreciative nod and flew to grab a fresh pan. She added a dollop of butter to the oil, adjusted the pan to sit higher on the fire, and when it sizzled, added the onions. Undercook an onion, and it lacked sweetness. Overcook it, and it became bitter. The secret was a slow fry until the onion turned golden and crisp. It needed a deft hand and patience, neither of which the vegetable assistant seemed to possess.

As the onions fried slowly, she stirred the legumes and tasted a few. They were just soft enough. She set the pan aside. The herbs and noodles would cook quickly. She would add those a half hour before the meal was served. The aroma of frying onions filled the kitchen. They looked golden, just as they should. She removed them from the heat.

Over the past two days, they had managed to serve five regular meals without creating a disaster, and completed most of the braises, sauces, and appetizers on Cook's list. But time was tight. She still had the final braise to make, the one designed to be one of the centerpieces of the dinner. Only four hours before the king arrived. She went to fetch Cook's recipe scroll from the box where she kept it.

She opened the lid. Nothing but dark shadows inside.

She frowned. Had she forgotten to replace it the last time she took it out? She whirled around, trying to spot it on the counters where she had worked.

"What?" Sisy asked from the doorway where she sat, elbow-deep in a vat of water, washing pots.

"Cook's recipe scroll. Have you seen it?"

Sensing the desperation in her voice, Sisy dropped a pan back into the water and joined her in the search. They looked everywhere: the counters, the back room, the vegetable baskets, even inside clean pots.

"You're in trouble now," the vegetable assistant said, his voice dripping with satisfaction.

The dairy assistant looked over his shoulder. "Cook will take your head off for losing his precious recipes."

He would have every reason. She had lost a treasure trove of culinary genius. An invaluable resource. As if that weren't bad enough, she was one braise short for tonight, with less than four hours to make it. What was she supposed to do now?

She could either waste more time chasing after the scroll—or make a braise using her own recipe.

She straightened her shoulders. "Sisy, are the ducks ready?"

"All plucked and cleaned."

Roxannah sautéed more onions and garlic with turmeric, adding roughly chopped walnuts to the sizzling butter before transferring them into a large mortar.

Halpa gently removed the pestle from her hand. "I'll do this. You see to the duck."

She cut the ducks into large pieces, trying to plan her next steps as she worked. The usual recipe required the duck to cook in water. Boiling made the meat tender. But it also meant that most of its flavor leached into the sauce, leaving the flesh of the fowl tasteless and stringy. She could roast the duck. But that would leave the sauce bland. Besides, roasted meat was never as fall-off-the-bone soft as boiled.

It seemed stupid to try something new tonight of all nights. *God, give me wisdom! Give me counsel so I know how to proceed.* She waited for a moment, head bent low, trying to discern what to do. She felt a release, a sense of rightness about going forward with her risky plan.

Nodding to herself, she added a dollop more butter to the same pan where she had fried the garlic and onions, which still held their lingering aroma. Sprinkling the duck with salt, she set it carefully into the sizzling pan.

Halpa held the mortar under her nose. "Is this the consistency you want?"

"Perfect." She fetched the jar of pomegranate molasses she had brought from home and added a heaping tablespoon to Halpa's paste, seasoning it with salt and a dash each of turmeric, cinnamon, and cardamom. In the pan, she flipped the pieces of duck. Their skin had turned the color of bright copper, gleaming with melted butter. By now, the whole kitchen staff had gathered around to watch her. Even the Immortal craned his neck for a better view.

She ignored them, keeping her attention on the duck. When both sides had fried evenly, she removed some of the excess fat, remembering Amestris's crack about the king's sleepless night.

Pomegranate juice and a rich, gelatinous broth made from chicken bones would enrich the duck's flavor. She hoped the fried skin would seal in enough of the juices that simmering the fowl in liquid would not rob its flavor. Finally, she spooned in the paste from Halpa's mortar. Covering the pan, she lifted it over the fire to reduce the heat. It would simmer gently and, hopefully, be ready just in time for the dinner.

Sighing, she stepped away. She had done her best. She could do no more.

Hathach walked in, catching everyone away from their counters. "Why are you not at your work?" he asked coldly.

Everyone scattered. Over his shoulder, the vegetable assistant said, "She lost Cook's recipe scroll, Master Hathach."

"Did I ask you?" But Hathach threw Roxannah a quick glance, his brow knotted in a deep furrow. "Should I worry?" he whispered in her ear.

"That's my job, Master Hathach. And I do it very well, I assure you."

She decided to make use of the eunuch's presence while she could. The assistants would be less inclined to snap at her with him here.

She checked with the vegetable assistant first. "Could you cut the herbs more finely, please?" He gave her a disgruntled look but obeyed. She tried a piece of the grape leaf, which he had boiled earlier. "These are good." She spread one open and pointed to the tough vein in the center. "Could you cut these out, please? Not too far, or the leaf will split."

"I know how to do it. I don't need your meddling."

"Just do it," Hathach snapped.

Roxannah made a slow circuit of every counter, making sure each individual element was ready, adding seasoning, preparing the details for last-minute decorations. She wrapped the grape leaves herself to safeguard them from falling apart when cooked.

Time to visit the spits.

She did not dare trust the assistants with what would be another centerpiece of the meal—a delicate cut of venison from a stag the king himself had hunted the previous morning. She had seasoned and soaked the meat in a bath of wine and shallots early last evening. A few weeks earlier, Cook had explained which was the tenderest part of the meat and had shown her how to find it under the backstrap. If roasted well, it should be almost as tender as boiled meat.

Several other roasts would also be prepared. But those would be served to the royal attendants and servants. This meat was for the king, and she had a smaller piece of lamb, courtesy of Avraham, for the queen.

Miletus welcomed her with an unpleasant smile. "I knew you'd be back. Missed me, did you?"

She kept the meat in front of her like a shield. It did not slow him down. He took two large steps in her direction, arm extended like a hammer ready to descend. Without warning, he came to an abrupt stop, snapping back a step. The Immortal tightened his grip on the scruff of his neck. "Close enough, Spit Boy."

Miletus gave the Immortal a wide-eyed look. "Leave me alone!" His voice emerged comically high, making Roxannah grin.

The Immortal tightened his grip on Miletus's thick neck. The tip of his spear had somehow found its way under Miletus's chin. "Promise to be a good boy? I hate to get blood on my clean tunic."

"Fine. Get off me."

The two muscle-bound men eyed each other. The Immortal smiled and stepped back.

The white-haired spit master ran out of his shelter. "What goes on here?"

Roxannah had no time for explanations. She held out the venison and the lamb. "For the king's dinner tonight."

Miletus reached to take it. His master slapped his hand away. "Go on with you. This work is for me." He examined the piece of venison, nodded once, and turned to the spit. "I'll deliver it myself."

Roxannah exhaled the breath she had been holding. "I am grateful for your help with Miletus," she said to the Immortal as they jogged back to the kitchen.

He shrugged. "He's an annoying gnat."

"You know him?"

"Tried to get into the army and was rejected. I enjoyed putting him in his place."

"You are more useful than you look."

The corner of his mouth twitched. "You're a better cook than I thought."

Roxannah served the thick noodle soup in a silver bowl. Keeping her hand steady, she drew crisscross lines with white fermented yogurt on top, forming a checkered pattern. Within each square, she added elements of her decoration: golden fried onions, dried mint fried in oil, saffron sauce, fried garlic. Each square held a different color and texture—red, green, gold, white—carrying extra flavor into the soup when served.

She waved, and a white-garbed server carried the bowl to the queen's apartments. One after another, she decorated each dish and sent them with the waiting servers.

She would now have a little extra time for the desserts since they would not go out until dinner was complete. Cook had told her that the king was not fond of too much rosewater, so Roxannah had used very little in her custard. Now she worried that it might prove too bland. She tasted the milky-white concoction, rich with the flavor of almonds and cream.

It was too late to change anything now. She had to trust

that what she had prepared would meet with the king and queen's approval. The jiggling custard had set in individual glass bowls, each one a priceless treasure. Arranging dried pink rose petals and slivers of pistachio in a flower pattern at the center of each bowl, she then turned her attention to her miniature almond cakes, sweet-chickpea flowers, and date-filled cakes, which she had made with Halpa's assistance. And, of course, the marsh mallow candy specifically requested by the queen.

Everything had to look as beautiful as it tasted. She covered the platters with palm leaves and decorated them with fresh flowers, dusting her cakes with ground almonds and pistachios before sprinkling the top with rose and violet petals.

The dishes from the main meal were starting to return to the kitchen. Everything had been tasted. Some of the platters looked more than half empty. Roxannah's stomach clenched. Had she done enough to please the king? To justify Esther's trust? She sent the desserts with the servers and sank on the stool, head resting in a trembling hand.

"Well, are we going to eat or what? The leftovers are here." Sisy clapped her hands to her waist. "I'm starved."

Roxannah sat up. "Of course. Everyone, take your share." She looked at the half-empty dishes and fought a wave of nausea.

It seemed an age went by before the dessert platters were returned to the kitchen. She had not heard one word from the royal couple. Not a single compliment. She sat ramrod straight, probably looking as green as the crushed pistachios that sat forgotten in a wooden mortar.

A single server ran into the kitchen with the final tray carrying the empty glass bowls of custard. "The king requests the presence of the cook," she said as she placed the tray softly on a counter.

Roxannah's hand spasmed as she snapped to her feet, sending the bowl of crushed pistachios spinning into the air. The

Immortal caught it mid rotation and returned it unharmed to the table.

She stared down at her old, stained tunic. "Good Light! I forgot my fancy robe in our room."

"I didn't." Sisy smiled smugly. "I knew they would send for you, so I fetched it this morning." She pointed to Cook's corner. "It's behind the curtain where Cook keeps his clean tunic. You better change fast."

Roxannah's hands were trembling too hard. If not for Sisy, she would probably still have her head stuck in suffocating folds of blue and cream fabric. She wiped her face and hands with a wet rag and hoped she smelled more like roses and cardamom than raw onions and garlic.

Hathach met her at the door, the junior handmaiden at his side. "Do something with her hair. It's sticking out everywhere," he said.

The junior handmaiden rolled her eyes. "What else is new?" She did not waste time on a formal design. Instead, she pulled Roxannah's hair loose, ran her comb through the curls without regard to her scalp and braided it into an orderly pillar at the base of her neck.

Roxannah shifted her weight from foot to foot. "Did the king like the food?"

"Do I look like I am his boon companion? Hold still, girl." She sprinkled Roxannah with something fragrant, wiped a bit of flour from her forehead, and shoved her through the door.

36

The king's heart is a stream of water in the
hand of the LORD;
he turns it wherever he will.

Proverbs 21:1

The king had abandoned his solitary curtained alcove, where he had eaten his meal in private, and sat with his legs casually sprawled on an elaborately carved couch, the queen tucked against him.

He sat up in surprise when Roxannah stumbled in. She bent at the waist and, upon rising, held a formal hand before her mouth according to the custom of the court.

"Who is that?" His voice was deep and pleasant.

The queen leaned into his side. "You asked for the cook. Well, there she is."

The king leaned forward, and Roxannah found herself the focus of his scrutiny. Her legs turned to custard as the ruler of two-thirds of the world paid her the compliment of his undivided attention. He had wide, guarded eyes and a hawkish nose in a face that had inherited the famous good looks of his

Achaemenid ancestors. She found nothing friendly in his expression.

He pointed a finger at her. "You made our meal tonight?"

"I and the other assistant cooks had that privilege, my king."

"You seem young. And very female." He waited for an answer.

"Yes, Lord." He raised a dark eyebrow, seeking more of an explanation. She cleared her throat. "Time will deal with one, though I fear it's helpless against the other, my king."

"Light spare us. A philosopher as well as a cook."

The queen wrapped her fingers about his elbow. "She's shaking. Put her out of her misery."

The king grinned. The unfriendly cast of his face melted away in an instant. Though the caution never left his eyes, his expression grew warm. Heaven help her, he was unleashing his charm upon her. Roxannah felt the tug of it, supreme power wrapped in kind humor.

"You did well, girl. The duck might even have shown a small spark of genius. And I liked your custard. Not too rosy. Some desserts make one feel like a horse chomping on a clump of flowers. The marsh mallow candy, though . . . that was close to perfection."

Roxannah's eyes widened. Had he just praised her? "You are too generous, Sire." She bowed and remembered to add, "Cook was the one who told me how to prepare the custard to your liking. The praise is rightfully his."

"Talented and humble. Perhaps I'll pinch her from you, my dear."

The queen sat up primly. "I would be honored to please my lord. Of course, you would have to chomp on horse food every time you come to visit me. With Cook on his sickbed, I would be left with no one competent in my kitchen were Roxannah to leave it."

The king gave a mock shudder. "Preserve us from such a fate. I shall leave her where she is."

291

"Magnanimous as always, Lord." Esther turned her face to Roxannah. "Very well done, little cook. I am delighted with the meal tonight. I will send a sheep to your home as a reward."

Roxannah felt her clenched muscles loosen. The queen had been pleased! Walking backward as she took her leave, she caught a glimpse of the king gently capturing Esther's hand in his. The hawkish, unfriendly mien had grown soft. And shockingly tender with love.

Taking a deep breath of warm night air, she leaned against the wall.

"You still have your head, I see," the Immortal said.

"He liked the food." Her voice shook with wonder.

"You doubted it? Don't you ever taste your own cooking?"

She huffed a weary laugh. A wave of exhaustion made her want to sit down and not move for a whole week.

The worst had not happened! She had not let the queen down. She had not been fired. She would be able to hold on to their ancestral home. Come tomorrow, her mother would receive the gift of a fat, woolly sheep from the queen's own flocks.

The thought shot a burst of fresh strength through her veins. She wasn't ready to retire after all. She wanted to share this moment. "Let's go visit Cook," she told the Immortal.

Sitting up on his pallet, Cook was examining a cup of something green with glum apprehension. The sight of her seemed to cheer him. He set the cup on the tiny table next to him. "How did you fare?"

Adin closed the scroll he was reading. "You have your new tunic on. I take it they sent for you?"

Trust him to notice the details of her clothing. She nodded happily.

"Sit here, and tell us everything." He rose from the single stool in the room so she could take his place and, with the same motion, handed Cook his cup again. "You can drink as you listen." He held up a finger when Cook opened his mouth. "Don't argue, old man, or I will send her away."

"Cruel and savage treatment. See if I make you those barberry lentil balls ever again."

"I am trying to keep you alive so you will do just that. Now drink up and quit griping. I want to know what happened."

The weariness left Roxannah's bones as she began to describe her day. Cook wanted to know every detail of the meal and its preparation. Adin asked how the assistant cooks had behaved. Cook questioned her about the decorations for each dish. Adin wondered if she had had time to eat.

They both leaned forward when she began to describe her meeting with the king and queen.

"Genius? Perfection?" Adin crowed the words as if he was personally responsible for adding them to the general vocabulary. "You can't have better than that."

"Only a *small spark* of genius and *close to* perfection." She did not want to exaggerate her triumph.

"The king is not a man for grand compliments," Cook said. "A *small spark* in the mouth of Xerxes is a towering flame on someone else's tongue. He must have really enjoyed the meal."

Listening to Cook and Adin's praise, watching the delight on their faces, finally made the events of that evening real. What she could not quite absorb with her own eyes and ears began to sink in as she listened to the men. As she saw the evening through their eyes.

"I forgot to thank you for the advice about the rosewater, Cook. The king mentioned that especially. I did tell him the credit belonged to you."

Cook's pale cheeks colored. She could tell he was pleased, although he waved away her accolade. They all basked in the triumph of the meal for a few moments longer.

She could not delay her ill tidings anymore. Her stomach clenched with dread. "But, Cook, I have some bad news."

"What?"

"The scroll with your recipes. It has disappeared." Her eyes filled with tears. "Before making the final braise, I went to fetch it from its box and found it gone. I have looked everywhere, Cook. It has simply vanished. I will search again tomorrow. But I wanted to tell you myself before you heard it from the others. I am so sorry."

Cook's brow furrowed. "A scroll doesn't just evaporate."

"I know, Cook. I ask your pardon. It must be there somewhere. I never took it out of the kitchen."

Cook's cheeks filled with air. "*You* never took it out, maybe. I bet one of those rascals did."

"The other assistants?"

"They weren't too thrilled to have you in charge, I wager."

"I wouldn't say thrilled. Hathach scared them half to death, though. They did their work."

"Perhaps. But they would have enjoyed seeing you stumble." He frowned. "Didn't you say the scroll disappeared before you started making the third braise?"

"That's right."

"Then how did you make it?"

She pulled on her braid. "I used my own recipe. Well, I modified it a little."

Cook stared at her. "The duck?"

"Yes, Cook."

He huffed a laugh. "Your first meal for the king and you used your own recipe. Wait. Isn't that the dish that won the king's praise? The one he declared had a spark of genius?"

"A *small* spark, Cook."

"I think that's a big enough spark for your first time, girl. Not to mention that your candy recipe rated close to perfection."

"Thank you, Cook. Thank you for trusting me with this responsibility. And please never do that again."

Adin laughed. "She doesn't learn, does she?"

Cook leaned into his pillow. "Very thickheaded."

"Cook, what do I do about your recipes?"

He frowned. "I will send for the meat assistant."

"You think it was him?"

"Never. I took him on when no one would. He may be an annoying toad. But he is *my* toad. If he knows anything, I will get it out of him."

Roxannah chewed her lip. The recipes had been lost while in her possession. She should never have allowed them out of her sight. Even if someone stole them, they did so because of her carelessness. "I am so sorry for the trouble, Cook."

"Yes, well, I'm sorry for your trouble, too."

"What trouble?"

"You're still in charge."

"What?"

"I can't return to the kitchen until this tyrant who calls himself a physician releases me. For now, you stay in charge."

Roxannah groaned. She had barely made it through the king's dinner, and that by virtue of Hathach's threats. The other assistants would surely rebel if she tried to manage the kitchen for weeks on end. "Why don't you ask your meat assistant? Remember how loyal he is?"

"Because he is a second-rate cook. What's the problem? You've already shown you can handle that kitchen."

"I can handle the food. The men are another matter."

"They will learn to respect your place. And if they don't, just tell them they are out on their ear."

She groaned. She wasn't Cook. She couldn't go around threatening people. But she could tell by the obdurate angle of his jaw that he had made his decision and there was no swaying him. She was to remain in charge.

Tomorrow, she would have to face the anger of the assistants again. Somehow, she would have to coax them to cooperate with her.

Cook waved a tired hand. "Out you go, little spark of genius. It's long past my bedtime. The physician says I won't be pretty in the morning if I don't rest enough."

Adin followed her into the courtyard. He lingered silently as though loath to say good-bye. She felt a sudden warmth at the realization. That deep gut knowledge that he didn't want her to leave. He wanted to remain in her company.

It made her smile even wider than the king's compliments had.

37

Adin

He who opens the breach goes up before
  them;
they break through and pass the gate,
going out by it.

Micah 2:13

She had done it! In spite of the lost scroll and the thick-skulled assistants and Amestris's would-be assassin on the loose, Roxannah had managed to make a magnificent dinner that had pleased the king and made Esther's household shine. Adin remembered how, that first evening in Lord Fravartish's chamber, she had not flinched as he had explained the gorier details of tending her father's wound. She had stood her ground.

Here she was, standing again.

He wanted to cheer. He wanted to shower her with accolades. He wanted to hold her and not let go.

"You are right, Adin," she whispered. "God *is* faithful. He helped me with that dinner."

Something in his chest tightened. He had sensed in her the slumberous awakenings of new faith. Underneath the objections, the polite questions, he had seen the hungry way she looked when he prayed. When he spoke about God.

But he couldn't allow her young faith to cling to a false notion of God. "Yes," he said. "He is faithful. And he did help you. Then again, I've learned that God's faithfulness does not always look like success. It doesn't always lead to victory."

Adin knew better. God's faithfulness could also look like Joseph's pit. Like Joseph's yoke of slavery. Like Joseph's wasted years in prison. It was tempting to think of Joseph at the conclusion of his story, arrayed in his rich Egyptian robes, holding the reins of unimaginable power as he saved thousands of lives. It was easy to brush Joseph's crushing years of loss under the carpet of time, as though they had flown by in the blink of an eye.

It was tempting, but it was dangerous. That kind of oversight could break the back of young faith.

God, make me a good ambassador.

"Roxannah, in this world, sometimes God's faithfulness looks like success. Like healing. Like open doors. And sometimes, his faithfulness looks like a pit of suffering. It looks like injustice and pain. Sometimes, God's faithfulness looks like the years the locusts strip to the nub until you feel you have nothing left."

Her eyes widened. Before he could finish, she burst out, "If God's faithfulness is cruel and uncertain, then why should I trust him?"

"You misunderstand me. God's faithfulness can sometimes seem hard. But it's never cruel. God is not Lord Fravartish. Though he may allow tribulation into your life, he never leaves you in that pit, abandoned and alone. Those are the times he draws closest. The times he adds his strength to your bowed-down heart. The times his love is so tender, you can rest against it like a feather pillow.

"You didn't have that experience with your father. The experience of being safe and loved even when the world was one long storm. So, perhaps, it will be hard for you to imagine it now."

She jerked her head down in agreement.

"God is neither a bully nor weak and helpless, Roxannah."

She rubbed her forehead with a tired hand. "Sometimes that is hard to grasp."

"Faith will start your journey to these truths. A journey I sense you have already begun?"

"Yes," she agreed softly.

"Yes." His heart skipped at this simple confirmation. He grinned and kept grinning like a callow youth.

"I believe in God," she said, "but I don't think I understand him as you do."

"To reach the deeper waters of faith, you have to take one step at a time—sometimes a hard, slogging step that is pushed back ten times.

"It takes time for your soul to learn these deeper truths. To learn what your mother could not teach you: that God is an eternal refuge and underneath your life are his everlasting arms, so you don't have to keep charge of your own safety. It takes time to undo what your father *did* teach you: that love can be cruel and cold and uncertain. In time, you will learn that the Lord is worthy of your trust."

Roxannah brought her hands over her chest as though she were cradling her heart. As if she wanted to press his words deep into her inmost being and not let them escape.

He understood how she felt. Understood it with a shock that made him stand rock still, pale as the sails of the ship that had carried him across the waters of the Aegean Sea into Ionia.

The words he had just spoken to Roxannah were not for her

benefit alone. God had hammered them into his own heart with fresh insight.

He had needed them as much as she.

He had come through the storm of Hulda's passing with a new faith and an attachment to the Lord that went to the depths of him. But he had withheld one thing from God. He had decided to keep his own heart safe from another loss. Another sickbed. Another Hulda.

He had closed the doors of his life to the possibility of love and marriage because he could not trust God's faithfulness. Not with his heart.

He exhaled. Instead of forging safety, he had paved his way to loss. He had robbed himself of the possibility of God's blessing.

He stared at Roxannah, at the dear face that had haunted his prayers.

Forgive me, Lord. Breach whatever wall I built in your way.

38

Roxannah

You shall not fear them, for it is the LORD
your God who fights for you.

Deuteronomy 3:22

Roxannah cradled her head in her hands. Around her, chaos ruled. Every counter had a pile of unfinished work: vegetables not peeled; eggs not beaten; meat not chopped; herbs not washed; fire not tended. Sisy moved her sweep around a too-clean floor, the only one actually putting effort into her work.

For the second day in a row, the dinner preparations were unraveling.

It had begun when the Immortal had left Roxannah in the kitchen with a stiff warning not to leave the confines of the building until he returned to collect her in the evening. He had been reassigned to the king's detail when a company of his comrades had come down with some digestive malady, leaving too many holes in the king's protection.

Without him, the unspoken threat of punishment vanished, giving the assistants no compelling motivation to put any effort into their work.

It did not help that Hathach had not come personally to announce Cook's decision to leave Roxannah in charge. Instead, he sent a letter. A puny scroll that hardly captured the growl in his commands or the fire in his eyes.

No Hathach. No Immortal. No order in the kitchen.

The assistants had pranced about like mischievous children, paying Roxannah no mind at all. She had managed the morning meals with Halpa's assistance. The lunches had been a stretch. Not only did the assistants refuse to help, they made sure they were underfoot at every turn. They grew more meddlesome and harder to manage with each meal.

But tonight's dinner had become impossible. They had misplaced her tools. Dropped her washed vegetables. Doused her fire. She had gone from six dishes to three and barely managed those.

Esther was eating with her handmaidens and Hathach tonight. A meal for nine, plus leftovers for family and staff. Roxannah had devised a plan for nine different dishes, plus desserts. Two hours before service, and all she had was one dessert and one soup.

"Please," she told the meat assistant, "I need you to start the lamb."

"I started it already. Not my fault these walls are so puny. A piece of brick fell into the water."

The men howled.

"You were supposed to start a second pot."

"I'm getting to it."

"Where are the soaked chickpeas?"

The vegetable assistant shrugged. "I thought you were preparing those."

"You never soaked them?"

She felt sick. Even if the legumes cooked in time, without proper soaking they might cause stomach pain. She had to scrap that dish.

"Sisy, please set aside your sweep and cut these onions." They wouldn't be even-sized. Sisy could peel onions, but her cutting skills left something to be desired, which meant the onions would be half cooked if she wanted to prevent the other half from burning. But at least she would have something.

She went to fetch the eggs. The dairy assistant slammed a hand in her way, making her jump back. "Get out of my way, woman. This is my counter."

She wanted to scream at him. To put him in his place. Instead she kept her mouth firmly closed. She would work around him. She would work around all of them.

But they made it impossible.

By dinner time, Roxannah had swallowed so many tears, her throat felt raw. She could not manage these men. She could not take charge of this kitchen. Cook was dreaming.

And now she would have to serve the queen one soup, two meager half-baked dishes, and one dessert. At least Halpa had made enough bread that morning to ensure the queen and her companions would not go hungry.

Roxannah sent the dishes with the servers and collapsed on her stool. She had survived the king's dinner only to bungle everything now. Esther would send her packing.

She sighed and disappeared behind Cook's curtain. Dragging off her work tunic, she put on the pretty blue and cream robe that Esther had given her. She knew she would be summoned, though it would be for a very different reason than the last time.

Tonight, the queen would dismiss her.

She would have to return home in shame. She would have to confess to her mother that she had failed. She had failed to meet the high standards of the court. She had failed at her job. She would have to tell her mother that they would lose their home.

In the stormy wail of her fears, Adin's words came like a whisper. *"Sometimes, his faithfulness looks like a pit of suffering."*

If Adin was right, if God's faithfulness didn't mean that life came wrapped in a net of safety, protected from pits and prisons and loss, then perhaps God's faithfulness was with her in this moment. In this shame. In this failure. She wasn't alone in it. He was with her to help her through the next hour. The next day. The next year.

Adin had told her that these were the times God drew closest. The times he added his strength to her bowed-down heart.

The thought quieted her. It shut the mouth of the roaring fear.

When the serving girl arrived to fetch her, Roxannah rose, her heart composed, her back straight.

The men snickered. The sound of their laughter shook her for a moment. It reminded her too much of the power they had wielded over her.

Then she remembered. Even this failure could serve as a thread in God's faithful weaving if she allowed it.

The junior handmaiden did not even bother to comb her hair or spray her with perfume. Wordlessly, she accompanied her into Esther's formal chamber and walked out. Esther waved everyone from the room.

She seemed all queen tonight. The gracious friend had disappeared behind a curtain of royal formality. "I am disappointed. You served us a small disaster on a tray tonight."

Roxannah flushed. "Your pardon, my queen. I am so ashamed."

"Well? Explain to me how the woman who made that heavenly meal for the king served me this one tonight."

"I tried to tell Cook. I am not qualified to have charge of your kitchens, lady."

"No?" She arched her perfect brow. "We know you can cook.

304

We know you can create delicious flavors and beautiful feasts that impress even the king's choosy palate. What is it you cannot do?"

"A royal kitchen has many cooks, my queen. It's not enough to know how to prepare food. You must lead others. You have to inspire them to follow you."

Esther narrowed her eyes. "You imagine I don't know that? What do you think? I became queen the moment they set the fluted tiara upon my head? I may have gained the title that day, but I had to earn my position. I had to learn to lead. A nobody commoner sitting on the throne. I had to inspire men and women to look on me as worthy of that honor."

"Everything about you inspires loyalty, Your Majesty. You were born to be queen."

"Rubbish! I was born an ordinary Jewish girl. My lineage is lower than yours. I *learned* to be queen, and you can learn to have charge over a handful of donkey-headed men. There are greater rascals in the king's court than there are in my kitchens, let me tell you."

Roxannah exhaled. How could she make this woman understand the differences between them? "I do not have half your strength, lady."

Some of the formality drained from Esther's expression. She patted a stool with a fat cushion next to her. "Come. Come and sit by me."

Gingerly, Roxannah obeyed. If she were to lose everything, at least she would do it on a comfortable seat.

"I have inquired about your family. I know about your father. Lord Fravartish loved his wine a little too much, I understand."

Roxannah pulled the sleeves of her undertunic over her knuckles, hiding bruises that were no longer there. There was no place to hide from her past. Not even in the queen's peacock-blue chamber.

Esther patted her half-hidden hand. "There is nothing in

that to shame you, my dear. Though I grew up with a loving and gentle man who became father and mother to me, I know a little something about what wine can do to a man. How a man turns to the ruby contents of his cup to find strength and instead finds only weakness. I know how a man may try to find a hiding place in the depths of his chalice and instead only finds the worst of himself exposed. I know the frustration and anger that bubbles out of these discoveries. I have not suffered your bruises. But I have tasted the disappointments that a wine-soaked life can bring."

The king! She was speaking of the king.

The heartbreak of loving a man who, like her father, had turned to fermented grape in hopes of discovering a remedy for his pain. Xerxes might not beat Esther as Roxannah's father had done her. But his brutality revealed itself in different ways—in thoughtless edicts and rash decisions that harmed the lives of those he should protect.

She had little in common with Esther. Yet, in a strange way, the queen understood her better than any friend she had ever had. She did not judge her or her family because Esther understood what it meant to live with a man who had come to the end of himself and seen the worst reflected back at him.

Except that the king also knew how to rise from the ashes of his failure. He had done everything in his power to help the Jewish people in his kingdom once he had understood Haman's perfidy. He had tried to reverse the damage he had caused. He did what he could to protect Esther from Haman and Amestris and a thousand wagging tongues that meant her ill.

The king was not her father. He was stronger. He still knew how to hold on to love. How to bend to the weight of responsibility. He was by no means perfect. But he tried, in spite of his flaws, to shield those he loved.

And yet, she thought, he would have understood Lord Fravartish the way Esther understood Roxannah.

"Little cook." Esther patted her hand again. "You can allow your father to rule you for the rest of your life. Or you can rise from under his shadow. I tell you again, you can run my kitchen. You can stand up to those sniveling assistants. They don't have a fraction of your talent. But you must learn they are not your father. You must stop acting as if they are."

Roxannah blinked. Is that what she had been doing? Avoiding every possible confrontation because that was the pattern she had learned with Lord Fravartish?

"They are merely scared little boys, afraid of being bested. Stubborn men who do not know their place." She grinned. "You have to show it to them." She reached behind her and picked up a bundle wrapped in gold-embroidered red linen. "This arrived for you. From the king."

Roxannah gasped. "The king sent me a token?"

"Yes. And you had better take it, or I shall be tempted to keep it myself. He is a man of elegant tastes."

Roxannah felt something rounded and heavy within the cloth's folds. Slowly, she unwrapped the linen, revealing a single chalice, exquisitely wrought from pure gold and decorated at the base with a swan's head. The swan's eye winked with a single blue stone.

Roxannah pressed a trembling hand against her lips. The king had presented her with a royal gift!

Upon rare occasions, the Persian royals had a custom of bestowing their most faithful or talented retainers with a generous gift. Not practical, commonplace items, such as the sheep the queen had given her. Rather, a more luxurious offering that conferred upon its receiver a sign of the king's highest favor.

The king's favored officials sometimes received pieces of priceless jewelry, woven garments, even horses with a longer and more noble lineage than Roxannah's. Royal magnanimity was not reserved for the higher classes, however. She had once heard of a gardener who had received a gold necklace for turning a plain wilderness into a flower-drenched haven. Cook had received a silver platter and a small gold chalice from the king, items he displayed in the kitchen with great pride.

Roxannah shook her head. Against all reason, against all possibility, the king had presented her with the mark of his honor. The last piece of her impossible dream falling into place.

She clutched the cup painfully. "Does this mean you are not dismissing me?"

"Not today," Esther said dryly. "Tomorrow is up to you."

For most of her life, one man had told her that she was useless and incapable. That nothing she did was worthy of his approval.

The golden cup told a different story.

It said that a king disagreed with her father's assessment. The ruler of two-thirds of the known world thought her gifted. Worthy of his special favor.

Now she had to decide whose voice she would listen to. Whose voice shaped her world.

Against every expectation, she had not landed in a pit. Somehow, God had turned the threads of her failure into a precious moment of redemption.

She did not want to waste this grace.

39

Adin

And keep their hearts loyal to you.
1 Chronicles 29:18 NIV

How is Cook?" The queen placed her fan in her lap and sat perfectly still, as if the smallest breath of air might break something in her.

"He is better, my lady." It was the first day Adin had felt comfortable leaving his patient for several hours without worrying about a relapse.

Her shoulders relaxed. "The king's chamberlain informs me that the palace in Ecbatana is finally ready for occupation. The king is impatient to be on the road in one week. The court has already been packing in preparation of this news. I expect we will all be more than ready by then. Can Cook accompany us?"

Adin contemplated the question. "No, my queen. It would

309

put too much strain on his still-fragile body. Even if he does no work, the rigors of travel might prove too much. I suggest he remain here for the summer to recuperate."

He hesitated. Leaving Cook to his own devices for months at a time would probably lead to trouble. "Also, you may wish to consider leaving one of your women with him. He might not acknowledge it, but he still needs help. It will have to be someone with a backbone. Cook is bound to ride roughshod over anyone who doesn't have an iron will."

Esther gave her junior handmaiden a considering look. "I think I know just the person."

"He will not like it."

"Most of us have to live with things we do not like," she said dryly. "It is called adulthood."

Adin grinned. "I will tell him you said so."

"Yes. Do add insult to his injury. No doubt he will accuse me of giving him a nursemaid." She took up her fan and gave it a vigorous shake, making the colorful crystals glint in the light. "Any updates from the affair with Amestris?"

Adin had had to neglect his promise to look for the conspirator in the Apadana. Amestris's concerns had to wait while Cook's life had hung in the balance. He would have to remedy that now that Cook was growing stronger.

He realized he'd had no opportunity to update Esther on his latest conversation with Amestris. "I have much to tell you about the princess, my lady."

Esther jerked on her seat when Adin revealed Amestris's suspicion that the king's fall was no accident. "She believes it was an attempt on his life?"

"She has no proof. I suspect that is why she has not tried to alert the king of her misgivings. She would look foolish if proven wrong."

"Still, I best warn my lord to increase his guard. I will compose a letter to his . . ." She let the sentence dwindle. "I cannot, can I?"

"Not until we know who is behind this plot. Your letter might fall into the wrong hands. The people we think his closest friends and allies may prove false. Whomever wants to kill Amestris occupies a high position—very high indeed if he has access to the king's horse. Any letter of warning you compose could prompt him into taking rash action. The king is safe for now, in any case. With the book in Amestris's possession, Xerxes poses no threat to the assassin. It's the contents of that book that our conspirator wants hidden."

She nodded slowly. "That is why Amestris took it. She is trying to protect him."

"By placing herself in mortal danger. That was my thought. Although when she first took the book, she had no idea it would stir such a hornet's nest. She felt more curious than truly concerned. It wasn't until we overheard the plot that she realized how volatile a matter she had embroiled herself in."

"As much as I hate to admit it, Amestris has her good traits. She is fiercely loyal to Xerxes. In this, I trust her."

"But why not simply tell the king what she knows and let him read the book for himself? He seems to be the one person who can solve this mystery."

Esther's face pinched. "Who do you think she suspects?"

"Someone very close to the king?" Adin's heart skipped a beat. "Someone very close to *her*?"

Esther sighed. "The king's inner circle of trusted men grows ever smaller. I could name four, perhaps five, men who have easy access to him. Two of them are related to Amestris."

"Her father and her brother."

"Precisely. She would have to betray them to shield Xerxes. And if she brings them down, she may bring herself down. Family ties speak loudly at court."

"That's an impossible position." Who could navigate such an internal war? Then he realized that Roxannah had had to make a similar decision and, in the end, had chosen him. His chest expanded.

"Impossible, yes." Esther slapped her fan against her palm. "But she is doing what she can to protect him. She keeps him safe as long as she holds on to the book. For now, the danger remains only to herself."

"What happens if she discovers her father or brother are at the bottom of this? What if they both are?"

The tension drained from Esther's face. "She will place the king above them. Why else try to uncover the plot herself? I think she wants to present the king with the identity of the guilty man, even if that man is closely related to her. By being the one who reveals the plot, she might be able to prove her own innocence. She might even win Xerxes's favor for the depth of her loyalty."

Esther's lips softened. She bent toward Adin. "You better do all you can to help her succeed."

"For the king's sake?"

"And for hers. If she brings an end to this plot, she will gain the king's respect even more than she already has. That is a gift she can treasure. We should help her gain it if we can."

Adin stared at Esther. "Lady, it is my honor to serve you."

40

Roxannah

Rise up; this matter is in your hands. We will support you, so take courage and do it.

Ezra 10:4 NIV

Roxannah arrived at the kitchen so early, she supposed even Halpa must still be dreaming in his bed. Her Immortal sat in one corner, trying to keep his eyes open. He would leave her as soon as Halpa arrived.

She stood at her counter, reverently setting the king's gift before her. Opening the folds of red fabric, she withdrew the golden cup.

The goldsmith had polished the curves of pure metal so smooth that her reflection looked back at her with eerie clarity. Curls subdued in a severe braid tucked at the nape of her neck, eyes grey as a rainy day, mouth wobbly and unsure.

She had a decision to make. Would she listen to the tale told by this gold cup, or would she believe the story that ran in her blood, born of countless lies spoken by a broken man?

Today, she had to earn her place the way Esther had learned to earn her crown.

The Immortal whistled next to her ear. "Is that what I think it is?"

She couldn't hide the twitch of a smile. "From the king."

He shook his head. "I am in the wrong business."

She extended a fat, juicy onion his way. "Be my guest."

He held up his hands and turned away with a shiver, making her laugh.

Returning her attention to the golden cup for a moment, she placed it on a small shelf above her head, where she could see it as she worked. She fetched the bowl of sour cherries Sisy had pitted the night before. They would make a lovely jam for the queen's breakfast.

As the sour cherries simmered gently with honey, she turned her attention to the apples. The queen liked sweet dishes. Roxannah planned to make a date and raisin omelet, using the apples that had been preserved in the deep cellars of the palace since the previous autumn. They were a bit wrinkly and thick-skinned. But cooked in butter, they would taste fine.

She dropped the apple peels and seeds into the jam to help thicken its juice. Nothing went to waste in her kitchen.

She prepared the sweet mixture for the egg dish, keeping an eye on the jam at the same time as stirring the apples frying in butter. When they turned golden brown, she added the dates and raisins with a pinch of cinnamon and set the mixture aside. All that remained was to beat the eggs and add them to the mixture just before serving so that they would be fresh and warm for the queen.

The jam had come together nicely, and after picking out the apple peel and seeds, she set it aside to cool.

Halpa came to stand next to her. His eye caught sight of the golden cup. "From the king?"

"Everyone worked hard. It's for all of us, really."

Halpa rolled up his sleeves. "No, it's not. It's for you. All of us did what we always do. You added the special touch."

The Immortal came to his feet. "My shift starts soon. Don't step out of this kitchen by yourself. I'll return to fetch you tonight." She grabbed a leftover piece of bread from the evening before and threw it at him. "Don't break your neck on an empty stomach."

He caught the square of tumbling bread in the air and took a bite of his cold breakfast. "Not up to your usual standard."

"What is, these days?"

She joined Halpa, who was working the bread dough. "It's a new day, Halpa."

"Looks that way."

"Let's make something spectacular."

"I'd settle for edible."

Roxannah's brows rose when the meat assistant walked in. It was still an hour before the assistants normally arrived. The man had dark circles under his eyes.

"Need to talk to you," he mumbled under his breath.

Roxannah wiped her hands on a rag. "Yes?"

"I had nothing to do with it."

"With what?" she said, alarmed.

"I didn't agree with what they did."

"What are we talking about?"

"I told them they were going too far."

Roxannah held very still. "What did they do?"

"They took Cook's recipes."

"Do you know where they are?"

He jerked his chin down.

"Oh please, will you show them to me? Cook shouldn't suffer because you want to punish me."

"Told you. I had nothing to do with this."

"Right. Will you help me get his recipes back? Before the others arrive?"

315

"That's what I'm trying to do, isn't it?" he snapped. He led her behind Cook's screen. "Cook keeps a hidey-hole here. He thinks nobody knows about it. But we have all seen it a dozen times." In the ground, he dug his fingers into the narrow seam of a stone. It buckled up. Underneath, she saw a neat rectangular chamber. Cook's scroll lolled in the middle like a baby resting in its crib.

She snatched it out of its hole. "It's not damaged!"

"Of course not. They were just trying to make trouble for you. They aren't stupid enough to destroy Cook's property. It would be more than their life is worth."

"You have my eternal gratitude."

"Didn't do it for you."

"I know. You did it for Cook. Now I can put his mind at ease, which means you have my thanks whether you want it or not." She cradled the scroll against her, afraid to allow it out of her sight for even a moment.

"Halpa, how is the bread for breakfast coming?" she asked.

"Headed to the ovens to bake it now. Made you an extra loaf of sweet saffron bread. Will taste good with your eggs."

"You are my hero."

The meat assistant pointed a finger at the gold cup. "That's not Cook's."

"No."

His eyes bulged. "For you? From the king?"

She gave him a cool look. "A gift in appreciation for the dinner."

The large Adam's apple bobbed in his throat a few times.

This was it. The moment she could gain an ally or lose one. The moment she established her authority or lost it. The moment she listened to the whispers of the cup or the bellows of her father.

She cleared her throat. She wanted to sound menacing like Hathach. She wanted to sound self-assured like the queen. She wanted to sound confident like Cook. Instead, her voice wavered, girlish and small.

"This is what happens when we band together." She pointed at the cup. "When we work as a unified crew. This is what we are capable of." The more she spoke, the stronger her voice grew. "This cup proves that together, this kitchen can be great enough to best the king's own cooks."

She squared her shoulders and whispered a silent prayer. "Now you have to decide what you want. Because you only have one choice. Either you work with me, or you don't work at all. Not in the queen's kitchen."

The meat assistant looked at her blankly. "You can't do that."

"I can. That's what Cook means when he says I am in charge. Your behavior—yours and the rest of the assistants—has not been disrespectful to me alone. You have disrespected Cook, who made the decision in the first place. And you have disrespected the queen, who has had to eat your handiwork. I might put up with what you do to me. But I will not put up with that."

She pointed to the gold cup again. "You can be a part of *that*. You can help me create great things. Or you can leave. Consider carefully before you choose."

His mouth had come loose at some point during her speech and hung open now as though he had lost the power to speak.

She waved the fat recipe scroll under his nose. "I am going to return this to Cook. I want to set his heart at ease."

She did not wait to see what he thought of her speech. Instead, she grabbed the king's cup and its cover and scrambled outside, desperate to get away for a short time. Her heart pounded in her ears. She felt half sick and half elated.

She had faced him down! She had not run away. She had not hidden. She had stood her ground.

By the time she arrived at Cook's chamber, she could almost breathe again. He was alone, writing on his ever-present scrap of papyrus. She placed the recipes carefully on his blanket.

"Look what I have for you. Whatever you said to the meat assistant worked. He showed up this morning insisting that he had nothing to do with its theft and showed me where they had concealed it."

Cook unrolled the scroll to ensure nothing was missing. "Where had those sons of darkness hidden my recipes?"

"Your little hidey-hole."

Cook gawped. "How could they know about it?"

"They have all seen you use it, Cook. Apparently you are not as stealthy as you think."

"What does a great cook need with stealth? I have better things to do with my time." He pointed at the red package in her hand. "Something else you want to show me?"

Carefully, Roxannah unfolded the red linen. "From the king. For the dinner."

Cook reached out to touch the cup reverently. Softly, he started to laugh. "Well." And then as if he could think of nothing else to say, he repeated, "Well." He looked up, and his sensible, shrewd eyes held a sheen of tears. "I'm proud of you, girl."

Roxannah's throat ached from holding back a sob. Her chest nearly punctured with the pressure of something trying to claw its way free.

Joy.

Cook had said the very words she had once dreamed her father would say. She felt as if God had put those words in Cook's mouth, as if God wanted her to know that this was what he had always meant for her to have. "Thanks, Cook. For everything."

He coughed and cleared his throat. "Enough with the blubbering."

She gave a watery laugh.

"You have a lot of work to do." He turned the scroll of recipes over in his hands. "You still need this."

"I was thinking perhaps I can copy one or two every evening

to use on the following day. That way, if any of them is damaged or stolen, at least the originals will be safe with you."

"One or two won't do you much good. Court is leaving in a week. You'll have to stay up all night and copy the whole lot. And before you ask, no, I'm not going to Ecbatana."

Roxannah rocked back. "You're not coming? You're not coming at all? I mean, not back to work in the kitchen. You need your rest, I understand. But won't you come just to be with us?"

"That physician friend of yours won't allow it. He and the queen have colluded together and forced a nursemaid on me over the summer months." He sighed. "She's that handmaiden who's in charge of you and Sisy. The one who looks like a griffin."

"The junior handmaiden? She's not so bad. And you shouldn't call her a griffin. She's quite attractive in her way."

"Whatever you say."

Roxannah put her head in her hands. "Now I won't even be able to visit you and ask for your counsel. Is it my job to oversee the packing of the kitchen?"

"Who else? You think Hathach is going to do it?" He gave a raspy laugh before handing her a scrap of papyrus. "Here is a list of what you have to pack. The kitchen in the palace at Ecbatana is well-stocked. You only need enough implements for the weeks you'll be on the road."

"And how long did you say that would be again?"

"About forty days."

"*Forty* days? But Ecbatana isn't that far!"

"The direct route contains too many narrow tracks and dangerous precipices. The lumbering baggage carts cannot manage the terrain. They have to stick to the royal road." He shrugged. "The younger courtiers and military officers often go directly across the mountains and arrive in nine days. The rest of the court goes in stages, crossing into the Babylonian plain, and then north, before heading back east through the Zagros Mountains."

"But that's like putting on your shoes by way of your hat. Why do they go so far west before heading north and east again?"

"The royal engineers neglected to explain themselves to me. All I know is that you have to prepare as sumptuous a meal while you travel as you do when you cook in the queen's kitchens."

Roxannah studied Cook's list and added packing to her growing responsibilities. Oddly, she did not feel overwhelmed by the thought of preparing meals while traveling. Their kitchen at home had been so basic that it was not unlike cooking in a camp. She knew she could cope with that challenge.

But whether she remained in the well-stocked cookhouses of Susa or set off on the royal highway for a forty-day tramp through the countryside, she needed the assistants. Running the queen's kitchen had never been a one-person undertaking, and it had just grown even more complex.

41

For you have delivered my soul from death,
yes, my feet from falling.

Psalm 56:13

Outside Cook's building, she lingered long enough to take a deep breath and compose herself for the coming confrontations. She had spoken to the meat assistant. She had to pit her will against three more men.

The thought curdled her stomach. But it also caused an unfamiliar thrill of excitement. She thought of the way she had stood up to the meat assistant. It had felt good! It had felt right. It had felt, oddly, like victory.

She took a step on the path and stopped. She had left the kitchen forgetting to arrange for accompaniment. The Immortal would skin her alive if he found out.

There was no help for it now. She would have to return on her own. But when she reached the crossroads that intersected one of the main arteries of the palace, she realized she had left the king's gift in Cook's room. She would have to go back to fetch it. Turning half a revolution, she froze.

A richly dressed man with a sharp, straight nose and bushy

eyebrows that poked out of his stern face was strolling in the opposite direction as a servant tripped behind, waving a giant ostrich fan to cool him. An ordinary sight in a palace teeming with rich aristocrats and courtiers. Nothing to send chills down her back.

Except that she recognized him. He was the man from the river.

She winced. She didn't even have Sisy for company. Perhaps she ought to simply go and fetch her cup and get on with work. Forget him.

Still, her feet lagged. Would Esther want her to follow? Would God?

Oh, where was that iron-jawed Immortal when she needed him? Or, better yet, Adin?

Lord God, remind me to have a chat about your timing one day.

She whipped around, tucked the packing list into a small pocket inside her wide belt, and followed the richly dressed man. She lagged as far behind as she dared without losing her quarry. This time, he did not enter the Apadana. Instead, he headed for the storerooms of the Royal Treasury. Another impossible place for her to enter.

But he had marked himself by this location. It was not nearly so crowded as the Apadana. Amestris would surely be able to pry his name out of the guards in her usual persuasive manner.

Roxannah huffed an irritated breath. The sun was rising. Although she had most of the elements of the queen's breakfast ready, she still wanted to return before the assistants had time to make mischief. Then again, she could not rest easy until she had done her duty by the princess.

And by God.

In the undersecretary's cubicle, Roxannah was relieved to see the familiar figure of Amestris's senior handmaiden.

"I need to see the duksis. Urgently, if you please."

The handmaiden motioned at the undersecretary to put his

roster away and wordlessly led Roxannah past the sleepy palace guard into Amestris's chamber.

This early in the morning, the audience room looked like a fallow field. At the sight of Roxannah, the duksis dismissed two handmaidens who were laying out her shoes and cloak.

Her brows knotted in a thunderous frown. "Do you know the hour?"

"Pardon the inconvenient time, Duksis. But I saw one of the plotters just now. With haste, you might be able to discover his identity."

"I thought only the physician had seen his face."

"When we overheard them by the river, that was the case. But later, when we pursued the man, I caught a glimpse of his profile, and I recognized him this morning."

"Where did he go?" Her voice snapped like a whip.

"Into the Royal Treasury."

Amestris made a silent gesture to the senior handmaiden, and she slipped to the back of the room. Behind them, half the wall yawned open. The secret door that Adin had mentioned! The handmaiden stole out like a cat, not making a sound, and the door whispered shut behind her, its seams vanishing into the wall once more.

"Now," the princess said to Roxannah, "describe him for me." Roxannah did her best. But Amestris could not identify him.

"We'll do better with the guards of the Treasury—" Amestris left her sentence hanging when Onophas stepped into the chamber through the secret entrance and swung the door shut behind him. Amestris's eyes widened. "What do you want here?"

Roxannah wondered at Amestris's jarred expression. Onophas was always coming and going in these apartments.

Then she saw the glint of metal in his manicured hands.

Onophas was holding a dagger.

Amestris rose from her chair in a smooth motion. Roxannah watched in horror as Onophas lunged.

Over a decade of dodging and hiding, of running away and calculating escape routes, made good training for such a moment. Time slowed, flowing with the leisurely pace of marsh mallow syrup.

Roxannah shoved Amestris. Hard. The princess stumbled and fell face-first just as Onophas was about to reach her. The fall saved her life. But it also knocked her out.

Onophas turned his attention to Roxannah. "Why couldn't you stay out of it?" he cried.

Roxannah feinted to the right but leapt left and, dropping on all fours, scrambled behind the golden chair. Onophas followed. She knocked the chair down into his path and screamed at the top of her lungs.

This early in the morning, the hallway outside might be deserted. But there should at least be one palace guard out there. Unless Onophas had managed to send him on a wild-goose chase. The palace guards were in the habit of following the eunuch's directives. They were unlikely to suspect him of foul play.

Amestris moaned and started to rise. Onophas shifted back toward her. She made an easier target, still unsteady and weak from her fall. She would be like a lamb waiting for the slaughter.

God, help me!

Roxannah grabbed Amestris's silk-embroidered pillow from the floor and swung at Onophas's head with all her might. His neck snapped back from the force of the swing. He stumbled backward but managed to steady himself with a quick step.

"Leave her be!" Roxannah yelled. *Surely someone has to hear this commotion!*

The eunuch growled and turned back toward Roxannah, leaving Amestris once again. For a moment, the world stood still as his dagger, long and narrow, glinting silver in the lamplight, swiped malevolently. At the last moment, she shoved the pillow in front of her.

The dagger ripped through silk and priceless embroidery. If

the strike had been head-on, it would have killed her. But because the eunuch had slashed at her sideways, the thick expanse of feathers within saved her life.

Fat white feathers rained around them, dancing prettily in the air, as if they were engaged in a childish pillow fight rather than a battle for life. Onophas roared like a frustrated child.

Roxannah dove for the golden table behind her, crawling underneath. The eunuch ignored her and, whirling, headed for Amestris instead. Roxannah slithered back from under the table and grabbed the only thing she could reach: his ankle. She pulled with all her might, and he stumbled. Then, recovering his balance, he kicked viciously. His foot caught her in the chest and the chin. She could not breathe. Her vision went black. But she clung on to that ankle with all her might.

Swearing, Onophas turned back to her, kicking and squirming until she felt her hold loosening. Roxannah cried out, her throat hoarse. "Run, Duksis!"

Amestris did not.

Instead, she retrieved her own dagger from some hidden pocket in her ruched skirts. Though the handle displayed delicate, bejeweled carvings, the blade was all business. Onophas was still turned around, preoccupied with Roxannah. He missed death coming.

Without hesitation, Amestris sank her dagger into the eunuch's back. His eyes widened. An odd burbling sound came from somewhere deep in his belly. Like an axed tree, he toppled, missing Roxannah by a handsbreadth.

Amestris knelt by his side. "Who? Tell me who sent you."

"Forgive . . . Duksis." The deep voice had become thready.

"His name?"

"He has my nephew." A shivering breath, hard won from a ravaged chest. "Said he would kill him if I did not obey."

"Who?" Amestris screamed. But it was too late. The eunuch was about to answer a higher authority than that of the princess.

Roxannah came to her feet. Her knees shook. Her hands trembled. Her mouth quivered. "Are you harmed, Duksis?" Her voice emerged half-choked.

Amestris drew a hand down the side of her face, where a long bruise showed an angry red. "You saved my life." She looked to the door. "Where are the palace guards? Why did they not come to my aid?"

She took three long strides, her back rigid. When she reached for the door, Roxannah noticed that her hand shook violently. So, she was human after all.

"Guard!" she bellowed.

A young servant dashed into the hall. At the sight of Amestris, hands and tunic spattered with blood, she froze, forgetting to bow.

"Fetch me those imbeciles who call themselves palace guards. I don't care where you have to go to find them. Now! Understand?"

"Yes, lady." The girl sprinted off. She must have known exactly where to find the princess's guards, because within moments, they were crowding inside Amestris's audience chamber.

Roxannah slithered out of the room while the princess screamed at the guards. The woman's tongue clearly matched her dagger's sharpness. Fortunately, she was too busy to notice Roxannah beating a hasty retreat.

42

Adin

Behold, you are beautiful, my love.

Song of Solomon 4:1

The sun had dawned golden-red in the eastern sky as Adin emerged from Cook's building clutching Roxannah's royal gift. Cook had shown it to him, looking as proud as if he had earned it himself. "Return this to the girl," he said. "Can you believe she forgot it here? She'll be too busy to come and fetch it herself."

Adin stretched, wincing. In spite of sleeping in his own bed the night before, he still had a sore back, courtesy of the evenings spent on Cook's floor.

Last night, he had finally returned home. He smiled at the remembered pleasure of his well-stuffed mattress and soft pillows. The recent years had spoilt him with the comforts of home and the luxuries of the court.

His wry smile froze at the sight of the limping figure walking toward the kitchens. The droop of her shoulders gave her a forlorn air. What was Roxannah doing, traipsing about on her own at this hour? Had she forgotten she was still in danger?

"Roxannah!" He sprang toward her before he had time to form a single thought.

She came to an abrupt halt when she saw him. Then, without a word, she catapulted herself against him.

At the feel of her shaking body, something unraveled in him. Fear and tenderness collided in his chest. Of their own accord, his arms wrapped around her, pulling her into him. "Roxannah. What is it, my dear?" The endearment rolled off his tongue without his permission.

She shivered against him, her skin cold in spite of the film of perspiration on her brow. He drew her more tightly to him. "Are you hurt?" The words scraped out of him like a burr on his tongue.

"No." He felt the slight move of her head against him.

Thank you, God! The knot of terror loosened a little. He caressed the lush ridges of the braid hanging down her back, his fingers not quite steady.

She drew her head back to look at him. Her eyes held a hint of something wild. "Adin, Onophas tried to kill Amestris."

"The eunuch?" Part of him had no interest in Onophas or Amestris. They could take their troubles and jump together into the Karkheh River for all he cared at that precise moment. Another part of him registered her meaning and went rigid. "While you were there? In her chamber?"

She nodded. "Not half an hour ago. He snuck into her audience hall through that secret passage you told me about."

His hands tightened spasmodically around her. "What were you doing in Amestris's audience chamber so early in the morning?"

She bit her lip. "After I dropped off Cook's recipes, I saw the man. The one we chased to the Apadana that day."

"Wait. You recognized him?"

"What with you looking after Cook and me busy in the kitchen, it plain went out of my mind to tell you that I had seen him the day we chased him. This morning, I followed him to the Royal Treasury."

A knife of fear stabbed him as she described her morning's adventures. "You could have been killed! Where is that Immortal Esther assigned you?"

"He has another job during the day. I was supposed to stay put in the kitchen until he came to fetch me this evening. Only, I forgot."

"You *forgot*?" The words burst out of him, fierce as the desert wind. "What do you mean you forgot?"

"I mean my memory suffered a minor lapse when I ran to return Cook's recipes to him." One small dimple emerged like the sun from a bank of clouds. "Don't tell my mother."

"Your mother is the least of your problems." He slipped his hand around hers and held on like a drowning man to a line. "I am not going to let you out of my sight for a while."

"What about Cook?"

"He no longer needs my constant attention. But you must promise never to go unattended again, not until we get to the bottom of this enigma."

To his relief, she did not argue. "If I hurry, I can still arrive in time to make a decent breakfast for the queen."

Adin's brow knotted in thought as they walked. "What I don't understand is why Onophas attacked Amestris the way he did. It seems like an act of desperation, unplanned and messy. Not like Onophas at all."

"I think the undersecretary reported to him that I had gone to see Amestris. I'm guessing he eavesdropped on our conversation, which provoked him into taking rash action. He knew that the princess would be able to identify at least one of the men in the plot." She fisted a hand. "Do you think we may be close to solving this mystery, Adin? I am ready for an end to this benighted affair."

He pressed her hand. Her legs were not steady as she leaned into him all the way to the kitchen. He was barely starting to bring the thrumming of his own heart under control.

"I will find Hathach and ask for an audience. You must report to the queen as soon as possible. Esther should know what happened."

Roxannah gave a small nod. He tightened his hold on her hand, drawing her closer to his side. Holding up the linen-covered bundle she had missed in the excitement of running into him, he said, "Your royal gift, mistress. You left it at Cook's." He grinned as he handed it to her. "So. An assistant in three months, a royal gift, and now the savior of a princess. What great feat have you planned next?"

Her cheeks turned the exact shade of pink that was fast becoming his favorite color. "I would be happy if I can make an edible breakfast for the queen."

He laughed. As fear banked, gratitude welled up. God had preserved her.

More. God had used her. Her courage had saved Amestris.

It dawned on him that she had won something beyond her safety in this battle. The daughter of Lord Fravartish had not run. She had faced an angry man armed with a dagger and saved Amestris by choosing to fight.

He gave her a sidelong glance. Her color remained high, her hair in wild disarray, her tunic askew. He had never found her so beautiful.

He wasn't won over by the curve of her jaw or the delicate turn of her lips or the luminescence of her complexion. It was the woman inside who shone through like a shaft of light.

Her beauty came from the courage to stand when everything said she should fall. From the joy that rose out of her depths, refusing to be conquered by her past. From the way she chose the good, the best, the honest.

From the first day he had met her, he had been drawn to her. He realized now that the pesky attraction he had fought with all his strength had always gone deeper than skin and bones. From the beginning, what he felt for her had been more than he had been willing to admit. More than a passing desire.

He had always been drawn to the woman she was. The lady who spoke with the regal accents of the gentry and had the rough hands of a servant. The woman who laid down her life to care for her mother and provide for her fractured family. The friend who sacrificed her heart to keep him from harm.

He had been a fool to try and deny it.

He loved the daughter of Lord Fravartish.

43

Roxannah

> You guide me with your counsel.
> Psalm 73:24

Having Adin at her side, his large hand wrapped tightly around hers, set the world to rights somehow. She felt like she could breathe again. Like she could face the next hour. She leaned into the solid strength of him and exhaled.

Tomorrow, when she was capable of clear thought, she would no doubt turn scarlet with mortification. But for now, it did not matter that she had thrown herself into his arms. It did not matter that she had pressed against him as they walked to the kitchen. It only mattered that he was here. And he seemed to be holding on to her with the same insistence as she clung to him.

At the door, Adin said, "I will return as soon as I have had a chance to talk to Hathach and check on Cook. Try not to make any trouble while I'm gone."

She shrugged. "Can't promise."

"I know." He let go of her hand and waited until she entered the kitchen. Her chest squeezed at the look in his eyes—half tender and half fierce, like he might crush anyone who dared to harm her.

She caught the assistants studying the golden cup as she placed it on the shelf. The sight of it had certainly snagged their curiosity. She hoped it was enough to keep them out of trouble for a few hours. After the events in Amestris's apartments, she did not have the strength for another wretched confrontation.

She whisked a bowlful of eggs, expending the anxious energy that still coursed through her body after wrestling with Onophas and almost dying. She stiffened when the meat assistant came to stand at her elbow.

He shuffled his feet. "I thought I could make lamb porridge for lunch. I can start working on it now, if you want. It takes three or four hours to cook properly. If I begin right away, it will be ready in time for lunch."

Had he just offered his services? She swallowed a cough. "Fine idea." It was a good recipe for Esther since it did not mix the meat with milk products. "Use the meat that Avraham the butcher sent. The queen is partial to it."

The dairy assistant grabbed his arm. "What are you doing? You're supposed to stick with us."

He shook the clutching hand loose. "I'm sticking with her, like you should be." He pointed at the cup. "That's from the king. A proper royal gift."

"We don't need her for that. When Cook comes back, we'll receive better things than her puny cup."

"Are you blind? In all the years we have worked with Cook, he has received two gifts from the king. She got one in three months. Obviously, she deserves her position here, even if she is a woman."

"It's not like she got it on her own. We all worked hard for that. She couldn't have done it without us."

"Maybe not. But her dishes were what earned her that cup. The king said that duck might have shown a small spark of genius. We had nothing to do with that. Just stood around and gawped as she made it. And he thinks her marsh mallow candy is perfect. None of us raised a finger to help with that, neither."

Roxannah's lips parted company. Cook had been busy!

The meat assistant started to collect the ingredients for his porridge. "Anyway, Cook isn't coming back any time soon. He told me so himself." He smashed cloves of garlic on the counter with the flat of his knife. "You should never have touched his recipe collection. You went too far. I want no part of it anymore. We do our jobs. That's what we were hired for, with or without Cook. Now, get out of my way."

Roxannah bit back a smile. It appeared she had won her first recruit. Only three more to win to her side.

Thanks to her early preparations and Halpa's competence, she managed to send off an acceptable breakfast to the queen's chambers in spite of her tangle with Onophas. Adin arrived soon after the food had been served.

"You look pale."

"Is that your medical opinion?"

"No. It's personal."

Her belly curled at that look. *How personal?* she wanted to ask. *As personal as I feel about you? As personal as the way I want to wrap my arms around your neck and never let go?*

Her brush with death must have shaken her more than she realized. A turnip had more sense. "I'll be all right."

"I spoke to Hathach. Esther's day is full with several court obligations. He said she will not be able to meet with us until tomorrow late morning."

"Good enough. Surely there is nothing urgent in my account. She is bound to hear the news of Onophas's treachery in any case."

Adin frowned. "Why don't you go to Cook's cubicle and rest for a while? You have earned a quiet moment to yourself, surely."

"I think I will."

She scrambled into Cook's kitchen alcove, closed the curtain, and sank onto the wobbly stool, exhaling. She dropped her face in her hands and shocked herself by promptly bursting into tears. God had saved her life. As unlikely as it seemed, he had even used her to save Amestris.

Half an hour later, feeling more composed, she wiped her face and came to her feet. She had to make lunch as well as begin preparations for dinner. And she had to convince three men to accept her as their new leader. Until then, Halpa, the meat assistant, and Sisy would have to make do.

Of course, she could always put the physician to work. The thought made her grin.

The smell of the lamb porridge, at first gamey and unappealing, had settled into the pleasant aroma of well-cooked meat mixed with slow-simmered wheat. The meat assistant had not left his pot once since the wheat had turned tender. He stood guard over the large iron cauldron, stirring the contents with a long-handled spoon.

Roxannah gave him an approving nod. It was the constant stirring that gave lamb porridge its signature creamy texture. Even a few moments' neglect could turn the whole pot into a singed ruin. "That looks excellent. I will grind the cinnamon for it."

He did not respond. But his mouth tipped up in the corner.

The dairy and vegetable assistants refused to participate in the lunch preparations. But after a hard stare from the meat assistant, they did not interfere either. They hung in the background, speaking in low tones.

"What are you making now?" the dessert assistant asked Roxannah. He had stayed with his recalcitrant friends for the first hour of the morning. But increasingly, he seemed drawn to the busy heart of the kitchen.

"Chickpea and carrot patties glazed with grape molasses."

"I could make you a date and walnut purée for dessert, if you want, along with almond pudding."

Roxannah's hands, wrist-deep in mashed chickpeas, went still. "That would be a fine accompaniment to the meal."

The dairy assistant made a hissing sound. Undeterred, the dessert assistant waved a hand and set to work, whistling a cheerful tune under his breath. Next to Halpa, he was the most capable assistant in the kitchen. Roxannah suspected that he truly enjoyed baking. He must have decided that working for her would be better than not working at all.

The meat assistant brought a spoonful of the lamb porridge for her to taste. "What do you think? More seasoning?" It was the first time since she had begun working for the queen that he had asked her opinion.

She threw an appreciative glance at the golden cup. The king's judgment had made itself felt even in the queen's kitchens. She tasted the porridge and nodded. "This is a fine porridge. Cook couldn't have done better. Another hour of stirring, and it will be just the right consistency."

The man flushed. "A bit more salt, you think?"

"Not for the queen. I've noticed her palate runs more to the sweet. She will want hers served with honey."

Lunch that day lived up to the high standard the queen had come to expect under Cook. Roxannah felt exhausted by the time the last dish left her counter. It had been a full day, and she still had dinner to make.

But before that, she had one more chore. "Everyone, to the table please," she called.

Slowly, Sisy and the assistants gathered around the rectangular table that occupied the center of the back kitchen. Even the two unruly assistants came, too curious to hang back.

"We are leaving for Ecbatana in a week." She unrolled the packing list that she had tucked into her belt. "Cook has told me what we need for the journey. He won't be joining us. I need you to help with the packing, as well as food preparation."

She gulped a deep breath and prayed for courage. It was becoming easier to turn to God through the day. To reach out to him and lean into his strength. "You two." She addressed the dairy and vegetable assistants. "You have to decide if you want to come."

"What do you mean?" The dairy assistant took a threatening step toward her. "Cook already said we were going."

In the back of her mind, she heard the voice of her father, shrieking. She took a half step back. But something held her in place. Something bigger than the memory of Lord Fravartish. She had been given a place in this kitchen for a reason, and she would not just hand it over to this bully.

"I'm in charge now, and I say who goes." She straightened her back, tamping down the temptation to flinch. "I have already made a change to the original plan. The meat assistant is coming to Ecbatana. He has proven his worth today. You two have been nothing but a thorn in my side. You want to come to Ecbatana? Then do your job. One more outburst out of you, one more interruption in our work, and the only place you are going is home." She pushed out her chin. "Do I make myself understood?"

Roxannah tried to hide her shock when the vegetable assistant nodded quickly and headed for his counter, grabbing a large bunch of spinach as he went. From the corner of her eye, she noticed the dairy assistant crossing his arms mulishly and retreating to his wall, refusing to budge the rest of the day.

Adin made a show of pounding his fist into his hand and wagging his brows at her meaningfully. She grinned and shook her head. This was her fight. She had seen how having Hathach and the Immortal by her side had paved the way for a short time. But as soon as they had left, problems had returned to haunt her.

Unless she won this battle herself, she could never take her place at the head of the queen's kitchen.

That night, everyone, save the dairy assistant, banded together to serve the best dinner they had made since the king's visit. Roxannah could have danced when Esther sent her compliments to the kitchen with an extra ration of wine for everyone as a mark of her appreciation. The cheers that met this announcement drowned out the groans from aching backs and sore arms.

Before she left for the evening, the meat assistant sought her out. "Shall I go to Miletus in the morning to get the list of the meats for the day? It should really be my task, after all. No reason for you to have to deal with the boy."

Roxannah was touched by the man's thoughtfulness—and tempted by it. But here was another battle she had to fight alone. One more fear she had to face. "Thank you for the offer. I will see to Miletus tomorrow. After that, you have the job."

44

You will be blessed when you come in and blessed
when you go out.

Deuteronomy 28:6 NIV

The next morning, Roxannah had just enough time for
her unpleasant chore. Before breakfast, she headed for
the spits with Sisy. Straightening her back the way she
had seen Esther do, she hardened her face and marched over.

God, give me strength.

"Miletus!" she called, making her voice steady. She had had
a lot of practice in the kitchen and no longer sounded like a
mouse.

He swaggered toward her. "The snooty one."

She narrowed her eyes. "Mind your manners. And I need the
list for the queen's kitchen."

He leered. "Come and take it from me."

She forced herself to stand without flinching. "The cheek,"
she snapped. One finger pointed straight at him. "Now you
listen. You give me that list, and I'll hear no more lip from you.
Understand?"

Miletus blinked. "Eh? What did you say?"

"You best hurry, Miletus. I report to the queen, you know. One word from me, and you are out on your ear."

The mean look turned into one of uncertainty. He pulled on his ear, and she was surprised to realize just how young he looked. "Fine. It's nothing special. Mutton. Pheasant. Trout. Venison. The ox won't be ready till tomorrow."

She turned around and walked away, realizing there wasn't even the hint of a wobble in her knees. God had kept her steady. He had helped her face her foe. Suddenly, Miletus seemed very small and unimportant.

Adin straightened as soon as she came through the door to the kitchens. "Shall I beat the boy to a pulp?"

She gave him a bright smile. "My thanks. I did my own beating."

Roxannah dismissed the assistants after breakfast so they could snatch a brief rest. She was about to turn her attention to the travel itinerary when Amestris's senior handmaiden stepped through the door. "My mistress requests your presence."

Without a word, Adin planted himself at her side.

The handmaiden wrinkled her nose. "She didn't ask for you, Physician."

"And yet she is blessed to have me. After what happened yesterday, Mistress Roxannah is not going anywhere alone."

Hurriedly, Roxannah donned her best tunic, Sisy's nimble fingers turning her duck's-nest of a hairdo into something acceptable. The handmaiden made no more objection to Adin's company until they stood outside Amestris's audience chamber.

"You go no further, Physician."

The place had guards crawling out of every orifice this morning. There was even an Immortal overseeing their activities. After yesterday's upheaval, they obviously weren't taking any chances. Roxannah gave Adin a reassuring nod. "I think these rooms are safer than the king's own chambers."

"That may be." He crossed his arms and leaned against the wall. "But I will wait right here. Any sign of trouble and I will come."

Warmed by this uncompromising reassurance, Roxannah walked through the double doors. Once again, she found herself in Amestris's chamber, alone with the princess. All evidence of the previous day's treachery had been wiped clean by diligent hands. Someone had managed to wipe away the large bloodstain from the stone floor and lay down a new carpet.

Amestris did not even wait for her to rise out of her bow before launching. "You left rather abruptly yesterday."

She had regained her composure in the hours since she had almost died at the hand of her eunuch. Yet even the folds of a fresh gown and her newly washed and curled hair could not hide the bruises on her face.

"Pardon, Duksis. I had to return to work."

Amestris frowned. "Under the circumstances, I am sure your mistress could have spared you for a little longer. It's not as if you run her kitchens."

"Well, actually, my lady, it is precisely like that."

The princess gave her an arrested look. "I was told you were an undercrassistant or some such."

"It is how I started. I received a rather meteoric promotion when Cook fell ill."

"I see." She adjusted the folds of her green robe. "She runs an odd household, that woman."

Roxannah ground her teeth. "How may I be of service, Duksis?"

"No need to get your bowels in a twist, girl. I meant no offense."

That sounded so close to an apology, Roxannah almost swallowed her tongue.

Amestris walked to a loom where an exquisite length of purple and white fabric was starting to take shape. She played with the loose threads hanging at one end. "You saved my life yesterday. At the risk of your own. When my guards were nowhere to be found, you threw yourself bodily in the path of Onophas's dagger to shield me." Her lips twisted in a bitter smile. "Had I not been the target, I might have enjoyed the sight of you wriggling under the table to get away from him one moment and chasing after him to clutch at his ample ankles the next. However ineptly done, it was a brave showing. I owe you my life."

An apology followed by gratitude, given as only Amestris could, with the sharp side of her tongue and just a dash of disparagement.

Still, it was more than Roxannah had expected. "I am glad I could be of service, Duksis. I only pray we can put this business behind us."

"Before that, I must repay my debt. As I said, I owe you my life. As a reward, I have decided to give you a choice." Amestris swung away from the loom. She pinned Roxannah with an intense eye. Something in that gaze sent a shiver down Roxannah's back.

"You owe me nothing, Duksis."

"On the contrary." She took a few restless steps toward her golden chair but did not sit. "A favor from me can change your life. Your father racked up considerable debt, I understand. I can take care of that, for one. Remove the threat that hangs over your home. Make those unpleasant debtors disappear for good. Or if you prefer, I can give you a proper dowry to attract a man of your own standing. You need not work like a commoner in anyone's kitchen. You can become mistress of your own." She paced back to the loom, her fingers restless on the half-finished weaving. "I can also set up your mother in comfort. Gift her with beautiful robes so that she no longer needs be ashamed before her old friends. Think on that."

Roxannah had hardly taken a breath since Amestris began

laying out her favors, each more tempting than the one before. But like the knots in the weave that tied the loose threads to the weft and warp, she felt the knots in this one.

Amestris turned suddenly, her face growing still. "Or you can make a different choice altogether. You can use this favor for your mistress. Instead of receiving the personal benefits I mentioned, you can offer it to *her*."

Roxannah's eyes widened. "To the queen?"

"Esther, yes. I know she is not in need of riches. She owns her own property, I understand, thanks to the king's generosity. But she does not have everything. I *can* make her life . . . easier. As a favor to you, I can withdraw my enmity from her. Cease any plans to topple her from her throne.

"If you ask me, you would be wasting a great opportunity by choosing this gift. She will lose her crown regardless of what I do. Her childless womb has already decreed that. Six years as consort and her name has not been mentioned once in any royal decree." She shrugged. "They only record the names of the women who bear the king children."

Roxannah's mind whirled. God alone could have opened this door.

Esther had already saved the lives of a generation of her people thanks to her position.

She had saved Adin's life.

Who knew what God could do through Esther in the additional months and even years that this bargain with Amestris could purchase for her? How many more people would the queen help if she could retain her crown? For surely without Amestris's active needling, her position would be more stable. Would the Lord who set her upon her throne not be glorified if she remained there a little longer?

She considered Amestris's tempting offers. Had not God already looked after Roxannah and her mother better than she could have imagined? Had he not provided for their every need in spite of Roxannah's fears? Their debts were paid for the year. Her job made enough to feed and clothe them. In Adin and Darab, they had found friends who were better than brothers. Undoubtedly he would look after their needs next year with the same dexterity as he had this one.

She had the Lord. What need had she of Amestris?

"I choose your gift to the queen, Duksis. I choose for Esther."

Amestris looked like she had been slapped. "Think on it, girl. Think what you are giving up. For yourself and your mother. Think of the life you could have, no longer as a servant, but as befits your bloodlines. Why would you lose so much? For a Jewess who is not even one of us? For a throne that is wobbling on three legs as it is? Think what you are choosing."

Why had Amestris given her this choice if she felt so wildly opposed to it? Perhaps it was the thought of owing Esther anything that scraped against her rigid sense of honor. After all, if the queen had not given her permission—and indeed, command—Adin and Roxannah would not have approached the princess in the first place.

Perhaps she felt indebted to Esther, though it obviously grated on her.

The way Amestris stood, her shoulders rigid about her ears, her expression tight with sharp emotion, hinted at something more than debts and honor.

In a flash, Roxannah had the answer.

Esther had told Adin that loyalty meant everything to the princess. Yet the head of her own household, one of the most trusted people in her life, had proven unfaithful. This gift, this unusual offer, was as much a test as the payment of a debt.

Amestris wanted to know if Esther's people were more trustworthy than her own. If they honored her enough to lay down their own well-being for hers.

She wanted to know if Esther had what she herself had never managed to gain. Not merely loyalty. But love.

Something in Roxannah melted as she studied Amestris. Beneath the exquisite clothing, the priceless jewels, and the trappings of her position was simply . . . a woman. A lonely woman who sometimes found her schemes and devices not enough to keep her warm when the sun went down.

Roxannah softened her voice. "I choose for Esther, Duksis." She bowed, not for show or out of fear, but with genuine respect. "You have my gratitude."

From the Secret Scrolls of Esther

> There is a friend who sticks closer than a brother.
>
> Proverbs 18:24

Thirty-Two Years Later
The Twenty-Fifth Year of King Artaxerxes's Rule

Things belong in their proper place. Whether you are a queen or a slave, you expect to find the moon in the sky and water in the sea. You can count on the certainty of these matters. It's part of the little comfort allowed to us in this world.

For me, one of those comforts was the knowledge that Amestris would never, ever darken my door.

It was like the greenness of grass. The fact that your feet stay on the ground when you walk instead of floating in the air. The kind of certainty you could bank your life on.

Imagine my horror when the princess showed up unannounced, her pale senior handmaiden tripping in her wake, carrying a great basket of fragrant tuberoses.

I had been holding an audience with the physician and my little cook, vacillating between entertainment and surprise as they made their latest reports. They were a long way from finished when some noise outside brought our conversation to a halt.

"D . . . D . . . D . . ." It was never a good sign when my senior handmaiden stammered. I witnessed it three times in the whole of my residence at the palace, and it always boded ill.

I sat up straight, wondering what had brought on this bout of stuttering shock.

Then I heard Amestris's voice. We had never spoken in person, though I had glimpsed her many times in the opposite corner of some vast chamber at one of the king's sumptuous feasts. Still, I recognized that voice the instant I heard it.

"Step aside, woman. I have business with your mistress."

Roxannah and Adin were obviously familiar with that particular tenor and pitch, having both attended her more than once. I noted the sudden stiffening of their bodies.

Only years of royal training kept me from toppling on my face when Amestris glided in.

I had the presence of mind to come to my feet. I gave a subtle bow of my head, a concession to her position as mother of the crown prince. A mark of respect not strictly required, according to court protocol. But between you and me, I felt she deserved it.

Of course, she did not return the favor.

"Duksis. This is a surprise." I was quite proud to note that my voice did not tremble.

"Couldn't be helped," she snapped.

I smiled, trying to pretend my heart was not clawing

its way out of my chest. Turning, I made a motion to dismiss the physician and the cook.

To my astonishment, she waved me to stop. "Let them remain. If nothing else, they have proven that they can be trusted."

I could not return to my chair, which having been set upon a dais, would place her in a lower and therefore inferior position. Nor could we keep standing in the middle of the room like a couple of domestic chickens searching for grain. In the corner, I had two chairs, both the teal of a peacock's feather and of matching size. Motioning, I invited her to take one, noting that she lowered herself at the exact moment as I.

She was a woman for games, even to the bitter end.

She turned her regal head and took in my chamber with undisguised interest. "Smaller than I expected. Plainer too."

I nodded in agreement. My rooms suited me. I needed no approval from her. I waited patiently for her to speak. I had already expressed my surprise. What else could I say that did not feel redundant, unless to join my handmaiden in stammering?

She exhaled. "That one"—she pointed to Roxannah— "saved my life yesterday. I suppose you know."

I did not, as it happened. She had not worked her way around to telling me yet. I had, of course, heard of the great commotion in Amestris's chambers. According to rumor, she had almost been killed by her eunuch. But I had not realized that my little cook had been involved in the drama.

I was not about to admit my ignorance to Amestris and simply smiled.

"I have come to pay my debt."

I veiled my surprise. If Amestris wished to reward my

348

cook for a great service, she need not have troubled to come all the way into my apartments.

Amestris fidgeted, a sight so uncommon I almost missed her words. "I've come to offer you my peace."

My jaw came loose.

She cleared her throat. "Your servant chose to give her reward to you. Hence, it is to you that I must discharge my debt. Here is my gift to you: Enjoy your throne while you can. I will do nothing to topple you from it, nor will I bring more trouble to your door. On this you have my word."

A queen must face many unexpected circumstances. She must contend with enemies, as well as allies. Wrestling the startling shifts of fortune is part of the gristmill of her life.

Yet I can say that in all the years of wearing the crown of Persia, I had never been so stunned as in that moment.

Amestris had offered me a significant gift. She was no longer my foe.

I glanced at the little cook. Her pretty face wore an endearing flush. The large eyes, blue today like my walls, swam in tears.

My chest filled with unexpected warmth. It dawned on me that as of this hour, I had one less enemy. But I had gained something even more precious. The best gift a queen could have.

I had found a good and true friend.

45

Roxannah

I will place him in the safety for which he
longs.

Psalm 12:5

THIRTY-TWO YEARS EARLIER
THE THIRTEENTH YEAR OF KING XERXES'S RULE
THE SIXTH WEEK OF SUMMER

Roxannah tried to blink away tears. Weeping in the presence of royalty was considered an unacceptable breach of etiquette. The duksis likely had no patience for it. But the tears refused to be banished.

For so many years, Roxannah had longed to feel safe and failed. The world had remained inscrutable and harsh, full of monsters that could swallow her in a moment.

Adin had helped her understand that God would be with her the way her mother had once stayed by her side when she was recovering from a broken bone. Her pain hadn't vanished.

She had had to bear it. But her mother's ever-present care had made the pain seem manageable. Bearable.

She had started to think of God in that role. A comfort to have near. A consolation in the midst of pain. But that image of him had not fully assuaged the bite of fear. She was still not safe. Merely accompanied.

Now she realized that God's faithfulness meant so much more than his mere presence. More than his compassion and consolation.

His faithfulness meant that nothing in her life was wasted. Even the shattered things.

Her mind brought together all the different strands that had brought her to this moment, both the good and the bad. Her financial lack; her desperate circumstances; her broken childhood; her innate talent; the experience she had gained by dint of necessity; meeting Adin; her fight with Onophas. All of those different strands, the hard and the sweet, were being used in the unfolding of this extraordinary moment: Amestris offering peace to her rival.

Esther would remain queen a little longer. A simple Jewish woman used by God in ways they could not yet comprehend.

This was another turn of God's faithfulness. The safety only he could offer. Not a perfect protection from every tribulation flung at them by the mighty forces of darkness. But a gathering of the broken pieces to his will. Turning evil into good.

For a moment, she had been allowed this one tiny glimpse of God's plans at work. He gave her life a greater purpose. She felt an unshakable calm at that thought.

The buzz of incessant vigilance that always hummed in the back of her mind came to a sudden stop. She did not need to guard against every danger or watch for every hurt hiding behind the door. She need not keep herself safe.

An otherworldly peace replaced the roar of fear. A sweet silence reigned within. This was safety. God with her. God for her. God ruling over all. This was what Adin felt in the midst of every battle. This sense of everything being steady and solid even when the world was pitched sideways.

She gave him a bright smile. She wanted to tell him that she understood Ruth now. Understood what it meant to abandon everything and follow the Lord.

Your God is my God.

For all his talents, Adin could not read her mind. Still, he blinked, eyes widening at the look she gave him, as though something in her spirit had touched something in his.

Amestris gave Roxannah a piqued look. "Stop mooning after the physician and pay attention."

Roxannah choked on a laugh and tried to reel her thoughts back to the present. "Yes, Duksis."

"I found the man you saw enter the Royal Treasury yesterday."

"You *did*, my lady? Who is he, if I may be so bold to ask?"

"He is a cousin to the king, twice removed. No one particularly important, though he is in favor with a handful of the members of the royal household."

Roxannah was too caught up in the first real breakthrough they had enjoyed to mind her manners. She leaned forward. "Has he told you who hired him? What did he say about the book?"

"What could he say with a mouth full of poison?"

Esther's shoulders tensed. "He is dead?"

"As camel dung. His master got to him before we could. He must have realized we were close to discovering the man's identity and simply removed the threat. My people searched every nook in his residence and found nothing useful. We still have no idea who or what is the cause of this mayhem. Which brings us back to this." The princess extended a hand to her handmaiden. Rummaging under the tuberoses, she extracted a rectangular object wrapped in cloth. Spreading the thick wrapping, she revealed three tablets of clay sitting on top of one another.

Their surface was covered in a series of neat triangles and delicate lines, standing upright or lying sideways. The bottom of each tablet was marked by a golden seal.

Amestris addressed Esther. "Do you know what these are?"

The queen bent her head to it. "I would guess the particular Book of Memorable Deeds that has caused so much trouble of late."

"Quite." With exaggerated care, Amestris placed the tablets on her lap. "In spite of all my efforts, they remain inscrutable to me. I cannot eke out their secrets." Her mouth tightened as if she had just drunk a cup of verjuice. "I thought perhaps between us we might be able to solve this mystery. I have told you all I know. Perhaps you will now recognize something that I have missed."

Esther did not quite gape. She was too smooth for that. But something in her blank expression shook for a moment. "Certainly, Duksis. Although, if even you find the thing impenetrable, perhaps it is time we consider involving the king."

Amestris gave an annoyed *hrmph*. "Agreed. In five days, on the night before the court sets off for Ecbatana, I expect he will invite the family to the usual feast. We will have an opportunity to ask for a private audience then."

Her suggestion met with astonished silence. Amestris did not suffer Esther's limitations. Though she could not walk into the king's presence without being sent for any more than Esther could, she could ask her relatives for their help. Her connections spread to the king via dozens of contacts, like a spiderweb leading to the throne. Her brother, Hyperanthes, was one of the few men who belonged to Xerex's inner circle; and her father, no less. Amestris's desire to wait until she could personally approach the king demonstrated a chilling suspicion. The offender could be anyone.

Even someone amongst her own kin.

The princess tapped her foot. "Unless you expect a visit from the king before then?"

Esther offered one of her half-moon, narrow smiles. "His Majesty has not led me to expect such. With our imminent departure on the horizon, court matters keep him more occupied than ever."

How odd it must be not to have the freedom to approach your own husband, Roxannah thought. All in a day's work for someone married to the king of the greatest empire the world had ever known. She felt a renewed gratitude for her humble station.

Amestris passed the first tablet to Esther. "We have several days to solve this mystery ourselves, as there will be a risk to the king once we pass the book to him. If we fail, we can only hope he will succeed before another attempt is made upon his life."

That reminder had a sobering effect. It pressed home, more than ever, the gravity of the task before them.

To Roxannah's surprise, Amestris directed her handmaiden to pass the second and third tablets to her and Adin. "Make yourselves useful."

The princess came to her feet, forcing Esther to follow suit. "I cannot remain any longer or tongues will wag. It is one thing to stop for a short while. But it would not be wise to linger. Speaking of which, we need an excuse for my visit."

She tipped her head in Roxannah and Adin's direction. "Our enemy already knows these two possess some information regarding the book. Until now, the physician and your cook have been seen as functioning independently, setting their caps for a reward. No one would believe you and I could become allied in any matter. But now that I am here in person, that connection may be made. Which is why we must offer an iron-clad reason for my visit."

Esther pressed the bridge of her nose. "What do you suggest, Duksis? For myself, I am at a loss to explain away this unusual honor."

"I have the perfect explanation." Amestris gestured at Esther's flat stomach. "It seems I discovered that you lost a babe." She raised an ironic brow. "Everyone would believe that I came to gloat over your heartache and brought my flowers as an added insult. No one would suspect anything else."

Esther's head whipped back as though struck. "I will not lie," she said through white lips.

Amestris gave her the pitying look of a grown-up dealing with a child. "You needn't say anything. Leave that to me. The important thing is that no one suspect we are connected, or that you have the book. This story gives us the perfect cover. And since most of the court is already aware that your physician and cook have visited me several times in recent days, they would believe them to be the source of my information."

Roxannah felt suddenly sick.

"Your cook is looking green. No doubt she objects to having her good name besmirched by me. But it is the best way she can serve you now. Agreed?"

Esther looked a little green herself. "Agreed. Though we must try to put their reputation to rights once this matter is resolved."

"We can spin the matter one way or the other in time." She pointed to the book. "Send word as soon as you have something." At the door, she turned to address Esther one final time. "Throw that bouquet away where everyone can see it. The servants' gossip will take care of the rest once I plant a few well-placed hints. Consider crushing the flowers under your feet before disposing of them. Let them see how aggravated you are by my visit."

Esther's expression was all sweetness. "I will contrive to manage, Duksis."

Amestris's cackle rang as she stepped through the threshold. No sooner had Esther's senior handmaiden sealed the door behind them than Esther rounded on Roxannah. "You left a few details out of your report, I think."

"I was coming to them, my queen, when the princess interrupted us."

"You did not think that saving Amestris's life might belong to the top of your list?"

Roxannah pulled at the collar of her tunic. "Perhaps I should have started with that information."

Esther sank on her blue chair and patted the seat next to her. Roxannah found it still warm from Amestris's recent occupation. Lord's mercy. But she never thought her bottom would ensconce itself amongst such elevated company.

She began to make her report. Esther peppered her with questions, not satisfied until she had every particular of the last day's events.

When Roxannah admitted to choosing the gift for the queen over herself, Esther grew quiet. Without another question, she pulled Roxannah into her arms and held her for a long moment.

No words passed between them. But by the time they parted, Roxannah knew that they would never be quite the same. Once before, Esther had offered to speak to Roxannah as a friend. That exchange had felt like an aberration, an unusual departure from the reality of their positions. But now, something shifted.

Esther was still queen, and Roxannah the servant. Their stations remained unchanged. Yet in the place that hearts and attachments and loyalties occupy, they would now be forever, simply, friends.

It was midmorning by the time they turned their attention to the Book of Memorable Deeds, reading through each tablet out loud. As Amestris had said, they contained nothing save the dry details of the daily business of court.

By the time they finished, they were all parched and no wiser than when they had begun. Esther sent Hathach to the kitchens to inform the assistants that Roxannah was otherwise engaged.

"Request a simple repast for our noonday meal, dear Hathach. Bread and cheese and some herbs will do. We don't want anyone but you and my senior handmaiden to enter this chamber."

Adin studied his tablet with intense concentration. "Why did she do it? Why did Amestris entrust these to us? To *you,* my lady? If we discover that her own kin are behind the plot, you will be in a position to destroy her."

Esther swallowed. "By some miracle, it seems we have won the princess's trust." She stared at the tablet on her lap. "These were recorded seven years ago. What happened during that period? What are the larger events that surround these unimportant details?"

"The book was written shortly after the Persian defeat in Athens," Adin said. "Also, the same time period as the revolt in Babylon, followed by another uprising in the coast of Ionia."

Roxannah tried to recall her history lessons. "Wasn't that also close to the time the king's own brother rose up against him?"

"Yes." Esther lifted her head. "Masistes and his sons."

Roxannah felt a stab of compassion for the king. By then, Xerxes must have been reeling. Three defeats in a row at the hands of the Athenians and their allies, taking the lives of countless Persians, including three of the king's own brothers. He must have been heartsore. But he would have had no time to grieve. He had to put down two fomenting revolts before they spread across the empire. And just when he could finally breathe, his favorite brother stabbed him in the back.

The king seemed to become very human as she realized the depth of grief that had haunted him for long months while he also dealt with the pressures of state.

"Though the tablets do not directly mention any of these events, the entry in question must surely be tied to one of them," Adin pointed out.

Esther kicked off her shoes and stretched her feet. "You mean one of these entries may show that someone the king trusted might have actually betrayed us in Greece? Or was in league with Babylon?"

"Or with Ionia. Precisely."

Roxannah sighed. "How can we tell which? What are we searching for?"

No one answered, and the room filled with an uncomfortable silence.

Hathach returned, bearing a large silver tray. Roxannah smiled when she realized the assistants had sent a few extra dishes, not settling for mere cheese and herbs.

Adin came to his feet and bowed before the queen. "I must leave, Your Majesty. I can make excuses for a long morning visit. But I won't be able to explain eating luncheon with the queen."

Roxannah expected Esther to dismiss her also. Instead, she asked her to remain for lunch and, afterward, invited her for a stroll in the flower garden, a singular honor usually reserved for her handmaidens. "Perhaps a short walk among the roses might inspire us with fresh ideas."

46

He reveals deep and hidden things;
he knows what is in the darkness,
and the light dwells with him.

Daniel 2:22

Esther cut a cream rose with the small knife at her belt, tucking the silky bloom into the crook of her arm where a towel protected her from sharp thorns. "So, what goes on between you and the physician, little cook?"

Roxannah nearly swallowed her tongue. "Nothing worth mention."

Esther plucked another rose, this one a pale peach. "I beg to differ."

"He feels guilty, is all."

"Those burning looks he sends your way when he thinks no one is watching do not smack of guilt to me. You cannot be that oblivious."

"It is not so simple, Your Majesty."

"Explain it to me, then."

Roxannah gave Esther a sideway glance and saw only a friend rather than the queen. A friend who in some ways understood her better than any she had ever known. If she could not open her heart to Esther, then she might as well wrap herself up in stone and be done.

Slowly, she recounted the tangle of the past year. "I fear he is filled with guilt about my father. I am not sure if he can unfurl that blame from anything he might really feel for me."

Esther picked another rose, this one red, adding it to the growing bundle in her arms. "Do *you* blame him?"

"I did, at first. But that was when I did not know the whole story. Now, I think what happened might have been inevitable. My father made his choice. At some point, our bad decisions catch up with us. Adin did his best. But his best could not match my father's worst."

"Have you told him that?"

"Not yet."

"I would not delay. He deserves to know you do not blame him, no matter what happens between you." She cut another rose, palest pink, like a drop of pomegranate juice mixed in with cream. "And what is between you and Adin is a simple matter, Roxannah. It requires you to answer only two questions.

"First"—she held up the pink rose for emphasis—"do you love the Lord with all your heart? Not so long ago, you asked me a question about his will. About whether he wanted you to be an assistant cook in my kitchen. At the time, I thought it the question of someone who had opened her heart to God. Am I right? Because there is no future for you and Adin unless you belong to the Lord. Nothing less will do for our physician."

"I do belong to him, my lady," Roxannah said without hesitation. "My life is his."

Esther smiled and handed her the pink rose. "Good. An unequal yoke is a painful burden."

No doubt, she knew that from experience. Roxannah inhaled the perfume of the rose, feeling a little dizzy. "And the second question, my lady?"

"Do you love Adin? Love him enough to twine your life with his, to share in his trials, treasure his dreams, put up with his foibles?"

Roxannah pictured Adin, ebony eyes alight with tenderness. She had loved him for so long, though she had tried to deny it even to herself. "I do, my queen. I love Adin more than I can say."

Esther transferred her bundle of roses, towel and all, into Roxannah's arms. "Well, why are you telling me? He is the one who needs to know."

A thorn found its way into Roxannah's thumb, making her wince. "It's impossible, Your Majesty."

"And why?"

"You mean besides the fact that my father tried to kill him and rob him of everything? Or the fact that I am penniless and have no dowry to offer? Even the fact that my mother and I still own our home is thanks to a loan from him. I owe him too much. It muddies the waters between us."

Esther stopped her ambling walk. "*Your* house?"

"Yes, my lady."

"Adin's house, I think you mean."

Roxannah gave the queen a puzzled look. "No, my lady. *Our* home. The one that has been in our family for three generations."

"Tell me, what do you remember of the king's edict? The second one, I mean. The codicil to Haman's."

Roxannah cast her mind back, trying to recall the words of the king's second decree. "That the Jewish population had the right to defend themselves against any who attacked them."

"And?"

"And . . ." It came to her in a rush, the rest of that codicil, which she had forgotten in the shock of her father's death. "And . . . to take the property of their enemies," she whispered.

Esther nodded. "According to Persian law, your house belongs to Adin. But lest you accuse him of taking false responsibility for you and your mother, you should know that none of the

Jews living in Susa took any plunder from their enemies. They defended their lives. That is all. They would not stoop to what their enemies had intended. They would not kill for the sake of the spoils they might collect.

"In looking after you and your mother, and in leaving your home unmolested, Adin has merely followed the dictates of his conscience before the Lord. I do not think he confuses that with love. What he feels for you, he feels for you apart from this matter."

Roxannah could hardly take Esther's words in. All this time, Adin had known that he could take their home. He had far more power over them than their creditors. And yet he had chosen never to act on that power.

What manner of man could show so much grace?

She knew the answer before the thought was even complete. The man who loved God more than money. More than success. More than the law. Not many men had that spirit.

Her eyes filled with tears of gratitude. She had been blessed to have him in her life as a friend, though her father had done his best to turn him into foe.

Esther plucked another rose, this one scarlet, and laid it on top of Roxannah's pile. "There is one matter that must be addressed. You have done me a great service, little cook. By giving away the gift Amestris promised you, you have offered me peace. I wish to return the favor. I have arranged for Hathach to pay off your creditors."

She held up her hand to stop Roxannah from speaking. "That is the debt I owe. However, as your queen, I also wish to give you a gift. We do not want you to go to your husband's house empty-handed, do we? I will provide you with a dowry from my own storehouses.

"Now, if Adin wishes to marry you, you can go to him as an equal. Equal in faith. Equal in position. You owe each other nothing. If you love each other, it is without strings."

In the queen's chambers, in spite of Hathach's commendable knowledge of court history, they grew no closer to solving the mystery contained in the Book of Memorable Deeds. An urgent message arrived for Hathach, requiring his presence at one of the queen's properties.

"It's up to the two of us," Esther told Roxannah. "Look for something in the tablets that stands out to you. Anything that seems strange, however minor or insignificant."

Hours later, Roxannah's eyes felt gravelly with exhaustion. "There are forty-three names mentioned here, either directly or by inference. Four are dead. Five are currently in some far-flung corner of the empire and could hardly be suspected of pulling the strings behind these recent events. That leaves us with thirty-four suspects."

"Thank the Lord we have narrowed the field," Esther said with a wry twist to her lips. She reached for her chalice of apple juice. "I am with Amestris. I find nothing incriminating within these tablets. Why go to such lengths to lay hands on them?" She set the tablet aside. "Time for a rest, I think."

"May I see to the kitchens, my lady?"

"So long as you do not linger. I don't mind more bread and cheese if that is all your assistants can manage."

To her delight, Roxannah found the kitchen a hive of ordered activity. The meat assistant held up a spoon in greeting. "Hathach said you may be held up for a couple of days. We took the liberty of making a soup and some stuffed onions for dinner. And we have a custard for dessert." He dropped his head. "It's not a lot, I know."

"It's perfect," Roxannah said.

She was proud of the way the assistants had banded together in her absence to keep the kitchen running and told them so. And though she and the queen worked through dinner and long into the night, the sweet encouragement of her assistants' support helped buoy her through the exhausted hours.

———

In the morning, Hathach and Adin joined them again. None of them had slept more than a few hours, and Roxannah found her mind wandering. She stole a glance at Adin and found him already watching her. She felt the heat rising in her cheeks and looked away. She had turned into a ripe pomegranate.

Pomegranate!

Roxannah sat up with an indrawn breath. She pulled one of the tablets closer, trying to make out every syllable of the entry. "Here is a discrepancy."

Esther stopped reading. "What is it?"

"It has to do with food."

Everyone laughed. "Let's have it," Hathach said. "Did they cook their poultry with the wrong herbs?"

Esther joined in. "Did they use too much rosewater in their dessert? The king is sure to punish them for that."

Roxannah held up a finger. "Jest all you like. But explain this. How would one send fifteen cartloads full of sour pomegranates from Susa to Parthia?"

All traces of joviality wiped from Adin's face. "By the royal highway?"

Roxannah nodded. "By the royal highway. Which is why it has been recorded in this book. Here is a request for a special pass to journey on the King's Highway from Susa to Parthia."

Hathach squinted at Roxannah's tablet. "I see nothing strange in the request. Anyone who journeys on the King's Highway must requisition for a pass. It allows them to get past the checkpoint sentries and use the rest stations."

"Yes, but this petitioner requested the pass to be expedited because the pomegranates, being fresh, might rot if their delivery was delayed."

Adin gave her a curious look. "I still cannot see anything strange in the request. Their haste seems reasonable."

"Look at the date. This request was made not long after the defeat in Greece. They requisitioned their special pass toward the end of summer."

Esther laid down her fan. "And?"

"Sour pomegranates do not ripen until two months after this date. If you are not a gardener, you would not know that. There is enough early crop for the fruit to be available at a nobleman's table by late summer. Enough for fresh juice and salted seeds in a single household. But in no way will you have fifteen cartloads of sour pomegranates ready for transportation at that time of year."

Adin took a sharp breath. "Whatever he transported in those carts, it was not sour pomegranates."

"Right you are. Except that he was too ignorant to know that he had given himself away by his choice of fruit."

"Xerxes would have known that." Esther shook her head. "He is an avid gardener and spends many of his free hours with his hands in the soil. It must be a scribal error, else the king would have questioned it."

"The king was not there." Roxannah pointed at the entry. "See here? It mentions the name of the senior scribe who issued the pass. But there is no mention of the king. It would have been considered a simple enough matter to handle without His Majesty's direct input."

Adin examined the scribe's seal. "If the king were to read the book now, would he pick up on the discrepancy?"

"Without a doubt," Esther said. "He would know that something in that request is awry."

Adin gave Roxannah an admiring nod. "Well spotted. You have discovered the entry we have been searching for. Seven years ago, someone transported fifteen cartloads of something that was not pomegranates—and did so in great haste."

Roxannah threw up her hands. "But what is the significance?

Why Parthia? The region has no bearing on any of the events we mentioned. Babylonia is in the wrong direction, to the southwest, and Ionia is even farther to the west."

"But Parthia is more than halfway to Bactria." Esther opened and closed her fan without making use of it.

Bactria. Where Masistes was heading with his sons in order to incite an uprising. In order to make himself king.

Esther tapped Roxannah's tablet with the tip of her ivory fan. "That would explain their urgency. They needed to use the royal road because it provided the fastest and most direct route to their destination. From Parthia, there are good secondary roads into Bactria. Those ancient routes can accommodate carts and mules."

"Wily," Adin said. "They were throwing their lot in with Masistes and yet too cautious to name Bactria, lest the plot go awry. A wise precaution, as it proved. Fifteen cartloads of something other than pomegranates could supply a lot of help in the midst of an uprising—weapons, armor, equipment. Even the men guarding the carts might have been trusted soldiers. Fifteen cartloads of the right supplies could turn the tide of a great battle. And it would explain the haste. They needed to get to Masistes before the first clash. Only, the king's forces moved so fast, they intercepted Masistes before he arrived in Bactria."

Esther snapped her fan closed. "Who? Who made the request?"

Roxannah tried to swallow past a dry throat. "Prince Arsames, the king's half brother."

Esther's head snapped back. "Lord have mercy. His favorite. The one friend he thought he could trust. All those years ago, Arsames betrayed Xerxes. He helped Masistes in the revolt. My poor Xerxes. Another heartbreak for him to bear."

No one said another word for long moments. Finally, Hathach came to his feet and bowed before the queen. "If I may,

I believe this is where the Lady Amestris is best equipped to take over."

Esther chewed on her lip. With some reluctance, she nodded. "Adin."

"My queen?"

"Let the duksis know what we have discovered. And take these infernal books with you. You can hide them in your medical chest."

"How will I get that past her door? The new guards won't let a mosquito into her chamber since the attack on her life."

"Hasn't the lady suffered a fainting spell?" She smiled grimly. "If I am going to lose a babe, she can certainly swoon like a delicate lily."

47

Adin

You who seek God, let your hearts revive.
Psalm 69:32

Adin stepped in front of a pair of palace guards shielding Amestris's door. "I am here to see the duksis."

The taller guard frowned. "You aren't on my roster."

"The lady has asked for my services. I am a palace physician." True and true again, though not strictly connected.

The taller guard frowned. "No one told me about it."

"Did you hear that she had suffered a fainting spell?" A question to which the proper answer was a simple no. Hard to side-step an outright lie when working undercover.

The guards looked at each other. "I'll ask," the shorter one said.

The tall one wriggled his fingers to signal Adin to step forward. "I'll search you while he investigates." Adin hoped that

Amestris would send for him before the guard discovered the Book of Memorable Deeds buried at the bottom of his medicine chest. He held his breath as the man reached to remove the fabric covering the book.

Amestris's door burst open, revealing the senior handmaiden. "Leave that," she cried just before the man pulled the fabric off. "The mistress bids the physician to come immediately."

"I haven't finished my search."

"Did he have any weapons on his person?" She tapped an impatient foot.

"No. But I haven't gone through the whole chest."

"It's good enough. My lady is impatient to see him."

Adin gave the guard an I-told-you-so wag of his brows.

Amestris did not even let him finish bowing before pouncing. "You are early, Physician. That means you either solved the matter or your mistress has already given up."

"We have the connection to the book, as well as the name you seek, Duksis." Adin withdrew the annals from their hiding place at the bottom of his chest, glad to hand them off to the senior handmaiden.

Amestris leaned forward. "Speak. Leave out no detail."

Adin obliged her, describing the process by which they had solved the puzzle.

The princess threw her head back and laughed. "The two most powerful women in the court, a eunuch famous for his learning, a physician who studied in parts unknown, and who cracks the case? A cook! It certainly puts us in our place." She took the book and studied the passage pertaining to the case. "Never was much for gardening myself. I will go to see Xerxes as soon as I can arrange a meeting."

Her voice held a distinct thread of relief. Her family was innocent. She smiled with satisfaction. "He will be pleased to weed out another enemy."

Adin winced.

"Why the face? We have good news for the king. At long last, we can celebrate catching the rat in our net."

"A rat he loves, my lady." Trust her to miss that important detail. He weighed his words carefully. "The king is sure to mourn the loss. I suspect he would appreciate comfort more than celebration. A little commiseration might go a long way toward softening the blow."

Amestris cocked her head. "Did *she* say that?"

"She was concerned for his broken heart, Duksis."

"I see." She gave a bitter laugh. "Comfort and commiseration. Does no one understand the business of ruling?"

"Even rulers have hearts, my lady. It's good to remember he is a man as well as a king."

She gave him an uncomprehending look. "Well, in any case, his throne shall remain safe for a while longer."

Adin cleared his throat uncomfortably.

"What now?" she snapped.

"I needed an excuse for coming to see you, Duksis, since I had to bring my medical chest along."

She raised a brow. "And what excuse did you offer?"

"My lady thought a fainting spell?"

He thought Amestris might slap him. But on the way out, he heard the tinkle of her laugh just before the door closed.

At Roxannah's request, Adin had picked up a hen and some lamb from Avraham's stall for the queen, and Roxannah was putting the finishing touches on each dish. The other assistants seemed to be falling in line, returning to the smooth rhythm Cook had created for them.

She was more emotive than Cook in her leadership, readier with a compliment, and the assistants had warmed to her approval. The kitchen had taken on a friendly atmosphere. Everyone worked hard and seemed eager to please their new leader.

That afternoon, Roxannah had dismissed the only remaining creak in her well-oiled hinge: the hardheaded dairy assistant. Adin had almost laughed aloud when he saw the way she stood, back ramrod straight, her sweet face turned hard. He had seen the exact expression upon Esther's face not so long ago. Before he knew it, the dairy assistant was out on his ear, a stunned look on his habitually self-satisfied face. No one seemed to mind the loss very much.

Adin was supposed to be making a salve for one of the king's concubines who suffered from back pain. But he found his gaze landing on Roxannah again and again, his concentration like a feather in the wind, flitting about aimlessly.

How he loved that woman.

When the leftovers returned to the kitchen, she made up a plate for him from Esther's special meal and set it up in a corner so he could eat by himself. He prayed before eating, his appetite desultory in spite of the delicious meal.

They had not had a moment to themselves since he had returned from his meeting with Amestris. As he walked Roxannah home that night, he suggested that they return to their favorite bench in the herb garden so he could tell her about his visit with the princess. She seemed quieter than usual this evening, an air of distraction about her as she sat next to him.

She smiled when he quoted Amestris's line about no one understanding the business of ruling, but made no comment, not even when he told her that he had been afraid she might hit him.

She must be exhausted. None of them had slept much the night before. He gestured to the path. "Shall we go?"

"In a moment. Do you mind if we linger here for a while?"

"Of course not."

She was sitting with her profile to him, a faraway look in her eyes. "Adin, I must tell you something."

His chest tightened. It was something important, he could

tell. An ending now that their part in the mystery of the book had been fulfilled? A good-bye?

"For a long time, I blamed you for my father's death."

He stilled, her words a kick to his gut. He had known it, of course. But hearing her say them made the pain worse.

"I blamed you for not protecting him, and I blamed myself for my disloyalty."

He ground his teeth. "You had no fault in the matter. I should have—"

"No. No, Adin. You should have done nothing differently. This is what I want to say. I have thought long about the events of that night. About what you revealed. And this is what I want you to know: I don't hold you responsible. You did all you could to keep my father from bearing the consequences of his loathsome actions. No one could have done more.

"You and Leah are not at fault here. Even I do not bear the responsibility of my father's death. We all did our best to protect those we love. We all failed.

"Ultimately, it was my father's own actions that resulted in his brutal end. I have thought about the man he was at the last. His final words. They are a comfort to me, as I hope they are to you. Receive them as a benediction from him, Adin.

"My mother and I do not hold you responsible. Not in the least. I hope you can accept that. Be released from the pain of a guilt you have not earned."

Adin felt the burn of salt in his eyes, in his throat. A tear escaped its boundary and trickled into his beard. With it, something bitter and putrid seemed to leave his body.

"Thank you." His voice had turned gravelly with emotion. "Thank you for that."

She reached for his hand, and he held on tight to those delicate fingers, calloused from years of work. "I needed it as much as you."

He nodded.

She gave him a quick sideways look. "I followed Ruth's example, you know."

He tilted his head in confusion. There was a Ruth in his neighborhood. But when could she have met her? "Ruth?"

She gave him a pull-yourself-together look. "King David's great-grandmother."

"Oh, that Ruth." He sat up straight. "Wait. You did?"

She turned so she could look him in the eyes. Softly, so softly he had to lean close to hear, she whispered, "Your people shall be my people, and your God my God."

Whatever control he had exerted over his heart for months, whatever walls he had built, simply crumbled. He tugged her until she laid against his chest, and for a long time, simply held her.

"I love you," he said.

She stilled. Her tongue moistened a trembling lip. "I fell in love with you the day you told me you had a weakness for pistachio cake, I think."

He had known—hoped—that she was not indifferent. But he had needed the words. The plain-as-day, holding-nothing-back, honest words that made her his. Slowly, he tangled his fingers into her untamable hair the way he had imagined doing night after night and pulled her tight against him until their lips touched.

Their first kiss. He felt the fire of it from the instant they came together, and it shocked him into taking a breath and putting a bit of distance between them.

She gave a little gasp. "I never thought we could be together." Her dimple peeped out, teasing him. "Does this mean that like Xerxes you are holding your scepter over me and offering me half your kingdom?"

"You can have the whole thing."

"You can have mine too. My debts—"

He didn't let her finish, knowing how sensitive she was about them. "I care nothing for that."

"That's a pity. Because the queen is paying them off."

He pulled back a little. "Truly?"

"She calls it a repayment of *her* debt, though she owes me nothing."

He grinned. "She is a worthy queen." He could not resist. He pulled her into his arms for another kiss, gentle and slow. It still set his hair on fire. His Ruth. His bride. He gulped like an adolescent and drew back before pulling her onto his lap.

She was quiet for a moment. Had he offended her? Gone too far? He winced and opened his mouth to apologize.

She cut him off. "Kissing is better than anything I imagined."

He laughed and kissed her again until they both lost their breath. "When will you marry me?"

She giggled. She sounded so carefree that he wanted to leap. "Don't make me wait," he said, his voice husky.

"In Ecbatana? If the queen is agreeable?"

He heaved a sigh. Forty days. It sounded like an age. "Whatever you like."

"Now that I have a dowry, I can buy myself a wedding dress."

"You have a dowry?"

"Didn't I say? Esther gave me one of those too."

48

Roxannah

For where you go I will go, and where you lodge
I will lodge. Your people shall be my people, and
your God my God.

Ruth 1:16

THE THIRTEENTH YEAR OF KING XERXES'S RULE
THREE DAYS LATER

Adin's hand tightened around hers as he tugged her closer
to him. "Watch that puddle, love."

Love. Her new name. She was Adin's love. The knowledge filled an empty hole until she felt like she had turned into an overflowing spring.

"I saw no puddle," she teased. "Just an excuse to pull me close, I think."

"There was a puddle, and you are right." He grinned back, face full of mischief.

She poked him in the ribs, and he jumped. She had been

delighted to find how ticklish he was. The past three days had been the happiest she had ever known. In between their duties at the palace, they had spent every hour together, getting to know each other better, already growing into a *we* and *us* instead of the solitary words that had defined them before.

They had decided to move into Adin's house after they wed. It would be easier to make the crucial repairs needed in her family home while it was unoccupied. But when the house was ready, they planned to make it their permanent home since it could comfortably accommodate her mother and Darab, as well as Miriam and Leah.

Roxannah had started to study the Scriptures with Adin's help. They had begun with the story of Ruth, which she had loved. Sometimes, in playful moments, Adin called her "my Ruth," though it didn't feel all that playful when his eyes turned hot and her knees turned into rosewater jelly.

Of course, Adin asked Esther's permission to marry Roxannah.

"When?" the queen asked coolly.

"Before we set out for Ecbatana, I hoped."

The queen narrowed her eyes. "And spend your honeymoon on the royal highway?"

Adin cleared his throat. "Well, yes, lady."

The queen gave him a withering look and told him to mind his manners. "A woman needs a proper wedding and a better honeymoon than what you can give my little cook in a dusty cart or some roadside station. Ecbatana is soon enough for you."

Her mother had been speechless when she found out about Esther's generosity. But she had almost swooned with joy when Adin asked her for permission to marry her daughter. "I thought you would never get around to it, my boy."

Adin rubbed his neck and turned a violent shade of red. "I thought I was moving fast."

"Fast is your Nisaean. You are more the plodding type."

"Like Donkey," Darab supplied helpfully.

In all the joy and excitement, Roxannah had not had a chance to speak to Leah yet. Today, she had left breakfast under the charge of the assistants and Halpa, and the two of them were heading home together to do just that.

She tightened her hold on Adin's hand. "I long for God to revive the child's heart. She can't even look me in the eye."

Adin slowed his steps. "Let's pray for her right now. Our words have no power to heal. But God can anoint them with his strength."

They stopped, and on the side of a dusty Persian road, they prayed for dear Leah to receive their comfort and be restored.

As usual, Leah hid behind Miriam as soon as she caught sight of Roxannah. Roxannah understood the depth of the child's distress better now that she knew the full story. Leah had lost her own abba, a bereavement she felt keenly. To her, the very worst misfortune could not compare to the loss of a father. The thought that she herself had caused the death of Roxannah's father had become a torment to her. A guilt she could not shake.

Adin called softly to Leah. "Come, my little friend. Mistress Roxannah and I have something we wish to say to you."

Gently, Miriam tugged on the child's hand until she stood before them, eyes downcast, fat tears already trembling on the tips of her lashes.

Roxannah knelt before her until their eyes were level. "Sweetheart, I know what happened that night. The night my father died." She reached for a tiny hand and held it fast. "Leah, it was not your fault."

Leah pulled her chin down. "Is too. I heard the grown-ups talking. That's what they said. It was my fault because I disobeyed my ima."

"They were mistaken, Leah. My father . . . my abba . . . he was a troubled man. You understand? He made bad choices. He should never have gone to Master Adin's house that night. You wanted to protect your friend. That shows you have a good heart.

"Of course, it's important to honor your ima. Obey her, yes. But the death of my father is not your fault. You must stop believing that lie."

Roxannah turned to Adin. "Master Adin and I, we have forgiven each other, and we want you to know that we forgive you too. We don't hold you responsible. Nobody here does. Do you understand?"

The little girl hesitated. She gazed at them with an uncertain look on her face. But at least she did not run away. Roxannah pulled her into her arms and held her tight. "I don't blame you, Leah. Stop blaming yourself."

It would take time. Months. Perhaps even years for Leah to fully grasp that truth. The blade of guilt had cut her sharper, gone in deeper than the edge of her father's sword.

Still, the first essential steps of healing had begun. She had received the words of absolution her little soul needed. She had even allowed Roxannah to give her a hug.

In the coming days and months, Roxannah and Adin would make certain to remind her of that absolution. To repeat the truth until her bruised heart could accept it.

Before returning to the palace, they stopped to share their news with Tirzah.

"I have become a follower of the Lord, my friend," Roxannah announced.

Tirzah stared in wonder. "The Lord?"

"Your God is my God, Tirzah. Your people, my people."

"I have more news," Adin said. "We are going to be wed."

Roxannah grinned. "In Ecbatana. As soon as we arrive with the court."

Tirzah's open-mouthed wonder turned into a whoop of joy. "Wait. But that means I won't be able to attend the wedding."

"It's my one regret."

Adin winked. "I'll save you a piece of pistachio cake."

Outside the seven-walled city of Ecbatana, at the end of a long dirt track that led off to another dirt track, Esther owned an orchard where green apples ripened amongst long serrated leaves. In the midst of the apple orchard, a modest mudbrick cottage painted white held pride of place.

According to legend, Lord Harpagus, King Cyrus's famed general, had at one time owned the land and the house. Cyrus himself, it was said, had studied there as a boy with his female tutor.

Whether the legend held any truth or was the stuff of someone's overactive imagination, the place held a special charm. Esther offered it as the venue for Roxannah and Adin's wedding. She had several workers build a special arbor, festooned with summer flowers.

Flanked by silver candelabra sent from the queen's own apartments, the quaint spot became a place of enchantment, the scent of apples and jasmine making Roxannah's head spin as she stood next to her bridegroom. For long years, the guests spoke nostalgically of the sweet ceremony and assured her that the food was the best they had tasted at any wedding.

No one, save Roxannah and Adin, knew that the woman who stood at the very back, her face half-covered in the folds of an unfashionably large scarf, was none other than the Queen of Persia, who winked playfully when Roxannah happened to look her way.

Roxannah felt beautiful in one of Esther's own priceless robes, its ruched skirts with their golden embroidery swaying about her like a bell, while her flowing sleeves fluttered in the cool breeze. Her mother had spent hours adjusting the dress to Roxannah's more diminutive height, making it look as though it had been made for her.

Roxannah stared into the tender eyes of the man she loved and whispered, "Where you go, I will go, and where you lodge, I will lodge. Your people shall be my people, and your God my God."

From the Secret Scrolls of Esther

But the Lord God helps me;
therefore I have not been disgraced.

Isaiah 50:7

Thirty-Two Years Later
The Twenty-Fifth Year of King Artaxerxes's Rule

Let me tell you a secret: Being king will break your heart.

When Xerxes discovered Arsames's treachery, he raged. He broke a few priceless ornaments. He jumped on the back of his Nisaean and went for a ride that lasted a day, his Immortals barely able to keep up. By the time he came to see me, he was like the foam edging the waves in the Caspian Sea. White and full of holes.

"He was never true to me." He grabbed a goblet full of ruby-red wine and stared into its depths. Trying to resist but finding its pull too hard.

All this intrigue. Murder and plots to murder.

All this ambition.

Can you have an empire without it? Can you conquer

half the world and force it under your dominion and not expect the same in return?

Gently, I took the goblet out of his hands and placed it back on the table. "What will you do?"

"Kill him like the traitor he is. Him and the fellow he hired to murder Amestris. That one is a snake of such vile venom, I cannot stomach the thought of him breathing."

I held him for long moments until he stopped trembling. Under the rage, I could sense his sorrow, pent up, refusing to release.

"Why not let Arsames live? Banish him instead."

Xerxes pushed me away. "What message will that send my enemies? That I am weak. That they can do as they like and receive no punishment."

"For a man like him, being away from the glitter and power of the palace is worse than death." I cupped his cheek with my hand. "Teach your sons the way of forgiveness. Set them a lesson in what it means to be brothers. Don't let Masistes and Arsames set the example for the next generation. Show them a different way."

He turned away from my touch. "You ask me that? You who wanted the Jews to have an extra day to slaughter their enemies in Susa?"

I flushed. "Not a man of them would have been harmed if they had not attacked first. It was kill or be killed that day. They fell to their own avarice."

"And how is Arsames different? All those years ago, he colluded to kill me, to say nothing of his plot to murder Amestris. He even killed his own man to cover his hide."

"Yes. But you have disarmed him now. He has no sting, no venom."

He released an explosive breath. "You don't know

what it is to be king. You don't understand what it requires to rule."

He did not listen to me then. Would it have made a difference if he had? Years later, would it have prevented his own blood from being spilled, thanks to another bleak scheme?

Who can tell? Who can unwind the threads of the future from the past?

I only know that he was mine for too brief a time. And though he did not take my advice, he did reach for me instead of the wine that night.

My little cook had purchased me more time with him, thanks to her generous heart. I hope the years show that I did not waste that gift.

Well, my dear Nehemiah, somehow you have managed to find me in my hiding. All the way from your governer's house in Judah, no less. I suppose it was not so great an achievement for a man who rebuilt the walls of Jerusalem in fifty-two days. As you asked, I have begun to set down my story in these scrolls.

It occurs to me that the God who brought you *out* of the palace to tend to his people's need brought me *into* the palace for the same purpose.

Palace or rubble, it matters not. As long as the heart is willing, he will use us for good.

Author's Note

(Spoiler Alert!)

Who was Esther?

In recent decades, historians, theologians, and writers have cast her in so many conflicting roles as to make her a riddle. Some portray her as a romantic heroine, others as a a rape victim, still others as a savior.

As usual, in writing this book I leaned heavily on the biblical account as well as historical evidence to try to do justice to this extraordinary woman who has been loved and admired by so many generations.

To begin with, I don't think it's fair—or accurate—to apply modern cultural values to a people who lived 2,500 years ago. I doubt Esther would have thought of herself as a victim of rape. Marriage to the king was considered an honor. The only time Esther complains of her marriage in the biblical account is to bemoan the fact that her husband has not sent for her in thirty days (Esther 4:11).

Rather than a victim, the book of Esther reveals a woman who battles her worst fears and emerges a confident, purposeful, and wily heroine. She is a queen who wields considerable influence in a vast empire and changes the course of her people's destiny.

Obviously, Esther was married to a king. At the same time, she was married to a broken man. The consensus among many scholars is that the Ahasuerus of the Bible is the king known to history as Xerxes. Most of what we know about this monarch comes to us from his most bitter enemies, the Greeks. Experts now warn that we need to approach these accounts with a grain of salt.

I wrote Xerxes by leaning on the biblical narrative coupled with what we know about him from history: his defeats, his heritage, the betrayals he suffered. The person who emerges from the mists of time is a complex, wounded man who is not always admirable. But when did that ever stop a woman from loving a man? Yes, my Esther is a romantic heroine, though not with the simple happily-ever-after we sometimes like to imagine.

Outside the Bible, we have no record of Esther. Nor, for that matter, is Vashti mentioned anywhere. Amestris is the only wife of Xerxes recorded in Persian or Greek documents. But I believe there is a simple explanation for this dearth of historical reference: The Persians only recorded the names of wives who had children. Hence, part of the storyline of *The Queen's Cook* deals with this detail.

For those of you who like to distinguish between fact and fiction in your historical novels, here are a few particulars: Darius and Xerxes's defeats in Greece are historical, as are the revolts in Babylon and Ionia. The rebellion of Masistes, Xerxes's brother, is also factual. That Amestris killed Masistes's wife seems fairly indisputable, although the explanation offered by the Greek writers includes some mind-bending motives rejected by veteran historian Pierre Briant (*From Cyrus to Alexander*). I offer my own interpretation of those events.

A couple of other historical facts worthy of mention include the Jewish mercenaries of Elephantine Island and the advanced medical knowledge in Cnidus (located in Asia Minor, in modern-day Turkey.)

Both Roxannah and Adin are fictional characters. Hathach, Esther, Xerxes, and Amestris are historical figures. The incident surrounding Arsames is pure fiction. We know very little about this half-brother of Xerxes. My apologies to the poor fellow. In case you wondered, the Secret Scrolls of Esther are purely imaginary. Nobody has found such a document. But a girl can dream.

I use the word *Greek* and *Greeks* for the sake of my readers' convenience. But it is an anachronistic term. The people who occupied the independent city states that we call Greece today would be better referred to as Hellenes.

A little bit about the food Roxannah prepares. No recipes from the Achaemenid period survive. However, ancient Greek historians describe the abundant luxury of the Persian royal table. There are references to foods served at the court (an ox baked whole in the oven, for example), the number of cooks, and several lists of ingredients. Persians, we are told, loved a meat-rich diet and a lot of sweets. Putting these clues together alongside regional and popular Persian recipes of today, I created the dishes that Roxannah prepared. I am a huge fan of Persian food, and I hope some of that love comes through in the book.

Modern Persian cuisine uses a lot of basmati rice. But at this early date, rice was not used broadly in Persia. It is entirely possible that Roxannah would have had access to rice as an exotic grain from the East. I had every intention of writing a scene that included her experimenting with a rice dish for the queen. Sadly, I ran out of pages! I share some of my biblical-era recipes in my book club kits and in the back of several books. (You can find these at TessaAfshar.com.)

An important note about Roxannah's background. In my

conversation with Dr. Jessica Sanderson (please see Author Acknowledgments), what became obvious to me was that childhood wounds cause us to break down differently. The same wound can cause one person to break toward control, while another breaks toward fragility. We break toward hyper-vigilance, catastrophic thinking, workaholism, or worthlessness. Our deepest wounds can wear a thousand faces. But *The Queen's Cook* is not a book about childhood trauma. It is the story of a woman who through hardship finds friendship, love, and a life-changing relationship with God. The scope of such a novel simply does not allow a deep examination of Roxannah's wounds. I merely skimmed the surface of her trauma. In doing so, I did not mean to underestimate the pain of those who have had to endure similar issues in childhood. If you grew up with a Lord Fravartish for a father or mother, I am amazed by your endurance and grace. You are extraordinary! Your story is likely much more interesting than any book I could pen.

One final note: The QUEEN ESTHER'S COURT series will tell Esther's story three times, focusing on a slightly different vantage point with each telling. My hope is to take readers deeper into Esther's world. At the same time, no version of any of my stories can compare with the original. For the original account of Esther's life, please refer to the book by the same name in your Bible. My stories can in no way replace the transformative power that the reader will encounter in the Scriptures.

For updates and to sign up for my monthly newsletter, please visit my website at TessaAfshar.com. I love hearing from my readers.

Discussion Questions

1. Family relationships can be complicated. In what ways does Roxannah's mother protect her? In what ways does she fail her?

2. How did the death of Adin's wife change his life? What are some positive outcomes of that loss? Have you or someone you've known gone through a loss that alters the trajectory of your life?

3. Why do you think Darab finds such dignity and peace in spite of everything he has gone through? Compare and contrast it with Lord Fravartish's experience.

4. What is the underlying reason for Esther's fear of approaching Xerxes when Mordecai tells her that the Jews are in danger (ch. 10)? What do you think you would have done in her position?

5. Adin, Leah, and Roxannah each struggle with feeling responsible for Lord Fravartish's death. Why do you think guilt is such a sticky emotion?

6. Why do Roxannah's efforts to feel safe ultimately fail? How does she finally find a sense of security? Have you ever struggled to feel secure?

7. Why does Amestris give Roxannah the option to choose a gift for Esther instead of for herself? Which would you have chosen?

8. Esther tells Roxannah, "An open door does not always lead to an easy path." What do you think she means by that? How does that statement speak to you personally?

9. Roxannah prepares a variety of different dishes for her family, Adin, and the queen. Which would you most like to try? What appeals to you about it?

10. Which character in this book did you enjoy the most? Which character did you relate to the most? Why?

Acknowledgments

First of all, thank *you*, dear reader. You are a gift, and I hope I never take you for granted. I am so happy you decided to pick up this book and spend your precious time romping around ancient Persia with me.

My deepest gratitude to Dr. Jessica Sanderson, LMFT, who patiently helped me understand Roxannah's trauma and how her wounds might have presented themselves in her life. I had the privilege of growing up with a kindhearted man for a father. Roxannah's particular trauma was a puzzle I could not have solved without Dr. Sanderson's invaluable help. Any shortcomings in capturing Roxannah's story are entirely my responsibility and no reflection on Dr. Sanderson's insightful grasp of the problem.

A special word of gratitude to Patrice Doten, who is an extraordinary beta reader. Her insights made this a better manuscript before it ever left the gate for the editorial team. My buddies Kim Hill and Rebecca Rhee helped brainstorm some of the plot points, and it is thanks to them that Leah was created. My precious friend and critique buddy Robin Jones Gunn read the early chapters and gave me some of the best advice and most heartwarming encouragement of my career. So thankful for you, Robin!

What a privilege to work with the marvelous Bethany House fiction team! My deepest gratitude to Andy McGuire and Rochelle Gloege for taking a chance on these stories and on me. I am especially grateful to my editor, Jennifer Veilleux, whose input elevated this book to a whole new level. Thank you for catching those pesky mistakes that I myself never seem to see. Kate Jameson, thank you for your clever insight into why Roxannah needed the queen's encouragement!

My sincere thanks to Anne Van Solkema and Raela Schoenherr, who have been so patient with me and keep coming up with seriously genius ideas. I owe a debt to the amazing Bethany House marketing and sales teams that ensures this book is accessible to readers: Lindsay Schubert, Joyce Perez, Rachael Betz. Thanks for making me look so good. Jennifer Parker, I appreciate the lovely cover design with all the ancient Persian touches. And you gave her the perfect hair! Also, design team, I *love* that awesome map. Thank you.

Always thankful for my spectacular agent, Wendy Lawton, who found the right home for this series, and the right home for all my books.

Utmost love and honor for my husband, who accompanies me on research trips, helps me plot ideas, gives me the strength to overcome the discouraging days, and champions me through life's highs and lows. Thank you hardly seems enough.

And above all, praise to God who opens impossible doors and calls us to impossible things.

Read on for a *sneak peek*
at the second book in

Queen Esther's Court

Available November 2025

In ancient Persia, a Jewish potter must risk everything to help the queen . . . and find her second chance at love.

Sazana's exquisite pottery graces Susa's tables. But her master, Lord Haman, does not know her secret: Sazana is really Shoshana—one of the Jews he loathes so much. Only Arta, Sazana's guardian since childhood, is aware of the truth. All seems lost, however, when Haman discovers Shoshana's identity and threatens her life.

In an unexpected reversal, the king condemns Lord Haman to death and transfers the ownership of the pottery workshop to Queen Esther. Arta and Sazana assume their troubles are over, but tragedy strikes when Arta is murdered.

In desperation, Sazana asks for the queen's help. The following day, Jadon, a former member of the king's elite guard and the man who once broke Sazana's heart, arrives at the workshop under the queen's order. Can Sazana and Jadon set aside their personal heartache and unite to help Queen Esther protect the lives of the Jewish people?

From the Secret Scrolls of Esther

And the young woman pleased him
and won his favor.

Esther 2:9

The Twenty-Fifth Year of King Artaxerxes's Rule

Let me tell you a secret: Being queen will not fill the empty places in your heart.

I arrived at the Persian court on trembling legs, a stranger to its rigid protocols and sharp-edged rules. All the priceless jewels and alluring clothing in the world could not chase away the chill of loneliness that plagued me those first days.

At eighteen, I was one of the oldest girls brought into the palace for that absurd competition. My age and my faith had garnered me enough wisdom to recognize a few things by the end of my first week at the palace.

My companions in the women's quarters were ruled by their longings. The longing to be the loveliest, the wittiest, the best liked, the most admired. The longing to be chosen, wanted, desired.

The longing to be queen of an empire.

Longing flowed over the polished marble of the women's chambers like an invisible river, its currents pounding at the walls, at the foundations, at the rooflines, demanding fulfillment.

But I knew that the way of my companions would lead to discontentment. To disappointment so deep, it would swallow them whole.

All their yearning, palpable in its reaching, snap-jawed hunger, rose out of empty places in hearts that had been starved of better things. My companions thought the crown would fill those old aches.

I knew better.

But looking at them, I felt the first quakings of real fear. I had my own empty places. The child of dead parents, I had learned loss at an early age. No heart is whole in this fractured world. I could easily fall into the same pit as the young women whose craving eyes looked upon me and thought, *rival.*

Which is why I determined I would never be queen, not even when Hegai, who had charge over the virgins, set me up in the best chamber. I had no desire to win the king's love, nor had I any interest in surrendering my heart to him.

I kept my own counsel and hid my Jewish heritage as my cousin Mordecai bade me. Like Abraham, I laid the Isaac of my hopes and dreams at God's feet.

I was twenty when I completed my year of beauty treatments. The night before my first visit to the king, I slept like a sated babe. I asked Hegai to dress me and went to the king not with the fluttering of desperate hopes, but with the ease of a woman who did not care.

Imagine my surprise when Xerxes stared at me as

though enchanted when I told him his beard needed a good trim and his lamb braise was too cold.

I found love when I had thought to protect myself from the pain of it. The pain came, sure enough. But love also brought something unexpected. It opened the door for the salvation of my people.

In that vast palace, I discovered that I was not alone after all. God had brought me the companionship of a few dear friends. And together we were able to stand up to dark forces that were greater than us as individuals.

I live a quiet life now. The life of Hadassah. The queen is forgotten, as I meant her to be. My hidden life keeps me safe from those who still wish me harm in a palace full of sharpened knives.

But even here, my friends surround me. Together, we sometimes remember the wonder of days when a fragile queen was able, against all odds, to save her people. . . .

Tessa Afshar's biblical fiction has been on *Publishers Weekly*, CBA, and ECPA bestseller lists and has been translated into twelve languages. Tessa's books have received the Christy, INSPY, and ECPA Christian Book Awards, and are Carol, Christy, and ECPA Christian Book Award finalists. Born in the Middle East, Tessa spent her teen years in England and later moved to the United States. Her conversion to Christianity in her twenties changed the course of her life. Tessa is a devoted wife, a mediocre gardener, and an enthusiastic cook of biblical recipes. Learn more at TessaAfshar.com.

Sign Up for Tessa's Newsletter

Keep up to date with Tessa's latest news on book releases and events by signing up for her email list at the link below.

TessaAfshar.com

FOLLOW TESSA ON SOCIAL MEDIA

Tessa Afshar   @TessaAfshar